STIRRINGS OF DESIRE

Daere rubbed the backs of his fingers along Star's cheek, eliciting a quiver that ran the length of her spine. Ever more daring, his hand dipped, tracing the graceful curve of her neck.

"Daere . . . I don't think you should . . ." she began, releasing a trembling breath.

"That's the first time you've said my name. Your skin is soft as velvet," he said huskily. His fingers, never still, found a sensitive spot behind her ear and stroked gently. "Let me hold you, Star. Just hold you, nothing more."

She trembled and pressed a restraining hand against his chest. "I don't think that would be a good idea."

"You've let me hold you before," he said, wooing her with the seductive timbre of his voice. It was impossible not to think about her fingers splayed against his chest; the heat of her flesh was like a balm to his soul.

His eyes were dark pools of despair and Star's heart wrenched painfully. She knew if she stayed, she'd be lost, but at the moment she didn't care. Later, there might be regrets, but right now she didn't want to think beyond this moment.

Placing her hands over his, she closed her eyes and slowly began to move his fingers over her face. "Touch me," she whispered.

"Once I do, I don't know whether I'll be able to stop," he said hoarsely. "You have to know that, Star."

"Then don't stop," she replied, her voice a mere thread of sound. . . .

MARY MARTIN

DESIRE'S EMBRACE

ZEBRA BOOKS
KENSINGTON PUBLISHING CORP.

This book is dedicated in memory of my beautiful, courageous mother, Sally O'Neill, who left me a legacy of love and laughter. I miss you, best friend.

And last, but never least, my father, Michael F. Molick, charming, witty; a man who truly lived his life with gusto.

Until we meet on the other side . . .

Once upon a midnight dreary, while I pondered, weak and weary,
Over many a quaint and curious volume of forgotten lore,
While I nodded, nearly napping, suddenly there came a tapping,
As of some one gently rapping, rapping at my chamber door.
" 'Tis some visitor," I muttered, "tapping at my chamber door—

Only this and nothing more."

The Raven, Edgar Allan Poe

Prologue

1860, Santa Fe, New Mexico

"There isn't anyone who makes love the way you do," the auburn-haired woman sighed as she surrendered to the man's ardent kisses, his skillful hands and mouth driving her wild. Sweet madness; yes, that was what he offered — exquisite sexual pleasure as she had never known before. She had willingly risked everything to spend this night in his arms and she wished that morning would never come.

Suddenly, a child's heartrending sobs invaded their privacy, abruptly ending the lovers' passionate tryst and eliciting an ugly oath from the woman.

"Damn her!"

The man lifted his mouth from the woman's bare ivory breast, and a tiny muscle twitched in his lean jaw. "Looks like the party's over, darlin'," he drawled, his hands falling away from her.

Cassondria Tremayne's gaze met his, then sparked with fury when she noted the amused ex-

7

pression in the depths of his eyes. She swore softly as her long, lacquered red nails fumbled to light the lamp on the bedside table. Her full lips, which only moments ago had been curved with pleasure, now thinned with anger. "I wonder what's the matter with her now? You'd think she could sleep through the night just for once. It seems I never have a minute to call my own anymore."

"Quit your bitchin', Cass," the dark-haired man said. "After all, she's just a kid, and it sure as hell won't kill you to act a little motherly toward her once in a while." He leaned back against the pillows. "Now go on . . . before she manages to wake up the entire household."

Cassondria's laugh was brittle as glass. "That's easy for you to say, lover. You don't have to put up with her twenty-four hours a day like I have to." Then, unable to resist, she bent down and pressed a warm, wet kiss on his lips. "And maybe I'm just not in the mood to be motherly right now."

"When are you ever?" he snorted, and added, "Go on, now. It shouldn't take you that long."

She looked down into his smoldering dark gaze and inquired softly, pleadingly, "You won't be leaving before I get back, will you?"

He laughed huskily, then threw back the covers to reveal a sleek, tanned body, rippling with sinewy muscle. He watched her gaze turn smoky as it fixed on him, his manhood jutting out proudly.

8

"Does it look to you as if I'm in any hurry to leave?" he queried.

Her glittering eyes roamed over his bare bronze flesh, then riveted on that part of him from which she derived such pleasure. She leaned into him and moved restlessly against his hip. "You really are a very sexy man, and I just love touching you . . . here . . . and here"—she purred throatily, her fingers skating feather-light along his taut belly and moving lower—"but most especially . . . here."

"You're a hot little bitch, Cass," he said not unkindly, his breathing accelerating as she manipulated his emotions.

"Yes . . . I am," she cooed, "and don't you ever forget it." She didn't add that if he did, she would surely die. He was the only reason she had to get up in the morning, to look forward to the evening. For it was then that he came to her. He had a way of making her feel young, sexy, and beautiful. When they were together like this, he enabled her to forget that old age was inevitable, as were the lines around her eyes that seemed to be appearing with more frequency. She didn't like to think about the fact that she was twenty-nine and would soon be thirty. Not old by any means, but it was compared to him.

He was barely twenty-one, although his youth didn't detract from his appeal; he already knew more about pleasing a woman than other men twice his age. But what thrilled Cassondria even more was her lover's endurance. He had more stamina than a racehorse, and for a woman with an insatiable sexual appetite, he was just what was needed to help make it through the long, lonely nights. Cassondria wanted very much to make love to him again, and her lips parted questioningly. Yet despite her concentrated efforts, he shook his head negatively.

Her eyes met his frantically. "Please . . . you know I'll make it well worth your while."

"Later, Cass," he said sternly. "Right now we have to concentrate on business before pleasure."

She sighed. "Mmmm, and such a shame, too." Brightening, she smiled coquettishly and lowered her head, placing a kiss where he'd remember it most. He caressed her bare thigh, dipping purposefully between her legs with deft fingers, but then he withdrew his hand, and she was left breathless and consumed.

"Two can play that game, sweet," he said softly, pushing her away from him once again. "But don't worry. There's more where that came from . . . after you take care of the kid like I told you." Then he swatted her rounded buttocks soundly, signaling an end to their bold foreplay in a manner in which she'd clearly understand. "Now get a move on it, Cass, before the girl comes looking for you and discovers who's been sleeping in her stepmommy's bed whenever dear daddy is passed out drunk in his room."

"Oh, all right, you've made your point," she

grumbled and, with a weary sigh, rose from the bed, slipped into her red satin robe, belted the sash, and shuffled sullenly out of the room into the hallway.

Cassondria pouted as she walked through the darkened corridor. She was sick and tired of having to sneak around in the dark, snatching stolen hours with her lover and watching him walk out the door at dawn's first light. But what she absolutely detested more than anything was the thought of having to endure another day, another hour, even another minute, with her drunkard husband and his sniveling little whelp. And after tonight, there were going to be some changes made. She'd absolutely insist on it.

It had been the anguished sound of her father's voice that had awakened the little girl, and Star Tremayne had known instantly that something was terribly amiss. It was then that she had cried out, "Daddy! Daddy . . . what's wrong?" And rubbing the sleep from her eyes, Star had sat up in bed, uncertain why her heart pounded in terror.

She had longed to go to her father's aid; she had sensed that he needed her as never before, but his bedchamber was in the west wing of the estate. A long, dark walk alone where *they* might be watching for her.

She felt trapped, suffocated, cowardly. But she

just knew that if she left her room, something vile and sinister would be waiting in the shadows to punish her severely.

Star continued to sob as though her heart were breaking.

Reaching her stepdaughter's bedroom, Cassondria opened the door, her body immediately tensing, anticipating an ugly scene. "What in God's name is wrong, Star?" And when the child just looked up at her with wide blue eyes, Cassondria snapped impatiently, "What has you so terrified? Is it the storm that's frightening you?"

Finding her voice at last, the little girl managed to whimper, "Daddy . . . I want my daddy and not you, Cassondria."

"Well, kid, this time you're stuck with me. He's fast asleep and I'm not about to wake him," Cassondria replied, glaring.

Seven-year-old Star Tremayne's cheeks flushed with temper. "No, he is not asleep. I heard him . . . and he sounded terribly sick. Please, couldn't we just check on him and make certain that he's all right?"

Her patience worn thin, Cassondria had to smother a curse and force herself to reply, calmly but sternly, "No, we cannot. He's a big boy who's perfectly able to take care of himself." She stared meaningfully down at the girl. "Now, go back to sleep and stop being a pest. Everything will be fine in the morning, you'll see."

But Star wasn't to be pacified. "I *won't* go to sleep! Not until I make sure my daddy is okay," the child retorted.

"I've never known anyone with such an overactive imagination," Cassondria snapped, her eyes wintry. "You have a bad dream and then you wake up certain that the world is about to come to an end. Well, I'm sick to death of putting up with you, and you'll not have your way this time, little miss. So just lie back down and go to sleep . . . or else. Have I made myself perfectly clear?"

Smoky aquamarine eyes darkened and clashed with Cassondria's narrowed green-gold gaze. "I won't . . . I won't!" the girl insisted, her chin jutting stubbornly, her tender emotions raw. Her pale blond hair, caught in the candlelight, shimmered like silvery moonbeams. "And if you don't let me see my daddy, I just might tell him what I saw the other day. And he'll hate you, Cassondria. He'll hate you very much," she threatened boldly.

"Is that so?" Cassondria drawled. The child had her absolute attention now. "And just what is it that you might wish to tell him, missy?" She towered over the slight figure in the bed.

Star sensed immediately that her slip of the tongue had been a dreadful mistake. "Nothing . . ." she managed to stammer, then quickly lowered her eyes. "I . . . really didn't see anything." She could still feel the woman's penetrating gaze and, worse, felt her seething enmity. She wished

13

Cassondria didn't hate her so, but Star had given up trying to please her long ago. Her stepmother rarely smiled, and when she did, it was only because she wanted her way with Star's father. Everyone said that Cassondria was driving him to the poorhouse with her free spending, whatever that meant. But Star knew one thing for certain: They hadn't been happy lately. Cassondria berated their servants every chance she got. They were really very devoted and loyal, and before her stepmother had come to live here, they had been like members of the family. Now they had to tread lightly and respond to Cassondria's every whim.

Suddenly, Cassondria's hand shot out and she grasped Star's chin, forcing her head up. "Spare the rod, spoil the child, I've always said. And you are a terribly spoiled little girl. You aren't stupid, and I think you know that it will be a cold day in hell for you, *nina,* if you should ever tell anyone, especially your father, what you saw." Then, Cassondria leaned over the lamp burning softly on the table next to the canopied bed and snuffed out the flame.

The room lay in puddles of blackness. She knew the girl feared the dark more than anything, and it was her intention to make certain that Star didn't leave her room for the rest of the night.

"Please . . . don't leave me alone," Star sniffed.

14

"You have only yourself to blame for this," Cassondria stated crisply. "Good night, Star . . . and pleasant dreams."

"Someday I *will* tell Daddy how mean you really are," Star mumbled under her breath, her eyes pooling and a single tear trickling down her cheek.

Cassondria paused in the doorway, her hard beauty rigidly defined in the pale lamplight from the hallway. "No . . . you won't, for if you should"—she jerked her chin toward some unseen threat outdoors—"something dreadful is waiting to punish you." She smiled coldly. "And I think you well know it."

Star could feel Cassondria's icy gaze boring into her and she shivered. Then the door closed, and she was alone again. Or was she? Tensing, the girl couldn't suppress a quiver of fear. Biting down on her bottom lip, she drew the covers up safe and secure to her neck. Hatred for Cassondria swelled in her throat until she felt it would choke her. Star turned her head and stared through the French doors that led out onto the inner courtyard.

The wind had stirred, heightened, and now moaned ominously around the doors and windows. Thunder boomed, and in the surrounding woods, wolves howled forlornly. In the darkness of her bedchamber papered in pale pink roses, the deepest shadows took on ghostly shapes, and even her dolls' faces no longer seemed sweet and familiar, but unknown and hostile. Star's gaze flitted around the room.

Something moved and scurried low across the floor. A bug? A mouse? A monster? Dark terrors threatened, and the little girl bowed her head and wept bitter tears. "I'm sorry, Daddy, but I'm so terribly afraid of the dark. I just can't bring myself to leave my bed," she sobbed softly.

Benjamin Tremayne had roused from a restless sleep and, before he had even opened his eyes, had sensed that something was amiss. He'd been in the throes of a terrible nightmare, but he knew it had been the dark force in the room with him now that had pierced his turbulent dreams.

"Is anyone there?" he called out. His wife's bedroom was in another wing, but she often came to check on him during the night. To his dismay, the silence remained unbroken and Cassondria did not appear.

Murky shadows danced against the wall, luring his gaze, firing his imagination. He was reacting like a child! There was really nothing to fear, he tried to reassure himself. Or was there?

To make matters worse, his temples throbbed unmercifully and there was the lingering taste of sour brandy in his mouth. He recalled having drunk himself blind after dinner. Now he wished he had shown more restraint. He knew that his drinking was tearing his family apart and slowly destroying his life, but even at this moment, he longed for a shot of bourbon to quiet his jangled nerves.

He vaguely remembered his son Alec—his progeny from his first wife—assisting him from the parlor and up the wide stairway to his room. His wife Cassondria had been playing the pianoforte as he'd stumbled past, but she'd worn an unhappy scowl and he knew why. He also knew that she would give him hell in the morning, and then Benjamin would try to reassure her by telling her that he'd never touch another drop of liquor again. As he'd done so many times in the past. But he really knew, as everyone did, that when the demon called again, he'd respond unhesitatingly. Nothing else in the world would matter but the next glass . . . and the next . . . and the next.

Then he heard that sound again . . . like a hauntingly familiar echo from some mist-edged nightmare he didn't wish to remember. He tried to rise but his limbs felt weighted, as if someone had tied heavy anvils to his arms and legs. The drink held him firmly in its grip, although he couldn't remember ever having felt so powerless before—and he'd done a lot of hard drinking over the years.

The night suddenly seemed alive, and he, damned. With a supreme effort, Benjamin finally managed to rise up on one elbow. His head pounded ferociously as he looked around the chamber through bleary, bloodshot eyes, his gaze darting anxiously here, then there, frantically searching for the invader.

The silver brilliance of the full moon spilled through the French doors and across the pale-hued Aubusson carpet. He cocked his head to one side, straining to hear, to determine the source, but at that moment a coyote on some distant ridge began barking mournfully at the moon. Benjamin swore under his breath.

After what seemed like an eternity, the beast finally ceased his eerie cries. Everything seemed quiet once more. There were no more strange noises; the night seemed in perfect accord. He suddenly felt terribly foolish, yet he still couldn't help sighing in relief. Lying back on his pillow, he closed his eyes and was soon resting comfortably once again.

Benjamin was just drifting off when the silk sheet covering him shifted and something stirred there in the darkness, whisper-soft against his skin. It was unlike anything he'd ever known before, and he knew that he could not have imagined it.

A quiver of fear ran along his spine. His panic propelled him, and despite his earlier lethargy, he managed to fling back the sheet, then struggled to sit up. He was almost afraid to glance down, but he had to see for himself if this was merely a delusion or something more.

The stark moonlight fell across his bare legs,

and he instinctively recoiled from the harrowing sight that met his eyes. It was black and twisted, like Satan's soul, a ghastly creature with fiery eyes that gleamed malevolently at him. He tried to tell himself that this could not be real! It was just a nightmare vision brought on by the drink and nothing more!

But even though he tried, he couldn't seem to force her name past his parched lips, and he knew he was literally choking on his own fear.

Shudders of revulsion wracked his body, and he could only stare wild-eyed at the menacing thing that was slowly, agonizingly, overtaking him. Then his legs began to burn excruciatingly, as though someone had just pressed hot coals against his skin. The pain seared beneath the flesh, the worst sort of torture he'd ever known. He made a hoarse, strangled sound that seemed to come from deep within his soul. Sweet Jesus, this was no dream or illusion!

Suddenly, he cried out, "Star! My darling girl, may God protect you!"

Minutes later, Benjamin Tremayne lay still.

One

New Mexico Territory, 1876

It was going to be a fine day for a hanging.

That seemed to be the phrase of the day, Star Tremayne mused as she'd skirted her way along the walkway back toward the hotel. A glance at the clear sky confirmed that indeed the morrow held the promise of being bright and sunny. People would gather from miles around to witness the lynching of Wade Matthews, the notorious outlaw who had terrorized the New Mexico Territory for the past year.

Star shuddered at the thought of watching a man dance at the end of a rope, and for just a moment she experienced a flash of remorse at the part she'd played in bringing the outlaw to his end.

Lifting her skirts to cross the street, she gave herself a good mental kick. *Remember Lucy Jamison and her three tiny children who have been left without a man to provide for them,* she scolded herself.

She was so caught up in her thoughts that she almost failed to see the horse that was bearing down on her; *didn't* see it until a hand gripped her from behind to pull her out of harm's way.

The warning shout of "Watch out!" seemed an unnecessary rebuke as she was practically jerked from her feet.

"You okay, missy?" the man asked.

Star turned her head to see the sheriff still holding her arm, a worried frown not helping his homely features.

Star put a hand to her breast, then flashed the man a grateful smile. "Yes, I think so, though I surely wouldn't have been if not for you. Thank you, Sheriff. I'll try to be more cautious until I reach the safety of my hotel room."

Another voice joined the conversation, and Star had to squint against the brightly setting sun to gaze up at the tall man who sat astride the horse that had almost trod her into the ground. "Sorry for frightening you, ma'am," the deep voice told her.

"My fault," she said.

"You looked mighty lost in your thoughts," the sheriff, Buford Taylor, commented, but Star hardly noticed as the stranger tipped his Stetson and drew her to him with his eyes. She was experiencing a strange breathlessness

In that instant, she felt pinned beneath that hard assessing gaze and mesmerized by the dark-haired rider's deep voice. Coal-black hair tum-

22

bled across thick, black brows and a shadow of a stubble darkened his jawline. He was a man different from the one she was standing next to, and she realized why. The cool, analytical keenness of those all-knowing eyes, the sense of violence kept suppressed just beneath the surface of polished manners, and the gun belted low on his hip revealed everything she needed to know about him. For an instant, she was aware of how chilling his eyes were as they held hers. Then, as if suddenly dismissing her, he bid her good day and turned his horse away.

Recovering her composure, Star swung around, favoring Sheriff Taylor with another brilliant smile. "Sorry for the fuss, Sheriff. I'm afraid all the talk about the hanging has upset me more than I realized."

"I'm just glad you weren't hurt, ma'am." He was looking at her with renewed interest. "Will you be staying around to see Matthews swing tomorrow?"

"Oh, no," Star said with a tiny gasp of protest at the notion.

"Pity," the rangy sheriff said, then tipping his hat much as the tall stranger had done, he added, "Well, then, I'd best be getting back to the jail. You change your mind, just come see me. I'll make sure you get a front row seat. Matthews might not mind that rope being put around his throat so bad if he had a pretty little thing like you to look at."

Star dipped her head, modestly refraining from a reply to the compliment, then hurried on across the street toward the hotel.

Her heart was still beating wildly in her chest, though whether the rapid staccato had been induced by her near accident or the handsome stranger who had nearly mowed her down she wasn't sure.

"Evening," the clerk said as she passed by the front desk.

Star acknowledged the man with only the slightest of polite nods, then raised the hem of her cornflower-blue dress as she met the stairs . . . and the stranger as he descended from the second floor.

No, she thought as their eyes locked for just a moment, she hadn't imagined the uncommon dark good looks. But this time, even in the brief instant of passing, she saw more: the slashing of his jaw with his lazy smile, his long ebony sideburns, and his deep-set green eyes that appeared warm at a glance. No wonder her heart had nearly leaped into her throat. Why, he was quite the most extraordinary man she'd seen in these parts! As she unlocked her door, Star laughed. Stepping into her room, she shut the world away behind her and began pulling the pins from her hair, loosening the silky silver tresses that cascaded around her shoulders with a shake of her head. She went to the looking glass to share a sardonic grin with her reflection. "Well, Star Tre-

24

mayne, if you weren't always so preoccupied with Raven's work, maybe you'd have time to notice more than what the end of a gun looks like. Handsome strangers, for instance."

The words provoked a twinge of conscience as she thought of Jake, the man who had been courting her for the past year. But just as quickly, she pushed the niggling worry away. Jake was a good man and an even better friend, but that was all he was ever going to be. And she was beginning to think that perhaps they would be better off if she simply told him the truth. Oh, he would be hurt at first, but he had a lot to offer a woman and it wouldn't take him long to find another companion. And it simply wasn't fair for her to keep going out with him when she had no intention of ever settling down and getting married. Better to tell him how she felt and let him build a future with another woman who would appreciate his many fine attributes.

It was only just approaching sunup when Raven slipped from the hotel room the next morning, but already the streets below carried the excited buzz of dozens of voices. The Raven's eyes glittered like wet turquoise as she hefted her valise and exited via the back staircase.

Her perfect features were set in a grim mask that little resembled the gentle loveliness of her alter ego as she watched the boy finish the saddling of her horse.

Pulling her hat low over her eyes ten minutes later, she steered the magnificent stallion from the stables, stopping only long enough to toss the boy who had cared for the horse for the past three days a coin. "For a job well done," Raven told him in a husky whisper.

The boy stammered a surprised "Thanks, mister," then raced outside after the black-clad visage whom he'd heard people whispering about. But he was only allowed a moment to stare after the gleaming ebony stallion and its master, as another of his charge's owners came to retrieve his mount. "That there's the fella what brung in Matthews," the boy told the tall stranger. "You gonna watch the hangin' like everyone else?"

Daere McCalister didn't answer as he stood staring after the rider the boy had pointed out to him. He, too, had heard the talk around town. Hell, that's all anyone had talked about the night before in the saloon. The Raven. Daere shook his head. Feet braced, he moved his coat in an unconscious gesture to grip the handle of his gun in the low-slung holster. It was men like that one who were making his life difficult.

With a sigh, he turned and made his way into the stables.

"What's the matter, mister? Ain't you excited about the hangin'? My ma tells me there'll be dancing in the—" The boy stopped in mid-sentence as his gaze landed on the six-shooter on

Daere's hip. Daere saw the fright in the youth's eyes.

With a soft laugh that reflected bitterness rather than amusement, he ruffled the boy's hair. "Sometimes it's not as easy as that to spot a gunslinger, son. Look at Wade Matthews. Seems to me I heard the man always shot his victims with a rifle."

The boy nodded, but he still looked unconvinced.

Daere took another route. "And look at that Raven fella. Didn't I see a bullwhip coiled up on his saddle? Could be a man might take one look and worry a mite that he was on the wrong side of the law instead of a bounty hunter."

This seemed to convince the lad, who grinned. "Yeah, that's a fact, 'specially all dressed in black like he is and riding that big black horse of his." The boy scratched at his scalp. "So what you saying, mister? You a bounty hunter, too?"

Daere laughed, and this time amusement danced in his green eyes. "No, son. Guess you could say I'm just a tired ole cowpoke who is gonna be real glad to get home to his ranch."

The boy's disappointment was reflected in his eyes. "Oh, well, guess that's okay."

"Glad you think so," Daere said as he took his horse's lead from the young stable hand. He put a foot in the stirrup, pulling himself up with the ease of a man who has known many years on horseback. "Well, son, you take it easy." He started to urge his mount toward the door, then reconsidered. "And son, don't put so much stock in the likes of that fella who calls himself the Raven. There's other things that are more important in life than being able to outdraw another man or wield a mean whip."

"Yeah?" the boy asked skeptically. "Like what?"

Daere's eyes roved over the barn for a moment before he answered. Then he grinned easily again. "Like having a way with animals," he said.

The boy beamed with pride at the obvious compliment.

As Daere steered his mount from the barn and rode away, he added to himself, "Or like having peace of mind."

The Raven paused behind the jail to pull a black silk bandanna over her nose and mouth. Then, freeing the bullwhip, she cracked it expertly against the bars of the cell window.

A muttered curse answered the whip's call.

She smiled behind her mask and waited for the man named Matthews to appear at the window. She wasn't kept waiting long.

The man's face reflected none of the fright she had expected with the approach of his execution. Most of the outlaws she'd brought in over the past few years since becoming the avenging Raven had been able bullies when terrorizing their victims but sniveling cowards when faced with answering for their deeds. But she realized now that Wade Matthews was one of those rare few who was incapable of feeling. That kind was the worst of the lot. They raided the weak, killing and brutalizing without thought to the heartache they left behind. And even facing their own demise, there was a defiant disregard that bordered on madness.

Raven was glad for the decision she'd made to pay the vicious killer one last visit. In that instant, she realized that for the first time in her alter ego persona as the Raven, she wanted him to know who had brought him down. Oh, not for the sake of pride. That wasn't what the Raven was about. No, she wanted to see his face, to know that he understood he was not invincible as he believed.

Slowly, she slipped the silk bandanna from her face, then swept her hat from her head, letting the silver mane of silky tresses billow around her shoulders.

"A woman! Sonofabitch," Wade cursed.

"I wanted to wish you a speedy journey to hell, Matthews," she said in a whispered voice that was all the more chilling for the quietness with which the simple statement was delivered.

She'd gotten the response she wanted, had seen the shock and humiliation . . . and yes, the flash of vulnerability. But it was gone in an instant, as the cold-blooded killer tossed his head back and laughed.

"Gawddamn, lady, I wish I'd known you was a filly . . . and a downright handsome one at that. Maybe we coulda enjoyed ourselves some while you was bringin' me in."

In spite of herself, the Raven shivered slightly with revulsion at the thought, but she passed it off with a gruff admonition. "Better to be thinking about that noose they're readying for you out there than what could have been, Matthews."

"Hey, you the one better be doing some worrying, little lady. I hear the devil lets his cronies come back to fix those who owe 'em a debt. Way I figure it, that be the case, you'll be the first one I come for."

With a shake of her head for the time she'd wasted, the Raven nudged her horse away and settled her hat back in place. The visit had been useless. Wade Matthews was rotten to the core. Well, she'd learned a lesson. From here on out, the Raven would do her job, then leave the soul-saving to the preachers. As she jabbed Midnight's flanks with her heels, giving him his head, she looked toward Tequila Bend and home. God, it was going to be good to get back to the mundane life as a seamstress. For a while at least, she hoped the Raven could rest.

Star was bone-tired, but she pulled her hair back with a sigh and a bright yellow ribbon, then went to the stairs that would deliver her back to her life in the dress shop. She was only halfway down when she heard her stepmother's voice below. Star almost turned around, but she knew Cassondria wouldn't leave until she'd talked with her. This time the sigh that she emitted was long and resolved.

Her spirits plummeted even further when she spotted her half-brother Alec also waiting for her in the shop, but she pulled a semblance of a smile into place as she stepped into the room. "Good morning," Star said with much more enthusiasm than she felt. "What brings you into town today? I would have thought you'd be much too busy . . . doing whatever it is that seems to keep you so entertained at the hacienda . . . to pay me a visit."

"Are we a bit acerbic this morning, sister dear?" Alec asked, his lips twisting in a mockery of a smile.

"Not at all. Just a little disappointed that my day seems to be getting off to such a poor start," she answered meaningfully.

"I do believe my sister is unhappy to see us," Alec said to his Aunt Hilda, who owned the dress shop with Star.

The rotund little woman made some guttural noise that bespoke her displeasure better than words, then disappeared to the back of the shop.

"I'm rather surprised to find you just now coming downstairs, Star," Cassondria said. "It's

31

almost noon. Do the ladies who depend on your services allow you such casual working hours?"

Star's turquoise eyes narrowed on the brassy-haired woman, but she kept her tone mild as she answered, "Juanita and Hilda are here even when other work keeps me upstairs."

"Or out of town," Alec said, his dark eyes probing. "We were here a couple of days ago as well, Star. Hilda said you were away. You seem to venture out of Tequila Bend more and more often lately. Is your business so good that you need travel so extensively? It *is* your dressmaking business that you are attending to on all these sojourns of yours, isn't it?"

Star ignored the question. "What do you want?" she asked. "As Cassondria has pointed out, it is almost the noon hour, and I have a lot of work to see to."

"I've decided to have some dresses made," Cassondria said with an imperious lift of her head, reminding Star, as she always did, that she considered her stepdaughter nothing more than another servant who should see to her needs.

Star let her eyes roam slowly over the other woman's voluptuous curves, before raising her gaze to her stepmother's hard face once again. "Ah, yes, I can see why you might need some new things. Gained a few pounds, have you, Cassondria?"

The woman's normally olive complexion reddened with the undisguised insult and her green-gold eyes flamed. "Why, you little—"

"Now, Cassondria, don't let her upset you. *She* is here to assist *you.* Just show her the fabrics you've picked out and discuss the designs you had in mind, so we can get back to the hacienda. I'm sure you'd like to have your afternoon siesta before dinner."

The supercilious woman was immediately mollified by her stepson's tone. Batting her long lashes in a coquettish manner that Star would have laughed at had her temper not been raised so high, she pointed at a bolt of red satin. "I need a gown of that. And another in that divine green. I wanted something in white, but everything Hilda showed me was too plain. Don't you have any white taffeta?"

Star sighed. Ordinarily, she would have pointed out that red would clash with the woman's fiery hair, but in Cassondria's case she knew it wouldn't do any good. Besides, why should she care if her stepmother's abominable taste made her look like the common whore that she was, for all her airs of superiority? "Most of my customers are the wives of hardworking ranchers, Cassondria. They have little need for yard goods such as white taffeta." Then, with a wickedness she couldn't resist, she added, "I only stock the more lavish fabrics for Rosalie's girls."

That shut her up, Star thought with satisfaction, though she felt a decided irritation at her brother's howl of appreciative laughter. She

33

hadn't intended on entertaining him. She glared his way as she hefted the heavy bolt of green muslin and carried it to a table to be cut. "How many yards do you want?"

"How should *I* know," Cassondria said. "You're the seamstress, after all."

The pair stayed in the store for another hour while Star was forced to measure her stepmother's ample proportions and listen to her demands for the dresses she wanted to have created. Star sank into a chair when they finally departed.

Why did she let them always upset her so? She knew what they were about. Good heavens, she should probably thank them. She owed the conception of Raven to them.

Leaning her head against her hand, she smiled. Just thinking about treating the pair to a visit from the Raven was a delicious diversion. Of course, she would never do that. Raven's secret was too important to be risked on them, but it was still fun to think about.

She frowned then. She owed them all right! Especially Alec. If not for all the mean tricks he'd played on her as a child, she might never have vowed to learn to defend herself.

The Raven had been born out of a desperate need within her to somehow make the territory in and around her home a safer place to live for the folks she cared about. Star had lost her father at an early age, and she well remembered her feelings of terror and helplessness on the night that he had died, how he had been screaming for someone to come to his aid. She had been too afraid of what she might encounter in the dark that night to leave her room, so she'd hidden under the covers and sobbed until his screams had stilled. Well, she wasn't hiding anymore. As Raven, she wasn't afraid to confront danger and death face-to-face.

Her role as the dark avenger was one she'd honed to perfection over the past seven years. The fear she'd known since childhood had slowly begun to disappear as her confidence had been restored. She had taught herself to ride and shoot just as well as any man, and Star vowed there wasn't anyone who would ever intimidate her again. But what she did best was wield a mean bullwhip, which was her weapon of choice.

Now the smile of satisfaction returned as she remembered her whip upstairs. How hilarious it would be to see the look on Cassondria's decidedly plump cheeks or her brother's cocky expression slip from place if they could witness the way she wielded the sharp-tongued weapon. And all because a frightened little girl left fatherless and to their mercy had been forced to find the courage to protect herself.

Star thought of Wade Matthews again as she stretched to rub at her weary back and saddlesore derriere. No doubt the man had long since met the devil by now. Perhaps she should have asked him to drink a toast to her half-brother at his first supper with Satan. After all, the Raven would never have come to be if not for men like Alec.

Alec was drinking a toast to his sister at that very moment. "To our lovely Star," he said, raising his glass in Cassondria's direction. "May her delicate little fingers not get too tired and sore as she works on your new gowns."

Cassondria didn't laugh. "She's an impertinent brat! Why, she acted as though she was doing me a favor by accepting my orders. She should be grateful for the business I throw her way! I could easily go to Santa Fe to have dresses made that would no doubt be fancier and more suitable for a person of my station than those simple rags she's capable of putting together. God knows the old frumps who live around here don't keep her in business. Why, she'd starve if not for me."

"Ah, but don't forget Rosalie's girls," Alec said, unable to resist ribbing his stepmother a bit.

"Oh, don't remind me of the insult that little chit paid me. Can you imagine her comparing me to one of those whores?"

Alec crossed the room to sit at Cassondria's side on the settee. Bracing the arm that still held the snifter of brandy on the back of the ornately crafted sofa, he caressed one of her full breasts. "You're certainly more beautiful than any of them," he said in a low voice. "And no doubt as talented in bed, though of course I don't have personal firsthand knowledge of their abilities."

Cassondria's eyes glittered possessively as she ran a hand over her stepson's lean jaw. "And you better never."

He grabbed her around the waist, pulling her against him. "Now, Cass, why would I need anyone else when I have you to warm my bed? And speaking of bed, how would you like to join me for that siesta we spoke of earlier?"

"Are you sure sleep is what you have in mind?"

"Eventually," he told her with a meaningful grin. Alec stood up, pulling her to her feet, but their progress to the bedroom they no longer gave the pretense of not sharing was impeded by a knock at the door.

Cassondria cast him a questioning glance. "You expecting company?"

"Probably just one of the men," he said, setting his glass down as he waited for the servant to show whoever was at the door into the room.

Marty Nichols, their hired hand, entered a few seconds later. "You told us to let you know if there was any word on McCalister," he said to Alec, then, to Cassondria, "Ma'am."

Cass bowed her head in regal acknowledgment of the man's greeting, then stood up to walk to the window, giving a talented performance at disinterest in the news he brought.

"And?" Alec asked shortly, irritated by the attention Nichols was paying his stepmother.

"Thought we weren't going to come up with

anything, but then I got a nice surprise. One of our men just got back from Matthews's hanging." He grinned, revealing tobacco-stained teeth. "Looks like we hit pay dirt. He saw McCalister there. I got curious, and so I went on over to his pa's ranch."

"Was he there?" Alec pressed.

Not to be rushed, the cowpoke took his time unraveling his story. "I rode on over and, big as you please, went right up to the door. Some old coot opened it, and I told him straight out I work on the neighboring ranch. Said I'd been riding by and had seen the horse. Came by to check and make sure someone wasn't inside who didn't belong."

"Oh, for heaven's sake," Cassondria said impatiently as she turned away from the window, giving up the pretense of not listening. "Who was it?"

"Well, ma'am, that's the whole point. I ain't sure. Fella just said that he knew Daere McCalister, but he ain't seen him yet. Didn't seem to want to offer me any more information."

"Do you believe him?" asked Cassondria.

"Reckon so. I never saw no one else around the place. But this fella seemed to think that the gunslinger would show up for his pa's funeral."

Alec and Cassondria shared a look of anxiety, but Alec quickly recovered to show the man out the door. "Good work, Nichols. You keep watching. Let us know if McCalister turns up or if you see anything suspicious."

When he returned, Alec stood in the middle of the room, running his hands over his dark hair. "That doesn't sound good."

"Why? Do you really believe Daere McCalister is going to want to hang up his guns and settle down?" she asked.

"On the contrary, Cass. I think he'll do just the opposite, and that's what makes me real nervous, considering our little role in this."

"Not *our* role, darling, *your* role. You're the one who scared old man McCalister to death with those vicious little beasts you keep as pets," she pointed out to him. "I wanted to woo him a bit, maybe charm him into parting with his land. But *no*, you didn't want to have to wait that long." She shot him a meaningful glare. "So, now we find ourselves in a bit of a predicament. However, if you'll let me handle McCalister and stay out of it, I think we can eventually come to a mutual agreement that will be satisfying to us both."

"And I guess I don't have to ask what *that* means?"

Cassondria laughed as she joined him in the center of the richly furnished room. She raised a hand, letting it rest on his chest as she tilted her head to smile deviously. "It will only be a brief interlude, my darling man. He's been away for a long time. I'm sure he isn't interested in settling down here, especially if the reputation that has preceded him is accurate. What would a gun-slinger want with a ranch? No, I think we have nothing to worry about. As a matter of fact, maybe it's better for us this way. If he shows up, then we can probably get everything settled within a matter of a few weeks."

Alec's lips twisted bitterly. "Always so confident of your allure, aren't you, Cass?"

"Yes, I am. As a matter of fact, I think we'll host a party soon after McCalister returns. Of course, we'll be good neighbors and make certain that we invite the man. Maybe even Star as well."

"Ha! As if Star would come out here for a party you and I would give."

"Of course she won't come," Cassondria snapped impatiently. "But we can invite her all the same, show our neighbors how generous we are in spite of her hateful attitude toward us."

"And what good is that going to do?" Alec asked.

"What good? Why, when the man sees how we're prospering, he'll be delighted to sell us his father's ranch." She snapped her fingers. "Just like that we'll own the biggest ranch in the territory."

"You're forgetting one little fact, Cass. We don't legally own *this* ranch."

"Oh, rubbish. The will has never turned up to disprove our right to it. I was your poor father's widow and you his firstborn. Who would contest our right to it?"

"Star."

"Oh, yes, my beloved little stepdaughter. Well, too bad she's never been successful in locating the hiding place where your father kept the will."

Alec scratched his neck, then retrieved his drink from the table where he'd left it. Bringing it to his lips, he downed the amber liquid in one greedy gulp.

"I do wish you'd try not to act like the barbarian you are," Cassondria complained.

Alec laughed. "That isn't what you told me last night."

She laughed with him. "How we act in the privacy of our own bedroom is a different matter."

"Then shall we go? I feel very barbarian at this moment."

"Still thinking of Star?" she taunted.

"Yeah, and that damn will. She's still determined to find it, you know."

"Of course, but we've talked about that before. We'll take care of her when we can."

"It would make it easier if she were more like other women. She's too damned independent. Look at the careless way she leaves the shop while she takes off whenever the fancy strikes her."

"Her unexplained absences are curious," Cass agreed. "But let's not worry about her anymore right now. Soon we're going to have everything we've wanted and a reason to celebrate."

"Not counting your chickens before they hatch,

are you, Cass?" Alec asked.

"Not at all. Just doing what any adept businesswoman does, as I always have. Planning ahead. How do you think I got where I am today? It wasn't by accident, I assure you." Her dark eyes had flashed with annoyance at his question, but she laughed unexpectedly now. "Your father was no fool, and I brought him to heel quickly enough." She smiled at her stepson. *You were the easiest,* she thought, though of course she kept that little morsel to herself. "I don't think McCalister will be much of a challenge."

Daere was gazing into the campfire at that moment, remembering the man he'd watched ride away from the stables earlier that day. It wasn't like him to brood on things as unimportant as a bounty hunter who called himself the Raven. But why did he have this nagging feeling that the encounter with the black-clad stranger was a bad omen? With a sigh of disgust with himself for his superstitious thoughts, he tossed the last of his coffee into the fire and prepared to break camp.

He was just bone-weary, he told himself. He had spent the better part of the night tossing on his bedroll, thinking a lot about the ranch house that he hadn't been inside for many years. *Too many,* he thought as he reached for his gear. Soon he'd be home, but what would be waiting there for him?

"I'm glad you're back, Star," Jake said, a wide grin on his face as he stood in the doorway of her dress shop. "I missed you."

"Wondered when you'd be coming around," Hilda said as she stood up behind the counter, where she'd dropped her needle and had been bending down to look for it.

Jake flushed crimson. He'd thought the beautiful shop owner was alone. He glanced around for Juanita, afraid that he'd been overheard by her as well, but she was nowhere to be seen. "Miss Hilda," he said, tipping his hat. "Didn't notice you at first."

Star cut her aunt off before she could embarrass the young man further. "I'm glad to see you, Jake, and I missed you as well." She felt a twinge of guilt for the white lie. She *had* missed him, only not in the way she knew the young man had hoped.

Jake grinned from ear to ear. "Have dinner with me tonight?"

Star started to refuse. She really was very tired, but then she reconsidered. As much as she dreaded hurting him, she knew that soon she had to tell him how she felt. She would always cherish Jake as a friend, but it was cruel to go on letting him think there could ever be more between them. "I'm very tired from my trip," she said honestly, "but I think I could meet you for an hour or so."

"I'll come by for you at eight. Will that be all right?"

Jake left with the assurance that eight o'clock would be fine, and Star watched him cross the street and enter the feed store. She was still thinking about the unpleasant task before her, when her aunt interrupted her reverie.

"When you gonna find you the man you want so you can stop leading that boy on?"

Irrationally, the face of a dark stranger flashed across Star's mind, but of course, that was foolishness. She sighed and let the bothersome question go unanswered.

Two

The bastard had been tracking him for well over two hours, but he had yet to make his move. It was only a slight sound that had alerted the gunslinger—a shod hoof glancing off the weathered lava basin—and he had known instantly what it meant.

It looked as if trouble had managed to find him again.

By his calculations, the tracker had picked up his trail about five miles back, not long after he had forded the Pecos River and headed due west.

It had become a grueling chase, the distance between them narrowing with every passing mile, leaving him to wonder when it would end. Whoever was back there had plenty of grit and determination, but it remained to be seen whether he had enough to stay alive.

Daere McCalister scowled darkly, his anger clenched within him like a fist. Earlier, he had chanced to glance back over his shoulder and had caught the glint of a bridle-bit in the moonlight. He had wanted to turn and make a stand right then, but instead had forced himself to keep riding onward, for he knew the timing wasn't yet right. Damn, but he had always hated the waiting more than anything. It wasn't easy contemplating who might live or who might die this night.

The gunslinger blew out the smoke from the cigarette he had rolled earlier, looked down at the glowing ash tip, then flicked the smoldering butt into a nearby stream. His luck had been holding until now. He hadn't encountered any trouble since he'd left Laredo.

It was too bad things were about to change, he thought. Daere wasn't anybody's fool; he'd been around long enough to know when a man had a bullet with his name on it, but he figured if he had anything to say about it, then his life wasn't going to end out here in the godforsaken wilderness, with the vultures and coyotes picking at his bones. He had always envisioned departing this earth in a far better fashion: at a ripe old age, with some sweet young thing snuggled up in bed beside him and a smile of satisfaction on his lips.

He knew that men like him rarely died peacefully or in the arms of a woman. Gunfighters usually met their ends violently, with no one to mourn their passing. Still, he intended to defy the odds until the bitter end. Dead men didn't talk, drink whiskey, or tumble a willing woman. Daere grinned devilishly. And that sure as hell wasn't for him.

Daere McCalister had always known exactly

what he wanted out of life and how to get it. He had also been defending himself for a good many years—too many for him to actually recall a number—and rarely had anyone ever taken him by surprise. He wasn't about to let things change. The tracker didn't know it yet, but he was the one in mortal danger.

The gunslinger pressed gamely onward, his steely gaze missing nothing, his mind constantly plotting his next move. He knew never to underestimate an enemy; there was no mistaking the caliber of the man on his trail or his intentions. The tracker would be out for blood and glory, and the latter couldn't be had unless he was primed to kill.

Daere let out a low oath. They were always the same, and so goddamn eager. Young, cocksure, hungry for fame, they'd do anything to make a name for themselves. Just the thought made him curse again. "Why are they always in such a hellfired hurry to die?" he wondered aloud.

A relentless hunter, the tracker didn't seem as though he had any intentions of giving up, but continued to pursue his quarry across the wilds of New Mexico, until sooner or later he'd manage to goad Daere into a fight. It was a deadly game of cat and mouse, which the dark-visaged gunslinger knew well. And he always played to win.

Despite the growing legend that depicted him as a trigger-happy killer, he'd reached the ripe old age of thirty-one due more to his brains than his brawn. He'd never taken pride in having to kill another human being, and he hoped to outfox the man on his trail before he'd have to outshoot him. Still, he'd do whatever was necessary to stay alive; he wasn't running, merely biding his time.

His chiseled countenance an impenetrable mask, Daere McCalister rode steadily onward, an icy calm settling over him. He quickly weighed the odds, then discarded any other options. Hell, let the fool keep on coming, it didn't matter to him. He'd been in situations like this in the past — countless showdowns, endless chases, blazing gun battles that had left men mortally wounded and cursing him as they lay dying. It was a way of life, though never an easy one; but he'd lived it for too long to change now.

Past experience had taught him well, and even though he might manage to give the man the slip, somewhere farther down the line they were destined to shoot it out. Kill or be killed. It was the simple, however violent code of men who lived by their guns. One of them would die before the sun rose on another day; the other would walk away.

His expressive green eyes narrowed to slits beneath his slanted brows. He couldn't remember a time when he had lived any other way, although once, long ago, his had been a face few recognized. He had kept a low profile then. Now it seemed he'd barely get settled in a town before someone would remember who he was and what he was, and then before he knew it, he had about as much trouble as he could handle.

At last count, in the past year, over a dozen men had challenged him. He had won each time. When cornered, he faced them over the barrel of a gun and showed them no mercy. He made them pay for their bad judgment in the worst way.

They had died by his hand, shot down in their prime by the wickedest man alive. A high price to pay for the glory of a gun. At least that was how the upstanding citizens always painted the picture.

Despite his seeming indifference, sometimes they made him feel lower than a snake's belly. Maybe it was because he knew it was far too late to change the course of his life. Not that he had ever actually considered it, but every now and again he would find himself wondering what it might be like to live on the favorable side of the law.

His reputation just seemed to precede him wherever he went, whether it was a town no bigger than a dot on the map or a place where he'd expect to easily lose himself in the crowd, and he'd never gotten the chance to find out.

He didn't recall exactly who had been the first to label him a worthless no-good, but the effect had been long-lasting. There wasn't a decent woman who would walk on the same side of the street with him anymore, and whenever he rode into a town, every mother was quick to caution her starry-eyed daughters about his checkered reputation. They called him bad, they called him wild; they said he was a mad killer. Yet the one thing they couldn't claim was that they really knew the man behind the legend. He could honestly say he'd never provoked trouble; he just didn't believe in turning the other cheek.

Pushing onward, he knew the gap between them was closing. Just as he had planned it. He had been deliberately slowing his mount's pace, luring his pursuer, drawing him ever closer. Survival at any price pounded through his veins. Soon, he knew, the hunter would become the prey, and then nothing in this world would save him.

"You may believe you're better than any of the rest, but you're dead wrong if you think you can outfox me," he muttered, his breath a misty cloud of white vapor.

Despite the chill of the day, the air was redolent with dust and sweat-lathered horses as the tracker and the gunslinger pushed determinedly onward. Hoofbeats thudded against gypsum sand, and loose rock skittered down the mountainside as they climbed steadily upward in an effort to reach the top of the ridge before the sun set.

One rider, dressed in black leather, was mysterious and compelling, every muscle tensed for the fight that seemed closer with the passing minutes. And beneath the brim of a black Stetson, wintry blue eyes scanned every rock and tree, missing nothing.

The other bore an animal alertness, a powdering of dust on his heavy chaps and a cold glint in his eyes. He had the collar of his sheepskin jacket pulled up to obscure lean, angular features, and the gun tied down on his thigh was never more than a hairsbreadth away. He was used to challenge and winning, his six-shooter notched and deadly, assuring him victory over his enemies. Wicked and welcome as a woman's touch, it was beyond any doubt his best friend; in bad times the only one he could count on.

Daere McCalister urged his horse onward, unmindful of the sounds that might alert his pursuer to his position. It no longer mattered. He knew there would always be someone at his back; it was the price he had to pay for his reputation. Just a little bit farther, deeper into the mountains, and he'd turn and make a stand. The time had come to end the pursuit.

The setting sun flushed the horizon a brilliant gold, then gradually paled. A purple haze stretched across the autumn sky and slowly deepened. McCalister's gaze riveted on the fading sun as it set behind the mountains, and the adrenaline surged through his veins.

It was the moment he had been waiting for.

The night shadows embraced him; dark, warm, seductive, and not without an element of danger. Daere felt the change in every fiber of his being, and his tigerlike eyes gleamed in the dim light of the new moon. He thrived on these unpredictable journeys where death stalked him at every turn. Risk worked to assuage the darker side of his soul that sometimes was beyond his control. A soft line of bitterness formed at the corners of his mouth. Tonight, he didn't want it to be.

Suddenly, the dark-haired rider drew rein on the crest of a ridge, and half turning in the saddle, he allowed his diamond-hard gaze to sweep the scrub and towering trees stretched out behind him. Tall pines rose as sentinels along the sloping ridge and the slivered moon hung suspended against a star-filled sky. The rugged trail that he'd ridden had come to a high point of the canyon, and the moon shed a pale halo of light behind him on the narrow pathway that wound upward to where he watched and waited.

Nothing stirred. Nothing seemed threatening.

But he was still out there. Several times, he'd felt his pursuer's eyes, hungry as a wolf, trained on his back, and it didn't seem as if he was going to make any impulsive moves. He was biding his time, determined that Daere wouldn't make good an escape.

Daere McCalister's jade-green eyes darkened dangerously. "Whoever you are, you seem mighty set on the two of us facin' off tonight," he thought aloud, staring hard. "So you just keep on comin', and I'll be right happy to oblige."

Rubbing a leather-gloved hand across his stubbled jaw, he didn't flinch as the cool breeze ruffled the shaggy black hair at his nape and caressed his sun-bronzed skin. An errant lock fell across his forehead, and he gave an impatient jerk of his head to toss it back. A restless energy seemed to form an aura of power around him and made the restriction of his movements seem calculated and controlled, as if he never did anything without first measuring the consequences. Daere McCalister was a man who didn't worry much about dying. He was too busy trying to control his destiny.

Lately, having grown bored with bedding women whose faces were soon a blurred memory, he'd begun to think he enjoyed these deadly games even more than a lusty go-around-the-sheets. Then he reconsidered his thinking and almost grinned. On second thought, maybe that was stretching it a bit.

A twig snapped no more than ten yards away. Daere's focus centered on the rocky trail. His lips lifted, his smile was humorless. Sometimes, no matter how hard you tried, life could be a real bitch.

They were never going to let him live in peace. Another one had come hunting.

Three

"It won't be much longer, McCalister," the husky voice murmured, "and then you'll be mine." The tall, leather-clad figure held the midnight-black stallion to a walk and scrupulously studied the narrow trail in the dim moonlight.

The chill of evening seemed reflected in pale turquoise eyes, but suddenly, a warm smile curved sensual lips as the rider leaned low over the horse's neck to stare at the hoof prints in the sandy soil. It appeared McCalister had passed this way no more than a half hour ago.

At long last, he was within reach.

The lone rider was known only as Raven, and everyone agreed the name suited the image, as did the wild-eyed black stallion the tracker rode. Raven had developed quite a reputation in and around Tequila Bend, a town some seventy-five miles south of Santa Fe.

Break the law, one wrong move, and Raven saw to it that the desperado never made the same mistake again. If there was a bounty to collect, then so much the better, although the money had never played a major factor. The West was often a violent, lawless place, but even here, sometimes, justice did prevail.

Making the territory safer for the good folks who settled it was Raven's primary motive. McCalister might not carry a price on his head, but that didn't mean he wasn't a killer. He was a gun for hire, and Raven knew that McCalister didn't have to hate a man to take his life. He murdered in cold blood, for silver. Raven didn't want him setting foot in Tequila Bend.

Cresting the steep ridge without incident, Raven wasn't surprised that McCalister was nowhere in sight. Yet he was here just the same, shielded by the darkness and, no doubt, already waiting somewhere up ahead. McCalister wouldn't worry about putting distance between them; he'd let his six-shooter and a shallow grave take care of his worries.

Raven's lips thinned with displeasure. Had someone in Tequila Bend sent for McCalister? Maybe even hired him to do a job? Or perhaps it was merely his intention to take over his pa's spread following the elder McCalister's funeral?

It was tragic the way Cap had died, broken and alone out in the desert. Alec Tremayne had found Cap's body after his horse had returned to the ranch without him. Apparently, he had been out riding and had either fallen or been thrown from his mount.

It was Alec's theory that he may have had a

heart attack. Perhaps, Raven mused, her expression darkening, wondering yet again just what Alec had been doing at the McCalister ranch when she knew for a fact that the two men had never had much use for each other in the past. And why did it seem that Alec was always around whenever trouble reared its ugly head?

Well, he might just meet his match in Daere McCalister. Cap's son hadn't been around in years, and although he had never seemed to give a damn about his father, he seemed mighty intent now on reaching Tequila Bend.

But it was a well-known fact that Cap had left behind a sizable ranch and a prime herd of mustangs. His son was the only likely heir.

Money and land were powerful incentives. Even the most honorable of men had been known to kill for less. How well Raven knew.

Questions stirred but went unanswered. It was unsettling to think how little anyone really knew of this Daere McCalister.

Ahead, suddenly, there was an ominous calm—the sighing winds, the rustling leaves, the sound of loose rock tumbling down into the canyon, were all still. The tracker drew rein in a thick stand of trees and glanced cautiously around. McCalister must have found a place to dig in, and now it was Raven's intent to force him out into the open.

Dismounting and moving cautiously through the shadows, Raven stared into the darkness, every nerve alert.

Moments later, an eerily chilling sound invaded the stillness. A mournful wail echoed faintly through the trees and wavered on the wind, as if a child wandered lost and alone in the wilderness. But how could that be? Raven wondered, stunned.

The frail sound came again; a lost, hopeless cry that drew the nerves taut. Despite the chill in the air, moisture beaded on Raven's brow and the silvery blue eyes reflected indecision, then mirrored suspicion.

Of course, McCalister knew well how to play on the nerves, and it could be just another form of a clever trick. The wind blended with the disquieting whimpers, making it difficult to discern illusion from reality. Raven knew there was only one sure way to find out.

Long, agile fingers closed around the smooth-handled weapon that Raven wielded with consummate skill.

It was time for the hunter to prowl.

Daere McCalister knew it was only a matter of minutes before his pursuer crested the ridge, and it was his intention to use the darkness to his advantage and lie in wait. He believed in fair play and confronting a challenger face-to-face, but he wasn't a fool.

He'd learned long ago that it paid to have the element of surprise in one's favor. Even though he knew he could easily pick off the tracker from his hidden vantage point and then ride onward without another moment of concern, he had never murdered wantonly like the back shooters who tracked him, and he wasn't about to start now.

He wasn't an executioner and only accepted a job if he believed strongly in the cause. Sure, he was paid well for his services, but laying one's life on the line for someone — often little more than a stranger — wasn't easy and deserved some form of compensation. Daere knew he provided security for many families who'd otherwise have to walk the streets in fear, and there were times when he was even able to feel good about himself and what he did.

Glancing around, he scanned the piñon and pine trees before his gaze was drawn to the woven straw basket tied to the pommel of his saddle. He was relieved the little orphan's cries had finally faded to a whimper, and he hoped he wasn't just catching his second wind. He knew it had been foolish to have brought him along this far, but at the time, he just couldn't leave him there on the banks of the Rio Hondo, hungry and frightened, cuddled up next to his mother's lifeless form. Daere had known he wouldn't survive alone in the wilderness and had been moved to bring him as far as the next town.

He didn't rightly know what he was going to do with him then, but he was sure looking forward to dropping off the troublesome bundle and then doing nothing more for the remainder of the night than whiling away a few pleasurable hours in Jade Soo Ling's big bed, with her, as always, eager to please.

This delay was going to put him in Tequila Bend later than he'd planned—but not too late for the evening that he anticipated. At the moment, nothing sounded better than a hot bath and a willing woman, but it didn't look as if he was going to get either anytime soon. At least not until he managed to get out of this godforsaken canyon.

His stallion Seguro's ears twitched nervously and he snorted his impatience. Daere laid a calming hand against the sorrel's sleek neck and murmured soothingly, "Hang on, fella, I promise you won't have to play nursemaid for very much longer."

The big horse nuzzled Daere's shoulder affectionately, as if to reassure his master that he would never leave him stranded. He was a magnificent animal, with more heart than a dozen of his kind. Seguro had been a gift from Daere's blood brother, Night Hawk, a Comanche chieftain, and there wasn't a mount better bred or trained.

Daere was drawn from silent contemplation by the soft scrape of a boot heel that had fallen on the rocky trail ahead. His senses sharpened, the sixth sense he relied on even more defined in the darkness, and he retreated several steps into a stand of shaggy pines. The shadows under the trees hid him from view and he waited, every steel-hard muscle tensed and ready.

As he'd figured, it was only a few minutes before a dark-clad form materialized from out of the shadows and trod cautiously toward his hidden vantage point.

The tracker stepped into a clearing in the trees, and a shaft of moonlight etched a youthful profile, delineating the soft curve of his brow and jaw and accenting high cheekbones.

Daere felt his gut churn. "Christ, not another foolish kid," he muttered in frustration, remembering the other young guns who'd been of the same mind. How they'd been so certain they could take him, and their vulnerability when their courage had failed them as they lay dying by his hand. He had to remember that none of them were ever as innocent as they appeared. It was a lesson he'd been forced to learn in order to stay alive.

Daere drew a deep breath and stepped out into the open. "You looking for me, kid?" he asked.

The tracker glanced in his direction and kept walking toward him.

"If you know what's good for you, you better hold it right there," Daere ordered. When there was no response, Daere cursed under his breath and snarled, "You trying real hard to commit suicide, kid, or just damned determined to get

60

under my skin?"

"Hold your fire, McCalister," the tracker replied, pausing several yards away, glancing at the silver-buckled gunbelt and the six-shooter strapped on Daere's hip, before adding, "You *are* him, aren't you?"

Daere's expression hardened. It was so senseless to take a life needlessly, but he had rarely been given any choice in the matter. Wearily but with outward calm, he faced the young tracker. "I reckon you've found your man, son." He didn't ask any more questions; he didn't need to. He'd learned a long time ago that the less he knew about any of them the easier it was down the line.

Daere didn't like lying awake at night with the ghosts from his past. There were some things better left unsaid, and he preferred that the dead stayed buried and didn't return to haunt his dreams.

"I been waitin' a long time for this, McCalister," the young tracker said, giving him a long, assessing look. "My name is Raven. It's one you're going to remember after tonight."

Daere didn't know whether to smile or to fake a shudder. This was the Raven he had been hearing so much about? The kid sure looked as if he were expecting him to tremble in his boots. "Look, I rarely offer anyone the chance I'm going to give you, but I figure you're young and too goddamn stupid to even know how close you are to dyin' where you stand," he said tersely. "And let me tell you, whatever you've got stuck in your craw isn't worth takin' a bullet for. So why don't you just turn around and walk away, and we'll forget we've ever met —"

"I don't plan on dying for a long time, McCalister," the tracker interjected, chin tilted stubbornly, "and I won't be walking away . . . at least not until I've accomplished what I set out to do."

Daere sighed inwardly. He wasn't of a particular mood to shoot it out with this kid, who undoubtedly was still wet behind the ears and didn't stand a chance of winning. He decided then to take his chances another day should they ever meet again, but for now, Daere had had his fill of killing.

Frustrated anger simmered inside him. Upon looking closer, he noted a slender figure dressed in a long black coat, leather trousers, tooled boots, and a dusty Stetson pulled down low over his brow. He couldn't determine the color of his hair, as it was concealed by his hat, but there was no denying the slivers of ice in those pale eyes.

If looks alone could kill, Daere figured he'd be a dead man by now. And he knew that he'd been right all along. This *was* just another glory seeker willing to risk dying for fame.

So, why then, was he willing to give him a chance when he knew better? He really didn't know the answer; he only knew that he was getting tired of facing down these young fools, watching them die, their innocence lost. Or maybe he admired the courage he noted in the youthful gaze staring back at him.

For whatever the reason, he paused with his fingers, strong and sure, resting on the polished ebony-handled Colt. Later, he would remember that he'd hesitated for only a heartbeat, but it had almost cost him his life.

Silence stretched between them for several seconds, and then Daere noted the barely discernible change in his opponent's eyes and watched as the tracker's hand blurred in motion. He held little doubt that he was going for his gun.

Reacting instinctively, Daere feinted to his left just as he glimpsed the tracker's lightning-fast movement. He didn't automatically fire from the hip, as he usually did, but held off.

To his astonishment, the tracker gave a graceful flick of the wrist, and a writhing strand of leather snapped dangerously near. Daere back stepped quickly, and the tasseled tip fell short of its mark, harmlessly stirring up the dust around his booted feet.

"You're not wanted in Tequila Bend, McCalister," the tracker said, the lash threatening, hissing like a deadly snake. "So you'd better make a change in plans, go back where you came from."

Daere knew he no longer had a choice. The whip undulated threateningly between them, then swiftly and with deadly purpose cracked again, and only Daere's catlike reflexes saved him. He had to admit that he'd never known anyone who could wield a cattle-cutting whip with such blinding speed.

He looked into the eyes of the stranger, who seemed determined to prove his merit, and saw a stubborn gleam he recognized well.

"Look, I don't have any quarrel with you. So why don't you go find somebody else to cut your teeth on?" Daere snarled. He'd reached an end to his patience, and he sure as hell wasn't going to stand here another minute and risk being flayed alive.

The tracker laughed softly. "If you think you can draw before I cut you in two, you're sadly mistaken, gunslinger."

Daere didn't doubt that for a minute! He dove for the ground and rolled several times, then reaching for leather, he came up with a handful of iron and opened fire. But to his stunned disbelief, when the acrid gun smoke finally cleared, the dark-clad challenger seemed to have vanished into thin air.

Rising to his knee, Daere gazed across the area, but he could find no sign of him. He'd deliberately aimed low, yet he couldn't have missed; he'd had the kid square in his sights. Staring at the place where his challenger had been only seconds before, Daere let loose with a particularly vulgar curse. He'd gotten just what he deserved for giving the kid a break, and remembering the cold, hard glint in the challenger's eyes, Daere felt certain the tracker would come after him again at some later date.

He wouldn't remember how close he had been to dying. Raven would only recall how Daere had tried to back out of the fight. For the first time in a long while, Daere's iron control had been shaken.

On his feet, Daere sprinted toward his horse. He was the hunter now; there could be only one grim conclusion. He should have known from past experience it could be no other way.

Ah, distinctly I remember it was in the
bleak December,
And each separate dying ember wrought its
ghost upon the floor.
Eagerly I wished the morrow; — vainly I had
tried to borrow
From my books surcease of sorrow — sorrow
for the lost Lenore —
For the rare and radiant maiden whom the
angels name Lenore —
Nameless here for evermore.

The Raven, Edgar Allan Poe

Four

*You'll never catch me, McCalister, Never. . .
never!*

The sibilant taunt seemed to carry on the unsettling wind, and even though Daere knew it
was only imagined, it took all of his self-control
to keep from sending his horse flying down that
mountainside in hot pursuit of his quarry. The
trail was precarious, particularly with thick
clouds scudding overhead obscuring the moon at
times, and demanded his concentration. But that
husky, ghostlike cadence kept whispering in
Daere's ear, driving him to distraction.

A look of implacable determination on his
face, Daere willed himself not to listen. Yet it
was the memory of that voice challenging him
that lured him onward, unmindful of the danger.
He knew it sure as hell didn't help his situation
to have his mind start playing tricks on him. Yet
that soft-spoken drawl seemed to haunt him,
goading him on as no other had before. While
he had only caught a glimpse of the tracker's

face, he was certain he would never forget that voice.

Calling on what little restraint he had left, Daere continued on his way, keeping off the main trail as much as possible. He knew it would be to his best advantage to travel in the deepest shadows, so he reined his mount around the mist-covered trees and boulders that lay strewn across his path, ever aware that his survival depended on which one of them possessed the better ability to track in the darkness. He was determined that it would be him. Despite his caution, nothing stirred or seemed threatening, although he well knew that that could change in a heartbeat.

The chill wind carried the ballad of night creatures: frogs, crickets, locusts, a wolf's forlorn cry from some distant bluff. Daere's gaze swept the darkened landscape for any signs of the phantom rider. There was none. He found himself wondering, too, just how the tracker had managed to disappear so swiftly and without a trace.

As time went by, he actually began to feel as if he were chasing an elusive phantom—a shape shifter, as the Indians would say. In Indian folklore, it was a mystical sort of creature able to assume any form desired, making it virtually impossible to be tracked by an enemy.

Then, upon realizing what he had been thinking, Daere almost had to laugh at himself. Of course, he had never really believed in the supernatural. But then he would come upon more tracks—clearly from the same animal as the others he had found—only to have them disappear once again farther down the trail, as if horse and rider had somehow melded into the night, leaving him wondering and ever more aware.

Riding through the shadows, every muscle in his fine-tuned body taut with expectation, he wasn't surprised when a prickling sensation suddenly raised the hackles along his neck. He had the feeling he was being watched, studied, almost as though he were the one actually being pursued. At any moment, he expected a bullet in the back, and he had to fight a strong urge to glance over his shoulder.

Daere swore softly, muttering under his breath, "Damnit, you know it's impossible for the tracker to have circled around behind you, so keep your eyes straight ahead."

The terrain was flat, dotted with mesquite and littered with tumbleweed. There were few trees, and these were scrubby and sparse. *Nowhere to hide, no place to run.* Nothing could get by him without his seeing it first. He would damn well stake his life on that! In fact, it was exactly what he had been doing. No one had ever managed to lead him on such a wild-goose chase before, and he begrudgingly found himself having to admire the youthful tracker's skill and cunning.

The moon slanting on the trail ahead carved pathways through the darkness. Daere's gaze scanned the crude trail, along with the area bordering it. Yet he saw only a big timber wolf standing off in the distance, a fresh kill hanging limply from its jaws.

The creature stared back at him, fiery eyes like live coals in an eerie tapestry of shadows and gray light.

He knew then that his night vision was as keen as it had always been. He saw everything, felt everything. Still, there was no sign of the rider he had been chasing.

"Who are you . . . what are you?" he was given to wonder aloud, an odd creeping excitement spreading through him, spurring him onward more than the fires of anger had earlier.

Finally, after several more miles of painstakingly careful tracking, the trail went stone cold. It ended abruptly, just as he rode over a slight rise and noticed the lights of Tequila Bend ahead of him.

With the slight pressure of his knees, he urged his mount along the narrow winding trail that led to the hard-packed road in the center of the town.

Daere felt another unfamiliar emotion well up within him. Frustration. He had been so sure he could overtake the tracker, but he had to admit that it didn't seem likely they would cross paths again tonight. His expression darkened, and he gritted his teeth. "We aren't finished by a long shot, *amigo*. You *won't* escape me the next time," he vowed.

Tequila Bend lay quiet in the predawn, the well-traveled thoroughfares and storefront board-walks all but empty save for two drunken cowboys who had just wandered out of the Birdcage saloon. Brushing past a trio of painted women, the men called out lewd remarks, but the soiled-doves ignored them and instead beckoned to Daere as he rode by. They were only interested in new customers they might entice inside.

"We got whiskey and the prettiest girls in town, cowboy. Come on in and let us show you a good time you won't forget," the boldest of the trio shouted after him. Daere never bothered to acknowledge her. The tinny sound of a piano sorely in need of tuning drifted over the swinging doors, muffling her shrill curse as she watched him nudge the sorrel into a trot, leaving her to stare daggers at his back.

The wranglers had mounted horses tied at the hitching post out front and never once afforded him a sideways glance, for which he was relieved. He had timed his arrival for late night in order to garner the least amount of attention. The news would travel fast enough, and he knew that by morning everyone in town would be waiting for their first glimpse of him . . . and to see if the resident fast gun—and every town had one— would challenge Daere. However, it was hours until morning, and there was still this night to enjoy.

Riding onward, he noticed that the town had grown considerably since the last time he'd been here. The West had attracted large numbers of settlers in the intervening years after the war, and along with them had come prosperity and growing settlements.

With a population of over five hundred— Spanish, Mexican, white Southerners and Northerners alike—Tequila Bend was a booming town and boasted two saloons, a fine two-story hotel, and a multicultural blend of businesses.

Daere wanted to avoid any further confrontations, so he kept on riding, his sights already set on his destination. At the moment, he only wanted a place to lay low and rest for a while. He had been on the trail for days, snatching sleep whenever he could, and sometimes that meant while riding in the saddle. He needed a drink, a bed, and a woman. And there was only one place to find that combination: The three-story house at the end of town.

As he passed on through town, he noticed that a blacksmith was now next to the town hall, which had recently been enlarged. And farther down the street he saw they'd erected a casino, and adjacent to it was a small variety theater, where for a penny you could see a performance of jugglers, mimes, and even pretty dancing ballerinas.

He caught sight of another new building, a dress shop, with a boldly scripted sign hanging above the door. Miss Hilda Higgenbothum and Miss Star Tremayne were listed as joint proprietors, and the name Juanita Tomas, seamstress, was inscribed in small, neat letters below theirs. Etched on the window glass were the words *Paris Fashions*.

In the apartment above the shop, a light burned dimly, and he assumed it was the ladies' residence. He wondered if the dressmakers were working overtime, or perhaps, maybe even entertaining a late night visitor?

Daere had never found himself drawn to quiet, soft-spoken women, as he had always imagined most dressmakers were, but he supposed even they had their fair share of male callers. He would just never be one of them.

Then glancing ahead at the bright, beckoning lights in the distance, Daere set his horse to a trot. He reined in behind a well-tended, clapboard house, and when a Mexican boy hustled out the door, Daere swung down from the saddle and readily flipped him the reins. Then after

73

slinging his leather saddlebags over one shoulder, he reached into the straw basket tied to his saddle and gently withdrew his sleepy-eyed passenger, cradling the plump, warm body tenderly in the crook of his arm. Daere noticed that the lad was staring at him, his mouth agape, and he couldn't help but smile.

Dipping into the pocket of his trousers, Daere withdrew a silver coin and tossed it at the boy, who deftly caught it in midair. "Take good care of Seguro, and if you do a real good job, there'll be another just like it when I leave," he called back over his shoulder.

The boy bit down on the coin, then smiled widely at the dusty traveler. *"Gracias!"* he called out. "I will give him nothing but the best care, *senor!"*

Daere was already bounding up the stairs, his wide-brimmed Stetson in hand. Again, for a fleeting moment, he had the strangest sensation that someone was lurking in the shadows at the window, watching his approach closely, but he couldn't really be certain.

He paused and glanced up, eyes searching, but there didn't appear to be anyone, only the draperies billowing at an open window. His hand still rested on the butt of the Colt, the challenge yet to die in his eyes, although he really was no longer in the mood to chase after man or phantom, whatever the case may be.

He simply wanted to forget their earlier run-in for a time and indulge himself in a soothing drink of aged brandy, a warm fire to chase away the chill in his bone, and clinging arms to ease the troubles from his mind. Then a humorless smile lifted the corners of his hard mouth. Daere knew he could expect to find that and more at Rosalie's.

There wasn't another place outside of New Orleans quite like her establishment. Tastefully appointed, boasting only the finest in food and drink, Rosalie's employed three chefs — French, Spanish, and American — who offered exotic cuisine as well as down-home cooking, to please even the most finicky of palates. Then when a man's hunger for food was appeased, there were other enticements to savor and enjoy.

Rosalie's girls were a mélange of races from around the world, expertly schooled in the art of lovemaking, each one with her own special techniques and secrets. They provided the clientele with anything and everything they might desire, all wrapped up neatly and refined in satin and French lace. At first glance, it looked as though Rosalie's had prospered well in the years since he had been away.

The structure bore a fresh coat of whitewash, and slate-gray gingerbread trim accented the upper and lower gallery. There were gleaming glass windows adorned with rich red-burgundy brocade, the soft flicker of candles behind the multi-paned windows welcoming a bone-weary traveler.

It had been a haven to him once in the past, when he'd needed a place to recuperate from gunshot wounds following a bloody gun battle with the Barlow brothers.

One brother had challenged him, while the other had hidden at a strategic point overlooking the street, waiting patiently, firing when the timing was right. Daere had thought he was a goner for sure that day. He recalled how Rosalie had not wasted a minute worrying what everyone else might think, but had immediately sent her most trusted servant, Abraham Johnson, to where Daere's broken, bleeding body lay sprawled in the dusty street—pointedly ignored by other passersby—with instructions to have him brought directly back to her place. He had been shot three times in the back, and at first the prognosis was grim. He was paralyzed from the waist down and was told he would never walk again.

Daere had been expecting to meet his Maker that day; instead, he had opened his eyes to find an angel of mercy leaning over him, with nary a hint of innocence in those night-black eyes. And no angel in heaven had ever smelled so sweetly or sworn so profusely.

The first thing she had said when his eyes had focused on her was, "You silly sonofabitch, didn't you know that when the Barlows go gunnin' for you, the odds are you'll get a bullet in the back instead of a fair fight?"

He hadn't, but he knew now, and it was a mistake he didn't intend to make twice. Rosalie had taken it upon herself to personally nurse him back to health, keeping vigil by his bedside and tending to his every need.

It had been touch and go for over a week, but with Rosalie's diligent care and enough money to convince the town doctor to operate and remove the bullets lodged near his spine, Daere had gradually healed.

He figured he would have died back then if not for Rosalie's kind intervention and her strong will, which had kept him going, even when he felt like giving up and lying in bed forever, an invalid. He didn't, of course, mainly because of Rosalie's constant nagging. He had well wanted to be on his feet to escape her constant diatribe.

But no one could say anything against her in Daere's presence. He worshiped the ground she walked on. Not many people in Tequila Bend would have dared come to his rescue that day, but then Rosalie had never cared what anyone thought of her. She lived life by her own set of rules, as did he.

In all, he had spent two months recuperating at Rosalie's, and he had gotten to know everyone who worked there very well. They were mostly good people whose path in life had taken a bad turn, leaving them down on their luck and desperately in need of money.

As for Rosalie, their friendship had continued, enduring through other dark trials and troubled years. Yet, despite their obvious attraction in those earlier days, they had never shared a bed. Not that it hadn't ever been mentioned.

They had discussed it quite openly, in fact, and had mutually agreed that sex and friendship were a lethal combination. They would never be lovers, but they would be great friends. And so it had remained, without question. They had never spoken of it again, knowing it was best to let sleeping dogs lie . . . and banked passions as well.

Suddenly eager to see old friends, Daere knocked briskly on the portal of the prosperous, luxurious brothel.

Almost immediately, a huge black man in a dark suit and pristine white shirt opened the door. "Why, Mistah McCalister," Abraham Johnson exclaimed with genuine pleasure, his astute coffee-brown eyes assessing the tall man at a glance. "It's right fine to see you again, suh. And I'm happy to say that you is lookin' fit as a fiddle." He stepped to one side and beckoned to Daere. "Do come in, suh. My, my, but it's been too long since you was here for a visit. Miz Rosalie, she's gonna be mighty pleased to see you."

"Thanks. It's good to be back, Abraham,"

78

Daere replied, flashing a grin. He crossed over the threshold into the red-carpeted entryway. Even though it was late, the brothel had a number of visitors.

Cigar smoke, voices lowered intimately, a seductive piano melody, all wafted through the dimly lit rooms, assailing his senses. He was genuinely pleased to be back in familiar surroundings.

"You picked a real good time to visit. It's been kinda slow this evening," the servant told him. Then taking note of the furry bundle secured in Daere's arms, Abraham's dark eyes rounded and he said, on a gasp, "Why . . . what is dat you got dere?" He took a precautionary step backward. "Maybe Mis Rosalie's not gonna be as pleased to see you as I thought."

Amusement danced in Daere's eyes. "I think maybe I can persuade the lady to come around to my way of thinking."

Abraham's inquisitive expression melted, and he chuckled. "Ah expect you can, suh. You know she never smiles as bright as when you pay us a visit." His dark face beaming, the servant motioned Daere ahead. "Go on now. I knows I don't have to show you the way."

Loping up the stairs and reaching the second-floor landing, Daere made an abrupt right turn and strode down the long, plushly carpeted hallway. When he came to the second door on his

79

left, he paused, then rapped lightly against the smooth wood.

Momentarily, a full-figured woman dressed in a prim navy gown and starched white apron, her skin the creamy color of café au lait, answered the door. Her face lit up when she recognized him.

Daere quickly placed a finger to her lips, his gaze warning her not to spoil his surprise.

Her eyes sparkled in response, and she whispered: "Good to have you back, suh. Been quiet around here for too long if you ask me." Then favoring him with a smile, she scooted past him and gently pulled the door closed behind her.

Daere noticed Rosalie immediately. She was bending over the hearth, busily stoking the fire, unaware, or uncaring, that she had a guest. She was gazing into the flames, raptly watching the orange-red tongues devouring the pinecones she had just added. The room smelled good, like the clean, fresh scent of a forest. It brought back fond memories, but painful ones as well.

He noticed, too, that the satin covering her behind was glimmering enticingly in the firelight, and he found his gaze drawn to the provocative vision of her firmly sculpted backside sheathed in an amber dressing gown that clung like a second skin.

"It's sure good to see that some things never change," he drawled.

Rosalie whirled about, startled at first, and Daere noted that beneath the robe her lush curves were amply displayed in a tightly laced black corset. Her expensive perfume wafted up to him. "How have you been, Rosalie?"

The woman's jet-black gaze riveted on the tall man walking toward her, and her lips quirked. "As if you actually give a damn," she snorted in a very unladylike fashion, but he noticed the beginnings of a warm smile easing the harsh lines that bracketed her ruby-red mouth. "I simply can't believe my eyes . . . after all this time . . . Daere McCalister! And just where in the hell have you been since you walked out without so much as a 'goodbye' or a 'thank you, ma'am, for the free room and board,' and that's not to mention the hours of affection that Jade lavished on you during your last stay here?"

He couldn't believe it, but he had missed Rosalie's bitchin' almost as much as he had missed Jade's loving arms. Daere found himself grinning at her. "Everywhere, darlin', but no place you'd care to hear about, I assure you."

"Well, why don't you try me and see if I agree?" she pressed scoldingly.

He helped himself to one of the Cuban cigars that Rosalie had shipped in for her best customers, kept in abundant supply in her suite, and reserved for her personal favorites—the ones who also got the best whiskey and women and could afford the upstairs prices. "Maybe later. Right now I'm not exactly in the mood for conversation," he replied, clamping an unlit cigar between his teeth.

"Guess I don't have to ask what you *are* in the mood for?"

"I've been three weeks on the trail—alone—except for my friend here," he drawled. "You of all people *shouldn't* have to ask that question."

Rosalie Valdez noticed then just what he held in his arms, and a slender eyebrow rose. "Don't tell me . . . he's one of yours?" she chortled, peering closer. Then her glistening lips curled. "You know . . . if you look real close, you can see a definite resemblance." She threw back her head, and suddenly, husky laughter resounded throughout the room.

Daere bore her good-natured chiding without complaint. Only Rosalie could say whatever she had a mind to and never have to worry that she might incur his anger. "He's an orphan," he explained, "and knowing how much Jade likes cats, I thought he might find a home with her. Is she free, do you know?"

"Even if she wasn't, I expect once she finds out you're in town, she'll make certain of it," Rosalie said, a twinkle in her eye.

Daere favored the madam with his most persuasive smile. "Rosalie, honey, you wouldn't care to help an old friend out and take this little fella

82

off my hands for the rest of the evening, now, would you?"

Rosalie's expression sobered quickly, and she placed her hands on her hips. "Do I look like somebody who'd get a thrill outta playing nursemaid to a baby mountain lion this evening? Just in case you've forgotten, I've got better ways to spend my time, and you damn well should know it."

"I'll make it worth your while," he persisted with that charming smile, taking a step toward her.

She extended her arms, fingers splayed, in an attempt to ward off his advance. "No! And I mean that, Daere McCalister," she insisted, glaring at the downy bundle in his arms. But she already knew that no matter what she said, it really wouldn't make any difference. Women just couldn't seem to say no to Daere.

As the gunslinger strode off down the hallway, silver spurs chinking softly on the Oriental carpet, Rosalie gingerly cradled the baby wildcat, wondering how in the heck he always seemed to talk her—and just about every other woman—into doing any manner of things they were dead set against.

Balancing the hissing kitten on one rounded hip, Rosalie glared accusingly at the gunslinger's retreating figure. "You're gonna owe me real big for this one, McCalister," she called after him.

"And just you remember it, too." After a distressed sigh, she added, in a softer voice, "Come back after you've sowed all your wild oats, honey. I've got a lot to tell you."

For as long as he'd been coming to Rosalie's, Jade Soo Ling had always made herself available to Daere without question, even shuffling her other customers around at a moment's notice in order to spend as much time as she could with him. Sometimes he got the feeling that Jade would have liked more than he was willing to give her, but he had told her once that he didn't have anything to offer any woman; although she had disagreed, it still hadn't changed his mind.

She had told him she had never met anyone quite like him, and that she admired a man who was wild and unfettered and determined to live life on his own terms. In that respect, she was right. But Jade wasn't exactly dull herself. She embraced life, she didn't just live it, and she liked to sample everything imaginable there was to offer.

Therefore, it didn't come as any great surprise to him when after reaching her room, he noted a thin ribbon of light showing beneath and heard the murmur of a soft female voice. It didn't sound like Jade. Puzzled, Daere hesitated, and for some reason he couldn't explain, he became uneasy, even angry. It was that certain voice he heard behind the door, and his gut kicked because he didn't like what he was thinking right then. Something about that voice sounded familiar but also left him with a bad feeling. He recalled his impression earlier of having been observed from the upstairs windows, and a red mist swam before his eyes.

Swearing under his breath, Daere didn't hesitate, but turned the doorknob and stepped into the room as if he had every right to do so. His volatile green eyes registered a flicker of surprise, one dark eyebrow cocked, and for the first time in a long while, Daere McCalister was stopped dead in his tracks.

Five

Daere barely remembered closing the door softly behind him as he entered the shadowy room. The bedchamber was dimly lit by a single lamp, but he could tell at a glance that he must have blundered into the wrong room.

For a moment, he teetered on the brink of retracing his footsteps and leaving before the woman on the bed might awaken. But then in the next breath, he threw caution to the winds, and his hand slowly fell away from the knob.

The hardness and cynicism drained from his face as his vision narrowed to pale silver-blond hair splayed against the silk pillows, and petal-soft lips, pink and dewy, slightly parted in slumber. She had one arm bent at the elbow and thrown across the upper portion of her face, shielding her eyes. She had a small, narrow nose, tilted at the tip, giving her an almost haughty air. He smiled to himself. Leave it to Rosalie to hire a girl with class and distinction. His gaze lowered, descending upon her warm, inviting mouth, and went no farther.

Her full lips hinted at a fiery, passionate nature and captured his rapt attention. Suddenly, he wished for more light, but he didn't want to turn up the lamp and wake her. And he really wasn't in the mood for conversation. At the moment, he didn't even want to know her name. Later, they would talk, but for now he only wanted to take her in his arms and make love to her. Body language was all he'd ever needed in the dark. It revealed far more than words could ever say. With a quick glance, he had already made certain there wasn't anyone else in the room but the two of them. He reasoned it must have been her voice he had heard cry out in her sleep.

Daere allowed his dark, scrutinizing gaze to slowly travel over her, noting how the swell of her breasts rose and fell rhythmically beneath her gown with each slow, even breath. His head began to swim and his thoughts narrowed down to one. There was no denying her allure. She looked soft and warm; the fresh scent of springtime lilacs radiated from her skin and filled his senses.

He stared at her with a deep, almost painful inner longing. It was something he hadn't felt in a long while. He wanted to bury his fingers in her wild mane and savor the smell and texture of her silken tresses.

In studying her, it came to him that what he could discern of her delicate features made her seem naggingly familiar. He couldn't imagine where they might have met before, but it wasn't of primary concern to him at the moment. The sort of interaction he had on his mind didn't require any type of introduction or even their needing to get to know one another first.

Rosalie's was a place where a man could be silent or boisterous, depending on his mood, and a woman wouldn't find fault with him.

Daere knew that whether he wanted her for an hour or for the entire night, the decision was simple. He simply had to cross the room and take her into his arms. In thinking this, the desire singeing through his veins precluded every other thought but one: *Possession.* His need to have a woman had lit the flames of passion in his belly and dispelled reasoning from his mind.

The lovely woman lying in the big feather bed looked pure and sweet in repose, like an angel, but it in no way diminished her provocative allure. Angels didn't exist at Rosalie's, although if a man felt so inclined, he might secure the next best thing. If he slipped her something extra for her trouble, she'd play any role he had in mind. And Daere McCalister was strongly entertaining such a notion at the moment. Here anything was possible and nothing was forbidden.

His eyes blazed, glinting with curiosity, and he

felt a familiar tightening in his groin. He promised himself that by the time he left this room, they would no longer be strangers. His thoughts whirled, his heart began to pound, and a wild excitement licked through his veins. Only moments ago, he had been certain he would open the door and find Jade. A hint of a smile touched his hard lips. There wasn't even a close comparison.

He studied her a moment longer, savoring her fragile beauty. The woman sighed, then curled one hand against her breast, her dainty fingers opening and closing, opening and closing, as though she were caught in the throes of a dream. Daere wondered what a woman like her dreamed about. And what were her innermost longings? She made a little gasping sound, inhaled sharply, then quickly drew her legs up, twisting her gown up around dimpled knees.

His avid gaze roamed over her at will, savoring her feminine appeal. She wore a soft ivory muslin night rail, a blue ribbon securing the gown at her throat, affording him only a scant glimpse of her creamy skin above the collar. He had little trouble imagining the ripe, willing body beneath the voluminous material, and thinking this, he crossed the room to stand by the bed.

The four-poster bed was draped and curtained in flaming silk that fluttered in the cool breeze drifting beneath the partially opened window.

At a quick glance, Daere noted that there were various articles of clothing draped over a flower-upholstered chaise at the foot of the bed: white cotton stockings, lace underwear, a forest-green high-necked gown with puffy sleeves, and various frilly, feminine things scattered about.

The beauty's soft, subtle perfume mingled with the heady scent of woman. Daere barely moved a muscle, just watched, waited.

In recalling how the other women here loved to play games, and the exotic and varied ones he and Jade had played out together, Daere felt his hunger sharpen.

There was a moment when he barely breathed, studying her with predatory thrall. In the next instant, his mouth twitched upward on one side, seductively, knowingly. She was every man's forbidden fantasy. Her face was enigmatic, but the glimpse of shapely leg drew his gaze and knotted his belly, hinting at sin.

Daere's jade-green eyes glittered with desire. She looked like a succulent peach, softly contoured, ripe for the picking, and he realized just how much he longed to take her in his arms. He couldn't remember ever feeling so aroused. The deadly chase had ended for now, but his craving for excitement lingered and his yearning turned to other fantasies, the black-clad tracker forgotten.

As quietly as he could, he washed up at the

small bureau where there sat a bowl and a fresh pitcher of water. He sighed with pleasure as he thoroughly washed the trail dust from his hard-muscled frame, then briskly towel dried his skin until it tingled. After running a brush through his hair until it felt silky to the touch, he retraced his steps to the bed and the woman.

He suddenly couldn't wait another minute to touch her. Turning a millimeter, Daere leaned over and blew out the lamp burning on the table next to the bed, plunging the area into darkness. The night belonged exclusively to him.

He had been weeks without the intoxicating smell and feel of a woman. She was a delicious combination of naughty and nice, and he wanted to sample everything she had to offer.

Something strong and warm and very male pressed against her willowy form. Star stirred from sleep but couldn't force her eyelids to open. She had been floating on a cloud, and strange sensations pierced through her heavy veil of dreams. Or was it a dream? Yes, of course it was, brought on by the sleeping draught that Jade had given her earlier.

Hands and lips and warm, moist kisses seemed to turn her blood to warm honey. Those lips began a heated exploration of her body, tasting her inch by inch, savoring her softness and sweet-

91

ness. She could feel warm, moist breath on her bare skin, the abrasion of a stubbled beard that tickled and aroused, and was struck at once by the clean, masculine scent that invaded her senses.

Star fought through the heavy mist of sleep. Her hands came up of their own accord, connecting with sculpted muscle and inflexible limbs. Arms and legs entwined with her own, sending an involuntary shudder along the length of her slight frame.

She tried to utter the words to tell him to stop, but the only sound she could make was a shuddering moan of pleasure. This was wrong, she knew it was, but somehow it felt right, too. Frightened but dreamily breathless, Star snuggled closer instead of drawing away.

Just one more kiss, she told herself, and then I'll make him go. But when that long, lingering kiss ended, his hot, sensual lips moved over her in other places, and she could only gasp in shock and, in the next breath, sigh with ecstasy.

It was as though he held her under some strange spell, or perhaps it was the side effect of the sleeping powder that Jade had given her. Yes, of course that must be it, Star thought dazedly. What other reason could there be for her lack of willpower?

Then, his hard mouth was on hers again, kissing her, his tongue ravishing her mouth, robbing her of the last of her will. My God, was that actually the sound of her own voice moaning low in her throat?

She felt lost and absolutely drained of any power. Star's body yielded even as her mind continued to rebel. There had never been another man who had kissed her in such a wicked way. It was absolutely indecent but also delicious, and Star was stunned to realize that she wondered what it might be like to make love with someone like him. But what really made her blush from head to toe was the way her tongue had instinctively mated with his, and her arms hungered to hold him ever closer. So close that the steely muscles of his body were molded to her every soft curve.

With a groan of desire, Daere cupped her buttocks with one big hand and pressed her hips against his throbbing need. Then she felt his free hand on the ribbons securing her gown, and she whimpered when he gave a sharp tug and the fragile ribbons fluttered free, exposing her breasts.

He lowered his head, his lips and strong white teeth sweetly menacing her nipples, then shifting lower, savoring the satiny texture and scent of her skin. But when he began stroking her inner thighs and his mouth moved downward, a cry of protest rose up in Star's throat.

"No . . . you mustn't," she gasped.

"I want to taste all of you, sweet," he murmured coaxingly, his lips brushing against her quivering belly. "Don't fight me . . . just let yourself enjoy. Then if you don't like it, just tell me and I'll stop. . . . But I think that you *will* like it"—he began nibbling at her flesh—"very much, in fact."

His lips probed deeper, hungrier. He tongued the sensitive bud gently in the nest of downy curls, suckling her, wooing her.

Star cried out as his mouth fused hotly against the very heart and soul of her, and her legs opened wider, the heat in her loins building, aching, starbursts of white-hot pleasure radiating throughout her body.

It was an emotion without control, a complete loss of will, and she shivered with passion and a trace of fear. But there wasn't any way she could stop the waves of ecstasy he was giving her. Star's body thrashed and writhed beneath his tender assault in glorious abandonment. When the last tiny flickering flame between her legs finally burned out and her body ceased to convulse beneath his mouth, only then did she realize what had just happened to her.

Dear Lord, she had given herself up in wild abandon to this man—a virtual stranger! For an instant, she couldn't believe what had transpired between them. Surely, she must be dreaming. But then she felt his long, lean body slide up and over hers, the rigid length of his sex burning between her thighs like a firebrand, and Star experienced shocking reality. She began shaking her head anxiously.

But he didn't notice. He was whispering intimately near her ear, saying crazy, sexy things that made the waves of heat start all over again. "And now that I've made you burn, you will do the same for me," he told her. "I'm going to come into you, and you'll take every inch I give you, then ease this need you've stirred inside me."

He said other shocking things that made her ears — and other places — sizzle, but Star's thoughts were fixed unwaveringly on that part of him that pressed at the apex of her thighs. She heard him emit a deep groan as the tip of his manhood touched the moist heat between her legs, and she felt the shudder that rippled along the length of his body.

Daere was so caught up in making love to her that he was lost in a haze of desire and unmindful of anything else. Having moved up and over her, he was poised and ready, his breath coming in short gasps. She seemed so small and delicate down there that for a moment he wondered if he might hurt her. And pain was the last thing he would ever wish for so exquisite a creature.

So he forced himself to ease slowly, gently, inside her, while at the same time bending his head and taking an aroused nipple into his mouth.

Her breath was coming in little pants once again. The intense hunger grew and enveloped them both. He caressed her belly with his hand, then slipped his fingers down between their bodies to part the silky folds and ease his entry.

She clutched at his shoulders and felt like screaming from the sensations rioting throughout her. It felt so good she could not believe it.

But then, just as she offered him total surrender, his body tensed and his muscles stiffened when he heard a feminine voice shriek, "Where the hell is he? I'm gonna make him pay big time for this!"

Daere clenched his teeth as that shrill feminine pitch rattled the bordello's windows and effectively doused his ardor. "Damn her, anyway," he growled, rolling away from the warm, willing woman, who had instantly gone rigid in his arms.

Doors opened, wide-eyed faces peered out curiously, and along the narrow hallway, men stepped aside as Rosalie Valdez stormed down the corridor, her corseted bosom heaving in rage.

"Daere McCalister, you'd better haul your backside out of bed right this minute and go pluck that damned little cougar off my satin draperies!" she bellowed.

96

With a disgusted sigh, he got out of bed and hurriedly stuffed his long legs in his trousers as Rosalie paused before the last door in the corridor. Their door.

Star had drawn the covers over her and lay quietly, studying him from beneath downcast eyes. Here, the moonlight slipped between the folds of the draperies and played across his hawkish countenance, finely sculpted bone, and sinewy muscle. It rippled over him, casting his nudity in bronze. She had never imagined that a man might be beautiful to behold, but he was. It bothered her to think just how much, and her eyes glistened with unshed tears.

There came a brisk rapping on the door. "I know you're in there," Rosalie called out. "And you got just about three seconds to get on out here."

Yanking open the door, Daere stepped over the threshold and stood face-to-face with the fuming madam.

Rosalie's dark eyes spewed fire as they stared heatedly at him. "Damnit, Daere, those draperies cost me a month's savings, and I sure as hell don't have a mind to see 'em end up on the floor looking like limp spaghetti!"

Running his fingers through his hair, Daere said more soothingly than he felt, "Calm down, sweetheart. I'll take care of it."

An anxious frown formed a wrinkle between

her ebony brows. "You'd just better, mister. And I mean pronto," she demanded, unyielding.

Muttering something caustic under his breath that expressed his displeasure at having been so rudely interrupted, Daere stepped around her. Slamming the door shut behind him, he strode off down the corridor, with Rosalie dogging his footsteps and grumbling to herself.

Star was shaking as she swung her legs over the side of the bed and willed herself to stand. She had to get out of this room before the gunslinger returned. The memory of lying in his arms taunted her, and a wave of defensive anger rose up inside her. She simply couldn't believe that she had let Daere McCalister take such liberties with her body, and the only way she could absolve her sense of shame was to tell herself that she had not been in complete control of her faculties.

Still, it was hard to accept the fact that a bitter enemy had been able to seduce her with such effortless ease. What kind of woman would have allowed him to do such things? And enjoy every minute of it, too! She flinched as waves of shock and distress washed over her. There simply wasn't any way she could bear to think about it another second or she would surely dissolve into tears. And Star hadn't allowed herself the release of tears in so long that she was afraid once she started, she would not be able to stop.

Frantic, she searched about for something to cover her bare body, and her shaking fingers closed around her rumpled gown. Hurriedly slipping it over her head, she drew a calming breath. She knew there was only one avenue of escape open to her, and she stumbled across the floor to a hidden panel in the room. When he returned he would find her gone, and hopefully, he wouldn't be able to recall in vivid detail what she looked like.

Once the panel had whispered closed securely behind her, Star hurriedly discarded her nightgown. Dressing quickly in the leather garments she had left on the floor of the secret corridor behind Jade's bedroom wall—the previous owners had constructed the house and had carved out the catacombs as a place to hide from the raiding Indians, but some of Rosalie's customers liked to use it for other reasons—she breathed a sigh of relief.

Only then did she notice that the sudden movement had aggravated the shoulder wound she'd received earlier. It was lucky for her that McCalister's bullet, which had torn through her leather jacket, had left only a jagged burn on her skin. But it would still leave a scar, however slight, along with a constant reminder of their deadly encounter on the mountain.

Recalling the feel of his body as he had slipped between her legs, then suckled her breasts, along with the combined scent of whiskey and tobacco that was so much a part of him, she knew there would be no forgetting this night.

Of the two encounters, this last had proven beyond her control. In her role as Raven, Star was used to always being in control. Never had any man stripped her of her defenses as McCalister had done. Moisture blurred her vision. What sort of fires had he kindled in her body that had made her want to surrender her every thought, will, and emotion to him? And now that he'd stirred passion to life, how could she forget that dizzying pinnacle of pleasure he'd given her. Even now, just thinking about his caress brought a tingle of heat running through her. Far more puzzling, though, was the odd sense of languor that had settled throughout her body, robbing her of her usual fire and vigor.

Startlingly, she realized it was satisfaction that had mellowed her and left her feeling as though she could purr like a kitten. *Sexual satisfaction.* McCalister had given her that. She vowed then that it would never happen again. It was just too helpless a feeling for her to accept. Raven could never rise to the challenge of her enemies if she walked around with her head in the clouds and her muscles so relaxed that the thought of any sort of confrontation at the moment only made her want to yawn.

Star was suddenly more weary than she had

ever been in her life, but she knew she couldn't afford to waste another minute. Sagging back against the wall, she forced her eyelids to remain open. She knew the sleeping powder that Jade had given her earlier had indeed helped her to rest, but it had almost proved her undoing as well. Jade and Star were good friends, and they had been for a long while. There had been many times in the past when Star had needed a confidant, and there was no one better at keeping a secret than Jade.

She knew that Jade had only been trying to help by doctoring her wound and convincing her to remain there, but Star realized she would have to be more careful about hiding out here in the future. The one thing she had feared most had come close to happening. Daere McCalister had almost learned that Raven was, in fact, Star Tremayne.

Daere McCalister! Damn him! Not only had he breached the sanctuary she had always found here in her role as Raven, but the blackguard had almost claimed her innocence as well! Suddenly, her pretty mouth twitched. Men! They were indeed all the same, she fumed, tossing her head, her silver-blond hair flowing around her shoulders. It had always given her such immense pleasure to lead the ones like McCalister on a wild-goose chase, but Star knew she would have to be more careful around him in the future.

Only a select few knew her true identity. And they would never betray her. She wanted to teach McCalister a lesson badly—especially after tonight—but she knew that now was neither the time nor the place. She just had to have patience, and he would come to her again. There was more than one way to tame the wild beast, and next time, perhaps Raven would emerge the victor.

Her eyes clouded as she remembered how she had lost someone very dear to her because of a lawless man very much like Daere McCalister. Then her lips tightened when she recalled once again what she had allowed him to do. Worse, she remembered her fevered gasps and moans, and at the end, her breathy sighs. Her flesh had felt as if it were on fire wherever his hands and mouth had touched her. And he had touched her in a very wicked way, in every place imaginable!

Suddenly, her palms grew moist, and she pressed them against her quivering belly. She could never tell anyone what had happened. Not even Jade, in whom she had always confided her hopes and dreams.

Her runaway emotions were because of him, the man she'd sworn to destroy before allowing him to remain in Tequila Bend. He had held her wildly mesmerized.

And now that the McCalister spread was his, there was no doubt in her mind that he would fight hard to keep what rightfully belonged to him. It would take someone equally as cunning and forceful to persuade him to sell out and move on.

Primal, savagely beautiful, he was as magnificent a man as she'd ever known. And it galled her to admit this even to herself. Worse, she didn't like to imagine that the singeing heat that had overflowed in the next room earlier was the cause of her quickened breathing and the heavy, prickly feeling in her lower extremities even now.

A footstep sounded in the distant corridor, and Star tensed. "Who's there?" she whispered low, standing poised for flight. She knew she should escape now, before he could possibly discover her hiding place.

"It's Jade," her friend replied, and Star sighed with relief as she noted the Oriental beauty's approach. Jade held a lamp up high, having come to assist Star just in case her friend needed her help. It was just the way they took care of one another. "I got terribly worried when I realized you were in there with McCalister. Are you okay, honey?"

Star nodded mutely, not trusting herself to speak. But she did trust the other girl with her life. In that, she was absolute. Jade worked at Rosalie's because she liked the freedom the money afforded her—having once been the concubine of a powerful warlord, before she'd managed to escape her country—and she had sworn never to become enslaved by another man again. In this, she was very much like Star.

Jade's dark gaze scrutinized her face. "He didn't do anything to you, did he?"

"I'm . . . fine," Star managed. "Let's just get out of here, shall we?"

Jade turned around and led the way, and Star followed. Freedom was near at hand. They only need turn and follow the narrow passage until it merged into another, then take that route to the stairs and head downward. From there, it was only a series of moves, and finally, she would pass through a door that opened onto a little-used trail by the river.

As Raven, she had traveled through these corridors many times. Jade Soo Ling knew the true meaning of friendship. She wouldn't betray her trust. Even for McCalister.

Then Star made a silent vow. *There will be another time and place, McCalister. And the next time, you won't stand a chance against me.*

Daere was to wonder later, when he returned to the same room, where the mystery woman had gone. But by then it was very late and he was extremely tired. He lay down on the bed and had barely given it a moment's consideration before his half-lowered eyelids began drooping closed.

104

Overwhelmingly exhausted, he was soon sleeping soundly, his dark head nestled into the plump soft pillow. Her scent was still in the room . . . and in his mind.

Hazily, he thought of sweet-smelling skin and firm, high breasts. He would have to remember to ask Rosalie who the girl was. For one thing remained clear in his mind: He wanted her again . . . more than he had ever wanted any woman that he could remember.

And the silken sad uncertain rustling of
each purple curtain
Thrilled me — filled me with fantastic terrors
never felt before;
So that now, to still the beating of my
heart, I stood repeating
" 'Tis some visitor entreating entrance at my
chamber door —
Some late visitor entreating entrance at my
chamber door —
        This it is and nothing more."

The Raven, Edgar Allan Poe

Six

The following morning dawned beautiful and cloudless. A good shopping day, Star Tremayne thought upon rising and drawing back the lace-point curtains that draped her bedroom window. Her sky-blue eyes gazed down on the street and she saw a number of townsfolk already up and about. Star hurried to complete her toilet, deciding to forgo breakfast, and was dressed within twenty minutes.

Business was always brisk at the town dress shop when the church held its annual supper dance, which was only two weeks away, and she knew she must be downstairs in time to greet the first customers. As she expected, several women were already waiting for the door to open when she arrived promptly at nine o'clock.

"Morning, ladies," she said warmly, swinging the door inward, smiling as they filed past her. "Go on in and have a look around while you're waiting. I've a few matters to tend and then I'll be with you shortly."

"Looks like it's going to be a busy day," Star said to their seamstress, Juanita, who had followed her into the workroom located in the rear of the shop.

"I expected as much," Juanita replied. She hung her cloak on a hook and sat down behind a long table, where she would spend her time cutting and sewing the garments that Star fashioned. "I told Carlos that I probably wouldn't be home tonight until after eight." Her brown eyes seemed troubled, even though she laughed. "Of course, the twins will undoubtedly have driven the poor man crazy by then, but he'll just have to survive somehow; I do whenever he's working nights at the hotel."

Star knew that Juanita's husband complained often about having to watch his twin daughters so that his wife could work, but she felt certain that it wasn't really his role of caregiver that upset him as much as it was the fact that Juanita had to work so that they might make ends meet. Carlos was a good man, but if he had a fault, it was his wealth of manly pride. "He'll be just fine," she reassured Juanita. "Both Carlos and the children can only benefit from the time they're spending together now. I still have many warm memories of the wonderful times my father and I had together. Your Carlos and the girls are making beautiful memories to cherish forever."

Juanita smiled gratefully at her. "You always

seem to know just what to say to cheer me up. *Gracias, senorita,* for making me feel less guilty about my having to leave them every day. If there is anything I can ever do for you, you only need ask."

"There is no need to thank me, Juanita. We're friends, remember? And you already do so much for me by helping out at the shop. Why, I just don't know how we'd get along without you." Hearing the bell jingle over the door once again, Star reached for her apron. "Speaking of which . . . I guess it's time we get started."

"I'm ready whenever you are," Juanita said cheerily.

For the rest of the day, there was never a moment when they weren't frantically busy. The flow of traffic continued throughout the morning and into the afternoon as well, and Star and Juanita had to work furiously to keep abreast of all the orders they received.

Never one to shy away from hard work, Star didn't resent the long hours she spent at the shop. She was a tall, slender woman with an elegant grace, who usually wore her pale blond hair drawn back in a smooth but flattering style. She always seemed to have a smile for everyone, and her expressive eyes sparkled with a zest for life. Framed by thick, sooty lashes, her eyes were a vivid blue and her most striking feature.

Not that she wasn't quite lovely, but she would be the first to admit that there were other girls far prettier, who attracted suitors easier than she. Star rarely went anywhere socially, except with Jake Fontaine, and lately, she had begun shying away from going out with him.

If there was one thing that Star did love, it was her work, and since the first day that the shop had opened, she had remained devoted to its success. She personally ordered all of their materials and also designed the shop's gowns — using her creative imagination instead of relying on patterns — and her work was always in high demand. So much so, that sometimes her eyes burned and her fingers were cramped from the long, tiresome hours she spent cutting and sewing. It was usually very late by the time she had closed up shop and gone upstairs, and she was often bone-weary and barely able to keep her eyes open. But she never felt better than when a day's work was done and their order book filled with new orders that just seemed to keep pouring in.

Star's Aunt Hilda, a plump, jovial matron, could generally be found working just as hard, right beside her niece. But she had been called away to Santa Fe earlier in the week to nurse her ailing sister, and she wasn't expected to return for several more days.

As the shop was shorthanded and there were over a half-dozen women still waiting to be fitted, Star was grateful that no one seemed in any particular hurry today and everyone was content, at least for the moment, to mill about or chat with friends.

Brushing a wayward strand of shimmering silver hair back from one smooth cheek, Star proceeded to finish pinning a bright pink bow onto Laura Meeker's hem. The flounced skirt and poufed sleeves with tiny velvet bows would be flattering, she thought, and would detract from Laura's ample hips, just as she had planned. The majority of their customers never realized the subtle tricks Star employed to make them appear at their best, but she really worked hard at it and was generally pleased with the results.

Star also knew that many of her customers had large families, and this often meant children who were underfoot all day and husbands who were too busy themselves to offer much in the way of relief. She had thought it would be nice if there was a quiet place in the shop, away from the mainstream of noise and chatter, where the ladies might retreat and wait their turn for a fitting, so she had had a section in the back remodeled for this purpose.

The ladies had been delighted and grateful, and business had improved even more. So much so, that Star sometimes had to remain open later at night.

Even now there were several women who had pulled their chairs up close to the cheery hearth, where a blaze crackled, and sat sipping tea from china cups, catching up on the latest gossip and exchanging news, content to just relax.

As she continued working, Star caught snatches of the ladies' conversation, and she wasn't at all surprised to hear them talk of little else but Daere McCalister. She, like everyone else, it seemed, had heard that he was back in town, unwanted but determined to remain.

The rumor was that McCalister hadn't been back more than twenty-four hours before the town's resident hothead, Billy Clyde Frazer—who, it appeared, fancied himself faster and deadlier—had begun to brag about how he was going to prove to everyone that he was faster on the draw.

To date, McCalister and the tough-talking Billy Clyde had yet to meet, but they were welcome to shoot it out anytime as far as Star was concerned. She hadn't forgotten their last encounter, but she had been trying very hard to put it out of her mind. Men like McCalister gave a town a bad name, and no one felt like shopping when there was a killer walking the streets.

Sitting back on her heels, Star's gaze flickered over Laura Meeker assessing her handiwork, and then she smiled approvingly up into the other woman's inquiring eyes. "There isn't a man at the supper who won't envy your Robert," she said, and was rewarded by the woman's grateful smile.

"You're always too kind, my dear," Laura replied. "But it's nice to hear you say so, anyway."

Finished with Laura Meeker's gown for the

time being, except for sewing the bows onto the hem, Star dismissed the woman. Laura wandered off to nonchalantly stand before the window that fronted Main Street, while her younger sister was fitted next.

Star couldn't help but notice that Laura's gaze avidly searched up and down the boardwalk, and moments later, she heard her exclaim excitedly, "Oh my Lord, girls . . . quick, come look. I . . . think this might be *him*."

Like a clap of thunder, the words disrupted the order of the fashionable dress shop. In a flurry of slippered feet and rustling petticoats, the young ladies forgot everything and hurried to join Laura before the window.

"Where is he?" her sister Rebecca asked, craning her neck for a better look-see, peering intently through the gleaming glass.

Laura withdrew the scented handkerchief that she had pressed to her moist brow, and she fluttered the tattered material in front of the glass. "Look . . . over yonder at that man who just came out of Riley's General. It's Daere McCalister—I know it is—and will you just look who he has on his arm!" Her prim little mouth puckered in disapproval. "I always did say that woman was bold as brass."

"Oh my . . . look, the street is beginning to clear," Rita Guillermo cut in anxiously. "I bet Billy Clyde's already on his way."

"I heard that he sent word for Daere to meet

him at high noon," Rebecca said. "But if you ask me, Billy Clyde was always more talk than anything else."

The boardwalks were nearly deserted now, but every window fronting Main Street was crowded. Bad news always traveled fast in Tequila Bend.

Word was out that Daere McCalister was on the street at last.

No one was certain whether McCalister had accepted Billy Clyde's challenge or not, but it was a fact that Daere McCalister was a man who made his living by his gun, and everyone knew that if he wanted to save his reputation, he'd have little choice but to confront Billy Clyde.

Star glanced at the clock sitting on top of the mantel. It was eleven-thirty—only a half hour until noon—and she was sitting on the edge of her chair. No one could say what the outcome would be this day or which of the two gunfighters would walk away, but McCalister was reputed to be lightning-fast on the draw and had yet to lose a gunfight. But Billy Clyde wasn't smart enough to let that worry him. He had listened to himself brag so much that he undoubtedly believed he would walk away unscathed. Star didn't know what made some men behave so foolishly, but it was a sad fact that their town already had its share of ruthless gunmen, and they hadn't needed another to come riding in. Like it or not, though, McCalister was here, and it didn't appear as if he were in any hurry to leave. Star had vowed not to be a party to any of the fervor his presence created, and she wasn't about to allow herself to be drawn to that window. Laura's voice carried to her.

"Well, what do you think, Star? Is it him or not?"

The women had remained determinedly before the window waiting for Daere McCalister and his companion to walk past. The tension increased, as did the women's nervous twitters.

"I really have no interest in finding out, Laura," Star said plainly.

"Well, I think you must be mistaken," Rita interjected, after having taken a long, close look at the tall, dark stranger. She had fully expected to see a man hard as nails, with the unpredictable disposition of a lobo wolf, swaggering down the street before her. But upon looking closer, Rita was disappointed when she didn't see anyone who measured up to her expectations.

"I know he's been away a long time and has probably changed somewhat in appearance, but I have to agree that *can't* really be him," Rebecca said.

Laura quickly cut into their exchange. "It's him, I tell you," she snapped. "I recall his picture being in the newspaper after that awful shootout in El Paso last year. I know you remember the incident, where that poor child accidentally darted into the line of fire and was killed." She pointed an accusatory finger at the couple who were now almost directly in front of the shop window. *"That's* the man responsible."

The women continued to observe him intently, their expressions dubious. The stranger was clean shaven and immaculately dressed in a tailored black coat. His trousers were tightly molded to long, firm legs and he wore beautifully crafted, tooled leather boots that gleamed from a recent shine. He had a thin black cigar clamped between full, sensual lips. His white shirt was silk, and the sunlight played off the diamond and onyx studs at his wrists. He had an easy, loose-limbed stride, and beneath the wide brim of the black Stetson, his chiseled features were quite handsome.

They couldn't believe it. He didn't look callous or threatening. Having heard of Daere McCalister's nefarious deeds, the ladies had envisioned someone entirely different, and now they were disappointed. *Just where was this savage they had been expecting?*

He certainly didn't appear to be the sort of man who possessed a deadly aim and killed in cold blood. But they knew that sometimes looks could be deceiving. At least they secretly hoped this was the case.

Rita Guillermo's dark eyes were still shadowed with doubt. "I don't know . . . I say that fella looks more like a card sharp than a gunslinger to me."

Their disappointment only intensified as they

watched him tip his hat to a young mother who passed by him, several youngsters in tow. And when her little girl accidentally dropped her rag doll on the boardwalk, the man left his companion to retrieve the child's doll for her.

Bending down, smiling, he placed it back in the child's arms with a tender smile and a pat on her head.

"Dear heavens, he seems to have manners and a warm heart as well," Rebecca blurted out, stunned.

The observers in the dress shop contemplated him silently for several more minutes, and now even Laura was beginning to have second thoughts. "Well . . . maybe I was mistaken after all," she admitted sheepishly.

The women continued to stare after him, but with considerably less enthusiasm. The man straightened, and after bidding the mother and her child good day, he continued onward. Just then a gust of desert wind swept the stranger's coat away from one hard-muscled thigh, revealing a hidden prize. The collective group at the dress shop window stood as if mesmerized by the gun tied down on his right thigh.

Laura's sober expression became animated once more. "I told you it was him!" She half turned, her gaze searching for Star, and noticing that she had finished with her sewing and had moved to stand behind the counter, Laura said coaxingly, "Star, come have a look-see. He can't know that we're watching him." They shared a silent look, and Laura grinned. "I should have known you wouldn't be interested. He really is rather handsome . . . albeit in a primitive fashion. But then I've always heard that some women find that attractive in a man. Of course, you wouldn't be one of those women in a million years, would you?"

Hot color flooded Star's cheeks at the insinuation, but then her blood chilled when she heard Rebecca gasp, "Lordy . . . I think he's headed for your shop, Star."

Her words effectively splintered Star's calm control. She whirled, and in her haste, her elbow bumped the tin of pearl buttons she'd yet to put away, scattering them underfoot. She barely noticed and was at the window in an instant, her earlier resolve forgotten. Air rushed from her lungs as she peeked through the window curtains. He was indeed striding toward the dress shop, and he was so close now that she could hear the clink of his silver spurs and the soft scrape of his boot heels on the wooden planks of the boardwalk.

Suddenly, as if he sensed her watching him, his gaze seemed to clash with hers. Star began to tremble. It was as though she'd been caressed intimately. She was amazed to discover that there was nothing chilling about those eyes that seemed to bore into her. They were a striking jade green in color, flecked and ringed with gold, like a forest pool kissed by the summer sun. And she didn't fail to notice, too, that his gaze bore a hint of sadness and pain. There was an underlying wildness as well, an unpredictability that scared the daylights out of her.

Worldly eyes; yes, that was what they were, and they'd seen things that would undoubtedly make her shudder, she thought. *How old was he?* Thirty-three? Thirty-five? Killing would come easy to him, and undoubtedly he was faster than most, for he was old in years for a gunslinger. They usually died violently, while still young.

Star continued to study him openly, for she expected that she was well hidden behind the swath of ruffled curtains that draped the window. Even if she'd wanted, she knew she could not have turned away. She'd seen her share of cowboy drifters and hot-blooded *vaqueros*. More than a few had landed in the jail house for disturbing the peace or shooting up the saloon, but they weren't killers, just rowdies.

This man was an honest-to-goodness gunfighter. It had been said that he killed people without the slightest provocation, that his hands and soul were stained with the blood from the countless numbers he'd murdered. *Oh, yes, he was going to give this town hell.* Star didn't doubt that for a minute. It snapped her to the present, and she swallowed the panic in her throat, ordering Rebecca, who was nearest to the door, to "turn the lock quickly!"

The girl fumbled with the key, panting from anxiety.

"For goodness sake . . . hurry!" Star urged.

"I'm trying," Rebecca snapped.

Too late, a footstep fell, Chihuahua spurs clanked, and Star froze as she observed the door-knob turning sharply.

Seven

The bell over the door tinkled and hinges creaked as it swung inward. Suddenly, a tall form, broad shoulders, and a dark face invaded Star's world. She caught her breath. How could she possibly consider such a scoundrel attractive? Forcing her gaze from him, she turned to the woman standing beside him. She was of Oriental descent and extremely beautiful. Star knew her well, but ever aware that Jade would not like to openly acknowledge their friendship before these women, she kept any greeting to herself.

"Good morning, ladies," McCalister said, keenly alert green eyes sweeping the room, the women, a watchful fixity in his face.

"Yes, it is," Star answered, trying to remain as calm as possible. "Is there something that I can do for you, sir?" She felt the blood drain from her face as his bold gaze settled on her once again, studying her closely.

"I certainly hope so, ma'am. I'd like something special for my friend," he explained, his voice deep and refined, and surprising her. He seemed to have dismissed everyone else in the room but her, even though the other women were still gaping ridiculously at him. "Something nice . . . something that befits a lady."

There was an audible gasp of disapproval and shock from the ladies in front by the window. Star found herself wishing the women would remember just who it was that they were confronting. He might shoot them all if they did something that displeased him. She breathed deeply and prayed there wasn't going to be a scene. "Ah . . . I'd be happy to find something, sir, but perhaps you might like to come back at another time . . . when we're not quite so busy." When he frowned, she hurried to explain. "You see . . . it's simply that we're shorthanded today, and I really hate to make you wait unnecessarily."

"But I'm a patient man, Miss . . . ?"

"Tremayne," she offered softly.

"And I'm not in any rush. I don't mind waiting, Miss Tremayne."

Buried memories, painful emotions, suddenly washed over Star, and she could only wonder why. For some odd reason, McCalister evoked images and impressions of another time. Agonizing emotions she'd repressed and thought she had buried now surfaced, washing over her. Yes, the man she'd known long ago had looked very much like McCalister, even though he'd been much younger at the time.

Tall, dark-haired, ruggedly handsome, with a winning smile, but really ice through and through. Star had understood years later, after her father's death, that the man who'd visited slipped into her stepmother's bedroom almost nightly, having been Cassondria's lover — but only one of many over the ensuing years.

Most importantly, she had never forgotten that he'd been there on the evening her father had died. The very same night she had heard her father cry out her name and had begged her stepmother to check on him. But Cassondria had refused, and she had frightened Star so badly that the girl had been terrified to leave her room. Even though it had been over seventeen years ago, the pain of that night would always remain with her, as vivid as if it had occurred only yesterday.

She noticed McCalister's eyes narrow. "However, if you insist, then Miss Soo Ling and I will return at your convenience, ma'am. Say, tomorrow afternoon?"

Star swallowed uneasily, her thoughts racing. She and Jade Soo Ling had become friends over the years, and Star had often sewn fashionable gowns for her to wear. She hated the fact that Jade had insisted they play down their relationship for fear of ruining Star's standing in the community. Star had abided by her friend's wishes, but she was sorely tempted at the moment to drop their charade and to heck with the consequences. She met Jade's dark gaze, noticing the warning message in the coffee-colored depths of her eyes.

Don't be impetuous, Star, and allow your heart to overrule your head. I won't be happy with you if you do, and it really is better this way for both of us.

Star nodded briefly, and Jade's lips twitched in a grateful smile. At that moment, Juanita hurried forward to her friend's aid, smiling and offering a solution that she hoped might be acceptable.

"Perhaps we can work something out, *senor*," she said kindly, standing next to her employer. "If you think it won't take you too long, then I will wait on the other ladies and *Senorita* Tremayne can assist you."

He inclined his head. *"Gracias,* that's mighty kind of you, ma'am." His inquiring eyes lit on Star. "That suits me . . . how about you, ma'am?"

"I suppose it's all right with me as well," Star replied. She vowed to have him out of her shop in less than twenty minutes, for in casting a quick glance at the clock, she noticed that it was going on noon!

To her surprise, McCalister was gracious and considerate of her time, but it was apparent that he wasn't going to settle for just anything. He had very good taste, Star couldn't help admitting to herself.

She had shown them several items: an Irish lace shawl, a flowery hat with a wispy veil, kid gloves. A pair of turquoise earrings. Jade liked them all, every one of them.

124

He considered her choices, then said politely, "They're all very beautiful, but just not quite what I had in mind. Would you mind showing us something more?"

"No, of course not," she replied and kept searching, displaying the fervor of a miner digging for gold. *Please, please let me find something that will absolutely satisfy him!*

A short while later . . . eureka! He ended up purchasing a very lovely and expensive silver-backed comb and brush set. He didn't bat an eye when she told him the price, simply peeling off several bills from those he had secured with a gold money clip.

Blood money.

Star hesitated momentarily before accepting it, and glancing up at him, she noted a brief flicker of something in his eyes.

She didn't know why she took the extra time to wrap the exquisite set in lilac-scented paper, securing the bundle with a bright yellow ribbon. Fluffing the bow with her fingers, she set the package on the counter before them. "Thank you, sir," she said and, glancing warmly at Jade Soo Ling, added, "I hope you enjoy it very much. It really is a lovely gift."

Jade assured her that she would.

"I am indebted to you, and I won't forget," he said, then exhibited that unsettling grin again. Star blanched. She thought it was downright indecent the way his teeth gleamed white in that sun-bronzed face. He reminded her of one of those pirates in the penny dreadfuls that her aunt read so avidly. She didn't trust him for a minute. Then he tipped his hat at the collective group, and he and his companion left.

The store buzzed like a beehive, and Star wilted. She never wanted to lay eyes on that man again! At least she didn't think she did. What was even more puzzling was the peculiar weakness in her limbs and the heat spreading throughout her lower region. That "place" where decent women weren't supposed to feel such sensations. And she found she was already recalling the way he walked, talked; the clean light scent of his cologne. Then again she only need think about the way he made his living—a killer who indiscriminately used his gun, snuffing out lives without conscience, as though he were Lucifer's own avenger—and her heart squeezed painfully. Foremost in her thoughts, however, was the memory of the night she'd spent in his arms.

No, it was better that he keep his distance and she hers from him, for trouble was sure to follow him, and Star didn't need more problems than she already had. Especially from a desperado like McCalister. Hopefully, he wouldn't be staying for long . . . just until he made certain that his father was properly buried. Although, if he'd already heard some of the rumors surrounding the untimely demise of the elder McCalister and if she were any judge of character, he wouldn't be leaving before he had some answers. Daere McCalister was just that sort of man.

"Humph, did you see the way his eyes raked over me? He's no good, that much is for certain," Laura was saying, her thin lips pinched with disapproval. She whirled away from the window and walked over to finger a bolt of delicate Swiss muslin that lay on the counter. "Got the light of the devil in those eyes. The sooner he leaves, the better off we're going to be."

"The man makes me tremble from head to toe," Rebecca said. "He's so . . . so . . ."

"Wicked," Laura blurted out, then blushed furiously.

She wouldn't have dared admit it, but Star silently agreed.

And by the sound of it, the real excitement was just about to begin. Billy Clyde had been as good as his word. It was twelve o'clock straight up.

"Your time's up, McCalister!" he yelled, stepping off the boardwalk directly across the street from Star's shop. "I'm the man who's going to teach you what real gunfightin' is about!"

It wasn't one minute later that his challenge was answered, and Billy Clyde, who fancied himself faster than any man alive, lay face down in the dirt, dead and soon to be forgotten.

"I wish you'd stay here with me a while longer," Jade Soo Ling said, brushing her long hair before the vanity mirror. She simply adored the brush and comb that he'd given her. And as women were wont since the beginning of time, she was in a particularly loving mood because of his generosity. "I don't like your being out there on your pa's ranch alone. It isn't a good idea, Daere, considering the way he died. I mean, do you really believe he fell from his horse and broke his neck? Well, no one else seems to think it was an accident like the doc says." She frowned. "Cap's property borders Cassondria Tremayne's, and it's no secret that she's been after him to sell her the place for years. And as for Doc . . . well, everyone knows he'll say anything if you offer him enough money. I'd just hate to think that something awful like that might happen to you." The brush paused in midair. "I don't know why you won't take me with you to the funeral tomorrow . . . Have you heard anything I've been saying to you?"

Daere had been drifting peacefully, eyes closed, in Jade's feather bed, but his ears were always attuned. She could carry on a one-way conversation like this for hours, and he didn't even have to say a word, just lie there and listen. He liked to hear the sound of her softly accented voice, the cute way she had of mispronouncing words.

Daere had been grateful for the quiet evening, no one else having dared to call him out after this afternoon. He knew Billy Clyde had two brothers, drunkards both, but loyal when it came to kin. He well remembered the Barlow incident, but he figured it was still early and he might relax for a while longer. He knew they had last been seen in the Birdcage. Hopefully, they hadn't had enough liquor yet to work up the nerve to come after him.

Slitting one eye, he noticed that the evening shadows were creeping into the room. The sun was starting to go down. It was that time of day when some men got reckless, even downright stupid, the liquor they'd been consuming since the saloon opened having had time enough to pickle their brains and override any common sense they might have possessed.

Not long afterward, he knew he'd been right.

"Hey, McCalister! Ya hear me callin' ya? If you do, then why don't you quit hidin' under the bedcovers and come down here and meet the man who's gonna whip your butt for what you did to poor ole Billy Clyde!" The voice turned sneering. "That is, of course, unless you're a yella' belly coward and are afraid of me!"

Daere roused from his catnap. Damn! Why did there always have to be trouble? He knew one of the other brothers was probably waiting in the shadows to ambush him. Not a exactly a novel approach, but for some reason no one ever seemed to come up with a better plan, so they used the same one.

He felt like putting his fist through the wall. His relaxing stay here was about to come to an untimely end. There was a braying jackass on the boardwalk below Jade's bedroom window—the two-legged kind were the worst—and it sounded as if he was just begging for somebody to put him out of his misery.

Frankly, at the moment, Daere didn't think it sounded like a bad idea. Yet he'd never found the idea of shooting down a drunk, even one who was asking for it, a fair game. Here his pa wasn't even buried in his grave yet and his son had already taken another man's life. Christ, would it never end?

Daere decided he just didn't need anyone else's death on his conscience today. Especially not some trigger-happy fool who thought he had the surefire way to rid the world of Daere McCalister, confirmed killer. Hell, hadn't they all felt the same way? But so far none of their bullets had ever had his name on it.

"Don't make me come up there and get you, McCalister!" the liquor-slurred voice threatened.

Stretching his long, lean form, Daere flung a muscular arm over his eyes and sighed in disgust. "He's just beggin' for it, isn't he, Jade?"

"I'm afraid so, honey," the raven-haired beauty seated before the dressing table replied, as she surveyed the damage her lover had inflicted on her coiffure. She ran the brush through her tresses once again. She sure looked a mess, that was for certain, but it had been worth it. They'd had themselves one fine time this afternoon.

Daere sighed, and rising up, he swung his legs over the side of the bed. "Sorry about the ruckus,

Jade. I guess I'd better head out the back way before the sonofabitch decides to come in here and tear the place apart looking for me."

Stunned, Jade swung around on the velvet-covered stool. "Did I just hear you right, honey?"

He didn't answer, just began buckling his gunbelt.

Questions gnawed at Jade. This wasn't the Daere McCalister she used to know. He'd never backed down from anyone in his life. An uncomfortable silence stretched between them. She stared after him, her eyes questioning. When it was obvious he wasn't going to offer an explanation, she couldn't help but query softly, "Daere?"

He held up his hand. "Don't," he warned her.

Without further comment, Daere McCalister quietly slipped out the door and headed down the back staircase.

Presently my soul grew stronger; hesitating
    then no longer,
"Sir," said I, "or Madam, truly your forgive-
    ness I implore;
But the fact is I was napping, and so gently
    you came rapping,
And so faintly you came tapping, tapping at
    my chamber door,
That I scarce was sure I heard you"—here I
    opened wide the door;—
      Darkness there, and nothing more.

The Raven, Edgar Allan Poe

Eight

Daere stood solemnly at the windy grave site, listening to the minister's words, his blood like ice water in his veins and his emotions, as always, unrevealed.

"Ashes to ashes, dust to dust. We now lay the body of our dear departed friend, Captain Shawn McCalister, into his final resting place. May the good Lord be with him, and keep him, and have mercy on his soul. Amen."

The minister's voice carried over the mournful sigh of the wind as the tiny congregation bowed their heads in a final prayer.

Daere didn't know why at the last minute he had decided to attend the services. He had never felt anything but anger toward his father, and he certainly felt like a hypocrite standing among these grieving people who called Cap McCalister a friend.

They had never been friends . . . hell, they hadn't even liked one another. So what was he doing here? Why had he come when his father had never given a damn about anyone but himself? Daere knew he should just put the ranch up for sale and move on; the sooner the better, since it seemed that every fast gun in New Mexico was out for his blood.

Daere had formed his own impressions about Cap McCalister long ago, and none of them had been favorable. There wasn't anything else he needed to know that he hadn't already figured out for himself.

His father had been a cold, selfish bastard, and it wouldn't surprise Daere in the least to learn that he had cut his only son out of his will and left the ranch to strangers.

Not that it really mattered if he had. Daere didn't feel as if he belonged here, although if anyone had a right, he supposed he did. His mother had sure taken the news hard. Even after everything that his father had put her through, to this day she still loved him. But there had never been any love lost between him and his pa. This was because of his mother and the despicable way that Cap had treated her.

Rachel McCalister was a soft-spoken, gentle woman, who had never uttered a harsh word to anyone, least of all her husband. She had always been a devoted wife and mother, who had rarely ever complained. She worked hard, mending fences and branding cattle, and still managed to keep a spotless house and set a fine table. How in God's name had she ever fallen in love with a man like Cap McCalister?

Daere had asked himself that question many times. He blamed his pa for her ill health, as well as for the hard times that she'd endured because her husband had refused to provide for her after kicking her out with only the clothing on her back and her teenage son to care for her.

Daere hadn't looked back as he had ridden away from the ranch that night, his mother weeping softly beside him. They had traveled as far as Santa Fe before Rachel fell ill. The doctor had said it was consumption. Daere had been certain she would die, but with his diligent care, she had slowly recovered, although she'd never been the same again.

Eventually, Rachel and Daere were able to put their shattered lives back together, although it hadn't been easy. He still recalled that time vividly and always with bitterness.

He knew that folks who had once been her friends believed that Cap had come home early from a cattle drive and had caught her in the arms of another man. A man to whom he had once provided a job and shelter. Hell, it had never been any secret that Rachel and their ranch foreman were friends, but Daere didn't believe for a minute that they had been lovers.

Daere knew his mother was a virtuous woman, and he had always believed wholeheartedly in her innocence. He was thinking of his mother now and how she just sat in her rocking chair before the hearth, reading passages from her Bible and humming songs she used to sing to him when he was a little boy.

He didn't realize his thoughts had drifted until he heard the shrill cry of a hawk soaring overhead, and his vision cleared of old memories.

Glancing up quickly, he noticed a brassy-haired woman standing next to the minister. Her face was partially concealed behind a wispy black veil, yet he still recognized her. She was tall and fair, with a harsh beauty and full lips that could still draw a man's eye. Dressed in a black gown with a low décolletage that emphasized her voluptuous curves, her lush breasts above the corseted taffeta were softly luminescent in the sunlight. He would have bet anything that she'd be here today.

"This concludes the services, ladies and gentlemen," the minister said, and the group of mourners on the windswept hill began to disperse from the grave site.

Snatches of conversation drifted back to Daere, who had been observing them from beneath hooded eyes. He held nothing but contempt for these narrow-minded people and had pointedly ignored them. Not that he expected anyone to walk up and offer him their condolences. Everyone knew that he had been estranged from his father for years.

Daere observed two rancher's wives, their heads together, walk past him without acknowledgment. They were engaged in conversation. He couldn't help but overhear what they had to say.

"I guess I'm not surprised that Rachel didn't come today, considering how he felt about her and all."

"I imagine she doesn't have the nerve to show her face, even after all this time. And considering how shamefully she treated the poor man, I can see why."

"Whatever happened to that Frank Colby, do you know?"

"Well, after Cap near killed him, he just disappeared, and as far as I know, he's never been heard from again."

"I've always said, people don't run away unless they have something to hide. Those two were foolin' around behind Cap's back, all right, and if you ask me, they got just what they deserved."

The women walked on, unaware of his killing look of fury.

Cassondria Tremayne approached him cautiously, her tone low and intimate. An emotion came and went in her eyes before her long golden lashes swooped down to conceal it. "It's been a long time. How have you been, Daere?"

He stared down at her. "I've had better days."

Her chin tilted up, and she met his gaze. "Don't pay them any mind." She added softly, "It helps them ease the boredom of their dreary little lives. I guess you know they're going to try and run you out of town."

The slight uplifting of his lips, teeth barely flashing, gave him a deadly appearance. "Your concern is touching, ma'am. I didn't think you'd care one way or the other anymore."

"I don't like to be called ma'am," she sniffed. "You of all people should have remembered that."

"Oh, I remember everything, darlin'," he drawled.

A sudden smile curved her lips. "Good," she purred. "I was hoping you wouldn't have forgotten. By the way, I'm having a small dinner party on Saturday evening. Some very important people will be there. I'd like for you to be there, too. And after the party . . . you and I will discuss a little business proposition. I think it's one you'll like."

Daere noted the glint of hunger in her eyes, and he quirked one eyebrow mockingly high. "It's been a long time. How can you be so sure?"

"Some things never change. I know how much you hate this place and the people here. Maybe I can help you out. It won't cost anything but a few hours of your time to hear what I have to say."

For long minutes he stood looking down at her. Finally, he said, "Hell, why not? Nothing would give me greater pleasure than to ruin everybody's evening."

Later, after everyone else had left, Daere stood there staring down at the fresh mound of dirt on the grave. He hadn't wanted to be here, but all of a sudden, he couldn't bring himself to leave. For some inexplicable reason, he longed to know more about this man who had shunned him for so many years. Even though he hated him, he still felt drawn to Cap McCalister and haunted by his past.

The day was growing warmer; the changing angle of the sun slanted across his eyes. His thick hair had been stylishly cut and gleamed blue-black in the blinding sunlight, which cast ghost-like shadows on the cliffs in front of him. Beads of moisture dampened his harshly planed face. He swiped at his brow with the backs of strong fingers and, with a jerk of his head, flung an errant lock of hair back in place. Then after unfastening the collar button of his linen shirt, he slipped out of his coat and tossed it over one shoulder. He didn't look like the same man who had first ridden into Tequila Bend, his appearance having been drastically altered.

He wore his fine clothes with casual disregard, as if he were accustomed to wealth and all its accoutrements, and really didn't belong in this sparse land that had once been his home. The gun strapped on his hip told another story, though, and the man at his back knew well to be wary.

Daere had heard the barely perceptible footsteps creeping up behind him, and he whirled about; in the next instant, the gun hammer clicked. He stood, legs braced apart, with deadly purpose in his eyes.

The intruder, who was visibly shaken, stared slack-jawed, his hands held wide in entreaty.

"Whoa there, son. There ain't no need to point that peashooter at me. I surely don't mean you no harm. I just came to see if it was true about Cap being gone and all, and if so, to pay my last respects. I don't cotton much to some of the folks around here, so I thought I'd wait a spell until they left."

Daere nodded and reholstered his gun. He watched as the barrel-chested old man, wearing a pair of scuffed red leather boots, moved a few cautious steps closer.

"You sure caused me a start at first, standing there by yourself like that. I knew I was crazy, but I almost thought it was McCalister himself for sure come back to haunt this place."

"Sorry. I thought everyone had gone. I wasn't expecting anyone else. Where'd you come from, anyway? I don't recognize you from being around these parts."

The old-timer motioned with a jerk of his thumb. "I'm from over yonder a ways. Got me a cabin up in the mountains. Been there a lot of years. You get used to the solitude. It's what I wanted after . . . well, you know."

They stared assessingly at one another across a ringing silence.

Finally, the man said, "He wasn't such a bad sort, you know. He just chose to believe all the wrong people instead of the ones who knowed the truth." He squinted his rheumy eyes. "By the looks of them fancy duds, I'd say you don't live around here parts. Special made, aren't they?"

"Yeah, they are," Daere replied, studying him closer. He concluded that he liked what he saw. There was a quick perception in the old man's piercing eyes and a ring of truth to his words.

"You're his kin, right?" the man asked, and this surprised Daere. He would have thought that everyone here knew who he was by now. Yet it seemed this man didn't have a clue.

"In a manner of speaking, but there was never any love lost between Cap and me," came the laconic reply.

"I got me some kin . . . somewhere," the man mused dreamily. "Not sure where they are anymore, though, and I guess they've probably given me up for dead a long time ago." He proffered a worn, red-knuckled hand. "I'm mighty pleased to make your acquaintance, son." He cocked his head. "Say, you know, you look so much like McCalister that you could pass for his ghost. Guess that's sure what startled me at first."

The two men shook hands.

"The pleasure's mine, I assure you. My name's Daere—Daere McCalister."

The codger's lips cracked in a smile. "Hot damn, I thought as much. I'm Frank Colby. I was your pa's foreman. It's been a lot of years since I last saw you."

Now it was Daere's turn to stare at him as if he'd seen a ghost, but moments later his mouth curved in a smile. "Do you believe in fate, Frank?"

"Nope, can't say as how I believe in much of anything no more."

"Well, you will. You see, I intend to stake my claim to this place and I want you beside me. I'll make it worth your while and then some."

Frank Colby stared oddly at him. "Why? . . . You know what they all said about your ma . . . and me?"

"Was any of it true?"

"Not a word," Frank replied unhesitatingly.

"*That's* why, Frank. We're not running away this time. You and I have come home to stay."

Daere was still experiencing mixed emotions later when he stood outside the ranch house that

142

had once been the only home he had ever known. Constructed of wood and stone, the structure sat silent in the twilight, although the memories seemed to call out to him. Daere tried his best to ignore them but found that it was impossible. In many ways this place seemed like a distant memory, but then in others, everything that had happened here still remained fresh in his mind.

The proverbial prodigal son had finally come home to stay.

His gaze swept over the house, the sloping roof, and lingered on the deep veranda, where he used to sit with his parents after supper until it was time for him to go to bed. His father would smoke his pipe and plan the next day's work schedule, while his mother would do her mending or help Daere with his book learning. She had always stressed to him the importance of learning to read and write. They had read many of the classics together. His father had objected, of course, but his mother had remained adamant.

Daere still enjoyed reading the works of Shakespeare and Shelley. Even now, whenever he needed to wind down, he'd reach for one of the dog-eared books he always carried with him and would read until he felt himself begin to relax.

Frank Colby stood beside him, and his voice interrupted Daere's silent reverie. "Go on in, son. The door's unlocked and it's all yours now."

"Care to join me in a drink?" Daere asked

him. "I reckon you're about the only one who knows what needs to be done around here and just where I should start."

"Sure, son, I'd be glad to pass the bottle with you."

The two men entered the house, and Daere led the way to the ranch office located at the end of the long hallway.

When he'd poured them each two fingers of bourbon, Daere handed one tumbler to Frank and carried the other to the rolltop desk that sat in front of a long row of windows. He took a seat behind it and stared thoughtfully out at the herd of fine horses in the corral.

"Looks like some quality stock," he said. "Guess my pa continued to do all right for himself." His shrewd gaze swept over the landscape. "It's too bad he never saw fit to share any of the wealth with his own wife."

Frank Colby studied him shrewdly. "Sometimes it ain't easy to come home, is it, son? Specially under the circumstances."

Daere sat in the leather-covered chair quietly, then shook his head. "It's harder than I ever imagined, but to tell you the truth, I've had my fill of moving around and never having a bed to call my own. I'm looking forward to settling in here. I've been thinking that maybe I can even talk Mother into coming home again. She really loved this place at one time, and God knows she did her share of hard work to make this ranch a success."

"I'll say she did," Frank agreed. "And there's money to be made here. Money that rightly should be hers, too." He frowned in concentration. "And I know someone else who would sure like to share in the wealth. I heard that Cass Tremayne's been lookin' to buy this place for some time. What with the Bar M bordering her spread, she'd stand to have better'n two thousand acres if she joined her place with this one. Explains why she was at the funeral today." He gave a short laugh. "She thinks you're gonna be eager to sell out. Hell, I'm surprised she didn't make you an offer right there at the grave site."

"She did invite me to a fancy get-together she's throwing at her place," Daere said, swiveling in the plush chair. He arched his eyebrow and smiled knowingly. "And if I remember anything about Cass Tremayne, I'd say she has plans to wine and dine me first, then later offer some friendly persuasion she feels certain I won't be able to refuse."

"You're probably dead right about that. Never met another woman like her in my life." Frank grimaced with distaste. "You just watch yourself real close if you decide to take her up on her invite. That bunch is meaner than a pack of jackals. There just ain't no telling what they'd do to get their hands on this spread."

Daere's expression was grim. "Even kill to get whatever they want, you think?"

"I reckon they might," Frank replied, staring at him with meaningful intent. His broad, stubby-fingered hand curled tightly around the tumbler of bourbon. "And I don't doubt that they haven't done so."

"You don't think my father's death was accidental, do you?"

"Your pa was an ace horseman. It's my opinion that something stinks to high heaven about that accident of his. Guess what I'm tryin' to say is, don't let their fancy manners fool you, and watch your back."

Daere's gaze met his in understanding. "I've been doing that for so long it's become second nature, Frank. But thanks for the warning. And don't worry, I'll remember."

Nine

The woman smiled softly in her sleep. It was the dream, the same one she often had, and even though it was a painful reminder of times long past, she welcomed it. Reality for her was far more grim, so she clung to these misty-edged memories and savored them for as long as they might last.

The little girl with the pale silver curls stood on the upstairs balcony made of intricately scrolled black wrought iron and waved her delicately stitched handkerchief at her beloved father. As always, her spirits lifted whenever she saw him. "Just give me a minute, Papa, and I'll be right down," she called to him.

Benjamin Tremayne tipped back his golden head and smiled proudly up at his offspring. "No rush. Bring your parasol, baby. The sun is brutal today."

She nodded eagerly and, whirling around, dashed into the airy bedroom furnished in rosewood and *objets d'art*. Reaching the four-poster heaped high with a snowstorm of clothing and a froth of petticoats, she snatched up a frilly parasol to match her day gown.

Her bright flowered day gown was the latest fashion—a Paris creation that her father had brought back with him from his last trip abroad. A blur of rose and apple-green blossoms flared around white kid slippers as she hurried down the wide center staircase and out the massive oak front door.

Benjamin Tremayne's eyes misted when he saw her and his chest swelled with pride. She was a fourth generation Tremayne, a refined and respected testament to a proud family bloodline. She'd lived on this land in quiet splendor for the better part of her life, her life actually having begun in the canopied bed in the high-ceilinged master bedroom all those years ago.

Sadly, her mother's passing had left Benjamin to raise his young daughter alone. Everyone knew he doted on his little girl and would do anything in the world to keep her happy. She was his cherished princess, born to wealth and protected always.

From the cradle, Star had been a rich man's daughter, Benjamin having inherited a tidy sum after his father's death and investing it wisely.

Star continued with her dream, snuggling deeper beneath the warm covers.

Benjamin Tremayne was a self-made man. Having always felt stifled sitting behind a desk in a stuffy accounting office and suddenly finding himself with the means to do better, he decided to move his young family out west, to New Mexico, where he intended to seek his own fortune. He made contacts there and a few months later traveled alone to Tequila Bend.

He found the land breathtakingly beautiful and remained there. Soon afterward, his second wife and his son Alec from a previous marriage settled in Tequila Bend with him. He took every cent he had in the world and bought a thousand acres of land bearing several mines. He had big dreams, and he told himself that one day he would get lucky and strike it rich, maybe even become a millionaire.

For a time, the little family lived in a small house that he had built with his own hands. But to his dismay, Benjamin soon found that he was far too busy with daily chores to work the mines for more than a few hours in the early mornings. Yet, he never gave up hope that one day his life would be as he'd always dreamed.

A year later, Star was born, and it was that first gaze into his daughter's big blue eyes that had so captivated him and gave him the added incentive that he needed.

He hired more men and a foreman to run his ranch, and Benjamin began mining around the clock for silver and gold. As added insurance, he also raised horses and prime cattle, often working without sleeping for days at a time. So no one who knew him was surprised when he struck a rich vein of gold and his fortune soon surpassed that of any of his neighbors.

Benjamin was a happy man, and he built a house like no other in a beautiful valley by the river. The Tremayne name was soon at the top of the social pyramid, and governors and senators were often guests at their lovely home. He entertained often and lavishly. Money didn't mean anything to him unless he could share it with those he cared about most. He was generous to a fault, particularly with those he loved.

Tragically, his lovely wife was killed in a riding accident, and Benjamin found himself grief-stricken and alone, except for his two children. Alec and Star had never gotten along very well, and without a mother's loving guidance, their petty bickering soon turned to bitter resentment and their relationship deteriorated even more.

Benjamin knew he must marry again soon, if for no other reason than to provide his children with a proper family environment. If he had ever had any one weakness, it was his eye for beautiful women, and it didn't take him long to fall in love with a much younger woman for the third time. He worried what his children would say, Star most of all, when he told them.

He cherished his only daughter more than any other human being, for she reminded him so much of her mother. Anything that money could buy was Star's for the asking, and even though she asked often, he had never refused her. He always saw to her every want and need with joy. He had never done anything that might hurt her in any way.

This was when her dream changed and always became painful. Star moaned softly and clenched her fists into the blanket.

Taking his daughter's hand, Benjamin said gently, "I have something that I must speak to you about, darling. Let's go for our walk, shall we?"

Star could tell by the tone of his voice that he had something pressing on his mind. She hoped he hadn't heard about the afternoons she and her Grandpapa Marceau—her mother's father, who had been visiting them for a few weeks—had spent closeted in the library, and how he had taught her many of the magic tricks he had performed the world over.

Grandpapa Marceau was a famous illusionist, and he taught her well the art of illusion; how the hand could be quicker than the eye, even though a person might be staring right at you.

Star reveled in her accomplishments, and her grandpapa said she was a quick study. That was theater talk for someone who learned quickly, he'd explained to her. She knew it really wasn't very ladylike to pop in and out of boxes and pull rabbits out of hats, so Star had decided she'd best not mention any of it to her father. Though now she had the feeling she should have, for then perhaps she wouldn't be feeling so miserably guilty.

She tried to smile gaily up at him as they walked along the path by the river, but her pulse was racing nervously and she finally blurted out, "Please, I can't stand it another moment! You must tell me this instant what you wish to speak with me about."

He became increasingly sober and was looking off toward the river, as if searching for the right words. "I expect there really is no better way to tell you, pet, so I'll simply say it." He met his anxious daughter's gaze. "Star, honey, I met someone very special. She has come to mean a great deal to me. Her name is Cassondria Gomez." He cleared his throat and hurriedly explained. "Star . . . baby . . . I've asked her to become my wife, and she has given me her consent. I realize my little girl needs a mother as well as a father. We'll be a whole family again. I've already spoken with Alec and he seemed very pleased. I wish you would be. Won't you at least try and be happy for me?"

"No . . . I don't want anyone taking my mother's place!" Star exclaimed, tears shimmering in her eyes.

Benjamin looked so distressed. "Please, just say that you'll give Cassondria a chance to prove herself. She really is a dear woman and I know her only wish is to make us all happy . . . *happy* . . . *happy* . . ."

152

* * *

Star became groggily aware of something warm brushing against her legs, moving slowly over her, and icy terror wrapped around her. Immediately, she found herself gripped with fear, and she sobbed softly in her sleep-drugged state. She couldn't seem to halt the images flitting through her dreams, of a ghastly creature whose glowing eyes and long, black legs made her flesh crawl.

A whimper threatened to rush from her throat, but she forced it back, knowing she could not risk showing fear. *They* would sense it immediately and attack. It was the nature of the species.

Carefully, muscle by tense muscle, she drew back the covers, and with her heart feeling as though it were in her throat, she glanced downward, her eyes mirroring fragile hope.

Star almost sobbed with relief when she saw the small, harmless caterpillar crawling along the curve of her hip.

A caterpillar! Not a poisonous killer.

Sighing with relief, she plucked up the wiggly invader, slipped from her bed, and tossed it out the window into the shrubbery below.

She swallowed hard, her breathing raspy in the calmness of predawn, and tried to still her trembling hands. She couldn't help thinking how lucky she had been to escape once again. Or had that other time merely been nothing more than a bad dream as well? The relief she felt at the prospect of this was so sharp she felt dizzy.

It had been so long ago and the memory was vague, but the one thing she would never forget was her fear that night. She remembered, too, how she had screamed and screamed, and yet no one had heard. She shuddered now in recalling the piercing sound of her own cries, how she had thought at the time that it surely had to be some other poor girl, because *she* knew that a properly brought up young lady never, *ever* screamed at the top of her lungs.

A flash of pain, and a horrifying thought came to her. *Father had screamed in much the same way on the night that he had died.* Star shook her head in bewilderment. She didn't want to know that! The memory flickered and died.

You're such a coward, Star mentally chastised herself. *You have been running away from life ever since the night your father died!* Her eyes narrowed, darkened to cobalt blue, and her inner voice emerged stronger, surer. *Not true! You've proven many times since then that you aren't afraid to confront life's challenges and dangers.*

Star felt a surge of renewed confidence and her spirits lifted. A tiny smile flitted across her lips. She had vowed long ago to one day resolve the conflicts within herself. With each passing year she had grown stronger, and she had never felt closer to achieving her goal than she did now.

Jake Fontaine took Star to dinner that evening. "You look absolutely beautiful. I bet every man here wishes he were in my place tonight," he told her as they followed their waiter to a table in the hotel restaurant.

Star blushed becomingly. "Why, what a lovely compliment, Jake. I'm so glad you asked me out this evening. I've been so busy lately that I haven't had much time for a social life, and I've just been waiting for an opportunity to show off my new gown." She was wearing a copy of a Parisian gown she had seen in a *Godey's Lady's Book* and had made for herself in less than three days.

Her dress was a blue taffeta, with yards of ruffles on the deep flounce and a snug bodice that complemented her lithe figure. She had deviated little from Jean Claude's design; however, she hadn't felt comfortable with the revealing décolletage and had altered the scandalously low neckline to suit her modest taste.

When they were seated and handed menus, Jake gazed at her and said, "You don't know how much I've been looking forward to seeing you. I can't remember the last time we were alone together. I've missed seeing you, honey." There was warm affection in his tone, and Star was moved to cover his hand with hers.

He was such a kind, thoughtful man, she told herself, and he deserved a woman who appreciated him. Unfortunately, she was beginning to think she would never be the woman for him. Not that she hadn't tried to love him, or at least, to tolerate his kisses. She had, if only to allow him chaste pecks on

155

the lips, and at that, she'd felt only a poignant regret that she hadn't been able to offer him a more passionate response. She supposed she was just going to have to accept the fact that she was never going to feel anything more than friendship for Jake.

He would always have her respect, for he was the perfect gentleman, but she longed for a man who would never settle for just brief kisses and holding hands.

Shortly, the waiter returned, for which Star was grateful, and they gave him their order of medium-rare beefsteak, mashed potatoes, apple-walnut salad, and a bottle of vintage red wine.

When the food came, Jake seemed to enjoy watching Star savoring every bite of her meal, and she caught him smiling at her several times, just like an approving father. She suddenly felt so self-conscious that she lost her appetite.

She had always enjoyed eating and never failed to clean her plate, but for a fleeting moment she was swept back in time, no longer a grown woman but a small child again, feeling ugly and humiliated. Instead of Jake's warm gaze, she felt her stepmother Cassondria's disdainful glare as she watched every bite Star put in her mouth.

You're going to get fat if you keep eating as much as you do, and then there won't be a man who will want you.

"Star, honey, is everything all right?" she heard Jake query.

Star hadn't even realized she had such a faraway

look in her eyes. "Yes . . . I'm fine," she replied, then on impulse hurriedly added, "I . . . was just thinking how much fun it might be to take in a show at the variety theater after dinner. Is that okay with you, or do you have other plans?"

"No, I think it's a great idea," Jake readily agreed. "I hear it's a very good show. They even have an illusionist on the bill who's supposed to make a leopard disappear. Now *that* will be something to see."

Star heard the doubt in his voice, and she smiled. "Are you one of those people who never believes anything until they see it with their own eyes?"

He blushed, then stammered, "Ahh . . . leave it to me to have forgotten that your grandfather was a famous illusionist. I hope I didn't offend you?"

"He was one of the best, and no, you didn't." She shrugged one shoulder. "I'm quite used to everyone saying it's nothing more than hocus-pocus." Her eyes sparkled. "Besides, I know better."

"I'm sure if I watch closely that I could figure it out fairly easily," Jake stated confidently.

She waggled her finger at him. "Not if he's a real magician," she scolded teasingly.

He snorted. "I don't believe what you're implying."

"Don't you?" she taunted him.

"Never," he scoffed. "No one can take a solid object and make it disappear into thin air and then have it reappear with the wave of a hand. It's impossible."

"It's a matter of the hand being quicker than the

eye, Jake," she said.

Jake was staring at her open palm, then his gaze flew to her face. There in her hand lay his gold stickpin, which only moments before had been firmly secured to his cravat.

"My . . . my word . . . how did you do that, Star?" Jake asked, his eyes wide in bewilderment.

Something flickered in Star's face and then was gone. "It's magic, Jake," she replied simply. "What else can I tell you."

He nodded, still looking rather dazed. "I declare, Star, you are the most intriguing woman I've ever met." He laughed somewhat uncertainly. "And here I thought I knew just about everything there was to know about you."

"We all have our little secrets, Jake," Star replied, having enjoyed the moment immensely.

To Star's delight, they were able to get very good theater seats. They had just settled in their chairs in the balcony when the gas lamps slowly dimmed.

Within minutes, the crowd quieted and a portly man in a bright red jacket stepped between the curtains onto the stage and announced the opening act.

During the first half of the show, they were entertained by a man with a dancing bear, jugglers tossing flaming swords to each other, and a raven-haired songstress who sang a very poignant romantic ballad that brought tears to Star's eyes. Embarrassed, she lowered her gaze to the beaded reticule in her lap, for she didn't wish Jake to notice.

After the singer walked offstage, the gaslights came up, and the same master of ceremonies announced there would be a fifteen-minute intermission before the final half of the show.

Star hurriedly brushed a hand across her moist eyes, but not before she caught Jake watching her closely.

"Are you all right, honey?" Jake inquired solicitously, peering oddly at her.

His concern was obviously sincere and she forced herself to smile. "Yes . . . it's just the cigar smoke. . . . I'll be fine," Star assured him, and managed to even convince herself as well that the smoky theater, and not the brooding love song, had been the cause of her tears.

She had no idea why a wave of sadness had washed over her like that. Even now, years after her father's death, there were moments when she still felt utterly alone and unloved. It wasn't true, of course. She had her Aunt Hilda, and even Jake, and any number of others who cared about her, but sometimes it just didn't seem to be enough.

As they stepped outside and away from the crowd, she was startled by the strangest sensation — a sizzle, like heat lightning, snaked along her spine — and she felt that someone was watching her closely. Her gaze wandered over faces in the crowd, studying them all, but she saw no one who seemed to be paying her any particular notice. She recalled having had these same feelings when in the darkened theater, while she had been fighting her emotions as she listened to the words of the love song.

She caught a brief movement out of the corner of her eye and glanced to her left, where she saw him. He was standing beneath a gas lamp. The pale yellow light cast his long, lean body in shadow. She felt the heat of his gaze, the fierce sensuality that he exuded, and the breath caught in her throat. She knew she should have the good manners to turn away, but she felt snared by that insouciant gaze and could only stand there helplessly, mentally tallying more than she ever wanted to know about him and clutching her white kid gloves.

It was the way he leaned one broad shoulder negligently against a wooden post that had first prompted her to involuntarily sweep her eyes over him. He held his arms crossed over his chest, had one muscular leg cocked at an unassuming angle, and appeared not to give a damn about the frenzy of humanity rushing past him. There was just that certain something about him that held her captive.

She heard Jake's gasp of outrage beside her. "If that devil is trying to prove how ill-mannered he is, then he's doing a good job of it. I have a mind to go over there and give him a piece of my mind."

His words broke the spell, and Star's gaze flew to her escort. "No . . . please don't do that," she pleaded. Jake was angrier than she had ever seen him and she knew he probably felt obligated to confront the man. It wasn't the stranger's welfare she was worried about. He looked more than capable of taking care of himself. It was Jake she didn't want to get hurt, Jake she didn't want to see lying dead in the street. Star had a feeling this other man could be deadly when challenged, and she would do anything to prevent that from taking place.

"Only after he offers you an apology," Jake insisted.

At that moment, the tall, dark stranger pushed away from the post and stepped out into the light. Jake and Star both watched him warily.

As he closed the distance between them with long, purposeful strides, Star was stunned when she recognized him. Daere McCalister. My Lord, it was the gunslinger who had caught her eye!

Unspoken words crackled in the air between them. Star's cheeks drained of color as Jake tensed at her side. She just knew there was going to be a terrible scene because of her, but she felt absolutely powerless to stop it.

"Lovely evening," the gunslinger said, as she stared wild-eyed at him, his deep voice like a caress.

He never gave her another moment's notice as he passed by. Star was mortified to feel both rejected and terribly disappointed. She could only assume then that he had recognized her as the town dressmaker and, knowing that she was a virtuous, respectable lady, thought she'd be exceedingly dull and not worth his time or trouble.

She should have known that a woman as common-looking as she never had trouble with ravishers, especially a devil like McCalister. She was even more stunned to realize that she felt affronted, and she couldn't stop herself from whirling around and staring after him.

Beside her, Jake gasped, "For God's sake, Star, what do you think you are doing?"

Star wasn't listening. She could only stand there and watch Daere McCalister walk away without so much as a backward glance in her direction.

Aghast, she saw Jake charge after him. "Hey, you! Didn't anybody ever teach you any manners?"

A tiny flare of excitement began to flicker beneath Star's apprehension.

McCalister slowly turned, bearing a dangerous glint in his eyes. "Are you talking to me?" he asked coolly.

Jake held his ground. "Yeah! Where I come from, a gentleman would never insult a lady like you just did! I believe you owe her an apology."

Star's cheeks were flushed and her eyes shone with an almost desperate light. She couldn't just stand by and do nothing, while poor Jake met the same fate as Billy Clyde. "No!" she cried and, within seconds, was standing firmly at Jake's side. "Please . . . it doesn't matter, Jake."

Jake didn't seem to be listening.

"Did you hear me? Apologize . . . or else!" he demanded.

"Or else what?" Daere queried stonily. Stepping away from the surging crowd, he quietly assessed his challenger, then as if dismissing him, his gaze shifted, sweeping over Star. He ignored Jake and inclined his head at her. Smiling ingratiatingly, he said, "No disrespect was intended on my part, Miss Tremayne. It was merely an unfortunate matter of timing, although I can see how it might have appeared as something more. I assure you, it wasn't intended to be." His deep voice was no longer low and menacing, yet it still hinted at an undercurrent of suppressed violence.

Star prayed that Jake would hear it, too, and keep his mouth shut. She stared up at McCalister in amazement. After having witnessed how he had shot down Billy Clyde in the street without so much as a hint of emotion, she thought of him as nothing more than a cold-blooded, ruthless killer, just as everyone did.

However, the man standing before her now was trying very hard to avoid a tragic confrontation, even though it was decidedly out of character for him. He had to know that Jake didn't pose any serious threat to him, but she was sure he wouldn't allow himself to be pushed too far before he became the savage aggressor she had seen confront Billy Clyde. She had to keep that from happening.

Staring up at him, she noted he was studying her closely once again, and she would never have dreamed that Deere McCalister's eyes could bear a kind, gentle light. But she wasn't imagining it. It was there.

Star was suddenly intensely curious to know more about this man. Wild rosy color flooded her cheeks when she suddenly realized he was watching her just

163

as intently.

His eyes suddenly took on a devilish light, as if he could somehow interpret what she was thinking.

Then his gaze settled on Jake once again and turned to ice. "Can we consider this matter settled?" he asked, his voice dripping sarcasm.

Jake started to open his mouth to reply, but Star interceded and answered before him. "Most certainly," she stated firmly, a smile pasted on her lips.

The crowd suddenly parted, and a redhead in an emerald-green satin gown, diamonds flashing on her fingers, sashayed out of their midst. A ripple of voices followed her. She was the sort of woman who was never ignored. When she moved, everything jiggled, and there wasn't a male head, except for McCalister's, that hadn't swiveled about to watch her approach.

"Now, now, boys. Let's not have any bloodshed this evenin'," Rosalie Valdez said, her heavily made-up eyes stabbing Jake. "It's far too lovely a night, and I for one can think of better ways to pass the time." She shot a glare at Star. "How about you, honey? Seems you should be doin' some of the talkin' here since you were the one makin' most of the eye contact, at least that's the way I see it."

The gunslinger's lips twitched despite his attempt at solemnity. "That's enough, Rosalie," he interjected smoothly. Cupping her elbow, he began to lead her away. "I believe the lady's had about as much excitement as she can stand for one night."

Rosalie started to turn away, but then she just

couldn't resist a parting shot. "And another thing: If my friend here *wasn't* such a gentleman, he'd tell you that it was *her* making calf's eyes at him that started all this fuss in the first place," she called over her shoulder.

At that moment, Star wished the ground might open up and swallow her. She felt like an utter fool as she realized there were faces she recognized in the crowd, and they were staring after her with the same expression. Shocked disapproval.

There was nothing more she could say or do to change things. It would only make matters worse.

Star ground her teeth in frustration.

She seethed.

She swore silently.

She mentally sliced Daere McCalister down to her size.

She would never again think that man might have had a kind bone in his miserable gunslinger's body! Even at this very moment, he was probably having a good laugh at her expense with that awful Rosalie Valdez.

Somehow, some way, she was going to make him sorry for this night. She just had to bide her time. They were bound to meet again.

"You've been awfully quiet since we left the theater," Jake said as he walked Star to her door. "Are you still upset with me because of what happened earlier?"

Star glanced up at Jake, and while her heart went out to him, she really knew for certain after tonight that they didn't have any future together. The enormity of what had transpired between her and the gunslinger had finally opened her eyes. She had been undeniably attracted to him, and poor Jake had almost gotten killed because of her. If she had truly cared about Jake, she wouldn't have thought to have looked in the direction of a man like Daere McCalister. There could be no doubt in her mind. It was time to say goodbye. She and Jake both needed to get on with their respective lives. "I'm not angry with you, Jake. Heaven knows, you should be the one who is upset with me." Star smiled sadly at him. "You're a dear man and I like you a lot, but we just don't belong together. We want different things out of life, and even you know it. You just won't admit that I'm right." She sighed. "I've been thinking about our relationship for some time. I really don't think we should see each other anymore. I hope you understand."

"I made a mistake tonight." Jake spoke in a low monotone, but there was a desperate light in his eyes. "I just got a little carried away. It won't happen again."

Star passed a hand across her forehead. "No . . . it wasn't anything that you did this evening that made me come to this decision. You haven't done anything. It's me. I'm the wrong woman for you, and I truly believe I'd only make you more miserable if I allow our relationship to continue." She hadn't intended for her words to sound so blunt and she hated the look of crushed defeat on his face, but she knew he would get over her in time. A nice man like Jake wouldn't be alone for long.

"I can't believe I'm hearing you correctly," he said, dazed.

"I'm sorry, but one of us needed to say the words. It's the only way. Please believe that," she said softly. "And don't hate me too much."

"So this is goodbye? Just like that?"

Star looked downward. "Yes, this is goodbye, Jake."

Jake stared at Star a moment longer as if he didn't understand the full meaning of what she had just told him. Then, slowly and with reluctance, he turned and walked away.

Star watched him, pain reflected in her luminous eyes. "I wish you nothing but the best, dearest Jake," she whispered. "You deserve so much better than I could ever give you."

Deep into that darkness peering, long I stood
　　there wondering, fearing,
Doubting, dreaming dreams no mortal ever
　　dared to dream before;
But the silence was unbroken, and the dark-
　　ness gave no token,
And the only word there spoken was the whis-
　　pered word, "Lenore!"
This *I* whispered, and an echo murmured back
　　the word, "Lenore!"
　　　　　Merely this, and nothing more.

The Raven, Edgar Allan Poe

Ten

Cassondria Tremayne was tired, despite having slept well last night. She stirred with a restless sigh and resisted the urge to stretch her cramped muscles. It was to her advantage not to awaken the man sleeping peacefully beside her. He would want to make love to her; he always did in the morning, and she was barely able to endure his touch any longer. At least not since Daere McCalister had come back to town. He had been handsome as a youth, but now he was positively magnificent, and she just knew he could be ruthless when he had cause to be. God, just the thought made her quiver from head to toe.

The early morning sun shone through partially separated draperies and along the curve of her back. She luxuriated in its soothing warmth and began to feel her nerves relax.

Yet she couldn't help but wonder how much longer she was going to have to live with her future so uncertain and with her current lover like a millstone around her neck. He spent her money freely and had never done an honest day's work since she had known him. Of course, he didn't know that she no longer had a vast fortune to rely on. And she had to admit that she had done her share of spending as well.

The one thing she feared more than any other was that she would end up dirt-poor again, as she had been as a young child in Mexico City. She could endure just about anything to keep from ending up like her mother. And she would endure, she told herself. If she had learned anything from her tramp of a mother, it was survival. The horrors of her former life were deeply etched like scars in her mind, and just to recall even a brief interlude from her past was hell. But it never failed to revitalize her when she thought she couldn't tolerate another day.

Her lover stirred beside her, and Cassondria stiffened. He mumbled incoherently and turned over. She held her breath for several seconds. Then, hearing him resume snoring, she relaxed once again and smiled. There wasn't a hint of warmth in the gesture. It was as frigid as the woman's soul.

There was a part of her that knew she would never find another man who revered her as Alec Tremayne did. He had proven his loyalty to her many times over the years. It had seemed practical to both of them to remain under the same roof after Benjamin had died. That they shared even more wasn't really anyone else's business but theirs.

It was really too bad, actually, that Benjamin had proven to be such a . . . what did the gringos call it?

A drunken sot, *si*, that was it. By far, he had been the easiest of her former husbands to manipulate, unlike his son Alec, who was just as ruthless as she was and could be a deadly adversary. That was precisely why she would never marry him. Of course, the fact that he was now virtually penniless was another good reason.

Men were a necessary evil in her life that she could not seem to do without. Her spirits lifted when she considered the dinner party this evening. She wanted everything to be just right.

Carefully, so as not to disturb Alec, Cassondria slipped out of bed, leaving him with his head buried in the pillows. She didn't wish to take time searching for her robe and slippers, so she tiptoed nude across the floor to her dressing room. Absolutely no one would be at her party tonight unless they had something to offer her. Not even Daere McCalister, although he probably didn't realize it yet.

Her smile was one of pure malice.

Cassondria was delighted to see Daere McCalister when she opened the door later that evening. He was the last of her guests to arrive—Star had declined her invitation just as Cass had figured she would—and she had begun to worry that he might not show.

"I'm delighted that you could make it," she exclaimed, swinging the door wide. From behind her, the sound of music and loud laughter drifted through the lavishly decorated rooms. "Do come in, Daere," she said, smiling, her cat-gold eyes sweep-

171

ing over him, widening in appreciation of the narrow cut of his trousers and the black linen jacket stretching across his broad shoulders.

"I guess you could say my curiosity got the better of me," Daere said, his eyes evaluating her at a sweeping glance. She wore a shimmering silver gown trimmed with flounces of vanilla silk. The clinging material hugged her ample curves and the scent she wore was cloyingly sweet. It was the same perfume she had always worn. It was a brand he had always hated.

Her gaze widened appreciatively, then surveyed him shrewdly. "I'm happy to hear that you were thinking about me." She slid a hand under his elbow and drew him farther into the foyer. "Let's have a drink together, shall we? It's been such a long time since we've had a chance to really talk."

Well, at least she wasn't going to waste any time getting to the heart of the matter, Daere thought.

"Margarita!" Cassondria called to a serving girl. "Bring a bottle of champagne and two glasses to my office right away."

Daere followed her into a darkened room at the back of the hacienda. He waited for her to light several candles, and then she turned back to him.

"We may as well get comfortable," she said, taking a seat on the settee and patting the cushion beside her. She stared up at him. He was so divine he made her heart lurch painfully in her chest. "Come sit next to me, handsome. I'd really like for us to get reacquainted."

Daere ignored her request, crossing the tile floor to stand in front of the windows. He stared out at the courtyard filled with guests and watched a smiling Alec Tremayne mingling in their center. "I would have thought you two would have killed one another by now." He chuckled caustically. "I guess you had to learn to share the spoils."

Cassondria nervously swallowed over the lump in her throat. He was the same old Daere. Hard as nails. "You turned me down, remember? A girl has to have someone she can count on."

He swung around to stand with his legs braced wide and a smirking look on his face. "Let's cut to the chase, Cass," he said in a lazy drawl. "Why did you *really* invite me here tonight?"

She smiled coaxingly. "I foolishly thought you might have missed me just a little bit, and I must tell you, it hurts my feelings to realize that you don't seem the least bit happy to be here with me tonight. That was always your trouble, Daere. You were all business. At least where I was concerned. I was hoping we might be able to change that." When she didn't get any kind of response in return, her smile faded and a certain wariness crept into her expression. "Well, I guess there's no point in our trying to make polite conversation. So, I'll just speak my mind. I know that you've never been one to settle down in a place for any length of time, so I thought as long as you were going to be here tonight, I'd make you a proposition before you decide to leave town again."

"Who said anything about my leaving Tequila Bend?"

She stared at him blankly. "Why would you want to stay?"

Daere's caustic laugh brought her up short.

"What's . . . so funny?" she asked haughtily.

"You never cease to amaze me, that's what's so damned amusing. I'm surprised you didn't make me an offer for the ranch at the funeral instead of waiting as long as you have." He looked at her as though she were vermin. "Well, I got news for you, sweetheart, and you can pass it along to the next of kin. I've decided to hang around for a while. Maybe even settle down here. And eventually, I aim to learn exactly how Cap met his death. You see, I think ole Alec knows more than he's been telling. And that goes for a lot of things that have happened around here."

A confused jumble of mixed feelings was pulling at her, not the least among them being a sliver of fear. "Is that a threat?"

"I don't make threats, Cass," Daere replied. "You can pass that along to Alec as well. And hear me well. The ranch isn't up for sale. Not now, nor in the future."

Pink cheeks clashed with her brassy hair. A knock on the door interrupted them. Cassondria went to it, opening the door to find the maid bearing a tray of champagne and two glasses. "We won't be needing refreshments after all," she told the girl. "I'm afraid Mr. McCalister and I have concluded our business. Will you show him the door, please?"

"No need. I can find my own way," Daere said, and didn't even pause to look back as he strode past her.

Cassondria watched him stride down the long corridor, her slippered foot tapping nervously. She was glad to see him go. Daere McCalister had always been trouble, and it didn't look as if he had changed. She would have to tell Alec that they would need to be extremely careful in the future until they might figure some way to get rid of him.

Silhouetted against the dusky shadows was a dark-clad figure, an interloper, who seemed perfectly at ease with the task that lay ahead. A restless energy seemed to form an aura of power around her, making the restrictions of her movements seem calculated or even defensive, as if she never dared do anything without first considering the possible consequences.

The warm desert wind ruffled the silky blond tendrils that had slipped from beneath her black Stetson. Raven brushed her hair aside and pressed the field glasses to her eyes. From a hidden vantage point in the hills, she studied the throng of people milling about the courtyard.

There were many prominent guests at the party, among them a wealthy widower from old money whose family had made their fortune in silver mines. This didn't surprise Raven, nor did the fact that Cassondria devoted her attention to the silver baron at the exclusion of her other guests.

She watched Cassondria smiling charmingly up at him, playing the part of sultry tease as only she could do. She wore her hair pinned up in a coronet of curls, her silver brocade gown wrapped around a voluptuous figure that many of the men seemed to eye appreciatively. She had an earthy sensuality, and even though Raven thought her features rather coarse, she had to admit begrudgingly that Cassondria still seemed to have a way of getting inside a man's head and letting him think of little else but her.

The pulsing rhythm of Spanish music vibrated across the dark green river that separated Raven from the partygoers. There was laughter and gaiety in the air. The ladies' silk gowns shimmered in the flickering light of the wall sconces, and diamond studs and stickpins sparkled on the men's formal evening wear.

Raven waited patiently, wanting to give the champagne that had been flowing freely time to dull everyone's senses. Then it was her intention to slip through the shadows and gain access to the house.

It was her plan to search the house for a valuable paper that she felt certain had been hidden there. It had taken many years for her to learn that another will indeed existed, one that her father had hidden before his death, which might very well exclude widow and son from any inheritance. If not for Jade, Raven knew she might never have found out, and she intended to have it in hand before she left here tonight.

She had loved her father very much, and in her estimation, she deserved to inherit what rightfully belonged to her. This ranch and his beloved family had meant everything in the world to him. As his daughter, she had understood and shared his love of the land. No, he would never have cut Star out of her inheritance and left everything to Cassondria and Alec. She was certain of it, and she didn't feel that it was right that the two people who had caused him nothing but heartache and grief had somehow managed to gain full control of his estate and were slowly bleeding dry his bank account.

Although, that could very well change after tonight. Raven's eyes suddenly gleamed in the moonlight, fixing on the hulking figure of her stepmother's bodyguard. "Santucci," she growled. With his bushy mustache and harsh features, Santucci made the role of venal bodyguard seem appropriate. Raven had lost a good friend years ago because of Santucci. Just to look at him reminded her of the painful incident.

She would never forget how long it had taken Tully to die after Santucci had finished with him. It had been one of the worst times of Raven's life, and she well remembered her vow: She would get both Santucci and Cassondria for what they had done to the people she had cared about.

Suddenly, her expression became intense, her eyes alive with anticipation. Yes, they were old enemies.

And Raven had waited long enough for this moment.

Raven moved stealthily through the shadows, careful to stay hidden from view. She had forded the river and had gone around the stables, keeping well away from the main salon, gaining access to the house through the French doors off the library.

The room was dark except for a low burning fire in the hearth. She looked around her, at the black wrought iron chandelier and wall sconces, the tiled floor with its bright red woven rug before the stone hearth, the plush leather sofa in front of it, and the eagerness she had felt only moments ago turned to pain and bitterness.

Once this grand house had truly been a home, filled with love and laughter and people who cared, but no longer. For years, Cassondria and Alec Tremayne had lived here, bound together by a common goal, their limitless greed. However, if Raven had anything to say about it, their long reign would soon be over.

Crossing the floor, her boot heels clicked softly on the polished tiles. It was very late, but the party was still in progress and the guests didn't seem in any particular hurry to leave. Raven could only hope that the music and loud voices would provide the diversion she needed to slip through the house undetected.

After carefully searching half of the library and

still finding no trace of the precious document she was looking for, Raven could only hope that the information Jade had passed along to her had been correct.

The last will and testament to Benjamin Tremayne's vast land holdings was supposed to be hidden somewhere in this house. Apparently, he had tucked it away where no one, not even Cassondria or Alec, had been able to find it. After his death, they had been unable to claim his estate without producing the document. So they had written up a new will, forging Benjamin's signature. Cassondria and Alec had inherited everything between them, leaving Star virtually penniless.

If not for her Aunt Hilda's generosity, Star might have been left at the mercy of those two heartless fiends. Only the good Lord knew what might have happened to her then.

It was time to right the wrong that had been done. And Raven didn't intend to leave here tonight until she had searched in places where she felt the original deed might have been safely hidden.

Jade had given her a few clues where to begin searching. It seemed that the Oriental beauty had added Alec Tremayne to her list of prominent clients about six weeks ago, and the more time that he had spent with her in bed, the more delighted he had become with their arrangement. Poor fool, he, Raven sneered.

It was a union of passion and enslavement. Jade, of course, knew only too well how to manipulate a man like Alec. She focused on his weaknesses and, ever so slowly, ensnared him in a silken web from which he could not escape. He was hopelessly under her spell and didn't care to leave her.

In some ways, Jade was ruthless, cold, and lacked scruples. In her country, family was revered and remained loyal to one another until the end. She did not like how Alec and his stepmother had treated the members of their family. She was only too happy to help Raven carry out her plans.

Jade knew they needed facts from Alec and that he was really a very weak individual. To loosen his tongue, she used every form of seduction known to her: sex, liquor, and finally, she introduced Alec to more addictive pleasures. In no time, he was a willing victim, and in the end, Jade had learned a few things about him that she hadn't known before. This information was passed along to Raven, who had sometimes listened to Alec's and Jade's conversations from within the secret corridor. Alec was being duped, but there had never been a more willing victim.

Raven couldn't say that she approved of Jade's methods, but in recalling how Cassondria and Alec had schemed and cheated many unsuspecting people out of their life's fortunes, crushing hopes and dreams, even going so far as to commit murder to achieve their goal of becoming millionaires, neither was she wracked with guilt. She was a hunter of such heartless fiends. They were criminals who preyed on the weak and unsuspecting, destroying anyone who stood in the way of what they wanted for themselves.

Benjamin Tremayne had been just one of their tragic victims; there had been several others after him. However, proving it had been another matter. It had taken careful planning, years of patience and perseverance, but at long last, there had come a breakthrough. A weak link had finally been exposed.

Raven's hunger for revenge had been sharpened by the years she'd had to remain in the shadows, waiting for that one mistake. At long last, Alec had made a wrong judgment call. He had trusted Jade, and she had happily betrayed his confidence.

Now the end was almost near for Raven, too, and she was ready. Cassondria and Alec were going to pay for every unjust thing they had ever done, and Raven planned to retire soon after. There were some things a girl just wasn't meant to do, even though for a while it had certainly kept her life exciting.

Raven continued searching, well aware of the fact that Benjamin Tremayne had never trusted banks or lawyers, having been quite eccentric by nature. Even after all these years, she held little doubt that the original document would be hidden in this house somewhere. It was certainly worth the risk to try and find it, for if indeed such a document did exist and could be located, it would give her great pleasure to expose Cassondria and Alec. To finally see their empire fall and their dreams destroyed! It was the only thing that had kept her going during the darkest days, and there had been many over the years.

Intent on her task, she had just finished checking the dark wood wall panels for a hidden safe and had begun searching through volumes of books, when there came a whisper of sound. Indistinguishable at first, but it signaled danger nevertheless.

A tingle of warning ran down Raven's spine and she barely had time to dart into an adjoining alcove, where she was concealed in darkness yet afforded a view of the library.

A door swung open on well-oiled hinges, and she saw the shadow of a man. A very big man! She knew she had to remain as coolheaded as possible, yet her composure nearly shattered when she recognized the bodyguard, Santucci, his expression murderous, poised in the doorway. He had drawn his gun; his beady eyes were avidly searching the room.

"I know there's somebody in here," he snarled, "and whoever you are, you'd better start saying your prayers . . . 'cause you ain't comin' out alive."

Raven knew he meant every word, and she didn't dare breathe or make the slightest sound that might alert him to her hiding place. She had confronted men like Santucci before. They held little respect for anyone, and the only thing they knew how to do well was kill.

Watching him from her hidden vantage point, Raven couldn't help but think how feral and threatening Santucci appeared. Aware that brute instinct ruled a savage man like Santucci, Raven knew he was going to prove a most formidable opponent. Any second now she expected he would step forward and discover her hiding place. Her hand moved smoothly, purposefully, to the handle of the whip, even as she coiled herself tightly, ready to spring into action. She didn't intend to surrender meekly, but would fight until she drew her last breath. The desperate glint in her eyes said she would never be taken alive.

Suddenly, from behind the bodyguard, came another voice. Crisp, authoritative, demanding Santucci's attention. "The *senora's* asking for you. She wants you to meet her in the main salon pronto."

Agile and quick despite his massive girth, Santucci whirled about, apparently recognizing the man at his back, and snarled, *"Perdición,* are you looking to get killed creeping up on me like some damned *gato?!"*

The tall man had to have noticed the gun leveled at his chest, but he didn't so much as flinch a muscle. "I'm merely passing along a message, *amigo,"* he replied calmly. "You can do whatever the hell you want. Matter of fact, I'll go back and tell the boss lady you've more important matters to tend." He shrugged negligently. "She probably won't like being kept waiting, but she can't expect you to jump every time she crooks her finger, now, can she?"

Santucci swore under his breath, then snapped, "You stay here and have a look around. I think we have an uninvited guest. Find him. I'll take care of the rest as soon as I get back."

Santucci left the room, and Raven was faced with a new threat, no less intimidating. His eyes stared coldly, gleaming with purpose, making her tremble. She shifted uneasily, sensing the dark, dangerous masculinity of the man standing in the shadows. He had yet to move or even draw the gun at his hip, but it didn't make him seem any less threatening.

"You might as well make it easier on both of us and come out," his deep voice commanded. "It's the only way you're going to leave this room in one piece."

Raven's heart was pounding. She closed her eyes briefly and sucked in a calming breath. There were no windows in the alcove, and the only way to freedom was now blocked by the man. She angled her head and watched him, sensing things that only heightened her unease.

He was a hunter himself and well versed in the rules of stalking prey. She felt a mixture of emotions, none of them reassuring. He was right; there was no other alternative for her. She released a pent-up breath. "Don't shoot. I'm coming out, mister," she said, her tone guarded and brisk.

He didn't say another word, just watched her approach.

Suddenly, Raven went still, her eyes focusing on Daere McCalister's face. For a moment, she was at a loss for words. His lips were set in that ruthless slant she'd come to recognize well.

"Well, well, if it isn't the young fella with the big bullwhip," Daere said, crossing the room to where

184

she stood. He had noticed Raven slip inside the house just as he had been heading for his horse, and knowing full well that the tracker's name wasn't on the guest list, he had decided to find out why he was here. Eyes narrowing, his gaze slid down and riveted on the long-fingered hand splayed around the whip handle. "Don't you even think about it, kid. You won't stand a chance this time."

"I seem to remember hearing those same words before, McCalister," Raven replied jeeringly. "They didn't scare me then and they don't now."

His eyes drilled into her. "You got lucky last time. It's not going to happen again."

Boot heels scuffed on glazed tiles and spurs chinked. He was close. Too damn close. Raven's gaze sliced the distance between them. She studied the sinister half smile that played about the gunslinger's lips. She had never felt as threatened as she did now, but she'd be damned if he was going to know it. A chill crawled up her spine. What was he thinking? Was he considering turning her over to Santucci? Or maybe he would just finish her off right here himself? She knew her identity, her very life, was in jeopardy.

He was studying her with the hard assessing eyes of a cunning raptor who had cornered a helpless prey. It seemed to her a challenge, clear and simple. But she was not entirely without defenses, and when it came to her survival, she would do whatever was necessary to stay alive. She could knock the pistol out of a gunman's hand, or slice hunks of flesh off a man so fast no one would recognize him when she was finished. McCalister might be fast, but then, so was she.

It was a moment when everything seemed to happen in the blink of an eye. "I can't surrender, McCalister," Raven told him. "We both know that Santucci's a cold-blooded killer. I won't leave here alive if you turn me over to him."

"Maybe you should have thought about that before you came snooping around where you don't belong," he said. He was watching her with those frigid eyes, judging her carefully. Tall, powerfully built, his shadow was ghostly in the moonlight spilling through the window, slanting across the floor.

Her pulse raced and her heart pounded. She only stood one chance at survival. How fast could she unfurl the whip before he cleared leather?

As if he could read her thoughts, he warned softly, "I wouldn't —" but Raven wasn't listening.

Everything savage and primal rose in her at once. Time hung suspended. The world ceased to spin on its axis. There was a blur of movement, then the lash cracked across the distance, but it was she who ended up surprised.

McCalister's hand shot out fast and sure, just as the whip undulated toward him. He grasped the strand of leather in his fingers and held on.

"Damn you," Raven spat, hanging tight to the whip handle, determined not to let him defeat her. Planting her booted feet, she rocked back on her heels.

His mouth creased at the corners, mocking her as he gave a jerk of his hand.

She lost more ground.

"Why is it whenever you're around, there's sure to be trouble?" he asked, shooting her a look from beneath ominously lowered brows.

Gritting her teeth, she seethed with frustration as he twined the length of leather slowly around his hand.

She knew the whip was her last grasp on security. Her eyes flashed. A heartbeat, a swift flexing of his wrist, and he had her on her knees before him, helpless but still fighting mad. She glared up at him. There was nothing meek about the silvery blue gaze she fixed on him. "I'll see you in hell for this. . . ."

"Behave," he interjected softly, but there was no mistaking the bite in that single word.

Furious, she hissed, "You rotten bastard."

"And you've known enough of 'em to recognize one, I bet."

She didn't flinch, but faced him with all the dignity she could summon. "I don't care what you do to me. I'll never surrender to that bitch."

"I think you'd better care, kid," he said as his fingers tightened on the leather strand, drawing her onto her feet, "because it could make the difference whether or not I take pity on you and let you live. You've been a thorn in my side since the first time I laid eyes on you. And now you've gone and messed up my plans for the second time."

Her eyes flew to the grim set of his jaw. There was

no doubt in her mind that if she gave him any more trouble he would make her regret it. Her strength was no match for his. For now, she had no other choice but to surrender. Maybe, if she played by his rules, there might still be an opportunity for her to escape. It was her only hope. Everything else had been taken away from her.

Her eyes momentarily lost their battle lights. Raven was so close to him now that the scent of man, along with her own fear, assailed her nostrils. He was regarding her with that hard, piercing way of his that had already become too familiar. She flinched noticeably when she felt those long fingers tighten on her wrist. There was nothing uncertain about his touch, and it frightened her to realize how it seemed to set her skin afire.

He was so damned sure of himself, and for the first time in many years, Raven wasn't. Standing so near him, her slender form was dwarfed by his. He was well over six feet, and every bit of him was sinewy muscle. She was strangely breathless, and her limbs felt weighted and unable to move.

"Maybe you'd like to tell me now what you were expecting to find in this room?" When she didn't answer, his eyes smoldered. "Okay, have it your way, then. We'll just wait around and let Santucci ask the questions."

Raven went still. Tension became a palpable presence in the room. She moistened her lips nervously with the tip of her tongue as her thoughts raced. *Go for his vulnerable areas. Strike quickly and pre-*

cisely.

As if he'd read her mind, he warned in a silky voice, "I don't think you want to try anything stupid, unless you have some deep need to commit suicide."

She stared up at him without answering, unknowingly mesmerized by the cocky thrust of his chiseled jaw. His face was stony, his eyes hard as agates. Slowly, defiantly, her lips parted in a cool smile. "So, what now, McCalister?"

There was silence while he studied her, then that meaningful glare again. He leaned toward her, and before she realized, bound her wrists with leather. "We're getting out of here. And one peep from you, and you're history."

There was menace in his words and steel in the relentless fingers that squeezed her wrist, and Raven knew he meant exactly what he said. His face was mere inches from hers, and she saw the certainty of death glaring back at her in those tigerlike eyes. In the suffused moonlight, dressed in a black dinner jacket and trousers, silk cravat loosened at his throat, his hair falling over one slashing eyebrow, he looked like the devil incarnate — but he was also her only way out of this room.

Raven swallowed her pride and knew she would have to comply with whatever he said for now. She had no idea what he intended to do or how long it would take him before he realized just who she was. She didn't even know if they stood a chance of leaving this ranch alive, but she needed every precious second that she could get until she might think of a way to get away from him.

"What, no objections?" he scoffed, teeth flashing. He was already shoving her in the direction of the French doors that led out onto the courtyard, the same path she had taken earlier. "Let's move nice and slow," he ordered. "And don't think for a minute I won't be right beside you the entire time."

They were making their way through the doors; he had snaked an unrelenting arm around her shoulders. Raven believed he would resort to violence if she tried to escape him, but what worried her even more at the moment was that his hand might stray downward, accidentally brushing against her bound breasts.

God in heaven, what sort of chance would she stand against him if he found out she was Star Tremayne?

Eleven

Raven was acutely aware of the hard muscle of his forearm pressed to the back of her neck. What was he intending to do? Where was he taking her? She had to know. This wasn't happening; the entire scene seemed straight out of a nightmare, and she could only hope that she would wake up soon. But the taut body close to hers was very real, and she would have been hard pressed to say which was worse — not knowing what fate awaited her or realizing the truth.

Her gaze anxiously searched the grounds, then she almost laughed aloud at herself. Did she honestly think there might be someone who would materialize out of thin air to help her? You've been living on the edge of reality for too long, she told herself. There is no one but you and this man.

She cleared her throat, mentally willing herself not to panic. "You aren't seriously thinking of turning me over to that cutthroat bunch?"

"Dead serious," he replied flatly, and she knew he meant every word.

191

She made her decision, shaking her head vigorously. "No . . . I can't go with you . . . I won't."

His fingers manacled her wrists, which were still bound by the leather bullwhip, and she winced. Pausing suddenly, he jerked her around to face him, his eyes gleaming with that all-too-familiar predatory light. "The way I see it, you really don't have any choice in the matter."

Her face paled, her chin lifted. Somehow she had to get through to him, make him understand. "I have a choice . . . but you'll have to agree. You see, I'd rather die here and now than by their hand later. I'm not afraid of dying, I just don't want to die slowly, begging for the end." Her body shuddered. "And I know that's a distinct possibility if Santucci has anything to say about it."

It was Daere's turn to tense. "Damnit, will you just quit talking and keep moving."

"No," Raven stated firmly, a determined glint in her eyes.

"Christ, I wish I'd never laid eyes on you," he snarled, but for an instant he was caught up in conflicting emotions, and his gaze clouded with indecision.

It was just the moment she had been waiting for. A shift of her hand, a blink of the eye, and Raven was free from the leather restraint binding her wrists. Her movements had been little more than a blur, meant to confuse him, and for a moment, she succeeded. Instinctively, she had thought of the revolver in his holster and reached for it. Feeling the smooth ebony grip clasped securely against her palm, she summoned the courage to jam it against his ribs.

He grunted softly when the hard steel jabbed him. At last, Raven felt a measure of control, but she knew she was far from safe.

"Stand aside, McCalister, or I swear I'll blow a hole in you big enough to see daylight through."

The malevolence underlying her words was unmistakable. Their gazes locked, warred.

"I don't think you intend to pull that trigger," he said at last.

"Only if you give me no choice," she reiterated coldly.

"You're making a big mistake, kid."

"I'd be making a bigger one if I didn't try and make a break for it, and you know it!"

In the distance, she could see the faint outline of trees bordering the river. This wasn't the path she had taken earlier, but it would just have to do, she thought. She didn't have time to backtrack now, not when Santucci might already be on their trail.

McCalister held out his hand, and she jumped back, startled. "Give me the gun," he ordered.

"The hell I will," she swore sharply. "Just go . . . Turn around and get out of here before you make me do something I'll undoubtedly have cause to regret later on."

He stared at her with that dangerous, unpredictable glitter reflected in his eyes, which she had come to respect as well as despise. "So you can shoot me in the back? Uh-uh, it's not going to happen, kid. I swore I'd never die face down in the dirt. So, I guess the next move's all yours."

At that moment, neither of them dared to even breathe.

Daere gauged the dark-clad tracker standing in front of him. Damn, it was going to be another knockdown, drag-out fight, but he couldn't help it. He knew what he had to do.

In a quick reflexive movement he swung his arm, catching the side of the tracker's wrist with his open hand, knocking the gun from his fingers.

She gasped as the Colt fell heavily to the ground at Daere's feet. He reached down, calmly picked it up, and slid it back in his holster.

Raven's face was bloodless from both pain and fury. She clasped her throbbing wrist. "Bastard!" she growled.

He sighed deeply. "Believe me, I don't like this any more than you do."

Raven drew herself up, eyes shining brightly. "Like hell."

His face revealed no emotion as he extended his hand to her. "Let's go. Time's wasting, and the guests will be leaving soon. I wouldn't want them to discover an unpleasant surprise."

There wasn't even a flicker of acknowledgment from Raven.

A muscle in his lean jaw twitched, and then he reached forward to encircle her waist with one sinewy arm. "You know, having to fight you at every step is getting mighty tiresome." Quickly, he jerked her toward him.

Raven could do little more than gasp as she was catapulted along in front of him. Too furious to speak, she stormed off ahead of him. She had never detested anyone more at that moment. Mentally, she tallied the degrading insults he'd inflicted on her since their first explosive confrontation, and she ended up quivering with outrage.

The hot stillness of the night hit her with startling reality as they circled widely around the perimeter of the house, passing by Benjamin Tremayne's flower garden, the ornate fountain he'd had placed there as a testament to the hopes and dreams he had wanted to see his family carry on. She heard a sudden release of laughter come from the dining room behind them, then the voices gradually faded as they continued onward.

Raven realized they were walking in the direction of the stables, the noise and laughter of the party guests fading, until there was nothing but the suffocating darkness around them.

She knew if she were going to have any chance at survival she would have to escape from him again. Yet despite her brave thoughts, she had never felt this way before, like her knees would buckle at any minute and she would faint dead away.

He was so close, and every steel-hard muscle was tensed to strike. But if she could break away and run like the devil, it was possible she could lose him in the darkness. Yet if she tried and failed, his wrath would be vengeful.

Raven breathed in deeply. It was now or never. They were heading down a gentle incline. The stables loomed in the distance. Summoning her courage, she moved quickly, bringing her elbow back sharply, jabbing him in the ribs with all the force she could muster. He grunted in pain and, for an instant, eased his hold on her, and she was free.

With a muttered imprecation, he reached for her, but too late. She had darted away from him, focusing her energy on reaching the stable and hoping to elude him there in the darkness.

The short distance seemed endless as she scrambled over the uneven terrain. Behind her, she heard him swear softly. Would he take aim and shoot her now? She cast a furtive glance over her shoulder, hoping she might have gained some ground, but she was stunned to find he wasn't lagging as far behind as she had hoped.

He was coming after her, determination stamped on his face.

Raven plunged onward. She'd never have another chance at gaining her freedom. In a burst of newfound energy, she darted to her right, confusing him, moving quickly around the woodshed, propelling herself onward. She was going to make it! She just had to!

Suddenly, McCalister was beside her, yanking her against him, his strong fingers curling around her wrists and jerking her arms behind her back. She gasped, then muttered a vile curse. He only laughed harshly. He was very good at inflicting pain; she had little doubt that he was a professional at it.

His harsh breath rasped in her ear. "Damnit! You and I are through tussling. I'm not wasting any more time trying to convince you to behave. One sound, one false move, and you're as good as dead," he fumed from out of the darkness. "Christ, but you're a pain in the ass."

He was pushing Raven ahead of him now, and there didn't seem to be anything more she could do to stop him. She was just too weary of fighting against overwhelming odds.

He was muttering angrily between his teeth, "Maybe I *should* just go ahead and shoot you. Hell, you deserve it after what you've put me through." Then, as if he had actually been entertaining such a thought, he suddenly seemed to have a change of heart. He paused, shrugged, then said, "Naw . . . the shot would draw too much attention. Maybe I'll just drown the little bastard instead."

She drew a deep, quivering breath. Now there was no doubt in her mind where he was taking her. They were walking down an incline to reach the banks of the river. She forced herself to fight, kicking out at him with her foot.

Without even breaking his stride, he sidestepped her. Raven lost her balance and would have fallen if he had not been holding her arm. She knew she was only making it harder on herself by resisting, but if she was going to die — and she was beginning to feel certain this was her fate — then she would do so bravely. For the first time in a long while, Raven was acutely aware of her femininity and her helplessness against him.

Filled with terror but angry as well, she couldn't believe she'd heard him correctly. When they reached the river, he ordered her to take off her leather jacket and boots. Raven balked, shaking her head.

"Take them off or I will," he stated with conviction, his face set like granite.

"And if I don't?" she snapped.

He favored her with a humorless smile, his fingers already grasping a fistful of leather, and to her horror, the top button on her jacket popped open.

Raven knew if he persisted further, she'd have a whole lot of explaining to do in just a few more minutes. "Wait . . . I'll do it myself," she said, forced to concede, trembling in the chill of evening.

She didn't know whether to feel relief or renewed terror. She noticed then that several of the guards were making their way toward them. "I think some of your friends are about to join us," she said, unable to resist a savage smile.

His head whipped around, then back again. She couldn't believe she heard him right when he said, "You *can* swim, can't you?"

"I thought you just said you wanted to drown me?" she couldn't resist flinging back at him.

"We're *not* going to argue about this," he warned, and not even waiting for a response, he shoved her toward the riverbank, ordering, "Damnit, quit standing there. Go on . . . jump!"

Terror squeezed her throat muscles so tight that she could hardly speak. They were on a bluff overlooking the river below. At least she could only assume there was water below them. "It's so black . . . I can't see the water."

"You don't have to see it, just be able to swim in it."

"No . . . I won't do it," she choked out. She had never been able to conquer her fear of deep water, and when it came to swimming in depths unknown, forget it. She wasn't going to. She'd rather be shot!

"I swear, I've never known another fella who could act so brave one minute and then be so damn squeamish the next." He was beside her, glaring at her. "Just go on and jump. I'll be right by your side." He was nudging her forward even as he spoke. "Go . . . before I strangle you, and then you won't have anything to fear ever again!"

At the moment, dying by his hand no longer seemed quite so bad compared to jumping into the river. Suddenly, Raven felt his big hand splay across her back and give her a hard nudge. She was falling . . . falling . . . so terrified she couldn't even scream.

"I'll follow right behind you!" came McCalister's voice.

Some consolation, she thought. They would both drown. Thunder roared in her ears, and pinpoints of light danced behind her closed eyelids. She was plunging feet first, down, down, and there was nothing but emptiness beneath her flailing legs. From somewhere off in the distance, she thought she heard voices shouting.

"Shoot, you fools! Don't let them get away!"

The staccato sound of gunfire ripped through the night, a multitude of pistols and rifles that went on forever, it seemed. Someone was screaming. It sounded very much like her own voice, but she knew it couldn't be. She was far too frightened to utter a sound.

Raven's descent into the icy cold river blotted out the madness above. The water surged around her, and she didn't think she would ever stop sinking. Then she instinctively struck out with her arms, and soon she was kicking her way up toward the surface. It came to her then that even more danger lurked above.

The guards would have gathered force . . . and McCalister, where was he? Had he survived or fallen victim to a bullet? If it didn't mean she'd be all alone here in the water, she would have preferred the latter. As it was, the very thought made her stomach lurch.

Finally, her head broke the surface, and before she had time to orientate herself, she felt something brush against her legs. A scream bubbled in her throat, and she had to remind herself not to cry out.

Her long hair streamed over her eyes and clung to her face. She could barely see. Grasping at her soggy hair, she smoothed it back from her face. She knew, too, that if McCalister was anywhere nearby, her charade would be as good as over. He would know that Raven was in reality a woman.

It was then that she saw McCalister floating down river, far enough away that she thought for sure she could swim to the other side and he would never see her. But in casting a final glance his way, she saw that he was drifting aimlessly in the current, and now he was face down in the water.

Raven didn't like what she was thinking, but she knew what she must do. He could have killed her or let Santucci do the dirty work, but he hadn't done so. For some reason, he had tried to save her life. A puzzling man, this McCalister.

Angry voices echoed overhead. "Can you see them?" someone questioned.

"It's too dark to see anything," another man said.

Raven swam toward McCalister. He was barely conscious when she reached him, and blood streamed down his face from a head wound. "Hang on to me," she told him. "I'm going to try and get us out of here." She didn't think her words registered, and she had to snake an arm around his chest and try to hold his head above water while she kicked with all the strength she had left. Her splashing alerted the guards to their position.

A rain of bullets zipped through the water, so close that she almost cried out. At any minute, she expected to feel one tear through her. If she didn't have McCalister, she might have easily escaped. But she heard herself saying, "Just rest against me. We have a long swim ahead." His head fell back on her shoulder. He hadn't even heard her. He might even be dead, but she wasn't going to leave him. That much she knew for certain.

As she continued swimming, she had to fight off a chill. She knew by the way his body trembled, that thankfully he was still alive. She despised him, had feared him, but for the moment, she was all he had to keep his battered body afloat. He didn't seem as intimidating to her anymore. Hurt and wounded, he became just an ordinary man who needed her protection in order to survive.

In the interim, an unsettling stillness prevailed, only the gentle flow of the river disturbing the quiet. Then something happened that turned her blood to ice. Santucci began calling to her from a place on the riverbank.

"Hey, *amigo* . . . let us help you. We will, you know. You only have to let us know where you are." He was trying to inject concern into his voice. But Raven detected something else in his tone, carefully disguised yet not quite concealed. Perhaps it had been the succinct manner in which he spoke that warned her to remain wary of him.

She forced her aching legs to keep kicking, doing her best to stroke with her free arm. She grew tired and wondered how much farther it could be until they reached the shore. There came the sound of a boat moving through the water and suddenly the beam from a lantern illuminated a path on the river not thirty feet away.

Raven turned her head and saw the craft was almost upon them. Her eyes widened with horror when she noticed one of the men held a rifle sighted on them.

The explosive concussions rocked her one after the other. A repeater rifle, she thought, and there wasn't any way for them to escape. Raven experienced a shuddering ripple through her body but felt no pain. Mind drifting, she thought hazily, *So this is how I'm going to die.*

"I don't know for certain what they were up to, but I do not think it matters any longer. It appears they are dead." Santucci stood before Alec Tremayne in the study of the hacienda. "It is unfortunate that we weren't able to recover their bodies, but the current is swift there and I guess they were swept downstream. We'll be able to search better come daylight. I can let you know more later."

The party had been over for hours; the guests hadn't even been aware of the life-and-death drama that had taken place. The music and wine had helped to dull their senses, but the man sitting behind the massive oak desk was stone cold sober. And angry as well.

"How could you have allowed him on this property without checking with me first?" he demanded.

"It was an unfortunate error," Santucci replied, "but I was only following orders."

"Orders! Whose, might I ask?"

"The *senora's*. She's the one who wanted him here tonight. She would not listen to me."

Alec let his eyes pierce Santucci's. "I pay you to do what you're told! You're not to think or to follow orders from anyone else. You should have come to me with this problem. I would have taken care of it. Your mistake almost cost me a great deal. For your sake, I hope they did not survive."

After Santucci left, closing the door behind him, Alec rose from his chair and walked over to a glass terrarium sitting on a gateleg table. Dipping his hand into the terrarium, he scooped up one of the black, hairy-legged occupants and held it aloft.

"You, my pets, I can always count on," he murmured with something akin to affection. "I hate having to keep you caged like this, for I know what hunters you are, the intensity of the hunger that must be upon you. Just like me, you know well how to stalk your prey and bring him down." His eyes glazed with sentimental tears. "Soon . . . Yes, very soon, your hunger shall be appeased."

Raven half carried, half dragged Daere McCalister's big body from the river. Scrambling up the sloping bank, she kept urging him onward, even though she knew how difficult it was for him. He was only semiconscious, his gaze barely focused. By the time they reached her horse and he had pulled himself up into the saddle, the last of his strength was gone. He slumped forward over the black's neck without a sound.

Raven swung up behind him and drew him back

in the circle of her arms. She would do whatever she had to in order to save both of their lives, but she wasn't sure it would be enough. Touching his cold, clammy cheek, she willed life into his body from her own. "Don't give up, McCalister. You and I still have things to settle between us first."

Determinedly, she kicked Midnight's sides and the black sprinted off into the night, the ground mist surrounding them as they rode alongside the riverbank.

It seemed to take forever to reach her destination, but in actuality, she didn't think it could have been more than a few hours. McCalister hadn't said a word the entire time.

Throughout the long ride, he had lain quietly in her arms, and it was all that she could do to keep him from tumbling off the horse. She noticed the pallor of his cheeks in the moonlight and knew that he couldn't last much longer. There wasn't a second to waste, she realized as she urged Midnight onward.

When she reached the cabin hidden deep in the mountains and bordered on three sides by thick, towering pine trees, she was finally able to breathe a sigh of relief. It was a peaceful, beautiful place, and this was home to Raven. No one but Jade ever came to visit her here. It was remote and secure, but Raven knew there were certain risks involved in bringing the gunslinger here. Yet, she'd had no other choice. He wouldn't have survived the long ride into town. There wasn't any other place for them to go.

She dismounted first, then carefully managed to slide his body down from Midnight's back and lie him on the ground in front of the stairs. After untying her bedroll, she pushed and shoved his inert form until she had managed to position him on the blanket. It was slow going and tiring as well, but at last she had managed to drag him up the stairs and into the cabin, where she collapsed beside him onto the floor.

Lying there, she turned her head and studied the unmoving figure next to her. His breathing was shallow, each breath he took a painful gasp. They had made it and he was still alive, but she knew the worst was yet to come. Thinking of the grim task ahead of her, she shivered in the predawn light.

Then into the chamber turning, all my soul
    within me burning,
Soon again I heard a tapping somewhat
    louder than before.
"Surely," said I, "surely that is something at
    my window lattice;
Let me see, then, what thereat is, and this
    mystery explore—
Let my heart be still a moment and this
    mystery explore;—
      'Tis the wind, and nothing more!"

The Raven, Edgar Allan Poe

Twelve

The warm sun slanted through the open window and played across the long, lean body of the man who lay sleeping. The tangled, sweat-dampened sheets were twisted around his bare, muscular legs, as if he had been tossing about a great deal.

With a smothered groan, he rolled over onto his back and lay very still. His eyelids felt weighted, as if he would never be able to force them open again. At the moment, he was too weak to even try. He wanted to surface from the swirling darkness that held him firmly in its grip and banish the litany of demons from the corridors of his mind.

His thinking was fuzzy and he wondered why, trying to remember what had happened to him. But it was impossible to come up with any answers. He was dazed, confused, and just didn't remember. He sighed softly. Right now, thinking was even too much of an effort, and it seemed easier to just let himself drift off to sleep and not worry about anything.

Sitting in a chair next to his bed, Star had heard his change in breathing and she hovered over him, doing a quick evaluation of his condition. She was watching for further signs that might indicate he was finally waking up. She prayed silently, her chest constricting with emotion. "Come on . . . you can do it. Try harder."

She was rewarded for her efforts when his lips moved, but he uttered only indistinguishable words.

"Listen to me . . . you're alive, you're going to be fine," she said.

There was no response from him.

"Can you hear me? If you can but don't have the strength to answer me, just move your hand. I'll know."

She watched. Nothing happened. Chewing on her bottom lip, tears threatening, she sat back in the chair. His injuries had been severe, life-threatening actually. A bullet had clipped his temple, then had deviated as it carved a nasty furrow just above his right ear. He'd been beaten so badly that his features were bruised and swollen almost beyond recognition. Thankfully, he didn't have any broken bones. She didn't know how he had been so lucky.

At first, she had been relieved when she had discovered a clean wound, which meant the bullet hadn't passed through his skull, whereby she'd be forced to probe for it. She didn't know for certain whether his skull had been fractured, but she was beginning to think it probably was. She would have been surprised if it hadn't been.

God, but she hadn't wanted the responsibility of taking care of him, afraid she wouldn't be able to give him the level of care that he needed. But it hadn't made any difference. She alone had been given the task of saving this man's life. There simply had been no one else.

So she had sat here for days, watching, waiting. Never giving up hope. Realizing, too, that she was beginning to care far too much about him.

He was awake again, and this time his thoughts were more coherent, even though he was still dazed. Where he was? Daere still didn't know, but now he did remember a dream that he'd had, although not very clearly.

Something clicked in his brain. Or had it been more than that? Alec Tremayne's hired thugs had been determined to kill him as well as someone else. Daere tried to recall who had been with him, but he couldn't put a face to any memory. He did remember the pain well, however.

Once again, he felt their punishing blows, recalled a blur of faces and fists. Adrenaline was a powerful force, and it had taken all of them to succeed in bringing him to his knees, which they had finally done. A savage bloodlust had gripped them. He had known they wanted him dead, but didn't want it to be quick and easy. He vowed he'd never make a sound.

And he hadn't, although the effort had been almost more to bear than the beating.

His face was pummeled repeatedly, with fists and booted feet. Excruciating agony tore at his brain, and within himself, he shouted vile curses at his persecutors.

The relentless beating continued.

He fought against their punishing fists, even managing to get in a few good licks himself, when suddenly he felt a crushing blow. Something hard as iron glanced off the side of his cheek, and a new wave of pain exploded in his head.

He stumbled blindly, fell, was dragged up again. The men had lifted him up, supporting him, then hurled his body forcefully off a high bluff.

God, it had been a helluva long fall. He remembered clenching his teeth in shock when he hit the icy river, recalled floundering helplessly in the swift current, knowing he would drown unless he could manage to swim or grab hold of an anchor. Unfortunately, his limbs refused to obey his commands.

The water closed over his head, filling his nostrils and claiming the breath from his lungs. He was in absolute darkness.

Daere knew then he was going to die.

Death was no stranger to him. He had felt its presence before, but he had never imagined his life would end at the bottom of a river. His survival instincts overrode everything else. He did what was only natural to him. Given his stubborn nature, he compelled his arms and legs to move and clawed his way through the water, swimming upward until his head broke the surface.

He couldn't remember that first lifesaving breath of air, he thought groggily, still confused. So, was he alive or dead? His pain was almost too much to bear, but at that moment, he welcomed it. It was a clear indication that he must be alive.

Finally, he managed to force his bruised, swollen eyelids open, and to his shock, he found that he couldn't see a thing. Nothing, not even a splinter of light.

He was blind!

He almost panicked then. Anything was preferable to going through life without his sight! At that moment, he wanted to be dead more than anything else.

An angel was whispering soothing words near his ear.

"It's all right . . . you're not alone. I'm here

for you, and I won't leave you."

His fingers clutched the crisp sheet beneath his bare buttocks. The texture was smooth, cool to the touch, and despite his distressed thoughts, he found it a pleasant sensation, the very first since he had opened his eyes. He forced himself to relax, to think past his panic and the searing heat that seemed to have enveloped his body and set him on fire.

Think, assimilate facts, try and find out where you are! he demanded of his half-conscious brain.

Drawing in labored gasps of air, Daere concluded that he must be lying naked in a bed, with only a blanket covering him. His head throbbed unmercifully. But whose bed? He strained his hearing to see if he might pick up any other sounds.

To his relief, he found there was no multitude of angry voices — one of the last things he remembered as he had bobbed in the river — and there was no hint of impending danger.

In fact, he got the distinct impression that he was alone — except for the angel with the silky voice.

He was safe, protected. The tightness in his chest eased. Dead men didn't have these sort of impressions, did they?

One by one, he forced his fingers to move, and then he wiggled his toes. Nothing broken

213

there. That much was very good.

The earlier events kept playing themselves over in his mind, and he vaguely remembered another voice, urging him to swim, to save himself. Or had that been a part of his dreams?

No. Someone else *had* been there in the water with him, reassuring him over and over that he wasn't going to drown and that they were going to make it safely to the shore together. Had that same person saved his life, dragged him out of the river, tended to him when he'd fallen unconscious? But who was this person? And where were they now?

He listened closely and couldn't detect anything that sounded familiar. There was also nothing to connect his rescuer with Alec Tremayne, or with any of those men who had so viciously tried to kill him. No doubt they didn't have any reason to think they had failed. At least he hoped this was the case and that they weren't even now trying to track him down. The last thing he wanted was to endanger these people who had taken him in and had provided him with the care and shelter he needed.

He lay there with his eyes closed, and despite the searing pain behind his eyelids, Daere let his senses explore his new surroundings, savoring the soothing sounds of the birds singing, the breeze rustling the heavily starched curtains at the window, and startlingly, the sweet, clear voice of a woman humming as she moved about in the next room.

There didn't seem to be anyone else about. Only her. He knew she was the *voice*. He mentally counted her footsteps. They were minimal, so if he could trust his judgment of distance, then the room she worked in would be quite small. He heard several pots bang together, along with the steam from a tea kettle.

Minutes passed while he let his mind roam the interior walls of his sanctuary. Long-buried emotions swamped him like a tidal wave. Suddenly, his throat squeezed tight. He was overwhelmed with an intense joy unlike anything he had ever experienced before.

God, it was so good to be alive! Why had he never taken the time to notice the little things that life had to offer before now?

Memories sharpened in clarity and returned him to the realm of semi-rational thinking. Daere began to recall hazy impressions and, with a gasp of shock, suddenly visualized the leather-clad tracker.

He wondered if Raven had managed to save himself or had been killed. He had survived, after all, and perhaps Raven had as well. Daere knew then whose voice had been urging him to fight in the river.

He felt a strange sadness that the feisty, rebellious youth might have died in that cold, dark river. It wouldn't have been a pleasant death for someone so terrified of water. Raven had been so young and so damned determined to right every wrong that he could.

Daere recalled how he had been the one to force Raven to jump into the river, despite the boy's earnest pleas. He had only been trying to save his life, but unknowingly, he might have been the one responsible for Raven's death. A mantle of guilt settled over him. He had worn this mantle in the past, but somehow it had never felt so heavy.

Daere swore under his breath and his eyes flew open in a desperate attempt to escape the painful images, but there was only the frightening darkness to behold. He couldn't see, he could barely move, but the only thing that terrified him was the possibility that he might be blinded for life. It was too horrifying for him to contemplate. He couldn't even consider it for fear he'd go mad! There was no worse sentence for a gunman, especially one who was constantly sought out and challenged, than to live the rest of his life without his sight. Blinded . . . an invalid at the mercy of his enemies.

Daere didn't realize at that moment how dazed and in emotional shock he was. It seemed there was just the black void of emptiness looming before him and the cold truth to be faced. He didn't think he had made any sound, but suddenly he sensed a presence there beside him. Someone who smelled like lilacs and springtime. The woman. Could it be the same woman he had heard humming in the next room?

A cool hand pressed his brow. It was soothing and he welcomed her touch. There was nothing threatening about her presence or the gentle sounds she murmured as she wiped his brow with a damp cloth. Some innate sense told him she could be trusted and that she was desperately trying to save his life.

His dry, cracked lips tried to form the words he wanted to say to her, but he was barely able to whisper hoarsely, "That . . . feels good."

"I'm glad to see that you're coming around at last, but please don't try and talk yet," the soft voice replied. "You need to save your strength. Just rest, and know that you're safe here with me."

He wanted to keep talking so that she would remain with him, but it was difficult to concentrate on anything other than her hands, her tantalizing scent. Her skirts rustled as she started to turn away, and Daere forced his hand to move and grasp hold of her wrist. "St . . . ay . . . don't leave . . . yet."

Having come so close to dying, he felt as if death were still lingering there in the shadows, almost as if it were waiting to embrace him while he lay imprisoned in the darkness. For the first time in a long while, Daere McCalister found that he needed someone. It was a startling revelation.

He felt the woman's slight weight as she sat on the mattress next to him. "If you wish, I'll stay with you until you're able to fall asleep. You must rest as much as possible, Mr. McCalister. You'll regain your strength faster."

"Why can't I see . . . ?" he rasped, forcing the words from his dry throat, his hard fingers squeezing hers, refusing to let go. Despite his grave injury, he was still very much in command of his faculties.

"I don't know for certain, but I'm hoping it is only a temporary condition. You were shot and severely beaten. There's been a great deal of swelling. Perhaps after you've healed, we'll be able to tell more."

"How . . . bad . . . ?"

"Quite serious, but I've seen worse."

Her voice was calm, and every time she spoke to him, he felt better, less alone. It was a familiar voice, and somehow he had immediately recognized her, but he attributed this to having heard her voice even while he had been unconscious.

"And the boy . . . did he make it?" he asked.

"Raven, you mean?"

He squeezed her hand in affirmation.

"Yes . . . he made it."

Daere released a pent-up breath. "I'm . . . glad. Tell me what you know . . . about that night?"

Clearing her throat, she began telling him about the night Raven had brought Daere here to her cabin. How he had been semiconscious as the tracker had half dragged, half carried him to his horse. Then they had lit out, and hours later they had come across the cabin.

"That's about all that I know," she said in conclusion. "Other than the fact that Raven wasn't seriously hurt and he left here the following morning." Her fingers closed around his. "I think Raven realizes he owes his life to you, Mr. McCalister."

"I'd say he's repaid the debt," Daere rasped. He wanted to concentrate, but the pain was drawing him downward to that deep black pit again. There was only one other question he needed answered, then he could rest. "Wh . . . who . . . are you?"

"There will be time enough later for introductions," she replied. "I really must insist that you don't tire yourself by asking so many questions. Just rest. I'm nearby if you should need anything."

Suddenly, there followed his soft, bitter laughter. "If you really want to do something for me, put me out of my misery now. A . . . blind gunslinger. I'll be nothing more than a hideous joke."

She touched his forearm, squeezing gently. "I'm sorry. I really don't know what else I can say. I know how terrifying it must be for you."

Daere didn't need her pity at that moment. It was more than he could endure. And he didn't know what else to say, either. In fact, he was no longer in the mood for company. Even hers. "Just . . . go away." He pushed the words through his tightly clenched teeth. "Leave me . . . alone." He felt broken, weak, worthless. And never more abjectly humiliated than he did at that moment. The forgetfulness of sleep beckoned, and Daere slipped down, down, toward it.

Star hovered just beyond the doorway leading to the main room of the cabin, watching him intently. She stared at his dark, masculine face with quiet regard. Even battered, bruised, and swollen, he was still quite an exceptionally handsome man. His hair still gleamed black as ebony, thanks in part to her efforts to keep it clean by daily brushing, and more than once she'd been tempted to run her fingers through his thick waves. So far, she had resisted the urge, but she didn't know how much longer she could do so.

The bruising around his eyes was at its worst, but it would begin fading soon. His nose bore a faint bump at the bridge, no doubt broken before in some saloon brawl. His mouth was firm and, when he was awake, seemed always set in a ruthless slant. There were several nasty-looking scratches along the right side of his jaw, but she had applied a healing salve to these and didn't expect them to scar. He needed a shave, which only heightened his sinister appearance, but that would just have to wait a few more days.

Finally, she observed his chest rising and falling rhythmically, and when she heard his soft breathing, she knew he was sleeping once again.

Only then did she allow herself to leave him. Turning, she crossed over the floor to the stone hearth and found herself staring broodingly into the flames.

She could only hope for a positive resolution to his dilemma, as well as her own.

And the sooner the better for them both, Star knew.

Over the next few days, she had to nurse him around the clock, snatching sleep whenever she could, and most often while sitting in a chair next to his bed. She had been expecting that he might develop a fever, but she had prayed it wouldn't last. She forced willow-bark tea down his throat through a hollow reed, holding his nose while he sputtered, cursed, and finally swallowed barely a teaspoonful.

It was the evening of the fourth day, and she was beginning to think that her prayers might go unanswered. His big body was burning up, heat radiating off his skin with such intensity that she didn't think he would survive the night unless she was able to lower his temperature.

His skin color was gray as ash, and even though he slept most of the time, whenever he did awaken, he was out of his head. She knew she should ride into Tequila Bend and fetch Doc Snyder, but it was better than a day's hard ride from the cabin she used in her role as Raven. And how might she explain the gunslinger's presence here to the sawbones?

No one even knew this place existed, except for Jade. Star knew she would undoubtedly have a great deal of explaining to do if she brought the doctor back here. And what if she just happened to encounter Alec's bodyguards in town and one of them should see her leave with the doctor? They might even become suspicious enough to follow them. The situation could well turn ugly. The gunslinger wasn't in any shape for unwanted visitors, and she had faith in her ability to doctor him herself.

In truth—if she dared to even admit the truth to herself—Star didn't really want to leave him alone. Not after everything that they'd survived together.

She wished that Jade were with her, but there just wasn't any way of sending word to her. No one even knew she was here. There wasn't any doubt that she could use an extra pair of hands, someone who felt more at ease around a man's body and who would be decidedly more familiar with his needs.

Star closed her eyes, swaying on her feet. Lord, she was tired. Glancing over at him, she sighed in despair at the sight of his uncontrollable shivering.

She retrieved a handmade quilt from the bureau drawer and laid it over him, tucking in the corners securely. Otherwise, with the way he was shaking, she held little doubt that he would not stay covered.

He mumbled something in his delirium.

Help me!

I will, I am, she thought fiercely, not trusting herself to speak the words aloud for fear she'd burst into tears.

The hands touching him were gentle and familiar against his bare skin. They moved over him with careful regard, somehow knowing where his bruised body ached the most, and applied a light touch. He stirred, and the comforting hands urged him to lie still. Once again, he felt no threat. It was the woman who smelled like lilacs, and once more he was comforted by having her near him.

223

Standing there gazing down at him, she couldn't help feeling an overwhelming measure of pity, even though she well knew he would hate her for it. He was a proud man, tough as nails, who couldn't bear sympathy or tenderness, but who'd had to learn to depend on a woman. Something he'd probably never done before in his life.

A vision of the harsh stranger she had encountered over two weeks ago in the mountains flashed in her mind's eye. They had almost killed one another that night, and there was no doubt theirs had been a violent first meeting. Certainly not the sort a woman exactly dreamed about when she envisioned meeting the man she would one day fall in love with. Her head jerked when she realized what she had been thinking. Love! Was she actually beginning to feel that she was in love with this man?

As it was, she would probably always bear an ugly scar on her shoulder where his bullet had grazed her flesh, and he'd probably destroyed any hope she had of finding the hidden will.

She was still puzzled over why he had tried to save her life the other night, at risk of losing his own. It would have been far easier for him just to have allowed the cards to fall where they might.

Instead, he had tried to protect her. She closed

MORE PASSION AND ADVENTURE AWAIT... YOUR TRIP TO A BIG ADVENTUROUS WORLD BEGINS WHEN YOU ACCEPT YOUR FIRST 4 NOVELS ABSOLUTELY *FREE* (AN $18.00 VALUE)

Accept your Free gift and start to experience more of the passion and adventure you like in a historical romance novel. Each Zebra novel is filled with proud men, spirited women and tempestuous love that you'll remember long after you turn the last page.

Zebra Historical Romances are the finest novels of their kind. They are written by authors who really know how to weave tales of romance and adventure in the historical settings you love. You'll feel like you've actually gone back in time with the thrilling stories that each Zebra novel offers.

GET YOUR FREE GIFT WITH THE START OF YOUR HOME SUBSCRIPTION

Our readers tell us that these books sell out very fast in book stores and often they miss the newest titles. So Zebra has made arrangements for you to receive the four newest novels published each month.

You'll be guaranteed that you'll never miss a title, and home delivery is so convenient. And to show you just how easy it is to get Zebra Historical Romances, we'll send you your first 4 books absolutely FREE! Our gift to you just for trying our home subscription service.

BIG SAVINGS AND FREE HOME DELIVERY

Each month, you'll receive the four newest titles as soon as they are published. You'll probably receive them even before the bookstores do. What's more, you may preview these exciting novels free for 10 days. If you like them as much as we think you will, just pay the low preferred subscriber's price of just $3.75 each. *You'll save $3.00 each month off the publisher's price.* AND, your savings are even greater because there are never any shipping, handling or other hidden charges—FREE Home Delivery. Of course you can return any shipment within 10 days for full credit, no questions asked. There is no minimum number of books you must buy.

4 FREE BOOKS

TO GET YOUR 4 FREE BOOKS WORTH $18.00 —MAIL IN THE FREE BOOK CERTIFICATE T O D A Y

Fill in the Free Book Certificate below, and we'll send your FREE BOOKS to you as soon as we receive it.

If the certificate is missing below, write to: Zebra Home Subscription Service, Inc., P.O. Box 5214, 120 Brighton Road, Clifton, New Jersey 07015-5214.

FREE BOOK CERTIFICATE

4 FREE BOOKS

ZEBRA HOME SUBSCRIPTION SERVICE, INC.

YES! Please start my subscription to Zebra Historical Romances and send me my first 4 books absolutely FREE. I understand that each month I may preview four new Zebra Historical Romances free for 10 days. If I'm not satisfied with them, I may return the four books within 10 days and owe nothing. Otherwise, I will pay the low preferred subscriber's price of just $3.75 each; a total of $15.00, *a savings off the publisher's price of $3.00*. I may return any shipment and I may cancel this subscription at any time. There is no obligation to buy any shipment and there are no shipping, handling or other hidden charges. Regardless of what I decide, the four free books are mine to keep.

NAME

ADDRESS _____ APT

CITY _____ STATE _____ ZIP

TELEPHONE
(   )

SIGNATURE _____
(if under 18, parent or guardian must sign)

Terms, offer and prices subject to change without notice. Subscription subject to acceptance by Zebra Books. Zebra Books reserves the right to reject any order or cancel any subscription.

ZB0693

GET
FOUR
FREE
BOOKS
(AN $18.00 VALUE)

her eyes, seeing his jade-green gaze, as volatile as a summer storm, and how it had blazed with fire just before he had nudged her off the bluff into the river. Now those same eyes might never look upon her again with any awareness. He could well die before this night was through.

Star swallowed over the lump in her throat. "You're more dangerous like this than when you held a gun on me," she murmured, and upon realizing she had spoken her thoughts aloud, her eyes flew wide and she stared down at his face. He hadn't moved nor could he have understood anything she had said, she realized with great relief. Star knew well she would have to be far more careful in the future.

Thirteen

She kept a constant vigil by his bedside, refusing to leave him for any longer than was absolutely necessary. He slept a great deal, which was good. Sleep offered him relief from the pain and escape from his burdens.

Star wished this were true in her case, but it was not. In the past, her troubles had always seemed lighter with the dawn, but these days nothing, not even the sunrise, could brighten her mood. The shadows of her past remained, blotting out the sun and lengthening throughout the day. She was concerned that nothing would ever be the same for her again. It was because of him, she knew, and in thinking this, Star felt the same disturbing sensations she experienced whenever she allowed him inside her head.

Although, of late, when wasn't she thinking about him? Thoughts of him filled her every waking hour and invaded her dreams at night. Of course, what she worried about more than anything was trying to save Daere McCalister's life.

She remained firm in her resolve to do so.

He was so weak he didn't stand a chance at survival unless she was here beside him, strong and sure, fighting the battle he could not win on his own.

Sitting here like this, hour after hour, having the chance to study him, he now seemed so different to her. No longer the hard, invincible gunslinger, he had become just a man, one made up of flesh and blood like any other, with the same strengths and weaknesses. Yet, even though he was pale, his face drawn with pain, he still exuded an aura of power.

She felt it, like a tangible presence. Without a doubt, he would always be one of those men who, just by walking into a room, could turn every head. She remembered how her gaze had been drawn to him on the street outside of the theater. In retrospect, it seemed that night had taken place years ago when, in fact, it had only been a matter of days.

Star shook her head. Too much time to think, and always without forming any conclusions. She wished she could turn her thoughts as well as her feelings off. It frightened her to realize just how important he was becoming to her with each passing day. Time had ceased to have any meaning for her. How long had they been here? Two days? Three? Or longer?

It was nighttime once again, and when the shadows had deepened in the room, she rose to light the lamp sitting on the pine table next to the bed. The pale yellow flame flickered against the cabin's rough-hewn walls, licked upward, and danced along the ceiling's mismatched logs. There were sections of the roof where gaping spaces revealed narrow slices of the sky.

A full moon cast its ghostly light in between the logs, carving out the shadows, drawing her gaze to where a single bright star twinkled. Star smiled, then made a wish. It was something she hadn't done in a long time.

Let him live.

There wasn't anything else that she wanted more at the moment.

Wearily, she slumped down in the chair and leaned her head back against the hardwood frame. Here, like this, just the two of them, the world as they knew it seemed so far removed. It wasn't, of course, and she had better remember that, Star told herself.

Her life, her identity, everything she had worked and schemed to obtain, was now threatened because of her dedication to see this man well. Danger existed on an entirely separate level for her than it had before.

As Raven, she had confronted the worst of men and had always managed to walk away unscathed. This time, she wasn't so sure.

Daere was one of the very gunmen she had sworn to bring down. She had had the opportunity. Instead, she was trying her best to save his life.

She closed her eyes, and her thoughts drifted back over the years to some of the outlaws she'd confronted in her role as the Raven. There had been many. It was an agonizing realization. So much bloodshed, so much pain. Raven had seen and heard just about everything. Still, it didn't make her job any easier.

The West was a violent place that seemed to attract an overwhelming share of bad men. Some were just born mean, while others had become outlaws simply out of desperation brought on by hard times.

Big Bobbie Carver had been one of the worst of the lot. She remembered him well. He had been an enormous brute of a man, with a moral disposition that was lower than a snake's belly. His biggest thrill in life had been beating up on women he considered "tarnished angels"—his reference to the girls who worked for Rosalie. When the need came upon him, Big Bobbie was quick to leave his shack and ride into town, pockets jingling with silver. He'd head straight for the brothel.

Jade just happened to be his choice of woman on that Saturday night five years ago. Rosalie had warned him before that she wouldn't tolerate any further rough treatment where her girls were concerned. He had promised her that he'd be on his best behavior, but after a few whiskeys, Bobbie's buried hostilities toward women surfaced.

Star could still remember the chilling sound of Jade's screams. It would remain forever imprinted in her mind. So would the look of astonishment that had been on Big Bobbie's face when he'd glanced up to find the Raven descending upon him like a dark avenger from hell. She had just entered the secret corridor after returning from a midnight ride, when Jade's anguished cries had resounded through the walls.

Big Bobbie was on the bed straddling Jade's tiny form, his hands encircling her slender throat, when Raven stepped through the sliding panel into her friend's bedchamber. There wasn't even time to think, only to react.

Raven cracked the bullwhip across a space of ten feet, the lash biting into his right ear just as she'd intended, ripping his flesh, blood spurting down onto his grimy shirt.

He howled with pain and fury, but he wasn't yet ready to give up. Instead, his wrath exploded, and swearing a blue streak, he jumped off the bed and turned on the figure garbed in black, a dark Stetson pulled low over fiery eyes.

His own gaze glittered with deadly intent. His were the feral eyes of a monster. Suddenly, a knife seemed to appear in his meaty hand from out of nowhere, and he snarled at Raven as he lumbered toward her. "I'm gonna carve you up into crow bait, mister, and then when I'm done with you, I'll finish the whore, and take my good ole sweet time about it, too. I like to start with their pretty faces and work my way down to their toes." He smiled like a mad dog, with a savage uplift to his top lip. "And you ain't gonna be able to stop me, neither, 'cause you'll be lying in too many little pieces by then."

"Don't come any closer," Raven warned, but Big Bobbie didn't listen. Men like him never did. They ruled with their brute force, and it never even entered their heads to think that someone might one day best them.

He stomped across the floor, rapidly closing the distance that separated them. Even from a distance, he reeked of horses, sweat, and stale whiskey. "You black devil, you're as good as dead," he sneered, lunging forward, the knife glinting as the blade descended toward Raven's chest.

It was too late to draw back her hand again and unfurl the whip, so Raven did the one thing she had always hoped she would never have to do. She grabbed the derringer from her boot and fired point-blank, hitting him dead center in his heart. To her horror, he flinched, but then staggered on toward her.

Jade sprang off the bed to aid her friend, landing on his back like an angry, spitting she-cat. The hold she had around his neck was a death grip and

231

her fingers went for his windpipe. It was a technique she'd learned while growing up in her country. The man screamed only once, a strange, gurgling sound, then sagged to his knees with Jade still gripping his throat. Big Bobbie dropped over onto his face, and the awful sound of his huge girth hitting the floor brought everyone in the bordello running straight for Jade's room.

Jade looked up at Raven from where she was half crouched on the floor beside his body. Her face was pale. "We had to stop him," she said woodenly. "Go on, get out of here before they burst through the door and find you."

Raven knelt down beside her, staring at the froth of blood slowly puddling on the floor beside the man's body. She shuddered. "I can't leave you to take the blame," she said.

Jade gave her a push. "You have to. You can't risk the exposure. I'll tell the sheriff how Bobbie tried to kill me. He'll believe me. Everybody knows that Bobbie was destined for a bad end. It just remained to be seen when and where, that's all." She trembled, averting her gaze away from his corpse. "At least there won't be any other women made to suffer because of him, but I can't say I feel good about taking a man's life. Even his, worthless as it was."

Raven drew her friend onto her feet. "Listen, Jade, it's never easy to kill anyone, no matter how evil they are. I know better than most how you're feeling right now. But what you did was unavoidable. He would have killed me and then turned on you again."

Unshed tears gleamed in Jade's soulful eyes. "I know," she sniffed, "but I don't think I'll ever forgive myself. Now go on, get. Your having been here will remain our secret just like always."

"You're the best friend a girl could ever have," Raven told her, squeezing Jade's hand.

"The same goes for you," Jade replied, smiling weakly. "He took me by surprise. I'd probably be dead right now if not for you."

Fists were pounding on Jade's door and it seemed everyone was shouting at once.

"I'll come back later, after things have quieted down," Raven said, and strode briskly toward the hidden panel.

Her friendship with Jade had been forged even stronger after that night. As Raven, she needed every bit of support she could get. In Jade, she had a staunch ally who believed in Raven's cause.

She had never longed for Jade's soothing influence more than she did right now. Daere McCalister posed a new and different kind of threat she had never before confronted, nor even completely understood. But one thing was becoming startlingly clear: If she remained here with him much longer, she would never be safe again. The danger that existed for her, that kept luring her, was desire.

The realization hammered in her brain with frightening intensity, and the shaky hold Star had on her emotions was weakened even more.

You won't allow yourself to even think about what your life will be like once again after he heals and you must leave here. That day will come, you know, so don't fall in love with him. You cannot stay here forever, and just remember, he'll walk away from you as soon as he's able, leaving you alone with your broken dreams and bittersweet memories of a love that can never be.

"I can't allow that to happen . . . I won't," she said softly, as a warning to herself.

Yet the longer she remained with him, the harder it was to think about a future without their being together. A bond, however fragile, existed between them. She couldn't allow it to strengthen, yet how was she to stop it? Their need for one another seemed to grow stronger by the hour. And really, hadn't it begun the moment she had pulled him out of the river, had quickly assessed his injuries, and then had made the decision to bring him here? But she'd had no other choice. She couldn't have walked away from him when he had needed her. He would have died without her help.

Soon she'd be able to put distance between them, and once away from him, she could effectively bring her emotions under control. He would no longer dominate her every thought and action. She'd be free of him once more. It was what she wanted, she told herself, and the sooner the better.

Yet, when she heard him groan aloud in his delirium, she was immediately beside him, her brow furrowed with worry, and any other concerns ceased to exist.

"Don't you dare give up," she told him, willing life into his body through her voice and the touch of her hands.

Throughout the rest of that long night, as she maintained a constant vigil, she bathed his body with a cool, damp cloth and forced liquids into him. His fever was still raging, but he kept telling her how cold he was . . . how terribly cold.

She was determined to save him, at any risk. She knew what she must do, but even as she kicked off her slippers, that little voice inside her head was already issuing warnings. She hesitated, knowing that what she was about to do would bind her even closer to him. But in the next instant, she slid into bed beside him, her heart thrumming like a hummingbird's.

His long body was hard, muscular, and *bare*.

Star gulped as she lay down beside him, her head resting gently in the firm hollow of his shoulder. In an attempt to force heat into his shivering form, she turned onto her side and began stroking him, but she was careful, *so very careful,* not to allow her fingers to stray far and touch him *down there*.

Tucking her leg in between his, she rubbed her

foot along his calf, his knee and, growing braver, his thigh.

Star didn't think she had to worry about arousing him in his present physical condition, but just the same, she remained cautious of where her hand roamed.

She became increasingly aware of the fact that she was having difficulty breathing, and every time his muscles quivered beneath the pads of her fingertips, she made a catchy little sound in her throat.

Star's eyelids automatically drifted closed. She applied a soothing touch, losing herself in the smell and texture of his skin. Her fingers, never still, found a knotted muscle just above his knee, where she kneaded the rigid flesh.

He moved suddenly, throwing a leg across her hip, an arm around her shoulders, and she was trapped before she knew what had happened.

Something warm and satiny smooth was pressed against him, and his heartbeat accelerated. The scent of springtime flowers and . . . something more . . . of woman, tantalized his senses. Soft, womanly curves. Willowy arms, firm breasts, and long, lithe legs embraced him. It was her. She had gotten into bed with him.

He needed this woman more than he had ever needed anyone before. Her body was warm and vital; she made him feel far removed from that dark place where his mind had retreated. He needed her to help him make it through the long, cold hours until dawn, when the earth seemed reborn and the air was once more filled with the sweet sounds of life.

Daere buried his fingers in the folds of her nightgown. The soft muslin was comforting to the touch and, oddly, provided solace to his tortured mind. The woman was indeed real; he hadn't just imagined her in his dreams as he had begun to wonder while drifting in his delirium. She was here, and she must stay. With her had come serenity. Nothing mattered to him more at that moment then keeping her near . . . as near to him as she was now.

"Don't . . . leave," he rasped.

She gently placed her cheek against his, some intense emotion welling up within her. "No, I won't. I promise," she whispered close to his ear.

Lying against him, with her nightgown twisted around her knees, every part of her pressed to every part of him, Star shockingly realized that his hand was seeking out the curve of her back where it joined her hips; urging her closer.

The pressure of his fingers was strong and sure, eliciting a quiver that ran the length of her spine. He dipped lower, down the back of her thigh, then slid up coaxingly between her legs.

That first initial contact was electrifying, and

Star's eyes flew open. "Oh . . . no . . . you shouldn't . . ." she protested.

"You're so soft . . . so warm." He twisted his fingers, and she arched against him. "Oh, God, you feel good. I need your warmth . . . don't pull away," he muttered, his voice rough, his fingers absorbing her moist heat.

She didn't think he even knew what he was saying, let alone doing, but she was shaking all over. Her emotions were at war, and she knew things were headed in a very dangerous direction. She had to make him stop. Yet, despite her best intentions, the words stuck in her throat. Her eyes felt heavy-lidded once again as the warm pleasure spiraled upward from where he was touching her, heating her belly, her breasts, making her nipples ache to have his lips suckle her.

It amazed and frightened her that he should be this strong when she had assumed otherwise. She brought her hands up and pushed against his shoulders, but his arms were like steel bands. There wasn't any way she could extricate herself from his embrace unless he decided he wanted to release her.

"No . . . I don't want you to go," he breathed against her hair, and she shivered convulsively but lay still in his arms. "Good girl . . . just want to hold you. I won't hurt you."

It wasn't long afterward that his strength ebbed, and his body went slack against hers. Soon, he was breathing normally and drifted off to sleep.

Star knew now was her chance to slip away from him, but she remembered how cold he had been earlier, and she told herself it would be best for him if she remained here for the remainder of the night.

Only to save his life, she kept repeating over again in her head, snuggling down closer to him, her head pillowed on his broad chest. *Only to save his life.*

For the rest of the night, she held him in her arms.

When dawn's first light spilled through the window, she awakened first to find that their arms and legs lay entwined, his long fingers threaded through her hair, which had loosened from its prim knot, its pale silver splendor shimmering in the sunlight on the pillow, a startling contrast against his sun-bronzed skin.

She turned her head the slightest degree and was confronted with the intimate vision. Something happened to her then, something she didn't entirely understand. There were only the two of them, and the world as she had known it seemed very far away. Her blood licked hotly through her veins, her breathing accelerated alarmingly. My God, what was wrong with her thinking? He was injured; she was supposed to be helping him recover, not thinking about what it might be like to feel him inside her, hot and vibrant and alive.

There was no longer any sense in denying it. She lusted for him . . . had for some time now, if she were being truthful. She'd only be lying to herself if she refused to acknowledge it. After last night, she could never be near him again without passion flaring between them. She had to get away from him, she must, if she were to keep from making a fool of herself again.

She was trying to figure out just how she was going to extricate her hair from his grasp without disturbing him, when his hand moved, and she heard him say faintly, "You always smell so damn good."

She almost leapt from the bed, he had startled her so. She had not known he was awake. Of course, she thought he would have been gentleman enough to at least remove his fingers from her hair. It was almost as if he had been lying there doing his best not to awaken her. Had he been enjoying holding her, sifting his fingers through her hair? Now it was her turn to feel as though *she* were burning up with fever.

"Let me go. Please," she stated firmly.

He released her without further argument.

In the next instant, she was out of bed and on her feet. "You . . . you could have let me know sooner that you were awake instead . . . of . . . instead of . . ." She was floundering for the right word.

"Instead of lying here like the lech that I am and enjoying the feel of you in my arms." His words were drowsily slurred with contentment and edged with humor. "I might have, but I chose not to. I hope you won't hold that against me."

Star moved with swift grace toward the door. "It seems that your fever's broken and you're feeling much better this morning. . . . I'll just go fix you some breakfast." She paused, half-turning. "What would you like?"

"Forget breakfast." His voice turned coaxing. "Come back over here. I think we were just getting to know one another better."

Her breath stopped, then came in a rush. "Really, Mr. McCalister! What kind of a woman do you think I am?" she shot back, but she was really more upset with her own reaction and the fact that his suggestion made her pulse leap.

"I won't compromise you, ma'am," he said huskily, then added, "that is, unless you want me to."

She drew herself up. "I most certainly do not."

"Mmmm, is that so?" he drawled. "I seem to have gotten the impression earlier that you enjoyed being held in my arms."

"Well, you were dead wrong, mister," she replied coolly, head held high.

Whirling, she forced herself to walk slowly from the room.

She had never intended for him to become this important to her. So much so, that she hated having him out of her sight.

Tears burning brightly in her eyes, she made it as far as the rocking chair by the hearth, collapsing in it, before allowing the silent teardrops to fall.

He slept through another entire day. She was touching him again, wiping his moist brow, when Daere stirred from sleep, already sensing who it was before he even opened his eyes. Each time he awakened, he hoped he'd find that he would see again, but as yet his condition remained almost the same.

He was, however, no longer trapped in the world of total darkness as he had been.

He hadn't mentioned it to her yet, but his vision was gradually returning; he could tell if it was night or day by the brightness of the light in the room. There were only hues of gray filtering through the window next to his bed, and he imagined it was just after dawn.

He had discovered she was an early riser. So was he. They had some things in common after all, but he knew they were insignificant factors and that a fine lady of her distinction would never be interested in anyone with his background. She had made that quite clear to him yesterday.

Looking up at her, he fought hard to distinguish her features. He wanted very much to know what this woman looked like. A tiny flare of excitement flickered to life within him every time she came near. In fact, he realized shockingly, he had never wanted anything more in his life than to see her gazing down upon him with something more than concern in her eyes.

To his bitter despair, there was still only a hazy image. He could tell her hair was light in color and that her eyes were beautiful. Well, he didn't know for certain whether her eyes were beautiful, but he just knew that they must be. Every time she looked at him he felt their warmth, every emotion that she was experiencing. Windows to her soul. That's what her eyes were, yet he didn't think she even realized it.

He wondered then if the day would ever come when he might look upon her face and be able to define every feature. Soon, perhaps, but not quick enough to satisfy him. Nonetheless, today was going to be a special day. She *would* tell him her name. He wasn't going to let her get away from him until she did.

At least, he hoped she would. He was beginning to learn other traits of hers, some of them not so pleasant. She had a stubborn streak, and sometimes it was either *her* way or *no* way at all. He didn't think there were many men who would tolerate such willfulness, but he had always admired strong women. He had found they were always tender of heart. She was, to a fault. At least with him.

Realizing how much he had begun to think about her, Daere sighed with frustration. Days, hours, down to his every waking minute. God, but she was under his skin but good.

She interpreted the exasperated sound as one of distress. "Are you in pain?" she inquired, touching his arm.

Feeling his loins aching with need, he almost snapped her head off, holding back a sharp retort. Damn right he was, but not in the way she thought. And he sure as hell didn't want her to know what he had been thinking . . . how much it would mean to him just to gaze upon her face and see her clearly. He said nothing about his true feelings. "Not like you think. I'm just tired of lying here, and I know you've got to be weary of having to look after me."

She rarely left his beside. He had come to know her footsteps, her breathing, her smell. The little things she did every day by rote, as most people did, but were generally never noticed. Everything about her was as familiar to him as his own body. Everything except the color of her eyes, the shape of her mouth, and how her lips might curve whenever she smiled at him. And she did smile; he had heard it in her voice.

"Nonsense," she replied. "You haven't been any

trouble at all. And it's good that you're growing bored with your confinement. It means you're getting well. Maybe in another week, you'll begin to feel more like your old self again."

"I will. I'm going to make certain of it," he stated with fierce determination.

"That's just what I've been waiting to hear you say," she replied warmly. She extended a cup toward him. "I've made you some breakfast. It's not ham and eggs, I'm sorry to say, but it won't be much longer until you can leave here."

He opened his mouth obediently. It was oatmeal, but it had never tasted better. His appetite was improving as well, and he had begun to look forward to mealtimes. He had to admit, she was a fine cook. Last evening, he had enjoyed his first solid food since he'd been injured: rabbit stew brimming with carrots, tiny onions, and potatoes. He had only had a few mouthfuls before he felt full, but it had been tasty and satisfying.

Having consumed little more than broth and tea since he had been here, he couldn't remember having ever enjoyed anything as much. Except perhaps for the enticing fullness of her breasts pressed against him last night. Christ, he had to quit thinking this way!

When he had finished eating, she removed the napkin from beneath his chin and gathered up the empty cup and spoon.

"I've never really thanked you, ma'am, for

everything that you've done for me," he said huskily, wanting to express his appreciation.

"There isn't any need. You were injured and I couldn't just turn you away."

"You know, I would like to be able to call you something besides ma'am. You do have a name, don't you?"

She had known this moment would come sooner or later, but she still was ill prepared to answer him.

"Tell me your name," he coaxed. "I'd really like to know."

Star drew a deep breath, then said softly, "Yes, I have a name. It's Star. Star Tremayne." She instantly regretted telling him the truth, when he grabbed for her and clamped unyielding fingers around her wrist.

"Lady, you'd damned well better be kidding."

Open here I flung the shutter, when, with
    many a flirt and flutter,
In there stepped a stately raven of the saintly
    days of yore;
Not the least obeisance made he not an in-
    stant stopped or stayed he;
But; with mien of lord or lady, perched
    above my chamber door—
Perched upon a bust of Pallas just above my
    chamber door—
        Perched, and sat, and nothing more.

The Raven, Edgar Allan Poe

Fourteen

Tension quivered throughout the room. She didn't answer him, and he forced himself to grow calm. Christ, of all the things he might have been expecting, this certainly wasn't one of them. Finding out that the woman who had literally saved his life was a Tremayne—even one estranged from the family—didn't make for an ideal situation. Just when he thought things couldn't get any worse, they had. Hell, he should have known.

He heard her draw a ragged breath, then release it. "Believe me, I wasn't trying to deceive you."

"What *were* you trying to do?" he asked, forcing himself to speak low and calm. He had heard the tremor in her voice and knew that he had frightened her. It made him realize her position. She was a woman alone with a man she didn't really know. She had provided him care and shelter, even at the risk of ruining her reputation. She certainly didn't deserve for him to speak so harshly to her. This woman had shown him nothing but kindness and tenderness, and how did he repay her? By turning on her without first giving her a chance to explain. He didn't want to snap at her again, but damnit, he did need some answers.

"I was just trying to help you," she stated softly, attempting to keep her voice calm. "And now you're angry because you found out I'm a Tremayne, and you think I'm like them."

"I'm not angry with you," he replied, but his tone was still gruff. He drew in a calming breath, then holding out his hand, he said, "Come here."

She blinked at him. "Wh . . . why?" Yet, looking at that long-fingered hand stretched out in entreaty, she felt she had no choice.

Because I can never restrain myself from touching you whenever you're near me, he wanted to say, but it was too hard for him to put his feelings into words. He had spent too many years mourning life instead of living it, and he had given up believing anything good would ever happen to him again. "I know I'm behaving like an ungrateful sonofabitch. I should be thanking you instead of demanding you answer my questions." Sensing her trepidation, his green eyes turned toward her. "We need to talk, though. And I'd at least like you sitting beside me."

There wasn't any response from her. His restless gaze roamed the room. "Are you still here?"

"Yes," she whispered, "I am."

He followed the sound of her voice, saw her slender form silhouetted in sunlight. Damnit, he wanted to see her. *Really see her!* Not just a figure in shadow and light. "Will you stay and talk to me?"

"If . . . you want." She no longer seemed torn with indecision, and in the next instant he heard her light tread cross the room, then felt her presence beside the bed. "You *are* safe here, Mr. McCalister. You must believe that I won't betray you."

He could barely restrain himself from touching her whenever she was near him. "I do, but tell me, just why are you here, Star?"

My God, what should she say? She felt a cold knot in the pit of her stomach, but Star knew she had to come up with an explanation, and she had to make it seem as close to the truth as possible. Lord, she was tired of lying, but most of all, she didn't want there to be any more lies between them. Still, she didn't think he was ready to hear the absolute truth yet, so she decided to tell him only what he needed to know. Fighting to steady her nerves, she wet her lips, then said, "I like the solitude here. Sometimes I need to just get away by myself for a few days. It gets terribly hectic running a business like mine, and as you well know, there is plenty of time to relax here."

"Don't you get ever get lonely being here by yourself?"

"No, never," she replied without hesitating. "Actually, I rather enjoy being alone. It gives me time to think. In fact, I've sketched some of my better designs while sitting at my worktable in the other room. When I'm in town, I rarely seem to find time for myself, because there's always someone or something demanding my attention."

He didn't say anything for several minutes, just seemed to lie there reflecting. Star's knees began trembling so badly that she sank down on the bed beside him without thinking.

"Then I come along and invade your privacy," he said, his hand closing around her fingers. "I'm really very grateful that you took me in, ma'am. I know there aren't many people who would have done the same, given the circumstances."

"You aren't exactly a stranger to me," she said softly.

His fingers caressed the inside of her wrist in a slow, circular motion.

"Don't . . . you shouldn't . . ." she began, and tried to draw away from him.

"Easy . . . easy. I would never do anything to hurt you. My God, I probably wouldn't even be alive without you."

Star had never felt more guilty than at that moment. He didn't know that it was because of her that he had almost been killed. What would he say if he knew the truth? She could well guess. He definitely wouldn't be so grateful then. He'd probably wish to wring her neck.

"Why are you trembling? You've nothing to fear from me." He spoke soothingly, sensing her anxiety, but of course he misinterpreted the cause of it. He seemed to want to reassure her as well that he would not go beyond her carefully drawn boundaries . . . unless, of course, she wanted him to.

He rubbed the backs of his fingers along her cheek, eliciting a quiver that ran the length of her spine. Ever more daring, his hand dipped, tracing the graceful curve of her neck.

"Daere . . . I don't think you should . . ." she began, releasing a trembling breath.

"That's the first time you've said my name. Your skin is as soft as velvet," he said huskily. His fingers, never still, found a sensitive spot behind her ear and stroked gently. "Let me hold you, Star. Just hold you, nothing more."

She trembled and pressed a restraining hand against his chest. "I don't think that would be a good idea."

"You've let me hold you before," he said, wooing her with the seductive timbre of his voice. It was impossible not to think about her fingers splayed against his chest; the heat of her flesh was like a balm to his soul. What had once been a healing touch, providing comfort and care, now seemed intimate, stirring flames of desire. At the moment, nothing else mattered but keeping her near him.

"Yes, but it was different. You were hurt and needed me then," she replied softly.

He brought both hands up and cupped her face, drawing her nearer. "I need you more now than I ever have," he replied, his breath warm on her lips. "I want so damn much to see you, to know the expression in your eyes, but I can't . . . maybe I never will. Nothing is very clear yet. Everything I see is shadowy."

"I know how frightening it must be. Yet I think what you're describing is a positive sign. It's a beginning, Daere," she said, hoping to encourage him. "Just give it some more time."

He let out a long, audible breath. "Maybe, but what if it doesn't get any better than this? God, I took so much for granted before." His mind drifted back, and his voice dropped in volume. "I remember thinking how lovely you were the first time I saw you. I can still see you in the dress shop that day, trying so hard to be accommodating and nervous as a cat because I was there. And then later, running into you with Jake Fontaine outside of the theater. If I ever regain my sight, I'll memorize everything about you this time."

His eyes were dark pools of despair, and Star's heart wrenched painfully. She knew if she stayed, she'd be lost, but at the moment she didn't care. Later, there might be regrets, but right now she didn't want to think beyond this moment.

Placing her hands over his, she closed her eyes and slowly began to move his fingers over her face. "Touch me, see me," she whispered.

"Once I do, I don't know whether I'll be able to stop," he said hoarsely. "You have to know that, Star."

"Then don't stop," she replied, her voice a mere

thread of sound.

Though he didn't answer, his expression spoke for him. The look on his face was a mixture of eagerness and tenderness. The pads of his fingertips whispered over her high cheekbones. Her feathery lashes closed over her eyes, feeling like silk fans against her skin, he thought. She had a small nose, turned up at the tip, and small dimples graced her cheeks. His fingers continued their lazy exploration, skimming downward.

Ah, but it was her mouth that absolutely captivated him and made desire coil tightly in his belly. It was a mouth meant to be kissed . . . and often. Her lips were lush and ripe, her top lip full and sensual, which made him think of sucking it gently.

Suddenly, the imprisoning darkness no longer seemed like forced confinement. It was intimate and evocative, conjuring up a feast of images for his mind's eye that tore away the last of his restraint.

Their lips were so close that their breaths intermingled, and white-hot desire ignited to a fever pitch.

With a soft snarl, he pulled her close in his arms, before he might reason with himself to stop. He just didn't want to stop. He wanted this woman more than any other in his life.

Threading his fingers through her luxuriant hair, he held her firmly as his lips moved over hers. Theirs was a hard, demanding kiss, which

254

was filled with the volatile emotions they had continually fought to suppress.

A half sob, half whimper bubbled in her throat as his tongue pressed against her lips, seeking entrance. He found himself marveling that her tongue accepted his invasion, caressing and exploring his in a dance of desire. Her lips, soft and succulent, had been formed to drive a man wild, he thought, as his kiss ravaged her, and his hands soothed even as they caught her on fire.

He ate at her lips, leaving her weak with wanting. Star wasn't ever certain just what it was that she so desperately wanted. His lips, his hands, were completely overwhelming. Merciful heavens, but she had never felt this way when Jake kissed her!

She breathed deeply of his clean, musky scent. She wanted to forget the rigors of the last week and the terror-filled hours when they had both almost died. It seemed only natural to touch his chest, to curl her fingers through the crisp hair.

Still, there was more. So much more. Star could feel his muscles drawn tight at her touch, the strong beating of his heart beneath her palms, and the searing heat from his body. Her right hand slid around his neck, drawing him closer, and her lips sought the hollow of his throat and pressed against the throbbing pulse point.

If Daere was stunned by her uninhibited reaction to him, his confusion quickly spun away when she pressed her warm, seductive body against his.

"Star, honey, you've got to know I won't be able to hold back much longer," he murmured. "You've never done it before, have you?"

"No . . . but I want to with you," she whispered near his ear, and her last measure of control slipped away.

"It has to be all or nothing, sweetheart," he stated thickly. "I won't be able to stop once I'm inside you."

"Yes . . . I know," she murmured, cradling her head against his shoulder, pressing her mouth against his neck. The salty male taste of him was like an aphrodisiac to her senses. She forgot her shattered nerves and their close brush with death, as passion was aroused in its most primitive state.

Their differences forgotten, the world outside the cabin ceased to exist for a time.

His blood raced through his veins and a certain savage urgency gripped him. He seemed to need her more at this moment than he had at any other. God, she felt good, so vital and eager to help him forget. There was no denying their need, but he knew somehow that this was wrong. He couldn't offer her anything more than this night, but at the moment, the only thing he wanted was to lose himself in her arms.

Long fingers drifted over the curves and delicate hollows of her body, moved feather-light over her hips, then cupped the firm swell of her buttocks, enticing her to allow him more. He wanted her, all

256

of her. He wanted the taste of her on his tongue, wanted to know every inch of her skin. She was the sort of woman a man could easily lose himself to in passion, but there could never be anything more.

Star wrapped her arms around him and let him lead. He did so masterfully, but she noticed that his heart was beating just as wildly as hers, and his hands were so gentle as they roamed over her in places she'd never before been touched.

Star felt a quivering desire that was so achingly sweet she became lost to everything but the pleasure he gave. She felt the length of his sex, hard and as searing as a firebrand against her belly. It made her stomach flutter and her breasts ache to feel his mouth there. She also wanted very much to feel his burning heat inside her.

In fact, she shockingly realized, she had never wanted anything more in her life. Her breathing had turned to short, shallow gasps, and his lips were making it impossible to think of anything else but him. Her hips were moving unashamedly against him in a silent plea to give her what she craved, and she bit down on her bottom lip to keep from begging for his bold invasion.

Star tried to suppress a strangled moan when he shifted her body and the weight of her hips fit snugly into his, sending shock waves rioting through her.

"Tell me that you want me inside you," he whispered.

"I . . . I can't say the words." Yet they raged inside her head. God, he was a fever in her blood that she could not control.

Finally, when she thought she might go mad if he didn't touch her, *really* touch her, his hands molded over her breasts, his fingers curling possessively around the lush mounds.

The feel of his big, sinewy body, the way her form so naturally cradled against his, and the seductive taste of him in her mouth ignited a raging inferno within her that blotted out all else. There was no right or wrong, only this consuming need. She could tell he felt the same way, and she also understood from his rough, urgent caresses that he would make love to her, here, just as they were, with no whispered words of love or promises that they might not be able to keep.

His hands were all over her, taking liberties she had thought she would never allow any man. Especially him. Where was her common sense, her iron will? Gone, just as her innocence would be after this night.

He did this. Overbearing, sexy McCalister, with every one of his shortcomings, made time stand still and her heart beat so erratically she couldn't catch her breath.

His fingers held her firmly as his mouth closed around her aroused nipple, suckling the quivering bud, coaxing it, hard as a berry, through her clothing.

"Oh God . . . I had no idea . . . it would feel

this good," she rasped.

She didn't yet, but she would, he promised himself. Almost without her being aware, his hand dipped lower, and the buttons on her gown slipped between nimble fingers.

He helped her slip the garment over her head then tossed it aside. She sat astride his hips, wearing just her chemise and drawers, her stockinged legs tucked beneath her.

The enticing fullness of her breasts above the scalloped neckline of her chemise hinted at their ripe, round beauty, luring his lips back to their sweetness. She arched her back and moaned softly, the small sound filling him with heady passion. His mouth couldn't seem to get enough of her. His tongue gently laved the rigid peaks, tasting, moving over her.

It was then, his mind hazy with desire, that his lips closed over a small puckered scar on her right shoulder. It came as a startling revelation, but even though he suspected how she might have come by it, he didn't want to think about it now, or the fact that her voice had always been too naggingly familiar. Daere pushed it out of his thoughts, unable to bring himself to ask her that one burning question.

No man had ever touched her like this or made her feel so reckless. Nothing mattered . . . only that he should go on kissing her, touching her. Her breathing grew ragged and her hands bolder as they returned his caresses.

A sizzling rush seared along her nerve endings when his fingers slid downward over her flat belly to touch downy curls. She was on fire with liquid heat flowing through her, melting the last of her resistance. Star bit down on her lip to keep from sighing in ecstasy. It felt so wonderful, everything else fading from reality.

Daere's body was taut with passion. Her warm core was eager for his touch, and when she rocked back on her hips and parted her thighs, he accepted her invitation.

Dimly, she felt him loosening the tapes on her undergarments, then after pulling her chemise over her head, he stripped off her drawers. She was nude, feeling the air on her skin, and couldn't resist stretching her supple limbs. The only thing she could think of was how she had never felt so free. Back arched, she eagerly urged his fingers to explore between her legs.

"I'm going to touch your sex, sweetheart," he said, because he wanted her to know what he intended so she wouldn't be shocked. Some women were the first time they felt a man's hands there, and he never wanted her to remember this night with shame or regret.

Slipping his hand between her legs, he explored and petted until his fingers were wet with her passion, then he withdrew them and stroked her slowly. Very gently, one long finger delved, teased, only to retreat when he met the resistance of her maidenhead, sliding over her quivering womanly flesh with agonizing thoroughness.

"I'm going to kiss you there," he whispered. Then slowly dragging her body upward, his lips and tongue began their own exploration, following the path where his hands had been.

Star gasped at that first contact and felt tears well up in her eyes. It was so beautiful, quite unlike anything she had ever been told. She wanted him, God she did. But the truth was so difficult to admit. He took her hand and placed it against the fullness of his erection.

"I want you to know exactly how I'll feel between your legs," he told her. "It will hurt at first, but I promise I'll try to be gentle."

"It's too big," she gasped, sucking in a deep breath and jerking her hand away. "I . . . can't."

Fighting to hold back his own urgent need, he explained with infinite patience, "Your body was made for me, sweetheart. It will hurt at first, but I won't cause you any unnecessary pain." He was trying his best to speak calmly, but it wasn't easy when he was as hot as he could ever remember being for any woman. "Just relax now, love. I'm going to make you forget all about your fear." Then he pressed his mouth against her mound and slid his tongue into her gently curved folds, flicking it in and out, until she could no longer control the writhing motion of her hips.

It was the most marvelous experience of her life, but the knot of desire curling within her belly frightened her with its intensity. Nothing was ever supposed to feel this good, she thought. She clutched at his arms, thinking that she might scream if he dared to do anything more, but knowing, too, that there could be no escape. He intended to possess her thoroughly and completely.

And indeed, he did more.

Much more.

He suckled her, his tongue stroking across the feminine nubbin of flesh, and her legs opened shamelessly wider for him.

She moaned. She just had to feel him deeper . . . deeper . . . Her body surged and bucked, and his hands held her firmly his prisoner.

Fearing she might die if he went on, Star cried out for mercy, but the only thing he gave her was more erotic torture.

"I can't stand it, Daere. Now . . . oh, God, yes . . . I want . . . need to feel you inside me," she panted hoarsely, leaning over and nipping his bottom lip impatiently.

He gripped her hips and lifted her, then positioned the thick head of his shaft against the tight opening between her thighs, pushing into her slowly.

Her body instinctively recoiled, and she gasped in startled awareness. He knew there wasn't any way he could avoid hurting her. It was her first time, and there just wasn't any help for it. Clenching his teeth, he tried not to let his desire overrule his thinking. Damnit, he had promised. And he intended to make it as memorable for her as he knew it would be for him.

She accepted the penetration of his flesh without a whimper of protest. When he lay sheathed at last in her wet warmth, he made love to her as he never had any woman before, and each time, just as he felt her muscles beginning to quiver in the first throes of her orgasm, he withdrew, prolonging her pleasure as long as he could.

Finally, he just couldn't hold back any longer, and he grasped her to him, hearing her cry out his name as she reached her peak. He joined her there, dying that little death and knowing that his heart would never again be free.

Fifteen

It was the middle of the night, and Star felt certain he was sound asleep. She was lying wide awake beside him, a flood of emotions rising up uncontrollably within her.

There was no denying what she was feeling, had been feeling for days but refused to acknowledge. She was getting downright starry-eyed about him. It was shameless the way she thought about him, lusting after him night and day.

Why, just a minute ago she had dared to think about what a child of their union might look like. If he, or she, would have raven-black or silver-blond hair, and what color eyes their child would have. Vibrant green, silvery blue, or maybe a blend of both?

Strangely, she hadn't minded the thought of having his baby. Was it foolish to dream of nursing his child at her breast? Of watching their child grow up, a legacy of the love she felt for the father? If she couldn't have him, she might at least have his child to remember him by.

264

Star experienced a gamut of perplexing emotions. My God, she was unequivocally in love with him! How could that be, when only a short time ago she had despised him? This wasn't like her. There had never been anyone before him who had made her behave so wantonly.

He only had to speak her name or hold out his hand, and she was in his arms, the world outside the cabin forgotten. There was no denying he didn't love her in the same way she loved him. If she had learned anything from Jade and her adventures at the bordello, it was that sex and love were two separate emotions. One didn't necessarily have to accompany the other for a man and woman to achieve physical gratification.

Sex with Daere was wild and wicked, yet beautiful; a bonding of their hearts and souls, as well as their bodies. It was also the most satisfying of pleasures, and Star didn't think she would ever be able to give herself so completely to any other man.

In fact, just the thought of another man making love to her was repulsive, but it never seemed so when Daere touched her, kissed her, made her throb with need.

Their being here alone had allowed her to view a side of him she would never have dreamed existed. The gentle, caring man that he had revealed to her in this room had shown her nothing but kindness and concern. Star just knew he had never before experienced this depth of intensity in a relationship. Yet, he stubbornly refused to accept her love, and she knew he was fighting the emotion.

But how could he keep denying it? Touching him, being joined as one in body, the soul-shattering climax that always followed was totally consuming in its intensity.

The things he had done to her, which she had repaid in kind to him, went beyond the two of them just having consensual sex. He knew every curve and hollow of her body . . . how her skin felt, tasted, and smelled.

She moved her legs restlessly, half stifling a moan. He had no right to have done this to her! She didn't even know who she was any more.

I want him even at this moment, she thought. Wanting him had become addictive, the only necessity in her life that mattered. Was there something wrong with her that she should lust after him every waking hour? Even at night, she would wake from a sound sleep, look over at him, and melt inside thinking about his hands and lips setting her afire. The surge of heat she felt between her legs just before his hard, thick length thrust up inside her filled her so completely that her nerve endings screamed in protest, even as his name sighed from between her lips.

Ah, but it was the sweetest sort of agony she had ever known. She felt the familiar wetness between her thighs, and hot tears welled up in her eyes. It wasn't right that he should make her body react in this manner. Star didn't necessarily believe

266

in class or distinction, but she knew that a real lady never, ever behaved as she had.

She thought that perhaps she was one of those hot-blooded women so many men jokingly referred to as a "hot little piece." Even in the dark, she could feel her face turn beet-red at the thought. She would have to talk this over with someone who had more experience in these matters.

Jade's image swam before her eyes. Star almost sobbed with her need to see her friend. Yes, Jade would know. She would listen without passing judgment, and like it or not, Star knew she would hear the truth.

But how could she be a hussy when she wanted but one man? No other would ever do. Just him.

Star turned her head, studying the savage male beauty of the man lying next to her. He was all she'd ever need. Sadly, she realized, he was the one man she would probably never have.

Late the following afternoon, Star was outside in the yard gathering up more wood kindling for the stove, when she heard the distinct sound of a horse's hooves on the trail that wound up the mountainside to the cabin.

Grabbing up Daere's rifle, which she always kept near at hand, she ran toward the front porch, where she used one of the posts to shield her. The rifle barrel balanced on her shoulder, she took careful aim. But to her surprise, when the rider topped the steep rise, she recognized that it was a woman. Her heart leaped in her chest. She lowered the rifle, cradling it in her arm.

"Jade?" she cried, hurrying down the steps to meet her friend. She stood waiting for horse and rider at the end of the yard, one hand shading her eyes against the bright rays of the sun slanting through the leafy tree branches. "Whatever brings you out this way?"

With obvious relief, Jade smiled down at her as she slid out of the saddle. "Star, you don't know how glad I am to find you here. I was getting real worried about you." Pivoting, she reached across the bay's rump and untied the length of rawhide securing the saddle packs, then slung the store of supplies she'd brought for Star over her shoulder. Turning to face her friend once more, she said, "You sure gave me a scare this time."

"I'm sorry, Jade, it couldn't be avoided. I was hoping you would think to look for me here."

"When you didn't show up at the shop, at first I just figured you might have needed some time here by yourself. But then Alec paid me a visit, and I heard all about the ruckus Raven caused at the party the other night. That was when I decided I'd better ride out here to see if you were all right."

"I hope Aunt Hilda isn't too worried."

"You know Hilda. Sometimes I wonder how the poor women can remember what day it is."

"Yes, the poor dear. She does get forgetful at times."

"And it's lucky for you that this is one of those times," Jade said. "Otherwise, she'd have the sheriff out looking for you by now."

Star began to lead the way toward the cabin. "I'm sorry if I caused you unnecessary worry. It couldn't be helped, though. I couldn't leave him here alone, so I took the chance that sooner or later you would miss me and ride out here before you did anything else."

Star was abruptly caught by the elbow and pulled around to face Jade, whose expression was one of total bewilderment. "Uh . . . let me get this straight. I take it by your reference to *him* that you're trying to tell me there's a man here with you." She pointed toward the cabin. "And he's inside even as we speak?"

"Uh-huh . . . and not just any man, I'm afraid. The man is . . . Daere McCalister," Star confessed, looking sheepish.

Jade paled, then her ebony brow rose fractionally as Star's words registered. "You have *the* Daere McCalister, the man you vowed to run out of town, staying here—with you?"

Star nodded woodenly.

"Have you lost your mind?" Jade gasped. "What if he finds out who you are . . . or rather, who you become when you're not being Star?"

Jade seemed awfully excited, even befuddled, which was not like her friend at all, Star thought.

"Calm down and let me explain," she hurriedly replied, hoping to soothe her.

Stunned by Star's disclosure, Jade stared back at her. "Yes, I think you'd better."

"And I *will,* but first let's put your horse in the lean-to. I'd rather talk out of earshot of the cabin."

Star relieved Jade of the saddle packs, and the two women walked off together, one silent and worried, the other thoughtful and anxiously searching for a way to explain to her friend how she had fallen in love with the wrong man and couldn't think rationally beyond one day at a time anymore.

Daere was damned sick of lying around in bed. He felt helpless and weak. It was time for him to take charge of his recovery. Most of all, it was time for him to think about leaving her.

For the first time in many years, he was experiencing a range of heartfelt emotions. He grappled with the unexpected revelation, wondering just when and how things had begun to change. He had never been close to falling in love, and even though he had always enjoyed the company of other women and what they had to offer him between the sheets, he'd never had any trouble telling them goodbye.

Love 'em hard, but don't be there in the morning when they wake up.

270

It had been his absolute rule when involved with the female gender. He had sworn never to let anyone get to him again. Until now, until her, it had worked perfectly.

He recalled everything about her, remembering only too well the feel of her, the scent of her skin, and the defiance in her eyes each time he'd force her to comply to his demands. She was a woman unlike any other, with more spirit than any he'd met and with intelligence to equal her extraordinary beauty. He didn't want to remember all of those things about her or allow himself to feel that kind of response. They were threats, these emotions, and he must force them to the far corners of his mind, bury them deeply as he'd done so many times before.

Once, long ago, he had tried to live an ordinary life. He had settled in a town and made friends he'd liked very much. But it hadn't lasted more than a few months, before another gunman had tracked him down.

In the end, the boy, Tad, had paid the price for having been Daere's friend. There wasn't a minute of the day that he didn't remember that awful period in his life. He *made* himself recall the incident. Damnit! He just couldn't allow himself to forget. Tad deserved to be remembered because he had sacrificed his own life for his friend. He had taken the bullet that had been meant for Daere.

Daere knew he couldn't expose Star to the same threat. He wouldn't be able to live with himself if anything happened to her. Just as soon as he was able, he had to leave her. It was the only way he might guarantee her safekeeping.

As if she refused to allow him to forget, Star's image flitted through his mind to taunt him. She was unlike any other woman he had ever known. Innocently seductive, she didn't seem to realize how easily she could make him want her.

Daere could envision the glint of silver in her pale blond hair, which beneath his fingers felt soft as silk. Her silvery blue eyes, ever changing and expressive, that could darken to sapphire whenever she became upset. In the next breath, he found himself wondering if her eyes would sparkle like jewels when she was aroused. Ah, now that was something he would give anything to see. She would be magnificent to behold, he knew, for he had already seen her a hundred times a day in his mind's eye.

Sleek, firm body, full round breasts, and long, coltish legs that seemed to start and never end. Always, the mysterious temptress, luring him ever closer to her burning flame.

She had offered him her innocence, and he had gladly taken it away from her. Just like he had always done with everything else in life. If he saw something he wanted badly enough, he would pursue it, until eventually it became his.

He should have kept his hands off her, for he knew they could have no future together beyond these rooms.

"Daere? Are you all right?" he heard her ask from the doorway.

His heart hammered in his chest, just as it always did whenever she spoke to him. Just the breathy way she said his name sent desire raging through him. He didn't realize that he was scowling.

Star watched him, afraid that he had overheard her conversation with Jade, even though they had tried to be as cautious as possible and had stayed out of range of the cabin.

Jade had only remained long enough to drop off the supplies she had brought for Star, and to see that her horse had been fed and watered, then she had been on her way again. She had promised to cover for her friend, and Star had no doubt that she would. Her gaze searched Daere's face anxiously.

"Something's wrong."

"No, I'm fine," he sought to reassure her.

She moved across the room. "I don't think so. Let me help you, please."

"Goddamnit, there are just some things you can't make better, Star. So just stay away from me and let me take care of myself just this once."

Her steps faltered, and she felt a moment of panic. She didn't come any closer to him. "You sound so angry. What did I do?"

He sighed, flinging his arm over his eyes. "It's not you. I have to get out of this bed and on my feet." He began groping around for the chair next to the bed. "Where are my pants? My gunbelt? Hell, I can't stay here forever, you know."

She did understand. Only too well. He was already anxious to leave her. She hesitated, then decided he needed her to be brutally honest at the moment. What he was talking about doing was madness. He wasn't in any shape to go anywhere yet. "So, you want me to bring you your things, and then you're going to get dressed and ride out of here. You're forgetting something, aren't you?"

"No! Not for a minute," he snarled. "I know damned well that I can barely see my hand in front of my face," he interjected, fury rippling over him. "It doesn't change anything. I need to get out of here." As if to prove to himself that he could still defy the odds and win if he wanted it badly enough, he pushed himself up slowly and swung his legs over the side of the bed.

Star let him, but her anxious gaze followed his every movement. "Whenever you're ready, say the word, and I'll help you to get dressed. But I *won't* allow you to ride out of here. Not yet, anyway."

"Then just get my trousers and my gunbelt. I've damned well lain here long enough."

"I declare, but you're the most ornery man I ever did meet, Daere McCalister," she fumed, despite her resolve to remain calm. Her thoughts and emotions were in turmoil—she was concerned, too, but she knew he didn't want her pity—and right now, her fury was quickly edging out every other emotion. It had been held in check for too

274

long. She was suddenly mad at Daere, and herself, for caring this much.

"It's keeps me alive," he growled. "So I guess I'm going to go right on being a no-good sonofabitch."

She let the fury come then, and after hurriedly snatching up his clothing from the chair, she flung it at him. His brow lifted. She ignored him. "There, get dressed, buckle on your gun, and get the hell out if that's what you want. But don't think I'm going to be here should you decide to come back. I do have a life, too, and if you don't want me, then I know someone who does."

He sat there saying nothing, then he stood up, wobbled a little, but persisted in yanking on his pants. His fingers fumbled at the buttons on his trousers. Glancing over at her, his lips suddenly twisted upward in a smirking grin. "I bet you look real pretty right about now, being all fired up the way you are." His voice turned coaxing. "Come here . . . I think I need help getting my trousers buttoned."

Watching him, she felt her anger melting away. He sure was an ornery cuss, but he was also the most courageous and wonderful man that she had ever known. Then her eyes darkened with another emotion. One she was beginning to recognize well. He was also sexy as hell, especially at the moment, standing there so proud and straight, with his black hair tousled, a shadow of a beard masking his lean jaw, and the unbuttoned placket of his trousers luring her gaze.

"I'd rather help you take them off again," she said, her voice weak with wanting. Dark passion simmered in the depths of her blue eyes, waiting for him to fan the fire.

"Later, I'll pour a bath for you," she said, and continued to tell him how she would pleasure him. "Then after your bath, I'll smooth warmed oil all over your body . . . everywhere . . . and rub it in very slowly. Would you like that, lover?"

"Sounds good to me," he replied, tensed muscles already relaxing, "but only if you allow me to reciprocate."

"I wouldn't have it any other way," she said, her voice a low, sensual rasp. "And, Daere . . . shall I play the siren or kitten tonight?"

His mouth smiled. "Which would you prefer?"

"I'll follow your lead," said the willowy beauty, her softly accented cadence a soothing balm that banished all thought save one from his mind.

"I assure you, you won't regret your decision," he murmured silkily, reaching out to draw her into his arms.

With deft movements, she tugged the trousers down the length of his taut buttocks, trailing a pattern of fire with her lips and tongue, stirring him to pulsing arousal. His eyelids felt weighted and heavy as her lips nibbled and possessed, and her tongue swirled around his rigid manhood.

With a feral growl of need, Daere threaded his fingers in her silvery mane and, drawing her upward, cupped her buttocks and lifted her. "Put your legs around me, love," he whispered.

She did so without hesitation, and he slid into her satiny sheath in one smooth thrust. His big hands held her firm as he speared her with all the powerful force of his need. Her body arched and shuddered, her head falling back as panting gasps escaped her.

Daere set the pace, his hips grinding against hers, seeking absolute possession in the only way he really knew she'd ever totally belong to him.

The things she whispered to him while he moved in and out of her body drove the breath from his lungs and reason from his mind. She was the only woman he had ever truly needed, wanted, more each time than the last. The corded muscles in his arms and neck strained from his effort to hold back his release until he had granted her her own. He didn't have to wait long.

Her slim hands grasped at his shoulders. "I need you now, Daere," she whispered harshly, arching her hips, drawing him deeper inside her and setting him afire.

The warm, womanly scent of her filled his senses and heightened his desire. Responding to her plea, Daere's hard driving rhythm heightened her desire, bringing her pleasure so exquisite it was unlike anything she had ever experienced before. She met his thrusts, crying out his name again and again when she reached her peak.

He caught her quivering body to him, capturing

her sigh of bliss with a kiss.

Lost in a haze of passion, they played out other sensuous games beyond the borders of thought and reason.

Then this ebony bird beguiling my sad
    fancy into smiling,
By the grave and stern decorum of the
    countenance it wore,
"Though thy crest be shorn and shaven,
    thou," I said, "art sure no craven;
Ghastly, grim, and ancient raven wandering
    from the Nightly shore—
Tell me what thy lordly name is on the
Night's Plutonian shore!"
           Quoth the raven, "Nevermore."

The Raven, Edgar Allan Poe

Sixteen

"You've been hell to live with for days, Cass," Alec Tremayne grumbled, his expression one of pained tolerance. Stepping from the brass tub, he began toweling himself dry. "I'm beginning to think you're getting tired of having me around. Maybe you'd even like to get rid of me . . . like you have all the others." His dark eyes clawed at her like talons. "Yeah, that's it all right, isn't it? Get me out of the way first, then you can spend as much time as you want with that old geezer you invited to the party the other night."

"Don't be ridiculous. I just have a lot on my mind right now," Cassondria replied, catching his sharp glare through the mirrored wall surrounding them, feeling impaled by his unwavering gaze.

"So I've noticed. You barely have time to exchange a civil word with me lately," he grumbled. "And I don't like the way you've allowed business to come between us. I don't like it at all."

"Well, that's just too bad, darling, because one of us has to keep an eye on things around here—especially since you seem more intent on other matters lately, like maybe what's happening in town at Rosalie's," she snapped, the angry retort hardening her features.

"There you go again, Cass," he growled. "Nag, nag, nag. That's the only thing I ever get from you anymore." The tensing of his jaw betrayed his deep frustration. He thought she had a lot of room to complain about his philandering, but he knew for a fact that she was already bedding down with that old goat—albeit a rich old goat—that she'd invited to the party the other night. The line of his mouth tightened a fraction more. "Maybe I should just quit discussing my plans with you. You're getting too goddamn high and mighty. I never did find that the least attractive in a woman."

"I do whatever it takes. I'm going to make sure I get everything I deserve out of life," she retaliated heatedly.

"We have this place, and we've got each other. Isn't that ever going to be enough for you, Cass?" he asked in a harsh, raw voice, then added in a lower, huskier tone, "I remember when it used to be."

For a long moment, she looked back at him. There was a desperate, almost maniacal light in his eyes now. She didn't like it when he looked at her in that way. It frightened her, and Casson-

281

dria didn't ever like to feel vulnerable. Alec had always been a very dominating man, even more than his father had been, which at times irritated her and made her lash out at him. Yet, she had never been as afraid of him or felt more threatened than she did at this moment. It hit her then, and oddly, she felt a measure of sadness. Poor Alec was beyond her help now. His addictive nature, so like his father's, had finally overpowered the little self-control that he'd possessed.

It was absolutely pointless to stand and argue with him. He was a loaded cannon just ready to explode. He just couldn't see the trouble he was heading toward. His hands were always trembling, his eyes glazed and bloodshot. And while she knew how much he enjoyed his drinking, it wasn't just the liquor that was making him this crazy. It was something more. He'd definitely begun to change, and none for the better. She was growing increasingly worried about his violent mood swings, the grimness that always seemed present around his eyes and mouth. He was closer to the edge than she had ever seen him. She suspected that Alec was doing far more than just drinking, but Cassondria didn't know if she even cared enough to try and convince him to stop. Right now, she just wanted to protect herself, and so she forced a smile she didn't feel.

"Don't get your *cojones* in an uproar, Alec," she said. "It won't be much longer, and all our troubles will all be over. We've gotten rid of the gunslinger, as well as Raven, so there are few obstacles left in our path. And just as soon as I sink my hooks into this latest catch, we'll get rid of him just like we did the others, and then we'll have all the money we'll ever need to live comfortably for the rest of our lives."

"Aren't you forgetting somebody? There *is* still Star. She could possibly put a noose around both our necks."

Cassondria quickly waved aside his hesitation. "After all these years, she isn't going to suddenly remember what happened the night her father died. Thanks to us, she's still afraid of her own shadow, and she probably always will be." She laughed throatily. "What a little coward she turned out to be. She was indeed the easiest to manipulate. Of course, I always give credit where it's due. It was you, Alec, and the terror of what you put her through that day in the woodshed." Her smile widened in approval, and Alec was amazed at the thrill it gave him. "No, dear Alec, Star is the least of our worries. If she would even dare try and cause trouble, we'd merely pay her a visit and shut her up. This time, permanently."

His eyes glittered. "We could just make certain she never talks. Let me get rid of her, Cass. I can think of several ways that would give me such immense pleasure. In fact, I won't even lay a hand on her. I'll just watch her die of fright."

"We can't, darling. Although it's tempting, I know. However, I've always hesitated to kill her unless it becomes absolutely necessary," she explained. "Someone might become too suspicious, and I don't intend to ever make a mistake, Alec. I've worked long and hard for what I've got. No, we'll just leave Star to her buttons and bows, where she'll remain out of our way."

He shrugged one shoulder. "Whatever you say, Cass," Alec replied obligingly. He was watching her from beneath craggy brows, and his eyes had darkened with another emotion she recognized only too well.

She tried not to flinch when he walked up behind her. Snaking an arm around her shoulders, he released the towel knotted at her breasts and tossed it aside.

Alec stood in the steam-clouded bathroom, staring transfixed at her bare body glistening with a fine sheen of moisture and scented oil. His loins ached to possess her. It had been so long since they'd shared any intimacy together. Lately, she seemed to avoid his advances, using any excuse she could to put him off. Well, not today.

Today, his hands and lips were going to explore every inch of her, until they were both throbbing with their need to possess, to devour.

He could feel himself getting hard just thinking about it, as he mentally explored her body. Yes, she'd soon be begging him for it, and he'd be good and ready for her by then, too. It wasn't often that he felt this confident of his sexual prowess anymore. He could remember a time when he had always been hard as stone for her, when she liked to run her hand along the length of his manhood, eyes shining almost in reverence. He had felt powerful back then, and he felt that way at this moment, too.

"Be nice to me, Cass," he said hoarsely. "You'll see, I'll make it real good for you."

Cassondria stood rigid as stone, feeling his heated gaze rake her pale ivory form. He leaned into her, beginning to knead the tense muscles along her shoulders. "When we make plans together like this, it reminds me of the good old days," he murmured over her shoulder, his lips nibbling the shell of her ear. "It also gets me hotter than hell." His voice turned coaxing as he slid one hand under her buttocks and pushed one finger up inside her. "Please . . . give me what I need from you."

Alec curled his fingers around her throat, and Cassondria bowed her head, remaining in a state of frozen stillness. She no longer liked making love in front of the mirrors as she once had. That had been a long time ago, when she'd been younger, firmer, slimmer.

His fingers began stroking the curve of her neck, and his voice turned silky. "I know you like it this way. You always have."

She shivered, but he mistook her body's reaction for one of desire. He didn't realize she was feeling vulnerable, unattractive, and worse, repulsed.

Ten years ago, she would never have felt like this. Now, she only felt exposed, stripped emotionally and weakened. It wasn't Alec's rough lovemaking; she had always liked it that way before and had given back as good as she had gotten. Of course, that had been when she had been younger, her body in perfect shape and this room her favorite retreat. She used to like to stand before these same mirrors for hours, gazing at her reflection. But no more.

She was no longer happy with the reflection of the woman looking back at her. She saw only an older woman, still attractive enough, but one whose past lifestyle was revealed in every deeply etched line marring a once-youthful face.

It was difficult to accept the fact that her youth had faded, and with it her confidence, but what distressed Cassondria even more was that younger men no longer looked at her with avid interest as they once had, Alec included.

Once his eyes had devoured her; now he only told her what he thought she wanted to hear. She suspected there was another woman he had been seeing for some time now. Even worse, Cassondria knew he was bedding the wench on a regular basis.

She had smelled her perfume on him whenever he returned in the wee hours of the morning.

Who was she? Most importantly, how much younger was she? Knowing Alec as she did, no doubt his new interest would be an accomplished whore, with a firm young body and a carnal mouth that would drive him wild for her.

She tried not to stare at their reflections in the mirrors; just the sight of him pawing at her was enough to nudge her simmering anger over the edge. He probably did it like this with the other one, too, she thought. A pang hit her heart, and Cassondria squirmed uncomfortably. "I'm just not in the mood, Alec," she said stiffly. "Maybe later."

"No, now, Cass. Don't lie to me. You won't be in the mood then, either. You never are anymore!" He pressed against her, pinning her between his body and the mirrored wall.

Cassondria gritted her teeth when she felt his erection pressing against her buttocks, and her hands clutched at the cool glass. "Stop it, Alec. Let me go—now!"

After several more minutes of humiliating effort, he suddenly shook his head in disgust and flung her away from him. "Who needs this nonsense! I got places to go where there are women who beg me to make love to them. I don't have to get it from you!" Spinning on his heel, he stalked into the bedroom, throwing her a murderous glare over his shoulder. Muttering under his breath, he began yanking on his pants.

She came to the doorway and stared after

him. "I suppose you're going to your whore?"

"I know where I'm not welcome," he growled.

"And where you are," she ground out.

He glanced up, sneering. "You're damned right. One whore's as good as another, I guess. One I pay money for, the other just sucks the life out of me. I'd rather give in cash, thank you."

Cassondria exploded in outrage, hurling herself at him, teeth bared, her long red nails curled into talons. "You damned bastard! Who do you think you are that you can talk to me like that? Nobody calls me a *puta!*" The fingers of her hand swiped out at the side of his face, catching him by surprise, gouging bloody furrows along his pale cheek.

He didn't even cry out, but merely knocked her aside and stood there, letting the blood drip freely onto his white shirt. Finally, he raised his hand and dabbed at the angry-looking wounds, then glanced at the blood on his fingertips and said, "You've torn me up so badly inside, Cass, that this really is nothing."

Cassondria lay sprawled on the bed where she had fallen, her face pale and drawn. "Get out of here before we both do something we're really going to regret," she said tiredly.

Alec grabbed up his jacket and, for a moment, stood staring coldly down at her. She thought she had him by the short hairs, but he knew he could fix her anytime if he really had a mind to. Once he had worshiped her, but she was just using him like she had the others, and all for the sake of the God-Almighty dollar. It was the only thing she worshiped in her life. For that, he reviled her. "I'm leaving, Cass, but I'll be back. And you'd better be ready for me by then. I'm going to put a spell on you, Cass, that won't let you ever get free. You're mine, and you're going to stay that way."

Cassondria waited until she heard the sound of the front door slam, before she gave in to a fit of rage and pummeled the mattress with clenched fists. "I'll fix you yet, Alec," she fumed, struggling with equal parts of fury and frustration. "No one ever gets the better of Cassondria Tremayne. Not even you."

Seventeen

As the days flew past, they became good
friends as well as lovers. And when he had
opened his eyes one morning and realized that
not only had he felt the warmth of the sun on
his face, but had actually seen it streaming in
through the window, Daere had to immediately
awaken her. She had cupped his face in her
hands and wept tears of joy.

He had watched her, mesmerized, his gaze following the path of those tears, and then he'd
tentatively reached out and brushed his callused
thumb across her cheek, capturing a teardrop.

The tiny bead of moisture glistened like crystal
in the sunlight and was the most precious gift
she could have given him. He wished he might
bottle it up and tuck it away, to retrieve later
whenever he desired. He wanted to remember
everything about this time they'd had together,
so much so that it hurt just to realize it.

Daere recalled the tender moment once again
as he sat on the porch stairs early one morning,

waiting for her to join him. Those tears had moved him in a way that nothing else ever had. Because she had been crying for him. He couldn't remember anyone ever moving him to such depths of emotion. It frightened him to realize how important she had become in his life. And there was something else that distressed him as well: the fact that when he left her, she would go back to her other life. As Raven.

There was little doubt in his mind anymore that Star was the black-clad bounty hunter. He had begun to recall details and images of the night he'd almost died in the river. Most of all, he vividly remembered how she'd held him in her arms, urging him to fight for his life. Body language. There wasn't anything about Star that he didn't know.

He recalled the hours they had laughed together, played together, and loved most passionately together.

This morning had dawned sunny and warm. Spring was in the air. She was inside packing a picnic basket. They were going to spend the day deep in the mountains.

His vision was almost perfect once again, and he was a grateful man. The first time he had looked upon her face and clearly distinguished every detail, he had to turn away from her, for he'd almost wept at her beauty. He wanted so much what she offered him, but he couldn't let himself start thinking about marriage and children and what life would be like with her. Even if he did give in and marry her, they sure as hell would never grow old together. He would give her nothing but pain and dreams never realized. The truth was crystal clear: One day somebody would come along who was faster on the draw. It was inevitable. Star didn't need to go through life as his widow. She deserved something better than to carry his name.

"I think I have everything packed at last," she said brightly, stepping through the door.

He masked his tumultuous feelings, and together they walked hand in hand to their horses.

This was Daere's first trip away from the cabin, and he was enjoying their leisurely ride through the verdant, green forest. But he had to admit his mind wasn't really aware of his surroundings. Not with the enticing vision of Star riding ahead of him, her hips swaying from side to side with the gait of her horse.

Like a man who had thirsted for too long, his eyes couldn't seem to get enough of her. She was a study in seduction, her long, lustrous hair cascading down her back unhindered by pins, the sunlight sifting through the shimmering tresses. It was a day he'd likely never forget, but one he would retain in his memory, to retrieve whenever he couldn't stand living his life without her. And he knew that day was rapidly approaching. They couldn't remain in their own private little Utopia forever. Someone would come looking for him, and he didn't want her to have to face the danger when they found him.

By the time they had reached their destination—a clear mountain stream flowing over tumbled rocks into a deep blue pool nestled among the trees, glistening like a sparking jewel beneath the blazing sun—Daere and Star were both more than ready to relax.

Daere hobbled both horses in a shady glen, where they could graze on tender shoots of grass, and turned to find Star waiting for him.

"Ready for that swim?" she queried, her voice husky.

"You go ahead," he said. "I'm just going to take a quick look around and make certain that we'll be safe here."

Star waded into the water in her satin underclothes—she seemed shy with him since he'd regained his sight—and began to swim slowly away from the bank. She seemed to be enjoying the water's cool caress against her flushed skin. Turning over onto her back, she floated about, her silver-blond hair like wet silk, drifting behind her on the water.

Having at last made certain their retreat was secure, Daere stood watching her from the bank.

She reminded him of a pagan water nymph. He wanted her, needed her at that moment with a ferocity unlike anything he'd ever known before. His eyes followed her movements, and every now and again he noticed that her gaze would slide to where he had retreated to a large flat boulder at the edge of the water.

She didn't seem to mind that he watched her. Of course, he already knew the flowery fragrance of her perfumed skin, how she felt and the taste of her on his lips.

He knew all that, but he still wanted to know more. Much more. Several days ago, he had accidentally come across a black silk bandanna tucked away in the back of the armoire. He knew the Raven wore the same type of scarf. Sooner or later, he was going to have to confront her with his suspicions. What would she say? How would it affect their relationship?

For the past week, he had been having flashbacks of the night that Raven had dragged him from the river and had brought him to the cabin. He remembered silver hair and soft skin, but most of all he remembered that voice urging him not to give up, to keep fighting for his life during that hellishly long ride. It was Star's voice, Star's hands, which had been the lifeline he'd clung to during the darkest hours.

There were other subtle similarities. Things that he'd noticed with startling clarity while trapped in the darkness. Their height and build, even their scent were the same.

Time and familiarity had led him to conclude that Star and Raven were one and the same. Soon, they would have to come to terms with his discovery. Daere didn't think he could allow her to continue her dangerous crusades. It terrified him just to think about what might happen to her. What was *she* going to say about this? Therein was his greatest dilemma. If he knew any one thing for certain about this woman, it was that she was brave and had more heart than anyone he had ever known. If she believed in something strongly enough, no one could convince her otherwise.

He watched her swim easily through the water, then stop just a few yards away and stand up. His hooded eyes didn't miss a thing, and they feasted on the perfection of her willowy body, the contours of her firm breasts and pebble-hard nipples delineated against the clinging wet satin. He thought, too, that even now she was just as elusive and mysterious as the first time he had met her. No matter how many times a man might possess a woman like Star, he could never master her. She was proud and free-spirited, and she would slip through his grasp like quicksilver should he ever try.

"I thought you wanted to go swimming," she said.

"I did, but now I have something better in mind," he called back, crooking his finger. "Why don't you come here and I'll tell you what it is."

She shook her head. "Uh-uh, I'm enjoying myself."

He began unbuckling his gunbelt. "I guess I'll just have to come get you, then," he said.

"I don't think you can catch me," she replied, unable to resist the taunt.

Before she even had the words out of her mouth, he was on his feet and shucking off his shirt, then his boots and trousers.

Star squealed as he did a graceful dive off the boulder, surfaced, and began swimming toward her.

"You'll never catch me!" she yelled, and began swimming away from him.

Daere allowed her to lead, knowing how she'd revel in the position and the measure of control. He watched her carefully, for he recalled well her aversion to deep water. And if she were Raven—as he'd suspected for some time now—she'd soon shift directions and head back toward the shore.

But she kept on swimming, seemingly without concern that she was in depths over her head. "Hurry up, slowpoke," she couldn't resist calling back.

"Keep that up, and you're asking for trouble," he warned with mock gruffness. He began to close the distance between them, and just as he drew within a foot of tagging her on the leg, she kicked out hard and splashed water in his face.

"Star," he growled menacingly when she kept it up.

"You complained of being hot earlier. Well, I was just trying to cool you off," she teased.

"All right, you've been asking for this, lady," he said, then disappeared in one smooth movement beneath the surface of the water.

"Daere, come on now, don't do that," she cried as she stopped swimming and bobbed there in the water, her eyes watchful.

Star's gaze was drawn at once to the clear surface, frantically trying to discern the outline of his body in the water. Her breathing accelerated. On impulse, she thrashed her legs under the water.

He was almost within reach of her now. She commanded her limbs to move. Just as she was about to strike out for the shore, his hands closed firmly around her legs, and he tugged with enough force to pull her down under the water with him.

She managed to take a gulp of air before she found herself imprisoned tightly in his arms. Suddenly, their teasing became something more. He laced an arm around her waist and one hand cupped the back of her head. Despite the thudding of her heart, she wanted what he offered.

His kiss was hard and hungry, his tongue slipping between her teeth to probe her mouth. He kissed her until her lungs felt tight from lack of air and her head whirled with emotions she could no longer deny.

Then suddenly she was free of his embrace. They surfaced together.

Gasping raggedly, she faced him, still trembling from the myriad of emotions that his kiss always evoked. His eyes were dark with passion; she felt weak with wanting him. No words were exchanged between them. None were necessary. Her arms reached out to him, and he moved to gather her close.

His hands caressed the length of her spine, then skated downward, slipping under her buttocks, searching inside her underclothes to touch her where she burned so hotly for him.

Blood was charging through her veins, and heat was burning her up from within. His fingers stroked and filled her, making her forget all other wants. She arched her back and whimpered in ecstasy.

Her throat muscles were so tight she could not say what she felt, but her body's responses to his seeking fingers had already answered for her. Looking up at him, she saw a flash of memory in his eyes. It worried her that she had been thinking more and more that he might have figured out the truth about her role as Raven. He had begun talking to her more about Raven lately, and only this morning, he had asked her if she believed what men like Raven did was right. Of course she did. Of course he wouldn't agree. And while it frightened her to think that her secret might be exposed, it was the thought of losing him that absolutely terrified her. She felt certain that he would hate her if he ever learned she had deliberately deceived him. Worse, had wished him dead.

She closed her eyes against the painful memories and said shakily. "Oh, Daere, you make me feel so confused. When you're holding me, touching me, it's wonderful, and the world is beautiful. But the other times . . ."

He held her tightly in his arms. "Shh . . . shh . . . Let's forget the other times for now. I want you, Star. That's all that's important right now."

Any doubts that she had at that moment whirled away like vapors in the wind.

By the time they had gotten back to the cabin, the sun was setting behind the mountains and the night breeze had cooled their sun-baked skin. They heated water over the hearth, and then Daere filled the big wooden tub that sat before the blazing fire.

When they were together in the tub, he held her against him with her face cradled in his neck. They stayed like that for a long time, saying little, just enjoying their newfound closeness. By the time they had washed with scented soap, the water was chilled, but they were flushed with desire.

Daere slung a towel around his waist, knotted it at the hip, then lifted Star out of the tub and wrapped her in a fluffy towel that had been left to warm near the fire.

Later, they shared a meal of grilled fish and roasted vegetables. They ate sitting side by side at the table, facing the wide windows overlooking the mountains. The moon was full and the sky glittered with stars. Star had never felt more complete.

Tonight their fragile trust seemed to have grown stronger.

It was very late when they finally fell asleep.

When she awoke, it surprised her to discover that it was still dark outside. She was also sleeping alone. Daere was gone.

Listening closely, she thought she heard him talking with someone in the other room. Pushing back the covers, she slipped from the bed and went to the door, careful to remain hidden from view.

Daere was standing with his back to her, and there was indeed someone else with him. An Indian. He was dressed in a fringed buckskin shirt and trousers. But he was no ordinary brave. She could tell that just by looking at him, and when he spoke, his voice was cultured.

His presence was as commanding as Daere's. Tall, broad-shouldered, and extremely good-looking, he was darker and even more fierce of countenance than the man facing him.

"It is always good to see you, Night Hawk," she heard Daere say. "Although I have to admit, I'm a bit surprised that you were able to find me here."

"It's good to see you looking so well, my brother," Night Hawk replied. He smiled, and the gesture transformed his hawkish features, making him seem less intimidating. "You of all people should know that I could find you just about anywhere."

"So, tell me. Why are you here?"

"A matter of grave importance, my brother. There's been a great deal of talk about your sudden disappearance," Night Hawk said. "My braves did a little scouting, and they tell me that Alec Tremayne has offered a hefty sum of money for anyone who can find the tracker known as Raven. Men are already out searching; they might even come here. I don't think you or the girl should be here when that happens."

Daere stood next to him, his face expressionless, his eyes cold. "That bastard. I wish I would have finished him off years ago. He's the one who should have a price on his head, and not Raven."

"I will return tomorrow. You can tell me what you have decided then." Night Hawk laid a hand on his friend's back. "I will leave now and go back to where my braves have made camp. Sleep well, my brother. And may the spirits give you guidance."

"Thanks for coming to warn me, Night Hawk," Daere said. "Peace go with you. I'll give you my decision tomorrow."

Star closed her eyes. Fear, grief, and a sense of hopelessness tangled within her. She fought to regain control. It was something she had to do. When she opened her eyes, she felt calmer, more rational, but her heart still ached. There just was no help for it.

Much I marvelled this ungainly fowl to
    hear discourse so plainly,
Though its answer little meaning — little rel-
    evancy bore;
For we cannot help agreeing that no sub-
    lunary being
Ever yet was blessed with seeing bird above
    his chamber door —
Bird or beast upon the sculptured bust
    above his chamber door,
    With such name as "Nevermore."

The Raven, Edgar Allan Poe

Eighteen

Star knew it was over between them. She'd given him back his health and his life. She had never wished for anything more at that moment than to be able to give him her love as well. Freely and completely. Yet, it wasn't to be.

Then there was no longer time for further reflection, for she heard the sound of his footsteps approaching, and her heart began to beat so rapidly she could hardly breathe. She managed to hurry back to bed just as his tall, familiar figure entered the room.

Star closed her eyes, feigning sleep. She felt his silent approach, his weight on the bed, and had to restrain herself from turning into his arms.

Slipping beneath the covers, he automatically drew her against him. He lay against her back, his arms and legs enfolding her, his lean body pressed close. He seemed to want her near him, reassuring him that for now, he wasn't alone.

Star had wanted to protest when he'd pulled

her close and had caressed the curve of her hip, but her heart would not allow her to do so.

"Let me make love to you," he murmured against the warmth of her cheek.

She trembled in his arms and surrendered.

The touch of his hands, teasing and warm, had the ability to make her forget everything. He moved his head to rub his rough cheek against hers. She caught her lower lip between her teeth, wanting him, at the moment, but also fearful he'd know what was in her heart if they made love this last time.

His fingers slipped inside her gown to cup her breasts and fondle the soft, responsive flesh. Star bit back a sigh of bliss. He touched her nipples, squeezing them gently, rolling one pink crest between his thumb and forefinger until it was taut as a ripe berry.

"Star."

Her name, whispered through the shadows, was an almost impassioned plea she could not deny. With an overwhelming urgency, she surrendered to him. His lips closed over hers and his hand moved downward, his fingers searching, finding, holding her his prisoner of desire. She quivered beneath him at the first sharp thrust of his hips. He filled her, moving smoothly, powerfully. Their mating had a sense of primal ardor.

"Say it . . . tell me how much you care," he

murmured hoarsely, driving himself faster, harder, her own hunger compelling him.

With a soft cry, she relinquished the final part of her that she'd tried so desperately not to give. Her fingers tunneled through his hair and held him against her breast. "Yes . . . I love you . . . God, I love you so much." It didn't matter that he might see the tears shining in her eyes. There was nothing she hadn't surrendered now. He'd taken everything; she'd given him everything. And in the end, she knew, it still would not be enough.

He would leave her.

He was sleeping beside her but she lay awake, staring up at the shadows on the ceiling. She'd told him how much she loved him, and it hadn't seemed to matter. He'd looked down at her, arms braced on either side of her shoulders, and those jade-green eyes had remained shadowed by doubt. She no longer knew how to reach him.

He couldn't allow himself to believe that she loved him. It was probably better that she was leaving. To save herself from unbearable heartbreak, she had to put space between them. She needed time to think and to nurse her injured pride. Damn him, why wouldn't he give them a chance? Somehow, they would be able to work through their differences. Still sorting through her troubled thoughts, she didn't realize when her eyes closed and she fell into a fitful slumber.

Sometime just before dawn, Star woke up to hear Daere mumbling incoherently, and then he began to thrash wildly in his sleep. At first, she thought he must be violently ill, but then she realized that his fists seemed to be striking out at some invisible menace.

Staring down at him, she saw that his features were contorted with anguish, his lips drawn back in a frightening snarl. He wasn't ill. He was having some sort of terrible dream.

His body trembled, and he sobbed softly, "No . . . God, please . . . don't let the boy die."

Star could only wonder what kind of nightmare could reduce this tough, hard shell of a man to cry out in such horror and anguish. Her hand reached out to stroke the side of his face as she murmured soothingly to him, "Daere . . . it's okay, I'm with you. You're just having a bad dream." Very slowly, so as not to startle him, she moved to light the lamp on the table.

The soft flame flickered over his face. It seemed to quiet him somewhat, but he still lay there very tense. Very gently, reassuringly, she reached out again to touch him, caressing him soothingly.

Suddenly, his eyes flew open and he quickly

scrambled away from her and out of bed, as if he couldn't stand to have her touching him. Star could only stare at him, uncertain what she should do. Never had she seen eyes that mirrored such human torment or murderous intent. He was looking at her but not seeing her. His big hands were clenched at his sides, every muscle in his body poised for attack.

She knew he wasn't awake, and that whatever held him captive in his subconscious must be very powerful. He was caught up in something so vividly terrifying that even she couldn't reach him. Assumably, when he slept and his defenses were down, he reexperienced some hellish experience that now wreaked havoc with his mind. She watched him, choked with overwhelming emotion, and his voice tore through her.

"Tad, I wanted it to be me . . . not you. Oh, God, why wasn't it me instead?"

Star couldn't stand it any longer. She sprinted off the bed and was before him instantly. Daere watched her, still dazed, wariness in his eyes. She reached out slowly with one hand. He caught her wrist in a viselike grip that threatened to break the bones. She gasped in pain but made no move to struggle.

"Daere . . . listen to me . . . everything's all right," she said, trying to soothe him. Strangely, she felt no fear for herself. Her concern was for him. She stepped closer, her fingers finding the sharp angle of his jaw, stroking while she continued in a reassuring voice. "Shhh . . . I love you, Daere. I love you."

He quieted, blinked several times, then all rigidness left him. He dropped her arm, and when he reached out this time, she knew he wanted only *her*. He jerked her roughly against his chest. But she did not try to draw away. She wasn't afraid. He clung to her as if his very sanity depended on her being there at that moment. Star thought that she had never known such anguish as she'd witnessed tonight in this room.

"It's all right, darling. It's only a dream."

Gradually, he stopped trembling and his breathing returned to normal. Still, he made no move to draw away from the comfort she offered. Star recalled her own near brush with death, when she'd been so overwhelmed, and had needed warmth and reaffirmation of life to help her through her crisis. He'd done that for her. Tonight, she wanted to be here for him as well.

His face was buried in the curve of her neck and his arms still bound her tightly.

"Christ, I'm sorry you had to see that," he murmured into her hair. He raised his head and looked into her eyes. His were clear and lucid, but still shadowed with grim memories. "I must have scared you to death."

Her eyes teared. "No, don't be sorry for *me*. I wasn't afraid for myself," she replied.

His arms fell away from her, and she held firm to his hand. Tugging gently, she said, "Daere, come back to bed with me."

His big body trembled. "Star, you can't really want to be near me. I almost hurt you; it could have been worse. And I have hurt someone before," he said softly. "She was a lady I had met in Laredo. She was lonely and in need. So was I. We had dinner a few times, and the last night we were together, she invited me to stay with her." He drew a ragged breath and released it. "I had the dream. When I awoke from the nightmare, she was huddled in the corner of the bedroom, her eyes condemning. She said I had tried to kill her. I won't have the same thing happen to you."

"I'm not afraid of you, Daere," Star persisted, drawing him over to the bed while whispering soothingly. When she felt her legs bump into the bed, she slowly reclined backward and pulled him down over her. She knew the scars on his body were minimal in comparison to those seared into his soul. She had never felt closer to him than at that moment.

Their eyes met for only an instant, but she saw the naked need mirrored there. He dipped his head and his lips sought hers, teasing, tasting, exploring the velvet hollows within. She felt his body pressed close to hers, and her hands began touching him, wanting nothing more than to give him pleasure and take away the pain.

She clung to him, feeling a different kind of longing this time. His breathing grew ragged as her fingers wooed his body with the teasing rhythm of touch. He kissed her eyelids, and the pulse beating rapidly in her throat. And he stroked her where she burned hottest for him, his lips nibbling a path from her breasts to her thighs, and slowly, very slowly, parting pale blond curls to kiss the secret heart of her womanhood.

"Yes, my darling . . . I told you we could get past the pain," she said breathlessly, her thighs parting, her hips arching upward in a primitive dance of passion. Star felt she would never get enough of him. Still, he gave her more than she might ever have expected.

His lovemaking was fiercely consuming, even rough, but always with an underlying tenderness that was his alone.

"Don't ever leave me, Daere," she whispered as he drove up within her in frantic hunger, their need consuming them both. She had never burned so hotly for him as she did this night.

He wouldn't make her any promises, but he filled her body with the very essence of himself. Still, she could not seem to draw him deep enough inside her. She opened her legs and he thrust harder into her moist heat, his pleasure so intense that it robbed him of breath. "More . . . I want more of you than you have ever given me before," she breathed throatily.

Slipping one hand beneath her buttocks, he speared into her with wild abandon, nostrils flaring on his face. After that, her thoughts were a blur of colorful images, hot, burning flames and smooth-textured, bronzed muscle beneath her fingertips.

Then the world as she had known it ceased to exist, spun away, and together they soared on a wave of ecstasy unlike any other they had experienced before.

She heard him cry out as the tension mounted, joining him where, as lovers, they might exist together. With her mouth and hands and from her heart, she had shown him how very wrong he was, and how much she needed him with her . . . always.

Nineteen

The following morning, he seemed like a different man from the one she had come to know. They were sitting at the kitchen table finishing the breakfast she had prepared for them.

Star had been picking listlessly at the scrambled eggs on her plate. She noticed that Daere didn't seem to have much of an appetite, either.

Through the windows, the morning sun shone brightly. It was going to be another incredibly beautiful day. Why, then, did she feel as if her world was about to come crashing in around her? They had so little time together. It didn't seem fair to lose him this soon. Not after what they had shared last night.

Looking at him, she thought, once again, what a stubborn man he was. Couldn't he see what they had together? Why did he keep pushing her away, denying the depth of emotion they had shared? Last night . . . God, they'd been so good for each other, despite his pain and the

313

awful helplessness she'd felt at having to watch him suffer.

This morning, in the revealing sunshine, they were once again distanced. She wondered just when the change had occurred; they'd been so close last night. Or so she had thought. What would he say if she were to ask him? He was sitting there calmly explaining how he'd made up his mind to send her away today. His voice was even and he gave no indication that it pained him to do so. It was so difficult to accept that this would be their last day together. His words seemed to drone on inside her head, and she had to shake herself to concentrate on what he was saying.

"It really is better this way. You know it as well as I do." He set his coffee cup down and met her gaze. "Aren't you talking to me this morning?"

Despite her firm resolve not to plead with him, her eyes misted. What she read in his gaze offered her no encouragement. His emotions were effectively closed off to her. Quickly, she looked down at her hands. Why couldn't she be like him? Why did she feel as if her life would never again be the same?

He released a frustrated sigh. "I don't want to hurt you. Believe me, I don't. You deserve so much better than what I've put you through."

You wouldn't be saying that if you really

knew. I'm not the woman you think I am, and I've been deceiving you. But I think I'm in love with you, and I'm afraid if I tell you the truth about Raven, you'll hate me. She wanted to say so much, but in the end, she gave a staggering little sob, then bit it back. "Would it really be so awful if we stayed together, like this, for just a while longer?" She was pleading! Oh, how she hated the sound of her own voice, but right at this moment, she was just desperate enough to grasp and, yes, to beg, if need be.

He looked at her, at her face so honest with emotion, and knew she was waiting for him to tell her the words she wanted to hear. He had taken everything she had been willing to give, and now he was leaving her with nothing in return. He couldn't say the things to her that she deserved to hear. They would just be putting off the inevitable.

Sooner or later, someone else would come gunning for him. He held no illusions about that. His age was catching up with him, and gun fighting no longer seemed as exciting as it had in his youth.

Back then, death was just a word, one he didn't worry over or expect might apply to him. Now he was older, wiser, and no longer felt immortal. One day, inevitably, there would come a man faster on the draw, and then that would be the end of the road. Daere shrugged mentally.

So be it then. He didn't worry about dying, never had, but he had always sworn he wouldn't leave behind a widow, perhaps even a child, to fend for themselves. Worse, to bear his name. He knew what everyone thought of him, how they had labeled him a cold, heartless killer because of that boy. It had been a terrible accident, one he still had nightmares over, but there wasn't one person who told the story the way it had really happened. No, he would never sully this beautiful, vibrant woman by making her his wife and thereby linking her to his sordid past. He knew what he must do, for her. So he forced the words, asking, "And what would we stand to gain by having a few extra days together? Let go, sweetheart, before you get hurt. Go back to Jake Fontaine. He's a good man, the kind that will give you the life you deserve."

But I don't love Jake Fontaine, she wanted to scream at him. Instead, she swung her gaze away to stare out the window, so he would not see how much his words stung. It was so hard to realize that he was discarding her. But, then, what had she expected? She didn't know . . . but certainly not this cold indifference.

She had always known he was a man to be wary of, one she should never lose her heart to. Even Jade had tried to warn her, and she had accused her friend of only being jealous. How awful she felt about that now. She had no one

316

to blame for this but herself. She had made the first move last night and he had made love to her, but he was never going to be *in love* with her.

So, that was it. There could be nothing in the future for them until he was ready to accept love, with its trial and error, warmth and caring. Daere had forgotten the beauty of love. Somewhere in his life there had been too much ugliness. She had wanted so to strip away the bad memories and show him how to really live again. But he was not going to let her.

Daere wasn't quite as successful as he'd thought in hiding his emotions. He was hurting inside, although he would never let her know it. He had sworn long ago never to let himself weaken and fall in love. Being with her, even when he had been flat on his back for days, had been some of the best moments of his life. But last night, she had gotten closer to him, to his shame, than anyone ever had. That shouldn't have happened.

Of course, how could he have known when to expect the dream to come and shatter his defenses. He'd been running away from that day in Laredo for months. He had to keep running. He couldn't stop. Weakness was his enemy. This woman, with her gentleness, warmth, and love, would destroy the warrior he had become. His shield would crumble, was crumbling already, and he would be fair game for the first tough gun that came along. Then everyone, her especially, would see how weak he really was. He could feel her watching him, and he knew a moment of panic. Did she see through him even now?

She was staring coolly.

He raked long fingers through his tousled hair. "You couldn't really have expected us to remain indefinitely. You know that's impossible." He plunged onward, hoping to ease the strain between them, wishing there were some better way to do this. "You'll be safer without me, and that's the most important thing. Your welfare is the only thing that matters to me, Star. Think of your aunt, your friends . . . Jake. They'll be glad to have you back, I'm sure."

Her heart beating rapidly, she lifted her chin. Her throat was so tight she could hardly speak. "So it's that easy for you just to slough me off?"

"No . . . I just wish you'd be sensible about this. Try to understand."

It was useless to try and deny her feelings of rejection. Foolishly, she had thought after last night that he might confide in her this morning, share his thoughts and innermost feelings. Obviously, he thought otherwise.

"You have to let go," he told her. "Take the

good memories and leave everything else behind here," he said, and for a moment she saw a glimmer of emotion in the depths of his eyes. Regret? Sadness? It was hard to tell.

She wasted no time, saying, "I'm not asking you to change for me, Daere. I can accept the way you are. You have no idea . . . but we could be good together. I'm not the sweet little innocent you perceive me to be—"

"Stop it! I said it won't work." His face was implacable, then, upon noticing her shocked expression, he added softly, "If it makes any difference, you've made me feel more alive than I have in years. I've never met another woman who makes me feel the way that you do."

"And *that's* precisely why you're leaving me," she said quietly, adding, "I heard your visitor last night. He said I was nothing but another warm, willing body to you." The words still stung. Moisture threatened behind her eyelids. "Is that closer to the truth than I want to believe?"

His eyes were vividly green and hard as emeralds as they roamed over her, committing to memory everything about her. "In some ways he is right, you know. I do lust like hell for you. I want you all the time. I think about you every waking minute. Right now I want to take you into that bedroom and tumble you back on the bed. For a man in my profession, a woman like

319

you could be lethal. My enemies—and I have many, as you know—would find a way to use you against me."

His eyes followed her hand as she fingered the edge of the yellow tablecloth. "If what you say is true, then you won't easily forget me," she said softly, lifting her eyes to his. "You can send me away, but I'll still be with you day and night, Daere. You can't keep running. One day you've got to stop."

"Maybe. But right now, I have to do what I think is best for both of us," he said somewhat wistfully. "You deserve a man like Jake, who can give you what you're looking for. I'm not that man. I never will be." Smoothly, without pausing for more than a second, he switched the conversation, leaving her sitting there feeling herself die inside a little.

"My blood brother, Night Hawk, will be back later this evening," he said. "I'll feel better when you're in his safekeeping. He's the only man I'd trust to take you back to town."

Frustrated anger kept building, almost choking her. His rejection was impossible to bear without lashing out. Her laughter was sarcastic, her tone bitter. "Just like that, we're finished. Daere McCalister's had his little dalliance. Now, you just go on with your life like before."

His eyes narrowed. "Don't talk like that. It isn't true and you know it." He felt like the lowest form of vermin. She looked hurt and angry and disappointed in him. With her next words, she found a way to wound him as deeply as he had her.

"I've interpreted everything you've said quite correctly, all right. I also have a very good memory. I know that you thoroughly enjoyed taking my virginity . . . making me your whore. You were very clear about all of that. But I've never heard you say that you care—about me, about anybody. The only thing you've told me is how you lust for me." She stared up at him, her fury prompting her. She could barely choke out the words. "Well, now that you've slaked your desire, you can just put me in the same category as the other women you've known." She extended her open palm, "They were all paid in silver, were they not?"

Daere shot to his feet so quickly he threatened to knock over his chair. There was fire in his eyes, along with denial. For a moment, she thought he might weaken. But he held back, firm in his resolve not to allow her a glimpse of his deepest emotions. He moved away to the window and stood staring out with his back to her. Finally, he spoke. "We've both said enough. It's pointless to go on. We'll discuss it another day, when we're both calmer."

Star's eyes were drawn to the back of that black head, the proud slant so achingly familiar to her now, and she said, "No, I don't think so. For, you see, I already know after I return to Tequila Bend, that you won't even act like we know one another."

He turned, drawing a long breath, then slowly releasing it as if it pained him to do so. His eyes were stormy with his suppressed feelings as they moved over her face. "How did this get so damned complicated? You weren't supposed to come into my life. Not now, when it's too late."

"Why won't you let me decide whom I wish to spend the rest of my life with? . . . Do you think you're so wicked a man that I'm incapable of caring about you?" She sighed. "If that were true, then we would never be having this conversation. Don't you see that? You're not a bad person, Daere. In fact, you're your own worst enemy. What we've found here in this cabin is pure magic and only comes around once in a lifetime."

"You're probably right," he replied huskily. "But I'm not any good for you, don't you see? I can't offer you what you're looking for." He took a step toward her before stopping himself. His voice was strained, gruff. "And I don't want to see the disgust in your eyes, as I've seen in others before, when you finally realize the kind of man you've gotten yourself involved with."

"That would never happen," she stated firmly.

"Trust me, I know. It would. It has nothing to do with my faith in you. It has to do with me. I'm not the man I appear on the surface."

Nor am I really the woman you perceive me to be, but we could bare our souls right here, start over, learn to trust each other. I could use a man like you on my side. She wanted to tell him the truth about herself more at that moment than at any other since they had been here. Yet, she held back, mainly because he was purposely shutting her out. She had revealed her true feelings before him, and he had denied his. The mere touch of his hands could set her on fire, had seared her so deeply that she was weak from wanting him every minute of the day. Here, the rest of the world had ceased to exist for a time. At night, after he invaded her body and brought her to a shivering climax, they'd fall asleep in each other's arms, and he'd invade her dreams.

"Go pack your things," he was saying to her. "There isn't anything else left to say."

Star wanted to fling herself into his arms, cling to him, make him take back the words. But she didn't. Her pride was already wounded enough. She just didn't think she could take another emotional beating.

Those were their last moments together. They

avoided each other for the remainder of that long day.

Her Comanche escort arrived just after sundown. He listened intently to Daere's instructions. He was to make certain that she arrived back in town unharmed. No one was to see them together, and Night Hawk was to take no chances with her life. If he felt there was a threat, then he should eliminate it. Clear, precise, to the point. She clearly understood his meaning. Kill anyone who tried to harm her.

When it came time for them to leave the cabin, Star and Daere parted without saying goodbye, for which she was glad. If he was sorry to see her go, it wasn't evident in the look he bestowed on her. Hurt and anger stood between them, kept them distant, but it was their mistrust and deception that had ended any chances they might have had to start over.

She found herself wanting to depart hurriedly, before the hot tears she'd so effectively held in check for hours could no longer be denied.

Daere had stood in the open doorway, saying nothing and making no move to keep her from leaving. It would be a long ride, she knew, but at the moment she didn't care if they rode off the face of the earth.

Night Hawk seemed to understand Star's introspective mood and did not attempt to draw her out of her shell. Dressed in a blue shirt and split riding skirt, she rode silently alongside her Comanche bodyguard for the first few hours. She couldn't help thinking about Daere. Was he still at the cabin, or had he left already? She knew that he would try to avoid seeing her in town as much as possible. Maybe he would even seek out Jade's company once again. A stab of jealousy pierced her heart.

"You've been awfully quiet. Are you all right?" Night Hawk was asking her, and she turned her attention to him, letting go of the painful memories. "I'm fine," she replied, but her voice sounded flat even to her own ears.

He glanced over at her, before turning his attention back to the trail ahead. Her delicate features were shuttered, but her distress was still evident. Night Hawk was married to a woman with a great deal of Comanche heart. He knew when something was pressing on a woman's mind. "Daere force you into a showdown, did he?"

"Is it that obvious?"

He smiled and shrugged. "When you've been married as long as I have, you become intuitive about these things."

"Yes, we had one all right," Star replied, deciding it was pointless to try and deny it. "I'm afraid I lost."

"He's a hard man to understand. But I think you're the only person who's been able to make him do some real soul-searching in a long time. It's what he needed to do, although I know how he hates dredging up the past. For years, he's cut himself off from everybody. It's not good."

"I agree, but try and get *him* to admit it. I was really beginning to think he might need me. But I was wrong. He doesn't need me any more than he does the other women who drift in and out of his life."

"There have been women, yes, but never anyone who has meant as much to him as you do."

She frowned with doubt. "I wish I could believe you."

"It's true," he assured her, then added, "The way I see it, Daere doesn't think he's good enough for you. He chose a way of life that keeps drawing him on endlessly, and while he thrives on the danger, he doesn't like the man he's become very much. What folks say about him doesn't help him, either, and he blames himself for the death of that boy over in Laredo, although we've been friends long enough for me to know for certain it was nothing more than an unfortunate accident. Daere wouldn't shoot any child, even if it cost him his life."

"He won't talk about that day with me, and as far as he's concerned, it's a closed subject."

326

"I had hoped he would. I guess it was too much to wish for. The way I see it, the only competition you have is from Daere . . . if that makes any sense to you."

She turned questioning eyes upon him. "Exactly what do you mean?"

"He's punishing himself by denying his feelings for you. I suppose you make him face the weaknesses within himself, and although he might not realize it, he blames you for stirring up emotions he thought he'd effectively buried."

Her frown deepened. Star remembered Daere crying out in his delirium and mumbling incoherently, but she had heard one name clearly. "Tad . . ." she mused aloud. "Do you know of anyone by that name?"

"It was the boy's name," he replied solemnly.

"The one that he . . . shot?"

Night Hawk nodded. "He wasn't just some kid off the street. They were friends. Tad worshiped Daere, and in the boy's eyes he could do no wrong. Daere and Tad had been out back of the dry goods store that day doing a little target practice. They were planning a hunting trip together. He was showing the boy how to improve his aim by shooting at bottles. It was the sound of gunfire that attracted the wrong attention." He glanced over at her. "Tad noticed the man, then the gun he had drawn even before Daere did. He yelled out a warning and flung himself

327

in the man's path, just as Daere whirled and fired. It was a fatal bullet. The boy died in Daere's arms. The other man disappeared by the time a crowd began to gather. No one believed Daere's story. They were only too eager to form the wrong conclusions."

"He calls out for Tad in his sleep. Now I understand who he was and why Daere reacted to me the way that he did."

"Do you want to talk about it? I'm a pretty good listener."

She nodded, glad to be able to tell someone who would understand what she had witnessed. "It was very late. Daere and I were both sleeping. Something woke me. A sound . . . I didn't know, at first. It was Daere. He was muttering incoherently, almost as if he were in pain. I thought perhaps he'd had a relapse, but then I realized he was having a horrible nightmare. He . . . he cried out for Tad." She drew a ragged breath, then continued. "He pleaded for God to take him instead. I lit a lamp and managed to wake him up. When he looked at me"—she was fighting for control—"there was death in his eyes. I reached out to him. He jerked away from me when I touched him. For a long while, neither one us said anything. Finally, I grabbed his arm. He was rigid as stone. It was an absolutely heart-wrenching experience to see him like that."

Night Hawk knew very well about Daere's nightmare, which, awake or asleep, haunted him, had made him a bitter man. He'd seen his friend in the throes of that awful torment on more than one occasion. Daere had stayed with Night Hawk in his village, lived among his people for a time after the accident. Yet, he still wasn't able to put that part of his past behind him. Night Hawk didn't know if he ever would. Like Star, he had felt just as helpless in the face of Daere's inner agony. Night Hawk liked this woman who had saved his friend's life. She was strong, had Comanche heart. His friend should not have sent her away. Night Hawk reached over and squeezed her hand gently. "You care what happens to him as much as I do. I hear the concern in your voice. If it's any comfort to you, I haven't been able to reach him, either. He has to want to help himself. Maybe he never will, and that's too bad." Their eyes met briefly. "He has a lot in his past to deal with, but so far he's done nothing but hold the pain at bay. With a man like Daere, it's a matter of pride. He keeps everything locked up inside him and just goes on punishing himself day after day."

"It must be devastating to carry such a burden."

"Yes. But it's not too late for him," Night Hawk said. "He isn't incapable of feeling emotion, he's just very effective at withdrawing into himself when he feels threatened. He cares for you, and your being around him threatens his carefully constructed wall of indifference. He's the way he is because at one time he cared *too* much."

A movement from the corner of his eye caught his attention. His keen gaze sharpened; and there was enough light from the moon to distinguish several murky shapes. Riders on horseback drawing closer. Night Hawk stared hard at the vague shadows, which took on menacing purpose as they drew nearer. They already had their rifles free from their saddle scabbards. He didn't waste time with a second glance, but reached over and whacked Star's mount on the rump.

"Ride," he ordered her, "and don't look back!"

Night Hawk waited until he was certain he had the attention of the riders, before he lashed his pony into a run. He wasn't certain if all the men would follow him, but he was going to do his best to lure them away from Star.

He called out a guttural taunt in Comanche, knowing how just the cadence of his people's voices could instill a killing rage in some white men. He was rewarded when he heard them

330

shout, "Over there, boys! Let's get that damned Indian!"

Smiling to himself, Night Hawk leaned over to whisper a command in his mount's ear, then allowed his pony free rein. They merged with the wind, and the Comanche smiled to himself.

Night Hawk's urgent demand still ringing in her ears, Star dug her heels into her mount's sides, and the big horse responded. They dashed through the night, guns cracking behind them. She did not know the identity of the men who seemed intent on riding them down, but there really was no doubt in her mind. Alec had sent his small army of scoundrels in search of them.

A barrage of rifles resounded in the background, and Star felt a bullet zing past her, so close that she ducked low over her mount's neck. She knew her only chance was to stay out ahead of the riders. They were outnumbered, but she still intended to give them a heck of a run before they caught her.

Riding like the hounds of hell were following her, she raced onward through the night, unmindful of the treacherous trail, relying on Midnight's keen sense and surefootedness.

Her thoughts were centered on survival. Star's eyes gleamed in the moonlight. Ahead, she saw a steep bank . . . her avenue of escape. The sound of gunfire still echoed behind her, and she knew that even though she had managed to outdistance Alec's men, she hadn't lost them.

Star rode onward, her eyes gleaming with intensity. A steep crest rose up in front of her, a barrier of rock that hindered her progress. Yet, she thought she recognized the lay of the land, having ridden over the terrain in the past. Ahead was a precipice that beckoned her onward. On the other side, many feet below, she felt certain lay freedom . . . if horse and rider could survive the free fall.

She knew no one in his right mind would even consider such a feat, but if memory served her correctly, this particular area would mean there was fifteen feet of blackness before freedom. It was something she didn't like to think about.

When called upon, the stallion had done next to the impossible before, but if she had miscalculated and the ground dropped away farther than she imagined, they would not survive.

The valiant steed thundered onward. "Go, Midnight. I know you can carry us through safely," Star murmured near his ear.

Without hesitation, the black horse lifted his hooves and soared gracefully over the brink, plunging them into the dark abyss below. Star's breath caught in her throat.

Then, she felt the ground beneath them. Landing on sure hooves and without her having to issue another command, Midnight tossed his head proudly, then raced off into the night.

Star's eyes gleamed with victory as her mount carried them both to freedom, leaving the enemy wondering how she had managed to disappear without a trace.

Reaching the crest, three riders jerked back hard on their mounts' reins and sat perplexed, wondering which way they should go next. One man turned to another and shrugged his shoulders.

Far off on the distant plain, a woman's bubbling laughter drifted on the wind.

Later that same night, Daere left the cabin behind, but the memories of what had taken place there remained firmly rooted in his mind. As he rode along the trail that would take him back into Tequila Bend, the time he had spent with Star in their mountain retreat, together with the closeness they had shared, came rushing to the forefront of his thoughts in a sweeping tide that was beyond his control.

Star was so much a part of him now, and he had allowed himself to care too deeply. After Tad's death, he had sworn never to let anyone get that close to him again. The emotional pain was too great when the bond was severed. He was a hard man to live with, worse to understand, and he knew it was easier on everyone if he kept distance between himself and the people he cared most about. Until now, he had been successful in his efforts.

For the first time in many years, he was feeling real, honest emotion for someone. He grappled with this unexpected revelation, wondering just when and how things between them had begun to change, amazed that it had all happened so quickly.

Draped in the gloom of night, the unpredictable New Mexico landscape stretched out in front of him for endless miles. He had never felt so alone in his life.

But the raven, sitting lonely on the placid bust, spoke only
That one word, as if his soul in that one word he did outpour.
Nothing farther then he uttered—not a feather then he fluttered—
Till I scarcely more than muttered, "Other friends have flown before—
On the morrow *he* will leave me, as my Hopes have flown before."
        Quoth the raven, "Nevermore."

The Raven, Edgar Allan Poe

Twenty

At the edge of town, Star reined in her mount. Pivoting in her saddle, she glanced back in the direction from which she'd just come. Her flawless brow was furrowed with concern for her friend. She lifted a trembling hand to her eyes and forced herself to think calmly. Had Night Hawk made his escape successfully? There was no way to be certain, but she had to hope that he had. He was a good man, and she hated to think that any harm might have come to him because of her.

Her shoulders rounded with weariness, she nudged her horse toward town at a slow walk. In the morning, after she'd rested, she'd make certain of Night Hawk's welfare. For now, she had to have faith that he was safe. A smile started on her lips. Of course he had escaped. He was like the wind, fast and deceptive. Even the devil couldn't catch the skilled rider if he determined not to be captured.

And what of Daere? Where was he at this

moment? Still at the cabin? Did he think of her? A ragged sigh escaped her lips as a profound sadness enveloped her. Why would he think of her? Because she had saved his life? Because they'd shared such sweet lovemaking? No, he wouldn't be thinking of her now. He'd sent her away, cast her from his life the same way a boy cast stones against the water, creating ripples that disappeared almost at once.

She was relieved to see that the streets of Tequila Bend were mostly empty, the town sleeping except for those who still drank and wagered at cards in the saloon. And of course, the bordello where Jade worked would still be brimming with activity. The first real smile Star had managed since leaving the cabin spread across her face as she thought of her friend.

Star turned her mount, deciding it safer to skirt the main street than risk having to offer explanations about what she was doing out alone at this late hour.

Fifteen minutes later, her horse stalled and fed, Star made the slow climb up the back stairs to her quarters above the dress shop. Her muscles protested every step. Her eyes were gritty with fatigue. Still, she paused on the landing to look up at the starlit heavens. Was Daere out there somewhere under the same stars? Rubbing fingers that trembled with weariness across her brow, she squeezed her eyes tightly shut. She had to quit thinking about him, remembering the feel of his hands on her skin, his lips on her mouth. It would do no good to wish for what could never be. He'd made it clear that the future held no promise for them together. With another deep, pain-wracked sigh, she opened the door, leaving the night and its memories behind.

Only thirty minutes later, her soiled clothing changed and her body cleansed from a hurried washing, Star pulled a nightdress over her head. She was just turning out the flame in the lamp, when she started at a sound behind her. Without turning, she listened. Nothing. Only the normal, familiar night noises. A dog barking in the distance. A horse's whinny. A man's shouted taunt followed by laughter as he and his companion left the saloon. Then the departing clip of horses' hooves as they passed in front of her shop.

In the darkness that shrouded the room, Star crossed the floor without mishap, the familiar route to the window as easily traversed in darkness as in daylight. Parting the drapes, she opened the window, welcoming the night air. Now starlight and moonlight mingled to cast faint rays of light into her bedroom. She stared heavenward once again for a long moment as she stretched and yawned. She was bone-weary. From her periphery, her bed beckoned, but as she turned, her bare feet making a padding noise against the floor, another sound — sharper, more distinct — accompanied her movement. Spinning on her heel, she gasped.

There in the doorway, a man stood watching her.

Fear coursed through her, and she took an instinctive step backward.

In the shadows, she could make out only his tall, lean physique. He wore a hat, so the features of his face were obscured. But as she stood there paralyzed with dread, he swept the hat off, revealing dark hair . . . hair the color of Daere's.

She was surprised at the relief that flowed through her veins, making her suddenly weak and giddy. And then she realized that it wasn't relief so much as joy. With a cry of happiness, Star took a step toward him. "Daere, I—"

The man laughed, and she stopped as she recognized the familiar mocking sound. "How dare you!" she hissed.

Again the derisive laughter. "It's been my pleasure." He took a step nearer and she backed farther away, her eyes darting to her dresser. She kept another of her bullwhips hidden in her drawer, but it was too far away. Panic rose in her throat, and her heart responded with a wild staccato.

"Get out," she whispered, as her voice

caught around the knot of anger that was quickly replacing her anxiety.

"Oh, I'll leave . . . when I'm good and ready," he said, taking a couple more steps in her direction before abruptly changing course and lowering himself onto the edge of her bed. "Such a pity, our being born to the same father. You're a beautiful woman, Star." Again the ugly laughter. "Oh, don't look at me like that. Do you think this is the first time I've watched you change your clothes?"

"You're despicable," she said. Then suddenly realizing she still stood in front of the window, where the shafts of light bathed her sheer nightgown, creating a translucency that revealed her nudity beneath, she took a step into the shadows. Her hands trembled as she willed herself to drop them to her sides, and she reached inside herself for calm and courage. Lifting her chin, she glared at Alec. "Do you think it would make any difference to me if we weren't related by blood? I find you as loathsome as those horrid spiders you used to taunt me with. Now tell me why you've come here, then get out. I'm tired. I need to sleep."

Alec smiled, but the shadows across his face created a mask that distorted it, creating a grimace of monstrous proportions. In spite of her resolve to call his bluff with a show of disdain and unconcern, Star shivered.

"Where have you been, Star? Cass and I

have been worried about you."

"Worried, or hopeful I'd met with an accident that would rid you of the only person who stands between you and the land you've always coveted?"

He clucked his tongue. "Such ugly thoughts for one so beautiful. You wound me to my core, sister, dear. But since you asked, no, I didn't believe you'd met a tragic end. I am an optimistic man by nature, but even I know that my luck doesn't run that smoothly. That's why I've been here waiting for you. As a matter of fact, you could have saved both of us a lot of trouble by surrendering when my men and I met up with you and that Indian. Instead, I imagine he's led my men on quite a wild-goose chase." He paused to scratch his jaw and offer a sarcastic grin. "An annoying waste of time that no doubt will deliver them back to the ranch in surly moods. Not very considerate of you to try and fool us like that."

"Obviously, you weren't fooled for long," Star bit out, her tone equaling his with its sardonic tone.

"Oh, not me, sweetheart. I knew you'd come back here, so I beat you to it. I was waiting when you arrived."

Star's eyes widened at that last remark. Suddenly, she remembered the tethered horse she'd passed in the alley. It wasn't like her to dismiss such a blatant caveat. Raven would have noticed, taken heed, and been warned that something was amiss. But Star had been too tired, too drained both physically and emotionally from her ordeal of the past several days.

Gathering the folds of her nightdress to shield herself from his bold gaze, she took a slow step nearer her dresser, her eyes on him. "Now let me guess what it is that you want. Could it be that you think I've found the will?" With a forced laugh that she hoped sounded convincing, she leaned nonchalantly against the chest of drawers. "That's it, isn't it? You and Cass became worried when I disappeared, thinking that I had found the will and had taken it to Santa Fe." As casually as she could manage, she turned her back to him and slowly started to ease one of the drawers open.

She shrieked as he grabbed her arm suddenly, spinning her back around.

"Is that where you've been?" he asked, his voice now as harsh and as cruel as ever. "Have you found the will?"

Star considered a lie, but what good would that do? She saw murder in his eyes. If she lied and told him that she had indeed uncovered her father's hiding place, what was to stop him from killing her and then searching for it even as her body lay still warm at his feet. She shuddered beneath his skin-bruising grip as she met his crazed gaze. His green eyes glittered with evil, and she felt courage abandoning her. She shrank away from him. "You're . . . you're hurting me."

"I'll do more than merely bruise your tender flesh if you don't answer my question," he snarled.

"No," she said in a strangled whisper. Then stronger, "No! But I will, and when I do, I'll drive you and Cass off my father's land so fast—"

He slapped her hard, and her head reeled with dizziness. "Kill me, Alec, and you and Cassondria will dance at the end of ropes."

With a cry of rage, he shoved her away from him. Her ribs crashed soundly against the sharp edge of the drawer, but she didn't cry out. Instead, she straightened to face him. "Our father knew how evil you were. Somewhere, his soul is screaming for revenge against you and your . . . your lover. I'm going to find that will, Alec, and then I'll see you both gone or in hell where you belong."

Alec tossed back his head and laughed, but just as quickly as it had begun it ended, and once again he grabbed her arm, this time tossing her across the room.

"Get your clothes on. We're leaving."

"I'm not going anywhere with you," she said.

"Oh, but you are. You see, Star, darling, I believe you when you say you'll find our father's will. Cass and I have turned the hacienda upside down looking for it, but as I said, I've never deluded myself into thinking that I possess the kind of luck that seems to travel at your side. I know it's only a matter of time until you chance on to it. And as you said, that would be the end of the dreams Cass and I have built our future around. I can't allow that."

"I won't go with you," she said, fear beginning within her again.

As casually as a snake striking at an unsuspecting rodent, Alec whipped out his gun. "Oh, I think you can be persuaded. After all, what choice do you have? Your alternatives are simple. I can kill you here, set the place on fire, then join the rest of the townsfolk in mourning the tragic accident of an overturned lamp that took the life of my only living relative, or you can leave with me."

Giggles bubbled from her lips. Hysteria perhaps, or maybe it was simply the combination of irony and fatigue. To think she had survived the plunge into the icy water just days before, only to die now at Alec's hand. She clapped a hand over her mouth and shook her head. "I'm sorry, Alec. It's all too amusing. Do you think no one would hear the gunshot? Doesn't it occur to you that one good scream from me would awaken the entire town?" She still cowered on the floor where he'd thrown her, but her voice grew stronger as courage returned. "After all, it was you who taught me to scream, with all the vile tricks you pulled on me when I was little."

Alec's answering laughter was low and demonic-sounding in the darkened room. "Scream if you like. Actually, the sounds of your shrill, terrified shrieks always delighted me. I don't suppose I would mind it now. Then I will simply shoot you and be found dashing up the stairs with any others who might hear. Imagine my devastation at finding my sister dead at the hand of some villain." He scratched his jaw again, this time with the muzzle of his gun. "You know, I could probably even convince the good folk of Tequila Bend to form a lynch mob for that gunslinger you've been seen with lately. Daere McCalister isn't too popular in these parts, is he? Some even say he's never been quite right since he gunned down that kid."

With a groan that was born of mingling outrage and agony, Star scrabbled to her feet and lunged for him, her fingers splayed like claws. "You bastard!"

But there was no contest as Alec knocked her back to the floor, this time with the butt of his pistol, which sent waves of disabling pain cascading from her shoulder, where she had been struck.

"I didn't have a chance to offer my alternative suggestion, did I?" he said as calmly as if they were sharing an hour or so of polite conversation across a table set with tea and biscuits. "Now, where was I? Oh, yes, the choice. You can get dressed, Star, and go with me."

"So you can kill me out in the desert and leave me for the vultures to pick my bones clean? I'd rather die here."

"You always were impetuous. But you misunderstand me. If you go with me, I won't kill you. You have my word."

In reply, Star spat, "Your word! Do you think I'd trust your word? You, a lying, conniving sonofa—"

"Now, now, little sister, is that any way for the well-mannered, delicate seamstress, whom people admire and respect, to talk?" He smiled, the grin of a cat as it toys with a trapped mouse. "It's your decision. You can die now, or take the chance I'm offering."

Her eyes going to the dresser drawers behind him, Star felt a surge of hope. If she pretended to agree to his terms, she would have to get clothes from the drawer, and with them her whip. "I'll . . . I'll go with you," she said.

"Smart girl. Now get up. Get your clothes on. We have only a few hours until daybreak, and I want to be back in my bed at the ha-

346

cienda when the sun comes up."

Rubbing her shoulder, which still throbbed painfully, Star pushed herself to her feet. "Will you turn your head while I dress?"

"Why? I've already seen you in all your glorious splendor. Besides, I wouldn't want a bullet in my back as a reward for chivalrous stupidity." He waved the gun. "Get dressed!"

"You'll have to move away so I can get some clean underthings and a fresh shirt from the drawers."

He obliged, taking several steps away from both the chest of drawers and her, but only to pick up the clothes she'd shed earlier and toss them to her. "Put these on."

Star felt her hopes sink to the bottom of her stomach, but she made a valiant last attempt. "Those are soiled, Alec. I have clean clothing right—"

"Put these on and get a hurry on. I've enjoyed our little playtime here, but I don't have any more time for toying with you."

Taking the clothing he held out to her, Star receded to the darkest corner of the room, where she turned her back to him. But she could feel his gaze on her as she pulled her nightdress over her head, and her cheeks flamed with humiliation. With the window open, the room had grown quite chilly. As she dressed, fumbling with her wrinkled undergarments, she began to shiver. By the time she had pulled on her riding skirt and was buttoning her blouse, her fingers were trembling so violently that she couldn't seem to manage the tiny buttonholes that she herself had stitched.

She jumped as his hand grasped her shoulder. "That's long enough," he said, spinning her around roughly. He thrust her boots at her. "Here, put these on and let's get going."

"I . . . I haven't buttoned my blouse."

"You can finish it while we ride," he said, reaching out with his hand to trail the creamy flesh from her throat to the revealed swell of one of her breasts. "Besides, I'll enjoy the diversion. We have a long ride ahead of us."

Several times during the next hour, Star considered asking where they were going, but each time she changed her mind. What difference did it make? He was going to kill her no matter what their destination was. She had to concentrate on making her escape. But how? He held her reins and kept his rifle lying across his lap as they rode.

She considered jabbing her mount sharply with the heels of her boots. Perhaps if her horse jumped forward with enough speed, she could surprise him into letting go of her reins. She had no doubt she could outride him. She'd always been a better horsewoman than he was a horseman. But her mount was tired while his was fresh. He could easily outdistance her, and at the very least shoot her in the back, and she knew just as he had threatened to do back at her place, he would lay the blame at Daere's feet.

Tears blurred her vision, and weariness made her light-headed. Fear and fatigue were taking their toll, and for the first time in her young life, she was beginning to admit defeat.

Oh, Daere, she thought, *I don't want to die without a chance to tell you how much I love you.*

They'd been riding west, across the desert, but now the terrain was changing, and suddenly Star understood what he had planned for her. In spite of the lethargy that had begun to envelop her, she jerked on the reins, causing her horse to rear up. She almost laughed as she saw Alec lose control of his own mount, who bucked in panic as her horse's hooves flailed precariously close to his muzzle.

Everything seemed to be moving in slow motion, and absurdly, Star felt as if she were watching the fiasco happen to someone else. Her legs locked tightly to her horse's flanks, to keep from being unseated and possibly knocked unconscious and left to her half-brother's mercy. She watched as his rifle fell from his grasp and he slowly slid from the saddle.

Leaning forward over the confused animal's neck, she urged him into a fast run, but they'd covered less than twenty yards or so of the uneven terrain when the horse stumbled, and she went flying over his neck.

She didn't know if minutes, hours, or only seconds passed, but at once she was opening her eyes and looking into the maddened gaze of her half-brother. "I could have broken my neck, you damned fool!"

She didn't answer, but struggled against a protesting cry as she tried to sit up and felt her leg give way beneath her, a sharp, shooting pain stabbing from her foot to her knee. "I . . . I think I've broken my ankle," she said weakly. Then remembering her horse, she looked around, sighing raggedly when she saw the animal standing, seemingly unharmed, a few feet away.

With a growl of anger, Alec scooped her up into his arms and delivered her to her horse's back. "One move and I'll forget my promise not to shoot you. You got that?"

Tears blurred her vision and stung her throat. She could manage only the slightest of nods, and then she remembered the caves where she knew he was taking her. "Please, Alec, don't do this."

He had remounted his horse, and as he pulled up alongside her, a lazy grin of pure delight spread across his face. "So, you've figured it out finally."

She was fighting very real panic now and

crying in great hiccuping sobs. "What . . . what have I ever done to you to deserve this?" she whispered.

"Done? Why, nothing. It's what you plan to do that has delivered you to this fate."

"I won't!" she said, dashing away the tears. "I swear, Alec, I won't look for the will anymore. You . . . you and Cass can keep the land, the hacienda, everything. Only don't throw me down inside those caves."

"I'm sorry, Star, but regrettably just as you didn't trust my word, I can't believe in yours."

"Then shoot me here and now," she pleaded.

He laughed. "You know, I'd quite forgotten how exquisite you are when you're terrified. Your eyes are quite luminous, rather like sapphires. When was the last time I managed to frighten you nearly witless, Star? Why, I do believe it was when I last took you to the caverns, wasn't it? Showed you my pets? Remember how you screamed that day, little sister?"

Of course she remembered, just as he'd known she would. As panic wrapped itself around her like a dark shroud, she opened her mouth and screamed, but Alec's mocking laughter sounded even above her piercing shriek of terror. Just as it had that other time, when he had taken such delight in tormenting her.

Star tried not to let the awful memories of

that day surface, but the raw and naked pain left her feeling emotionally exposed and completely at his mercy. It was impossible to extinguish her fear. This place, along with Alec, fed the flame of terror until it blazed uncontrollably and consumed her.

At that moment, Star ceased to be a woman and once again became that little girl who was so fearful of the dark. For she had known then as she did now what awaited her.

She recalled how on that particular day Alec had lured her to the caverns by telling her they were going exploring, and how he had made it sound like such a wonderful adventure.

He had told her that perhaps they'd even find their own buried treasure if they looked very hard. She had wanted to go then more than anything.

Star had been searching in one of the canals, chipping away at the colorful rock formations with a small pickax, while behind her Alec had stood holding the lantern so she had light in the area where she was working.

It was the first time they had done anything together in a long while and she was rather enjoying herself, although in the back of her mind, she did wonder why he should suddenly want to take part in any of her adventures. Still, Alec hadn't been this nice to her in ages, and she didn't want to spoil their fun time by questioning his motives or saying something that might anger him. As yet, he hadn't said one mean word and was even being very patient about holding the light for her.

Star had always imagined these caverns, with their twisting channels and shimmering pools, as a sort of Atlantis filled with riches just waiting to be discovered. And since her father seemed to worry more of late about the large sums of money her stepmother and Alec spent so freely, she wanted this more for him than for herself. It was her intent to turn over everything to her father, just seeing his face wreathed in a happy smile once again being treasure enough for her. Behind her, she heard Alec suddenly exclaim, "Star, look over there! I think I see something."

She glanced back and up at his face. "What is it, Alec?"

He was pointing to a narrow crevice on their right, his gaze searching. "I'm not certain. Look closer, will you? It might even be a cache of jewels that's been hidden here for centuries. Go on, check it out. I'll hold the lantern for you."

Star scrambled to do his bidding, and she was overcome with joy when she saw a small weathered chest wedged in between the jagged rocks. Eagerly, she plucked it out, turning to smile up at Alec, her eyes shining with excitement. "What do you think is in it?"

"What else could be in it? I have no doubt it's gold or jewels," he speculated, his tone spoken in levels barely above a whisper. "Isn't this exciting! We did find a treasure, just as we had intended. Open it, Star, and see for yourself what it holds."

Star could hardly contain her excitement, and her fingers trembled visibly as she pried at the lid. The only sound in the cavern was their quickened breathing, along with the scrape of her fingernails on the metal clasp. Finally, she gave a sigh of relief and cried, "I've got it, Alec!" Sitting back on her heels, her eyes rounded as she opened the lid, then her gaze slowly widened in dawning horror. Her fingers tightened spasmodically as large, hairy spiders scrambled free from their prison and spilled onto her feet, crawling over her hands and up her arms. Star was frozen in fear, but what she really wanted to do was fling down the chest and run away. She should have known never to trust Alec! With supreme effort, she willed herself to move, and tossing aside the chest, she brushed the horrible spiders off her arms, then rising, whirled to glare up at her half-brother. Tears shimmered in her eyes. "You had this planned from the beginning, didn't you? The only reason we came here today is so you could pull another one of your nasty tricks on me!"

Alec merely howled with laughter, the sound

echoing off the chamber walls. "What, no treasure, little sister!? My, but you are a silly goose and have always been the easiest of them all to dupe."

It was that same laugh that rang in her ears at the moment. Alec was the most evil person she had ever known. Still guffawing loudly, the sound as mad as the glimmer in his dark, obsidian eyes, he led her horse toward the mouth of the deep underground grotto, and the last of the fight drained from her. The caves that had terrorized her even in her dreams as a child were going to be her grave, and she was too dazed with shock to struggle against it any longer.

She stared straight ahead as Alec dismounted, then went unprotesting into his arms when he reached for her. *Funny,* she thought, *how gently he holds me as he leads me to my death.* There was a loud roaring inside her head that all but obscured his words as he spoke to her along the way.

"You see, Star, I am a man of my word. I told you I wouldn't kill you, and here you are, safe and sound. It's the same thing I promised old man McCalister, but his ticker gave out just when we were starting to have some fun. He hated my pets almost as much as you did. Poor, poor man . . . He should have listened

355

when I offered to buy his ranch. He might be alive today." They'd arrived at the edge of a great gaping hole. A large, long-unused miner's bucket rested on its side near the opening to the caves below. The rope that looped the pulley looked dried and worn, and as Star gulped convulsively against the fear she tasted in her mouth, she almost hoped it would snap as Alec lowered her, thereby offering a swift death.

He set her on the ground, his tongue making solicitous noises of concern as he noted her injured ankle, which had swelled grotesquely in the past several minutes since her fall. "Guess you won't be able to walk on that for a while," he said, then started the hideous hee-hawing laughter of lunacy, much as he had before.

Star watched with an almost disinterested gaze as he righted the bucket, then tested the rope with a couple of mighty jerks. "Looks sound enough to hold a tiny thing like yourself."

The wind had picked up and her long silver hair whipped about her face, but she made no attempt to hold it back. Alec crouched down in front of her, catching the fine flaxen tresses and brushing them from her face in a gesture that was almost tender, but which Star discovered was merely another form of torment as he chucked her under the chin. "Hey, don't look so devastated. I've kept my word. I'm not going to kill you. I'm merely hiding you for a few days." Stretching to the side, he leaned over the mouth in the earth's floor, which would swallow her up as soon as he lowered her into its bowels. " 'Course, I can't deny that your chances of survival down there won't be too good. Snakes or my little pets don't get you, a fall is likely to do you in. You remember how slick those ledges are down there? Sure you do. But who knows, with that ankle hurt like it is, you probably won't be doing much investigating." He lifted her into his arms and deposited her inside the large wooden bucket. "Then again, starvation is another worry."

For a long time, he didn't speak, but Star heard him grunting and panting as he struggled to free the knot that had kept the bucket above ground. And then she felt the basket move, not far, just an inch or two. She knew he'd succeeded in freeing the knot and was just holding her there for another few seconds of torment.

She squeezed her eyes shut, determined not to give him the satisfaction of crying out in protest. She would beg no more, but a shudder born of its own volition shook her, and she felt another scream pushing its way to her throat. She pressed a fist against her lips with so much force that she tasted her own blood as her teeth cut into them.

"Make you a deal," he said, then apparently noting her closed eyes for the first time, he shouted at her to look at him. "Open your eyes, damn you! Look at me when I'm speaking to you! I'm about to make you a deal," he added in a more reasonable tone.

The first rays of daylight were stretching their fingers of gold and orange on the horizon, and as Star obeyed him, she saw the truth of her suspicions in his twisted features. Alec truly was a madman. "Leave me alone," she said in a hoarse whisper. "Just do your deed and leave me be."

He slapped her then, snapping her head to the side, and she gasped as the rope slipped a few inches more. But he seemed not to notice as he shouted at her. "Don't tell me what to do! I'm your older brother! Hell, I was out working that worthless land the day you were born. Show me some respect."

Star averted her face, and Alec sighed. "Always so stubborn, so prideful, and so arrogant. He made you that way, always doting on you, favoring you, spoiling you. But he's not here anymore. He's been dead too long for you to still be putting on airs for me. It's high time you were taught a lesson."

She heard the creaking of the pulley as he began lowering the bucket, and Star clinched her fists in her lap as she pressed her head to her knees.

"I'll set your horse free in three days, Star," he said. "You've trained him well. He'll return to the spot where you last left him. With any luck, someone will see him and follow him here." He laughed then as she descended into the dark hole. " 'Course, you'll be dead!" he shouted after her. As the bucket hit the cavern floor with a hard bump and pitched to the side, sending her rolling out, the taunt echoed around her.

" *'Course, you'll be dead!*"

" *'Course, you'll be dead!*"

" *'Course, you'll be dead!*"

Twenty-one

At first, Star could only mewl in fright and pain. Her ankle had begun a steady throb of agony that was rivaled by the cuts and bruises to her shoulders and face. But in her pitiful state, it was the terror of the darkened cavern in which she had been dropped that consumed the last of her energy. And after a while, blessedly, weariness won the fight with agony and she slept.

When she awakened she was confused, but only for a moment, and then the memory of her brother's evil trick slammed into her. Alert and panicked, she sat up with a start, only to cry out as her injured ankle bumped against the hard rock floor of the cave. Rubbing it gingerly, she looked around her. The room that had been bathed in darkness earlier was now lit from a bright shaft of light. She gazed upward and recognized that the sun's beams came from the west. So she had slept through the morning. How many hours of daylight did she have left? Star wondered. She shuddered at the prospect of facing darkness again soon.

Her gaze traveled slowly around the large room, which was really a succession of ledges, each narrower than the one below it. Against the sun's bright rays, the walls of stalactites and stalagmites glittered magnificently in white and pastel shades. She remembered her father's lessons about the extraordinarily beautiful rock formations, which she'd forgotten in her earlier terror. But she hadn't forgotten her one and only visit here more than a decade before: nor the dangers that her half-brother had taken such delight in pointing out to her. With a faint squeak of renewed fright. she scooted farther up the ledge, until her back was pressed against the cool rock wall.

As she folded herself around her drawn-up knees she tried to forget her brother's treachery, but the fact that he had left her here to die wouldn't be pushed away.

She'd always known, even as a tiny youngster, that he resented her. But even in later years, when his pranks had escalated to mean tricks that were always potentially dangerous, she'd never realized that he hated her. Even when he'd brought her here the first time, when she was only eight years old, she hadn't understood that he'd really meant her harm.

That time he hadn't lowered her alone but had descended in the miner's bucket with her. At first, though she'd been nervous, she hadn't been afraid . . . not until he'd showed her the horrid creatures he called his pets. She shivered with the memory, hugging her knees tighter.

He'd laughed at her fright, calling her a baby, taunting her by pinning her arms at her sides and refusing to allow her to move even when the hairy spiders, some as big as saucers, approached.

When one of them had started up the hem of her skirt, and she'd twisted and turned trying to escape, her screams mocking her in their echoing return, he'd laughed. But that was when her daddy had found them.

And she, foolish girl that she'd been, had actually felt sorry for the punishment Alec had received.

Had that been when her father had first begun to realize the duplicity and evil that lurked in her half-sibling's heart?

Alec had been nineteen then and her father already married to Cassondria. She recalled the fight her parents had had that night, the shouting and ugly accusations.

"He's only a boy!" Cassondria had railed.

"He's old enough for you to flirt shamelessly with," the eldest Tremayne had countered, his voice bitter. "All that aside, the trick he played on his little sister was cruel. She shook all the way home, Cassondria."

"Oh, for God's sake, she's a spoiled, willful

brat who was playing on your sympathy. You've got only yourself to blame for the fact that she still acts like a baby. Why, Alec was only trying to entertain her. And wasn't it you who told her all those stories about the glorious caverns? He was only trying to please her by showing her the magical rock formations that you've described in such detail."

"When I arrived, there was a tarantula the size of my hand crawling up her skirt. She was terrorized, and Alec was laughing. Laughing, Cassondria! Does that sound like the actions of a loving, caring brother?"

Star swiped at the tears that trickled down her cheeks as she remembered that night. How she still missed him, the father who had always been her protector, her teacher, her guide.

It was in that instant of longing for a man long ago dead that she recalled the lessons he'd taught her about the caverns. He'd told her about the splendid rock formations, such as the fantastic Chinese temples and palaces, the strange beasts, heavy pillars, and lacy, dainty icicles. But it wasn't his description of the underground cavern's majesty that she thought about now. Rather, she concentrated on the Indian paintings he'd described to her. They hadn't used the bucket to access the large underground rooms, instead using a secret entrance. If only she could find the way out. Her heart began a steady thrum of excitement at the possibility of escape, but just as quickly her hopes were dashed away as she remembered his counsel: "For all their glorious beauty, Star, they are dangerous. Many a skilled explorer has been lost inside those caves and not found until only their skeletons remained. You must never, never go into them alone."

Now her tears ran in rivers down her face, and she curled once again onto her side, hope abandoning her. Her eyes closed, she lay there for a long time until she heard a decided noise, not above her on the earth's surface, but here, inside the cave with her. Spiders! Tens of them, coming out of the shadows to bathe in the heat of the sun's rays. She had to get away!

A scream rose in her throat but she pushed it back. She mustn't make a sound. Mustn't alert them to her presence.

Pushing herself to her knees, Star gasped in spite of her resolve to move silently, for she'd forgotten her injured ankle and put pressure on it, creating shooting, stabbing waves of agony and currents of dizzying nausea. Still, she moved. Inch by inch in maddening slowness, she crawled on one knee, dragging her useless foot behind her, pulling herself with her hands along the narrow ledge to a higher shelf away from the creatures, whose ugliness repelled her almost as much as the stories of their lethal bites frightened her.

"Oh, God," she whispered as the ledge that she traversed became narrower and narrower, and she

364

chanced a glance at the cavern's floor several hundred feet below.

Already half crazed with fright, she heard the telltale rattle of a snake just inches from her face. Barely moving her head, she saw it, curled up, its pointed snout raised and dancing.

Don't move, she warned herself silently. She held her breath and kept still, watching the darting forked tongue, feeling the strain in her fingers as they gripped the rock's edge ahead. Just when she thought she could no longer hold the pose, that her arms would give in and her fall to the rocks below would surely be her fate, the snake began to unfurl, then slithered away, winding along her side toward the sun's heat and the grotesque spiders.

Star collapsed in panting relief and exhaustion.

Alec was right. She was going to die here. Her tongue licked at her parched lips. If not from those horrid, hairy spiders or from a snake bite or even from a fall, then surely from thirst and starvation.

She wanted to give in to defeat. *Sleep,* her mind ordered, but another voice countered for her to go on, to get to the waterfall. *If you can drink, you can survive until you have your strength back and can think of a way out.*

The waterfall? Her conscious mind hadn't even registered the water's sound, but she heard it now, and lifting her head, she saw it. But with a cry that was half sob, half laugh, she pounded the rock with her fists. It was too far, and the ledges that led to it were too narrow and slippery. She'd never make it.

Coward! The same voice shouted from inside her head, its voice taunting and impatient. *Raven would never give in so easily, not without at least a good fight.*

Without further argument, Star began the slow trek to the wall several yards away and a good fifty feet above her, where water cascaded in a great, noisy gush.

She slipped twice as she pulled herself up on her one good leg, when the ledge she crawled along ended and she was forced to make the arduous, dangerous climb to the next level. Each time, the ledge above proved narrower, slicker, just as she'd suspected, and her progress became slower and slower. At least a dozen times she lay down, stretched full out to rest, to regain her strength, which was waning thinner and thinner with each passing moment. Twice, she glanced behind her, noticing each time that the light was thinning with every yard she advanced higher and farther into the cave. But she couldn't think about it, couldn't let herself focus on the darkness. She'd always been terrified of the dark, but she had to concentrate on getting to the water. It was her only hope of staying alive until help came.

But why would help arrive? Who would even know that she was here?

As she lay down for the last time, allowing her aching, protesting muscles to rest, she remembered Alec's promise to set her horse free in three days' time. But she had no assurance that he would keep his word, and even if he did and someone did indeed see the animal standing at the cavern's mouth, could she survive two more days in the dark, with only snakes and spiders as company, without losing her mind?

"Don't think of it now," she whispered in a voice that was dry and raspy with thirst. "Only a few more yards."

The waterfall roared now as she neared it, and Star moved faster, forgetting caution. It almost proved her undoing as her hand grasped a piece of loose slate, and she only narrowly escaped a fall that would have sent her crashing to the bottom of the cave. As she dared a look over the side of the ledge, a shudder wracked her aching body. And then her eyes widened with horror as she spied a nest of twisting, writhing snakes less than five yards below her, in a hollowed-out piece of rock that resembled a giant vat.

Now she scrambled to the next ledge, everything forgotten but her desperation for escape.

And then she was within ten feet of her goal. She was perspiring profusely as the first splatters of water hit her face and back, and she realized that the front of her blouse was soaked from the water-doused rock that she was lying on.

With a cry of victory, she licked at the wet

stone, then tossed back her head, sticking out her tongue to catch the spray.

The water-drenched slate floor of the ledge she was lying on was less than two feet wide now and as slick as ice, but she inched herself nearer the waterfall, until at last the shelf widened and she was able to crawl on all fours behind the curtain of water.

She laughed and wept as she cupped her hands to catch the water, drinking great gulps of it.

She wet her hair with it, then her face, and still her laughter bubbled and her tears flowed. *Perhaps this is what madness feels like,* she thought with another giddy giggle.

She was now in almost total darkness, but for the first time in her life, Star took comfort in the enveloping blanket of blackness. She wouldn't be able to see the snakes and the spiders or the bats her father had told her about. And what she couldn't see couldn't hurt her, could it?

Her hands, which were bruised and bleeding now and as sore as her ankle, throbbed painfully. She held them out, letting the icy water numb them, but as she withdrew them from beneath the water, she saw a trickle of blood bubble up from a deep gouge in her palm. With a primitive instinct, she brought it to her mouth to suck away both blood and pain.

Crouched there in the darkness, her knees drawn up to her chest, her hair wet and matted, her face streaked with grime and water and tears, she was suddenly, inexplicably reminded of another day, many years before, when she had sat crouched by her father's side in his garden behind the hacienda.

She'd been wearing a dress of aquamarine muslin, her silvery hair caught back from her little girl's face with a matching bow. Her father was making a fountain, and she'd asked him why.

He'd paused in his work to sit back on his haunches and look at her with a tolerant smile. "Did I ever tell you the legend of Ponce de León?" he asked.

She shook her head. "No, I don't think so, Papa. Who was he?" she asked, eager for another of her scholarly sire's stories that he weaved with such magic she could almost believe she could see whatever it was he spoke of.

"He was a great explorer who went in search of the fountain of youth, which he believed to be in Florida."

"Why?" she asked dutifully.

"Why? Because like so many before and after him, he hoped never to grow old . . . never to die."

"Oh, Papa, wouldn't that be wonderful to always stay young? Did he find it? His fountain of youth?"

"No, unfortunately, it is said that he searched until the day he died."

"How sad. So is that what you're doing? Making a fountain of youth?"

She remembered now how he had reached over to stroke her head with such tenderness, and she'd thought for a moment that his eyes looked sad, but then he'd smiled. "No, there is no such thing. But there will be a fountain of dreams, Star, right here on our land."

"Why, Papa?"

"Because, child, that's what this all is, my dream that has been realized. This fountain will always be here to remind us that as long as a Tremayne lives who is worthy of possessing it, the dream will continue to live as well." He'd dropped the trowel that he'd been using and grasped her shoulders. He'd looked into her eyes, his own gaze serious, his voice powerful in its softness as he told her, "Never forget, Star. Our dream will be held safe by this fountain, for you and your children and theirs."

But she *had* forgotten until today. She raised her face to the rushing water, then held out her bleeding hand in front of her face. Though she couldn't see it, she remembered the tiny scar at the base of her wrist. She'd cut it the day that he'd been finishing the last of his fountain. He'd hollowed out a hole on one side of the base, and as she'd reached inside, she'd cut her wrist rather badly on the sharp edge of rock. As he'd carried her inside the house to doctor the wound, she'd cried, but his gentle ministrations and soothing words had quickly calmed her. Only a few minutes later, with a fast recovery indicative of the very young, her curiosity had returned and she'd asked why he'd left a hole.

He'd put a finger to his lips, urging her to be quiet. "Shh, little one. That is a secret. Ours alone. Only you and I will know that one of the rocks can be lifted out. You mustn't ever tell anyone else. Can you promise me that?"

She'd nodded solemnly but had persisted in her questioning. "But why, Papa? Why won't that rock be sealed in place just like all the others?"

Her injured wrist cleansed and bandaged, he'd kissed her forehead, then answered her query as he lifted her from her seat atop the table. "Because, that way we'll never forget that dreams can be snatched away if we aren't smart enough to know how to keep them."

Now, as the last of the blood stopped seeping from her injured hand, she curled up in her hiding place and drifted off to sleep.

A loud thrumming noise awakened her a couple of hours later. From behind the cascading water, Star could make out little. She crawled a few feet to peer around the fall, and her eyes widened at the sight of scores of bats flying toward the opening where only several hours before her brother had dropped her.

The bright shafts of sunlight that had lit the cavern before she'd fallen back to sleep had dimmed now to dusky rose beams, and Star realized that dusk was settling over the land above. But oddly, she wasn't frightened anymore.

371

Rather, she was fascinated by the sight of the tiny bats.

But then she remembered the fountain and the dream she'd had while she slept, and her turquoise eyes widened with understanding. The will! That was where her father had hidden it! All this time she'd known the answer, but not until now, when she was most likely going to perish alone in the dark, had she remembered the clues he'd shared with her and unraveled the puzzle.

Laughter bubbled from her lips. "Oh, Papa, isn't it funny? Do you see the tragic irony? Alec left me down here to die so I wouldn't find the will. Now I've found it, but I'm going to die before I can save your dream."

"Well?" Cassondria demanded of her stepson when he finally joined her in the parlor after a daylong sleep, during which time she'd paced the floor.

He rubbed the sleep from his eyes, ignoring her demanding tone as he crossed the room to pour himself a snifter of brandy. "Did I ever mention how your voice grates at times?" he asked.

"Tell me about Star," she hissed. "I've been half out of my mind with angst while I waited for you to get your sleep out."

"Waited?" he asked sarcastically. "It seems to me that I remember you coming into my room several times and trying to wake me."

"Alec! Answer my question. Is the insufferable bitch dead?"

"Hmm," he murmured, his eyes raised to the ceiling as he pretended to study the query. "Yes, by now, I'd imagine she must be. I can't say for certain, of course, but it doesn't matter. If she isn't dead yet, she will be in the next day or so." He raised his glass. "Shall we drink to her unfortunate demise?"

"You fool! What do you mean she might very well be? I told you to kill her. What have you done?"

"Done? Why, I've just handled things with the finesse of someone of more superior intelligence than yours, my darling Cass." He sat down on the edge of the settee, then settled back to cross a booted foot over his knee. He draped an arm along the back of the furniture, assuming a pose of relaxed confidence. "You're still a very beautiful woman, Cass, but too impetuous at times for your own good . . . or mine.

"I took the men out as you suggested, intent on ambushing her, but that Indian, Night Hawk, was with her. With the sixth sense that those heathens seem to possess, he felt our presence before I could get a shot off. He slapped her horse, driving her in one direction while he took off in another. I sent the men after him to kill him, then went after Star on my own. But it suddenly occurred to me that an accident would suit our purposes better, so I've delivered her to a place where she won't be found for a few days."

"Where?"

"The caverns. A certain grave for anyone trapped down there without a way out."

A slow, catlike smile spread across Cassondria's face, and she shuddered with a soft laugh. "Ohh, how horrible for the poor dear. How deliciously horrible."

"I thought you might appreciate the plan," he said with satisfaction as he swirled the amber liquid in his glass, then sipped greedily.

"And what of Night Hawk? Did the men catch up to him?"

Alec frowned at the reminder of the only foible in his well-executed plot. "Unfortunately not, but it doesn't really matter. He didn't get a look at any of us, and he doesn't come into town. By the time he learns that my precious half-sister didn't make it back safely, it will be too late."

This time, the lines of worry appeared on Cassondria's brow. "They have to find her, Alec. Dead, of course. If they don't, we'll not be able to prove our right to the land."

"Relax, my love. I've thought of that as well. Day after tomorrow, I'll set her horse free." A devil's smile came into place. "I gave her my word that I would do that, and a gentleman of means always keeps his word. But back to the subject at hand. In two days, I will set her horse free. He will return to the place where he last left her. Someone will see him there, investigate, and find my poor dead sister's remains."

"Where is the horse now, Alec?" Cassondria demanded.

"In the barn. Where else?"

"In our barn? Are you mad? What if someone sees the animal? How will you explain that?"

"Don't be ridiculous, Cass. Who would be snooping in our barn? Who would be able to get past our men, for that matter?"

"I don't know *who,* Alec," she snapped. "But nothing is impossible. Have you thought of an explanation should someone chance onto the animal?"

"I hadn't, no. But it isn't such a difficult riddle to solve. I'd simply say I'd found the horse alone, and that my men and I had been looking everywhere for her since then."

Cass was silent for a long moment as she paced the room, considering every aspect of his plan. Finally, she turned back toward him, then crossed the room to lower herself to his side. "I don't know, Alec. Perhaps you or I should ride into Tequila Bend tomorrow, pay a visit to her shop."

"Surely you're not that stupid. Aunt Hilda knows Star can't abide the sight of either of us."

"I suppose you're right. But at the very least, I want you to return to the caverns tomorrow. Make sure she's dead before we free the horse."

Alec slammed the fragile crystal glass down on the table next to him as he grabbed her wrist to

375

pull her against him. "Don't give me orders, Cass. I'm sticking to my plan. I'll make certain of her sad demise when I lead her horse back to the caverns personally." His dark gaze met her green eyes, and she shivered at the coldness she saw in them. "Do you think I would miss the pleasure of determining exactly how terrible her death was?"

"Kiss me," she said, suddenly excited by the evil that gleamed in his eyes.

He obliged, a hand snaking into the low décolletage of her gown to cup one of her full breasts, then viciously pinch a nipple between his finger and thumb.

She cried out, then wrapped her arms around his neck as she whispered, "Yes, hurt me."

At that moment, Jade was entering the dress shop.

"I was just closing up," Hilda told her.

"Oh, that's all right. I'll just go on upstairs to see Star. She is upstairs, I assume."

Hilda wrung her hands as she turned to face the beautiful Oriental woman. "No, I'm afraid she isn't."

That was odd, Jade thought. When she'd last seen Star, she'd said she expected to be back at the shop in a few days' time. A smile that she didn't quite let go tugged at the corners of her lips. Perhaps she and that handsome devil, Daere McCalister, had found too much to occupy them for her to return as soon as she'd anticipated. To Hilda, she said, "Ah, well, I'm sure she'll return before long. It's quite like our Star to disappear for long periods of time, isn't it?"

"Yes, it is, and I wasn't worried about her until this morning."

"What happened this morning to alarm you?" Jade asked, not yet concerned for her friend.

"It isn't what happened this morning," the elderly woman said, "but what I worry happened during the night."

Jade shook her head as she tried to make sense of the confusing statement. "I don't understand, Hilda. What are you talking about?"

"As I said—" She abruptly ended the sentence without finishing. "Let me lock the door and turn the sign so we're not interrupted."

Jade waited impatiently as the rotund little woman waddled with annoying slowness across the shop to lock the store up for the night. Still, she knew it would do no good to hurry her. Star had often joked about how poor Hilda's mind was no longer alert. "Why, she's apt to be making tea, then abruptly decide to go off to the dry goods store while the kettle boils," Star had once said. Then on another occasion: "She's a dear, but Aunt Hilda is getting more and more vexing every day. I had two dresses that were to be completed on Monday. Hilda promised to have them done, but on Saturday, just two days before they were due, I asked her about them and she calmly admitted that she hadn't started them yet. When I asked her why, she said it was because the red satin for a gown another of our customers had ordered—it wasn't due for three weeks, incidentally—was so much prettier to work with."

With a resigned sigh, Jade leaned against the counter to wait out the slow process of closing business for the day. After another ten minutes or so, her patience was rewarded as Hilda returned to stand in front of her, one hand again twisting and wringing the wrinkled flesh of the other.

"Now, where was I, dear?"

"You were about to tell me why you were suddenly worried about Star's absence."

"Oh, yes. I know that, but did I mention that while she's gone, I always go upstairs to her rooms to tidy everything up . . . pour fresh water in the basin for her should she unexpectedly arrive back home?"

"No, you didn't," Jade said with a soft sigh of frustration.

"Yes, well, I do. I most certainly do."

"And?" Jade prodded gently.

"And this morning when I went up as always, things weren't right."

Jade pushed herself away from the counter, alarm beginning to register for the first time. "What do you mean, things weren't right?"

"Well, I didn't notice anything at first. I mean, the bed was still tidy and neat except for a

378

slightly wrinkled place in the quilt near the foot. I didn't even notice that at first. But when I went to the washbowl to empty it before adding fresh water, I found it had been used. At first, I thought maybe that worthless Juanita had gone upstairs and used the washbowl. I was all set to march back down here and give her a good dressing-down, let me tell you. Yes, ma'am, I was going to—"

"But?" Jade interrupted.

"Oh, yes," Hilda said with just the slightest of indignant huffs. *"But* that's when I saw the discarded nightgown lying crumpled in the corner of the room. And the wrinkled place at the foot of the bed, as though someone had sat there. I didn't know what to make of it. Still don't, but it seems to me she must have returned sometime last night, gotten ready for bed, then changed her mind and left again. But why would she do that?"

"I don't know," Jade answered, more to herself than to the other woman. She looked up at Hilda, offering an encouraging smile. Reaching out, she patted the woman's plump arm. "Well, don't you worry, Hilda. I'll look for her. I'm sure she had a very good reason for leaving, and when I find her, we'll know what it is."

A few minutes later, Hilda let Jade out, exacting a promise to let her know the minute she learned anything.

Outside the dress shop, Jade paused. "Where

are you, Star? And why would you have come back last night, only to leave again?" There were no answers to the puzzle, only possibilities, and none of them pleasant . . . unless . . .

As she lifted the hem of her skirt and stepped from the walkway, Jade's dark almond-shaped eyes narrowed. "You'd better have a ready explanation about where she is, Daere McCalister, because if anything's happened to her, I'll be exacting a measure of your hide . . . and not in the way you're accustomed to me doing or will find pleasant."

Wondering at the stillness broken by reply so
      aptly spoken,
"Doubtless," said I, "what it utters is its only
      stock and store,
Caught from some unhappy master whom un-
      merciful Disaster
Followed fast and followed faster till his songs
      one burden bore,
Till the dirges of his Hope that melancholy
      burden bore
                Of 'Never—nevermore.' "

The Raven, Edgar Allan Poe

Twenty-two

Daere had been consumed with guilt, remorse, and debilitating anger since the day Tad died, but the agony he experienced in the two days after sending Star away was worse than anything he'd ever known. She'd filled him up as nothing in his life had ever done before, and her departure left a hollow deep inside him.

It was on the eve of his second night that he decided on a course that might alleviate his hunger for the tempestuous, complex, silver-haired woman who had crawled inside his skin, starting an itch that he could only hope would be stilled in the arms of another woman.

To that end, he headed for the bordello and Jade, just as darkness settled over the desert town.

Rosalie Valdez opened the door to his demanding knock, a wide grin of welcome on her lips that was rivaled by the look of surprise in her jet-black eyes. "Daere, how wonderful to see you, but aren't you a little early? Most of my girls are just crawling out of bed."

He grabbed her, a hand to the back of her ebony tresses as he pulled her to him and kissed her affectionately. "You shouldn't make them keep such late hours, sweetheart."

"Ah, so true, but regrettably, it is a consequence of our line of work." She laughed then, the sound loud and boisterous and bawdy. "But, then, what are a few sacrifices when our work is so rewarding?"

Daere laughed, already feeling better. "True, and speaking of your girls, will you call Jade for me?"

She closed the door behind him and led him into her private salon, motioning him to a chair. As she went to the bar to pour him a hefty shot of cognac, Rosalie formed an apologetic moue with her mouth. "I'm sorry, Daere, but my beautiful sloe-eyed minx isn't here."

Daere disguised his disappointment with a wry grin. "So at least one of your girls crawled from bed at a respectable hour. I'm only sorry it was this one. She's special, our Jade."

As Rosalie handed Daere his drink, then offered him a cheroot from an expensive mosaic box on the table at his side, she watched him. He was not as relaxed as he tried to appear. "That she is, and as such I give her leeway I don't allow the others. She is independent, that one." She sat down on the edge of the settee to his right, carefully arranging the folds of her red taffeta gown. "I've often likened her to an exotic bird who, though captured, can never quite be tamed." Reaching over to pat his knee, she smiled provocatively. "But she'll be worth the wait, will she not, my friend?"

"Where has she gone?" Daere asked casually.

"She said something about going to visit Star," Rosalie replied, her brow furrowing slightly as she glanced at the clock on her desk. "But that was a few hours ago. I thought she'd have returned by now." She shrugged, offering a small dismissive laugh. "Ah, well, she'll return shortly, I'm confident. In the meantime, why don't I go upstairs and roust some of the others. I'm sure they can find ways to entertain you while we wait."

As she stood up, Daere stopped her with a hand to her wrist. "No need. I'm content to visit with you until she returns. Sit down here and tell me how business has been. What gossip have your girls picked up since I was here last?"

Rosalie complied, but she turned an amused gaze on him, one brow raised suggestively. "Actually, Daere, the only gossip we've heard concerned you."

Daere was immediately tense, but he managed to put only the mildest surprise into his tone. "Me? What have you heard about me that would have tongues wagging?"

Rosalie was not fooled. "Relax, *amigo*. Don't get your magnificent feathers ruffled. The rumors weren't that enlightening. Only that you'd been away from your father's ranch these past two weeks and that no one seemed to know where you were." She smiled then, a wicked, taunting grin. "Of course, I wondered about the coincidental absence of a certain seamstress at the same time."

"Rosalie . . ." Daere said, the slightest warning in his tone.

"Oh, don't get angry, darling. I was only teasing you. Besides, I couldn't see you and Star together. You're both too alike."

Daere sipped his cognac, then pulled hard on his cheroot, determined not to give her the satisfaction of asking what the hell she meant by that, but Rosalie didn't need encouragement.

"For all her ladylike airs, Star Tremayne is passionate and volatile. Willful, too, although I suppose blame for that must be laid at her father's feet. He spoiled her rotten before his unfortunate death."

Daere laid a booted foot over his knee, a devil's grin twisting his lips. "You're saying I'm passionate and volatile and willful as well." It was half statement, half question.

"No, rather you court danger the same way most men seek out common pleasures."

"I don't go looking for trouble, Rosalie. It just seems always to find me."

"That may be, but my point is, with a woman like Star, trouble would be sitting right in your lap."

Daere tossed back his head and laughed loudly. "I think you've just hit the nail on the head. You're a very astute woman, Rosalie Valdez."

"Ah, so perhaps it wasn't merely coincidence that found both you and our silver-haired vixen missing at the same time?"

The slam of the front door saved Daere from having to skirt the question as Rosalie excused herself to go investigate.

Daere was still smiling about the madam's summation of Star when he heard Jade's voice, usually softly modulated and calm, raised in apparent agitation. A few seconds later, she burst through the door, a worried-looking Rosalie close at her heel.

"Where is she, Daere?" Jade demanded.

"Where is who?" he asked, setting his glass aside and rising to his feet.

"You know perfectly well who I'm talking about. Star. Where is she?"

"Why, back at her shop, I suppose."

"No, she's not. I went by there a couple of hours ago to see her. Her aunt said she returned sometime during the night but disappeared again before Hilda arrived this morning. That isn't like her. I thought she must have changed her mind, deciding to return to the cabin, but of course I found the place abandoned by both of you. I've wasted two hours looking for you."

"Tremayne," Daere said in a tight whisper.

"No," Jade said with a quick shake of her head. "If you're thinking she's gone to the hacienda, you can forget it. I went out to your father's ranch, then went to talk with Alec and that wretched stepmother of Star's. They claim not to have seen her. I'm worried, Daere. I know she's not predictable, but she wouldn't have left again without saying

386

something to Hilda or me."

"I've got to find Night Hawk," Daere said, dropping his cheroot into the ashtray and brushing past the two women.

"Something's happened to her. I know it," Jade said with conviction.

Daere was almost to the door when it occurred to him to question Jade further about her visit to the Tremayne hacienda. "Tell me what her brother said," he ordered.

"Nothing really. He just kept leering at me, insisting that he hadn't seen his sister in weeks."

"And you believe him? The man is a lying snake."

Jade frowned, remembering the few minutes she'd spent in the presence of Alec and Cassondria Tremayne. "I don't know, Daere. Now that you mention it, he did seem more cocky than normal. But now that I think about it, it was her stepmother's reaction to my visit that was odd. She was clearly nervous about something. I thought at the time she just didn't like the way Alec kept leering at me, but perhaps it was more. And she kept insisting that the selfish chit — that's what she called Star — had probably found the will and had taken it to the attorney in Santa Fe. Do you think that's possible?"

"That would make Mrs. Tremayne nervous, wouldn't it?" Daere said. "But no, I don't think that's a possibility. If either of them even thought it remotely possible that she'd found the will, they'd

387

have been on the trail to Santa Fe after her. They're obviously lying, but I can't worry about that yet. I have to find Night Hawk first. He escorted her back to town. He might have seen something that will provide a clue."

"All right, you go find Night Hawk, but I'm going back out to the hacienda. If I have to, I'll beat the truth out of that pair," Jade said with uncharacteristic emotion.

"You stay put," Daere ordered. "They aren't going to tell you anything. You might stand a better chance of learning something from some of your guests tonight."

Jade and Rosalie promised to use their persuasive techniques on anyone who came to the bordello that night, then followed Daere to the door.

"*Vaya con Dios,*" Rosalie said.

Daere swung himself up into the saddle, turned his horse toward the road, then paused, a sardonic grin on his handsome face. "Thanks, Rosalie, but I think I'll be better off relying on my own resources."

It took Daere most of the night to catch up with his friend Night Hawk, who as far as anyone knew was the last person to see Star.

When Night Hawk told Daere about the men waiting in ambush a few miles from town, Daere felt dread knot in his stomach. He clapped his friend soundly on the arm as he turned on his heel, headed once again for his horse. "Thanks. You've been a big help. I think I need to pay a visit to Alec Tremayne. It's obvious he knows more than he's admitting."

Night Hawk stopped him with his next words. "More foxes are caught with traps than with the chase. Star's half-brother is a wily devil. I think we would be wise to set a careful trap."

Daere swept his Stetson from his head to brush back his hair, and he sighed with weariness and frustration. "I appreciate your point, but we don't know for sure that Tremayne had anything to do with Star's disappearance. For all we know, she may be off on some mission Raven has set upon."

Night Hawk grinned as he folded his arms over his broad chest. "So you know about the Raven," he said.

Daere nodded, then smiled as well, finding a moment's relief in the memory of his discovery. "Yep. It isn't bad enough that Star Tremayne is more woman than any man could handle, she had to turn out to be a she-devil in black clothing who wields a mean whip."

"Come on," Night Hawk said. "We'll discuss this and the trap we'll lay for her brother while we ride."

"You're going with me?" Daere asked in surprise.

"Of course. You didn't think I'd let you go off with only your white man's instincts to guide you."

"You may have the advantage of Indian blood, but you're half white the same as me," Daere pointed out as he mounted his horse and waited for his friend to pull his magnificent steed up alongside.

"Yes, which you must admit gives me the advantage. I have the white man's knowledge of books and history, and the Indian's instinct and cunning. A superior combination, don't you agree?"

Their tones had matched each other's in a reprieve of light teasing banter, but as Daere faced the uncertainty of Star's whereabouts, his face reflected the return of a somber mood. "I only hope it's enough to help us find her before it's too late . . . if it's not already too late."

The two men drew their horses up behind Rosalie's bordello. Daere handed Night Hawk his reins before throwing a foot over his saddle and jumping gracefully to the ground. "I'll only be a couple of minutes . . . unless I have to wrest Jade from the arms of some cowpoke. Then it might take me longer."

Night Hawk's even white teeth were revealed with his smile in the darkness, but he didn't bother with an answer that would slow his friend's progress.

Less than five minutes later, Daere exited the bordello with Jade fast on his heels.

"She understands what she's to do," Daere told the other man.

"But not until you hear my signal," Night Hawk told the beautiful woman.

"I understand. I'll give you a ten-minute head

start. When I arrive at the gates, I'll wait until I hear the sound of the owl. Three hoots for safe to proceed. Two as a warning to turn back."

"I'm thankful for your quick mind," Night Hawk told her.

Daere was already remounted by the time the exchange was completed, and without another word, the two men turned their horses around and galloped off into the night.

Jade followed after them exactly ten minutes later.

Jade was having trouble keeping her emotions in check, an alien experience for the Oriental woman, who was very nearly always in complete control. She'd learned the art of self-hypnosis as a child, and it had never failed her . . . until now. But when Daere had arrived back at the bordello only an hour before sunrise to tell her what he suspected, she'd felt a hot brand of hatred and fury well up inside her. As she rode toward the Tremayne hacienda, she struggled against the urge to abandon the plan and exact a technique of torture that would get to the truth more quickly than not, if she were any judge of the pair who unknowingly awaited her inside the hacienda.

She'd stopped her horse at the gate as agreed, and in the two or three minutes of her wait for Night Hawk's signal, she found the strength of will she'd been battling in her short journey. Her back stiffening, her flawless features settled into their normal mask of cool, unrevealing detachment. She would follow the plan arrived at by Daere and Night Hawk. But when Star was found, if it turned out that either Alec or Cassondria had had anything to do with her disappearance, she would return to introduce them to the exquisite torture of her ancient culture.

When the owl hooted three times, she contorted her features into a semblance of grief and anguish and kicked her horse into action. With loud cries, she banged on the front door of the hacienda, then practically fell into the surprised arms of one of the servants. "Please, oh, please, you must get Alec and Cassondria. Something terrible has happened to Star!"

But both Tremaynes had already joined her in the foyer, having been in bed together and awakened by the loud cries and insistent clatter at the door. "What do you mean, something terrible has happened to Star?" Cassondria asked, her hand at her throat as she raised her eyes in desperation toward Alec.

Jade shook her head frantically from side to side, taking in short, quick breaths, her eyes sliding frantically from one Tremayne to the other, desperate, panicked . . . and missing nothing. "I . . . I don't know exactly what happened. Only that Daere McCalister brought her into town less than an hour ago. She's been seriously hurt."

"But she is alive," Cassondria pressed.

"She was. I only hope she still is. She was muttering incoherently. She kept saying your names and was so agitated, the doctor sent me to fetch you. Please hurry. Please!"

"Where did they find her?" Alec asked cautiously.

Jade could scarcely contain a grin of satisfaction. So the blackguard did know something. Well, she would return for him later . . . and his lover as well, if she found out Cassondria was involved. For now, she had to continue her role. "I don't know. I didn't ask questions. I just did as I was told and rode like the wind to get here. You'll come, won't you? I know it's been tense between you and Star, but she's calling for you. You won't deny her when—" She let the sentence end abruptly, burying her face in her hands as she began to weep.

"Of course we'll come. She's with the doctor, you said?"

"Yes. That is, he's with her in her quarters above the dress shop. Please, you have to hurry."

"You go on back," Alec said, wrapping a solicitous arm around her waist and guiding her gently but forcibly toward the door. "We'll dress and follow after you as quickly as we can."

Jade didn't risk another moment, hurrying quickly from the room and back out into the breaking morning. She paused for just a second to look back at the house. A slow smile played across her lips. "You'd better follow after me, for if you don't, if you fall into Daere's trap, I'll return," she said aloud.

The promise made, she remounted and rode back down the drive, pausing at the gate to await the call of the owl, the signal that would tell her Night Hawk and Daere still watched.

Twenty-three

Inside the hacienda, Cassondria raged at Alec. "You fool! You stupid, stupid idiot! They've found her, and now she's going to tell them everything."

"Maybe not. Didn't you think Jade's performance a little overdone?"

Cassondria's face twisted with doubt. "She was distraught. No, I think she was telling the truth."

"And if she wasn't? If someone has discovered my beloved sister is missing, and is only trying to get me to go investigate and thereby lead them to her? What then?"

"But what are we going to do?"

"You, my dear *mother*, are going to go into town just as we told Jade we would. Take one of the men with you. If Star is there, you can send him back to tell me, and I'll join you. If she's not, the man can bring me that word as well, and I'll know that McCalister is setting a trap."

"You bastard! You'd send me in as the sacrificial lamb? I won't go!"

Alec grabbed her arm, bruising her delicate skin with the ferocity of his grip. "You'll do exactly as I tell you. If she's there, you can stop her from talking. If she's not, you can demand an explanation for this terrible prank that frightened us both nearly witless."

"They won't buy into that. They know how Star feels about us and that I can scarcely abide the sight of her."

"Use your head for once, Cass. You heard Jade. There's been tension between us, but we're still family."

"All right, but if she's already told them that you left her in the caves to die and they try to implicate me, I'll bury you."

Alec ignored the threat as he went in search of one of his men. His head was reeling from the combination of too little sleep, long hours of lovemaking, and his precious white powder, and he shook it, trying to clear his thoughts.

They couldn't have found her, could they? But who? McCalister? No. More likely that Indian, Night Hawk. He frowned as he stepped outside, his eyes narrowed as he scanned the horizon for any sign that Jade had not come alone. But he saw nothing.

Crossing the yard, he went into the bunkhouse, where he awakened his men. Alec issued hurried orders.

One was to accompany Cass into town. The others were to ride out, circle the land, and make sure no one was hiding out there in the shadows.

"And if we find someone, you want us to bring him to you?" one of the men asked as he scratched at his back with one hand, his scalp with the other.

"No, idiot! Kill him."

That said, he hurried back toward the house. He dressed quickly, strapped on his gun, then reached for his hat. He stopped to rub at his gritty eyes. He needed something to get him going, to sharpen his senses. He was just reaching for the vial that was hidden in one of his drawers when Cass reentered the bedroom.

"I'm leaving, but Alec, what do I do if she's made accusations against us? I'm not going to hang because you were a fool and didn't kill her straight out like I told you to."

His hands braced on the dresser, Alec didn't turn to face her, but muttered a curse before answering her query. "Who's the fool, Cass, my love? If she's been found, she's probably dead by now. No one could survive even one night, much less two, in those caverns. I told you, if the snakes or spiders didn't get her, exposure to the damp air and thirst will have done her in."

"And if you're wrong?" Cass persisted, albeit nervously.

"If I'm wrong, get the doctor out of the room long enough to press a pillow over her face."

Now he pushed himself away from the dresser and turned on his heel. "Do you want me to write it down for you?"

Tears filled Cassondria's eyes at his sarcasm, but she didn't cower as she knew he expected. Instead, she spun around and left the room. A few seconds later, he heard the front door open, then slam shut, and then the buggy pulling away from the house with another rider at its side.

His hands shaking, he turned back to his task of finding the vial and freeing it of its stopper.

Alec's mood was much improved by the time his foreman came into the house to tell him that they'd found no one on the land.

So it was true. She'd been found. Well, so be it. He'd spoken the truth when he'd told Cass that she couldn't have survived two nights in the caverns. But he'd best set her horse free lest someone come snooping around, asking questions and demanding answers about how Star had gotten into the caves in the first place.

But as he went to the barn, his mood almost euphoric now in spite of the fact that his sister had not perished inside the caves as he'd hoped, Alec thought better of merely letting the animal loose. He wanted to see for himself the hell she'd endured. He knew there would be telltale signs in the cave: strands of hair, splattered blood, bits of flesh, shredded clothing.

A smile of pure madness flitted across his face as he saddled her horse, then one for himself.

"Poor little Star," he said, then tossed his head back as he laughed with maniacal delight.

"There," Night Hawk said with satisfaction as he pointed to where Alec was just emerging from the barn on horseback.

Daere's teeth ground together with his fury as he saw the horse Tremayne led behind him. "That's Star's horse."

Night Hawk didn't answer except for a tight nod, but he motioned for Daere to follow him to their hiding place in a thick copse of mesquite.

They waited for Star's half-sibling to pass, then followed more than a half mile behind him, neither speaking nor taking their eyes off their quarry. But just as Star had realized their destination as soon as the desert had given way to rock and mountainous terrain, both men quickly knew as well.

Daere cast his friend a questioning glance when Night Hawk abruptly changed course.

"We know where he's going now, Daere."

"Hell, yes, we know where he's going. We've got to get there right behind him."

"So he can pick us off as we follow him down in the miner's bucket? No, we'll have to take the long away around and come in from another entrance, one long ago discovered by my people."

Daere shook his head stubbornly. "It'll take too long. If—" He couldn't finish his statement as his voice caught on the implication of all the ifs that lay in wait for them.

"It's our only chance to save her, my friend." Night Hawk said in a soothing tone. "Trust me, and we may know success shortly."

Daere gave a short nod as he gulped back fear. Pulling the bandanna from his neck, he wiped at his brow, then straightened in his saddle. "I trust you, Night Hawk. Let's go get her."

From somewhere deep inside the recesses of Star's mind, awareness of daybreak registered. Still, she didn't unfurl from the ball into which she had pulled her body hours before. She didn't move at all except for the frequent trembles that racked her body, which was chilled from the spray of water and the constant cool temperature in the far recesses of the caverns.

Her mouth was as dry as parchment, and her eyes were matted with tears long ago ceased. She thought of home, but had finally given up the hope of surviving her confinement to see the house her father had built and left behind as his legacy to her.

She thought of Daere, forgetting the pain of his rejection and cleaving to the sweeter memories she'd made in his arms.

Those were precious thoughts to die with, and she wondered if she would still carry them with her when the angels came for her. Would she be able to tell them of the two men in her life she had loved, or would one be forgotten, left behind like the shell that was her body, while the other came to meet her?

And then she heard a faint noise, different from the others she'd learned to distinguish from the water's rush. Still, she didn't stir. What did it matter if it was the angels she'd been awaiting during the long night she'd passed or merely another of the creatures that dwelled in the caves? She was past caring, past fear.

A man's voice called out, shouting her name, but she didn't respond. If the voice was really that of an angel come to carry her to heaven, he'd find her. If not . . .

She turned her thoughts to the dimming memory of pain that had consumed her body the day before. Odd, how it had disappeared. She felt nothing now but the slight rise and fall of her rib cage with her shallow breaths. She might have smiled then had the effort not been so taxing, for she felt wonderfully at peace. She thought death must not be such a terrible thing at all, or wouldn't she still be fighting it rather than embracing it?

"Star! I know you're in here. I know they tried to deceive me, make believe they'd found you! They think they're dealing with a fool, but I know it was a trick!"

She recognized the voice now. Alec. Strange that she wasn't frightened at the prospect of being discovered. Instead, she felt a profound sadness that wasn't merely for herself but for him as well. "Go away," she whispered, but the words came out only in a whisper that carried no farther than her lips.

She heard the click of his booted heels against the rock floor and considered trying to sit up to warn him that he mustn't try and reach her. The narrow ledges were slippery and dangerous. But she hadn't the strength to move.

"Are you dead yet, Star?" he shouted. "Is that why you don't answer me?"

Soon, her mind answered. *Soon, Alec.*

"It won't do any good to hide from me, sister, dear. I can't leave until I know if you're dead." Laughter followed the declaration. "Ah, you left me a trail. How considerate of you. It looks like you were bleeding pretty badly. Poor baby."

His voice was drawing nearer, she realized, for he was no longer shouting. Even over the steady thrum of the cascading water, she could hear him quite clearly.

She sighed deeply. *Poor Alec. He'll never make it up here. The ledge is not wide enough for him.*

Summoning every ounce of energy she could muster, she pushed herself into a sitting position, thinking to warn him. By leaning slightly to the left, she could see him now, pressed closely to the wall as he followed the trail of bloodstains left by the cuts on her hands.

His face, too, was pressed against the wall as

he inched nearer, but he paused and moved back to peer below, and in that instant their gazes met. "So it was the waterfall that you were climbing to. How resourceful of you. But you always were a clever bitch, too clever for your own good. I'm disappointed, though. I thought it was my pets you were trying to escape." He paused to glance down at the hollowed rock below and the hundreds of slithering reptiles. "Or these snakes."

He began to laugh then, and even in her state of shock, Star recognized the sound of derangement and shrank away from it by some innate instinct, but not before she saw him lose his balance and pitch backward into the air.

As the laughter changed to a high-pitched scream, then to a gargling noise of agony, Star was jolted from the lethargy that had assailed her mind as well as her body. She pressed her hands over her ears to shut out the terrible sounds of her own screams.

Daere and Night Hawk were within thirty yards of the chamber, which the white man had nicknamed the opera house because of its acoustics, the semicircular floor, and the narrow shelves that resembled balcony tiers. They quickened their steps, moving cautiously yet speedily toward her.

"He'll kill her," Daere said in a strangled voice of mingling outrage and fear.

"Not yet," Night Hawk said. "Her voice comes from high above us near the waterfall. It will take him some time to get near enough to shoot her."

Daere didn't answer. He knew that Night Hawk's keen senses were almost flawless.

In another moment, they entered the chamber.

Both men stopped at the edge of the floor, momentarily frozen by the grotesque sight below them. Alec's sightless eyes stared up at them for a fraction of a second before his face was obscured by the snakes, who seemed to be dancing in celebration of the sacrifice delivered to them.

Daere was the first to look up. He could distinguish only the outline of her body, the sparkle of silver that was her hair beneath the water's spray, but he could hear her. Her screams had given way to softer weeping, but the sound was carried to them by the water.

He turned, starting after her, but Night Hawk stopped him. "Let me. My moccasins are surer than your boots. I'll bring her down to you, have no fear."

Dare shot him a look of passionate gratitude, but his expression was resolute. "I appreciate your concern, Night Hawk, but she's my woman. I've claimed her, and there can be no other to make the climb but me."

"I understand, my brother," Night Hawk replied solemnly. He stood watching as Daere, his step almost as sure and as quick as a Comanche's, made the treacherous climb to Star's side.

It seemed to take him only a few minutes to reach her, but then all was silent. What was he doing? Night Hawk wondered. "Is she all right?" he called when he could no longer contain his impatience.

Daere didn't answer, but a few seconds later, Night Hawk was relieved to see him reappear from behind the waterfall. Star was draped over his back, her arms held with a sturdy hand around his neck.

Several minutes later, his progress descending the narrow ledges impeded by the delicate package he carried on his back, Daere descended to the cavern floor.

Daere caught her up in his arms. He stared down at her with such tenderness that Night Hawk turned away. Moments such as these between a man and his woman were private, and he wished to offer them respect by allowing them this. But he uttered a soft word of caution. "She needs medical attention, Daere."

Her hair had fallen over her face, and Daere brushed it away with trembling fingers. "Star," he said in a strangled voice.

Her eyes fluttered open, and her parched lips managed the slightest of smiles. "I was going to tell the angels about you."

He laughed then, a choked chuckle that was a half sob. "I'm glad we got here in time to save them the trouble of listening."

"I was going to tell them how much I love

you," she said before her eyes closed once again.

"Let's go," Daere told Night Hawk. He only hoped the tears that stood in his eyes didn't blind him on the treacherous trail out.

Twenty-four

It seemed to take Daere forever to reach town, although in truth, he knew not more than an hour had elapsed since they had rescued Star.

Night Hawk rode behind them, silent, ever watchful, his heart understanding his brother's pain.

During the return ride, Daere vacillated between fear and intense anger. He'd come so very close to losing Star, and he wanted nothing more at the moment than to have her open her eyes and smile up at him. Wishful thinking, he knew, for her body and mind had just gone through a terrible ordeal.

She lay pale and still in his arms. He saw her lips tremble and heard her whisper his name. It tore at his insides, and a low, rough growl rumbled deep in his chest. He thought about how brave she'd been when Alec had chased her down like an animal and then had imprisoned her in the caverns, and his fists tightened. It hurt him more than he could have imagined to have found her so helpless and battered. He hated the way the innocent always seemed to be the ones who suffered most, and not only was

Star innocent, but she was also someone he loved. Loved with his heart and soul.

Then his next thought made him tremble. Christ, what if she had died there? The rage flared up hotly, and that part of him that was savage and uncivilized wanted revenge, needed the satisfaction that it provided. But Alec, the bastard, had cheated him of it. He was dead, and there was no one he could make pay for Star's suffering.

Reaching down, he spoke soothingly as he gently squeezed her hand, lying so limp and unresponsive in her lap. He'd been able to staunch the flow of blood from the lacerations on her forehead with his neckerchief, and he didn't know for certain, but he thought her ankle might be broken. He'd been relieved to find that the numerous cuts she'd received didn't look serious, but she was still so pale and there was that nasty bump on her temple.

He began talking to her, needed to at least reassure her, even though he didn't know if she were aware enough to understand him. "You're going to be fine, sweetheart. We're almost there. I promise I'll make certain that no harm ever comes to you again."

And so he kept talking soothingly to her, until he saw the town of Tequila Bend looming up ahead.

Riding around to the back of the dress shop, he slid from his horse to the ground and, holding her against his chest, carried her up the back stairs. Night Hawk followed behind them, their ever-watchful bodyguard.

Kicking open the door, Daere strode down the

hallway and carried Star into her bedroom, where he gently laid her on the bed. Star's Aunt Hilda was beside them faster than she'd ever before moved in her life.

Her mouth dropped when she saw Star in the arms of the gunslinger, with the wild-looking Comanche Indian hovering protectively near.

"Oh, my poor Star. What . . . happened?" she demanded to know.

Daere's gaze sliced into her. "Alec," he snarled, and the tone of his voice and that one word told her everything she needed to know.

Aunt Hilda flushed and, fluttering her hand, shooed the men away. "Please, gentlemen, you must move back so that I might tend to her."

"I'll get the doctor," Daere said, then told Night Hawk to remain with Star until he returned.

"Oh, my poor, poor dear," Aunt Hilda crooned, smoothing the tangled silver tresses back from Star's face.

Night Hawk began to explain to Star's aunt the series of events that had led up to their finding her in the cavern.

Daere heard Hilda exclaim angrily as he bounded down the stairs, "I always did despise that Alec Tremayne. He's always caused nothing but trouble for the family. If you ask me, he was just bad through and through. I say the world's better off without him."

Cassondria paced the length of her bedroom in

agitated confusion. There hadn't been anyone at Star's apartment when she'd gone into town to do some investigating on her own. The chit was probably alive and well and, no doubt, already telling the authorities everything she knew.

She forced herself to try and think calmly. They needed a plan just in case Star had indeed managed to escape. Stupid, stupid Alec! she fumed. She had tried to warn him, but he wouldn't listen to her. And where in the hell was he, anyway? She had been expecting him to return soon, so that they might discuss whether to leave town or remain and try to figure out some way to discredit Star's story if it became necessary.

It shouldn't be too difficult, she thought. Everyone knew the girl had been afraid of her own shadow ever since the night her father had died. Alec and his gruesome pets had seen to that. Cassondria was beginning to feel more confident now. Yes, they could still maintain their credibility, and just as soon as Alec returned, they would launch this new plan of attack.

Her expression brightened when she heard the sound of footsteps on the stairway, and she turned, smiling. "Alec—"

But it was her bodyguard, Santucci, and not Alec, who stood in the doorway. His jaw was swollen and bore an ugly bruise; he looked as if he'd been in a heck of a fight. "He won't be coming back this time, *senora*," he said.

"Don't be silly. Of course, he is," she exclaimed, green-gold eyes wide with apprehension. She found it impossible to believe that something terrible might have happened to Alec. They had been through so much together, and despite their squabbles and petty differences, they were a team and had been for many years. She really couldn't imagine her life without him. Foremost, Cassondria couldn't remember a time when there hadn't been a man in her life. She was a woman who needed male companionship at all times. In her mind, a woman was nothing unless her name was linked with that of a prominent man in the community. She stood wringing her bejeweled fingers. It just wasn't possible that Alec was gone.

Santucci eyed her sadly. "Not this time, I'm afraid. His horse has returned to the stable without him. Our men just came back after having searched everywhere for him." He extended his hand. "They brought back his rifle. Bart says he found it lying at the mouth of the caverns. He must have fallen to his death, *senora*."

"And . . . Star? What of her?" Panic flashed in Cassondria's gaze as she waited with bated breath for his answer.

"She's alive, I'm afraid. I know, because I was watching her place and I saw McCalister carry her up the back stairway to her quarters."

Hysteria bubbled up in her throat. "And . . . you killed them, didn't you? Tell me they are dead."

Santucci shifted his massive bulk, settling his weight, searching for the right words to tell her that he had tried but failed. "That was my intention when I went into town. I figured if something went wrong and the girl managed to escape, then I would take care of her once and for all. I positioned myself across the alley in an abandoned building and waited. It seemed like an easy enough task. I would simply wait and see if she returned, and if she did, then I'd pick her off." He paused, drawing a deep, fortifying breath.

Cassondria's eyes glittered, and she hissed, "Yes, yes . . . tell me that's what happened."

"Unfortunately, that's not how things turned out." Santucci's thick brows drew together in a fierce scowl. "It was that damned Indian shadowing McCalister who ruined everything. The bastard almost killed me!" he exclaimed somewhat incredulously, before continuing. "I had the gunslinger dead in my sights, figuring I'd backshoot him, then kill the girl." Cold sweat, prompted by a dreaded memory, beaded on his brow. "But before I could squeeze off a shot, I felt this cold, sharp blade pressed against my . . . my *cajones,* and a voice from behind me warned that if I even moved the wrong way, I would go through the rest of my life speaking in a high voice I wouldn't recognize as my own." The big man shuddered. "He made me drop my weapon and turn around. It was the Indian, and I knew he meant every word just by the look in his eyes. He said he was letting me live so that I might relay a message back to you."

"Well, tell me, for God's sake!" Cassondria screeched, a vein pulsing in her forehead. "I don't give a damn about what happened, only what those bastards intend for me."

For a second, Santucci's gaze expressed surprise. He thought she was truly the vilest woman he had ever met. Someone should have washed out her mouth with lye soap a long time ago. "Night Hawk said to tell you that all of your forces are scattered and there's nowhere left to run. You should give up, before someone else dies." Santucci's shoulders sagged wearily. "It was then he told me that Alec had been killed in the cavern." He wiped the back of his hand across his torn mouth. "I won't go to prison for you, *senora,* so you'd better think of a way to get us out of this mess."

The anger and hatred that had been boiling up inside Cassondria for years erupted in a spew of gutter language strong enough to make even the tough bodyguard wince. At that moment, he was almost tempted to shut her mouth permanently. Stepping farther into the room, he thought he just might do so. But Cassondria's next words quickly altered his plan.

"You're right, of course, Santucci," she agreed, suddenly calm and in control once again. "And I will take care of you, but you must do the same for me. I need a big, strong man like you now that Alec is gone." She took a step toward him, a message clear in her eyes, then hurtled herself into his outstretched arms.

He caught her up in a savage embrace, almost squeezing the breath from her lungs. There were few words needed. They simply rejoiced in the fact that they were both alive and at least had each other.

He laid his cheek against hers and whispered,

"You feel so good, *querida*. I think you and I were made for each other. I'm never going to let you go."

In the next instant, Cassondria gave a breathy sigh and swooned in his embrace. The bodyguard hurried to lay her on the bed. Poor woman. She had been through so much today. A thread of pity stirred in the big man, and he murmured tenderly.

"I won't ever let anyone hurt you, *niña*," he vowed, staring avidly at her in repose.

It surprised him to realize just how fragile she seemed to him now, when only moments before she had been spitting like a viper. Ah, but maybe this was what made her seem so intriguing. He scratched his chin. Women . . . who could figure them out? Reaching out, he fingered a strand of her brassy hair, then brushed the backs of his knuckles across her smooth skin.

Moments later, he lumbered toward her bathing room to retrieve her smelling salts.

Instantly, green-gold eyes slitted and watched him from the bed. Cassondria couldn't resist a tiny smile, then quickly closed her eyes once again. Men . . . they were really all the same.

While she waited for Santucci to return, she let her mind drift and had soon formulated the perfect plan. It was just a matter of time before Star gained control of everything, and Cassondria just couldn't bear the thought of being penniless again. However, there might still be a way to secure her future. Suddenly, a brilliant scheme came to mind. She could, and would, have everything after all, but first she must make Star believe that she had had nothing to do with Alec's ugly plan. Somehow, Cassondria realized she had to convince her stepdaughter of her innocence, for she knew she could not survive locked up in a jail. Nor would she be able to enjoy her inheritance as she intended.

Such a shame that Alec wouldn't be here to share it with her. Particularly since he certainly had gone to a lot of time and trouble in the beginning to remove any obstacles in their path. It had been Alec's twisted mind that had first devised the plan to do away with his father and forge Benjamin's signature on a new will.

He had murdered Benjamin just as sure as if he'd pulled the trigger on a gun. In remembering Benjamin's slow, agonizing death, Cassondria thought it surely would have been more merciful of Alec to have simply shot him. Alec's pets were vicious little beasts with a relentless appetite—she shuddered every time she envisioned them—and Cassondria suddenly decided that she no longer even wanted them in the house with her. She would make certain they were removed from the hacienda, along with Alec's personal belongings, just as soon as possible.

In fact, she would take immense pleasure in securing his pets' new quarters herself. After all, it was the least she could do for her poor Alec, God rest his tortured soul.

The two women stared assessingly at one another. "I always did say I admired your nerve, Cassondria," Star said, glaring up at her stepmother, whom

Aunt Hilda had reluctantly shown the way to her niece's bedroom. Star was feeling much better, but her ankle, while not broken, still kept her confined to her bed.

"I tried telling her that you weren't up to having visitors, but she insisted," Hilda told Star. "Would you like for me to remain here with you, dear?" She kept a watchful eye trained on the woman who had caused her niece so much heartache in the past.

"No, I'll be fine, Aunt Hilda," Star replied. "I'm sure whatever Cassondria has to say won't take her very long."

Casting a final warning glare at Cassondria, Hilda said "Very well, but I'll be right in the next room if you should need me."

When they were alone, Cassondria prepared to make amends, but it was difficult for her to mask the fever of excitement in her eyes. "I know you must be wary of me, but I really did come to make peace, Star," she said, meeting her stepdaughter's stony gaze unflinchingly. "I don't blame you, of course. I know you probably never thought to hear me say those words to you, but after that unfortunate business with Alec, I've decided it's time you and I cleared the air between us."

"How touching that you should think so," Star said archly. "It wouldn't have anything to do with the fact that Alec's treachery and deceit has finally been exposed, would it? Or could it be because I know where the original will is hidden, which makes me the rightful heir to my father's estate?"

Cassondria didn't so much as blink, keeping her

feelings carefully masked. "Why . . . of course not, although I can understand how you might think such a thing. Let me assure you, I really had no idea what Alec was going to do to you. He made me believe that *he* was the heir, you see, and since he was your father's only son, I had no reason to doubt what he told me. Now, of course, I realize he was really quite mad." She withdrew a handkerchief from her reticule and dabbed at her moist eyes. "I hate to speak of it, but Alec had been abusing drugs as well. So you see, he couldn't be held responsible for his actions, Star. I'm sure if he had been in his right mind, none of this would ever have happened."

"I'm sure you'd like me to believe that," Star said, staring at Cassondria as if seeing her for the first time, fascinated by the resolve in her stepmother's eyes. "Sorry, but I don't really believe that Alec planned everything on his own. He wasn't smart enough for that. Someone else was behind him, prodding him from the onset. Although I can't prove my theory, of course, now that he's gone. So, you can relax. You're free as a bird." Rage flared up hotly within her and she couldn't help twisting the knife. Her mouth curled in a victorious smile. "Albeit, a broken, homeless little sparrow, however, with nothing but a pitiful existence and approaching old age to look forward to."

Cassondria bristled, a bitter viper of disappointment uncurling in her stomach. She took a deep breath and straightened her spine in the characteristic way that Star had come to know and despise.

"Well! I can see that you are still determined to think the worst about me, as usual," she huffed and, turning away, walked over to the window. "So, I'll simply just leave the little peace offering I brought for you and be on my way." She set a lovely potted cactus on a small table and glanced back at Star. "I want you to remember how I did so want us to be friends."

"You may have wanted to be many things to me, Cassondria, but *never* my friend. Now, if you don't mind, I'm really very tired. I'd like to take a nap." Star stifled a bored yawn behind her palm. "Oh, and by the way. I plan to take up residence in my father's house just as soon as I'm feeling well enough to move. I expect you to vacate the premises at once."

"Don't worry, my dear Star, I don't think that you and I shall ever cross paths again," Cassondria replied heatedly, the door slamming behind her with a final thud.

Twenty-five

On the sixth evening of Star's recuperation, when she should have been looking forward to a secure future, she tossed restlessly in her bed instead, the covers pulled tightly up to her chin.

Alec Tremayne had terrorized her so completely by placing her in the dark caverns and leaving her there alone to die that she wondered if she would ever again be the same woman. Her nerves were skittish since her abduction, and she couldn't seem to rest quietly for more than a few hours before she would break out in a clammy sweat and cry softly in her sleep. Fear had always proven her most powerful foe, and even as she slept, it sifted silently into her dreams like a primitive entity stalking her.

Star had fallen asleep around midnight, after having once again replayed her harrowing imprisonment in the caverns and Daere's bold rescue. Something was waiting there in the darkness. Old haunts were reawakened, drawing her from sleep.

The night suddenly seemed forbidding. *It is only the laudanum making me hear and see things that aren't there,* she tried to tell herself. She knew that Alec had fallen to his death. But even so, Star couldn't help wondering if somehow he might have managed to survive and would return to terrorize her again. She would then envision her half-brother's dark form, those fancy boots, silver trim glinting in the diffused light as he had stalked her. He had wanted to see her dead, but instead, he had fallen to his own death. Star could not say that she felt any sympathy for him.

Then the scene in her mind's eye changed, and she remembered seeing a flash of silver outside her door on the night that her father had been screaming—*dying*—with no one who would come to his aid. Star had felt so guilty for being afraid of the dark and not having rushed to help him. Someone else had been nearby, and he might easily have done so.

Alec! He had been prowling the hallways of the hacienda as their father's piteous cries resounded in her ears, pleading for one of them to come to his aid. God, Alec had truly been a coldhearted monster. He had probably stood just on the other side of their father's bedroom door, listening gleefully to the poor man's death throes.

A sound filtered into Star's nightmare, and she felt a tangible presence there in the room with her. The room was in darkness; the newly risen moon suffused through the wispy curtains at the window when she opened her eyes.

She lay silent, wondering for the briefest moment if perhaps Alec hadn't returned for her after all. A great despair like a blanketing mist shrouded Star. No, please, she couldn't go through that hell again!

To the right of her bed, the sound of a match flaring against a thumbnail sent the blood racing through her veins. There *was* someone in her room! Star's heart thrummed wildly and her bleary eyes searched the shadows frantically.

"Who's there? I demand to know," she said, although her voice faded barely above a whisper.

A long-fingered hand reached across the moonlight spilling through the window, lighting the lamp on the table before it.

Alecs!

No. Someone else. In the next breath, she knew immediately whose hand she had seen, and her heart did a peculiar flip-flop. The flame flickered to life and brightened the room.

Daere had come to her. She simply stared at him, relief and anger both surging through her. Like a sleek, dark panther, savage and beautiful, threatening and alluring, he had slipped through the night to invade her life once again. It was a most provocative combination, a blend of seduction and danger.

Her stomach clenched with foreboding. What did he want of her? She hadn't seen him since he had left her in her aunt's care and then had walked out with barely an exchange of polite words between them.

Now he was back, and she imagined he expected to simply crook his finger and have her at his beck and call as before.

"How are you feeling sweetheart?" The husky sound of his voice washed over her, and Star's gaze narrowed to the man sprawled negligently in the chair, his long legs encased in tight black pants and his booted feet, crossed at the ankle, propped on a footstool in front of him. His broad shoulders were covered by a black silk shirt and a leather vest. His hair was rakishly long and windblown. The wayward locks tumbled over his brow, much the same way as the first day she had seen him, lending him a rakehell air. Yet, despite his renegade appearance and the concealing stubble of his black beard, there was a familiarity about him that calmed her almost immediately. She would never let him know this, of course, but she couldn't deny it to herself.

Star watched him blow out the match with that manner of infuriating arrogance she remembered so well. Oh, yes, it was so like Daere. She would know his actions anywhere. Then, to her dismay, she found that she felt like bursting into childish tears. Lord, what was wrong with her lately? Her emotions no longer seemed to be her own, but felt exposed and raw, and she could not control her moods from one minute to the next.

Relief quickly turned to resentment. How dare he stay away for so long, then think that he might waltz back into her life, and bedroom, at any given hour of the day!

"How am I feeling?" she said mockingly. "How do you think?" She angrily pondered his hawkish profile for several seconds, then snapped, "At least you might have waited until morning to have asked such an ignominious question."

Her less than cheerful greeting didn't seem to affect him. He sat back and laced his fingers behind his head. "I wanted us to have some time to ourselves."

She hid her turmoil behind clipped tones. "Why now? You haven't been to see me in over a week, Daere. I'm sure whatever we have to say to each other could be said in front of my aunt or Jade." Her eyes skimmed over every inch of him, and suddenly her stomach felt hot and heavy, as if she had a pound of molten lead inside her. The realization of it made her even angrier. Why did he have to be the one man who made her feel this way? Why not some decent, honorable man, like Jake? He had been to see her several times in the past week, but never had his visits elicited this sort of response from her. Only Daere. What they had shared together was wicked . . . lustful . . . indecent . . . but had also been wonderful . . . exciting . . . blissful. Always these conflicting emotions. All with the same message. Daere McCalister was not a man to give her heart to. He didn't wish to love anyone, and he *had* been truthful with her about that. She assessed him coolly. "What could possibly be so important that you had to come to me in the middle of the night?"

"We need to talk about a . . . ah, delicate matter." He took a deep breath, as though he was suddenly reluctant go on.

She felt his gaze on her and wondered why it always had to feel like an intimate caress. Looking back at him, her eyes touched on every plane and angle of that harsh face. She could tell that he was remembering their time together in the cabin, just as she was. His was a questioning look. She suddenly understood very clearly why he had come.

"I'm *not* carrying your baby, if that's what you're worried about," she stated bluntly, conscious of a sudden feeling of emptiness within her. She had thought about it a lot in the beginning, but she knew it really would be the worst thing that could happen right now. He didn't want to get married. Hell, he couldn't even hang around long enough to see her well.

He planted his booted feet firmly on the floor and leaned forward. A scowl creased his brow. "Always blunt and to the point, aren't you?"

"Not always, but since you seemed so worried about the possibility, I thought it best to ease your conscience for you immediately. Put you out of your misery, so to speak," she replied flippantly.

He sat forward, his gaze never wavering from her face. "Would you tell me the truth if you were?"

"So you could be gallant and do the right thing?"

His face darkened. "Despite what you might think, I would do the honorable thing. I wouldn't want my child to grow up without a father." He peered hard at her face, then his gaze drifted downward to where her hands lay clasped on her abdomen. "So, are you being truthful with me?"

The words had been clipped, but Star was suddenly too overwhelmed by her own feelings to pay his much notice. After her discussion with Night Hawk the other night, she was never more aware that Daere wasn't capable of loving anyone right now. Above all, before he could be free to love, he had to understand what drove him so relentlessly to continually take risks no other person would. Every hour was a test, every day he breathed and Tad did not, another penance paid. He hadn't said one word about loving her, needing her, *wanting* to spend the rest of his life with her. Only that he would do her and the baby a favor and marry her if it became absolutely necessary. Star stared at Daere, tight-lipped. "Go to hell, Daere. And get out of my room. I wouldn't have you as my baby's father even if I were pregnant, so that's the only answer you're getting from me."

The anger in her tone nettled him. "Is that so? Who would you choose as a good father for my child . . . if there was one? Jake Fontaine?" His voice had risen sharply.

"Keep your voice down," she snapped at him. "If Aunt Hilda should awaken and find you in my bedroom, she'll think me compromised for sure and then neither of us will have anything to say in the matter. She'll *force* you to marry me."

He didn't even realize that he'd been thinking it until the words just seemed to pop out. "Good, then I'll raise my voice some more. I'll even shout it at the top of my goddamned lungs if that's what it takes. I love you, you little hellcat! And pregnant or not, I want you for my wife."

Star couldn't believe what she'd just heard. She could only stare at him. Somewhat dazed, she said, "Now you've gone and done it for sure. She'll be in here any minute."

As if on cue, Aunt Hilda's voice drifted down the hallway from her bedroom. "Star, dear, are you having one of your nightmares again?"

"No, I'm fine, Aunty. There's no need for your concern," Star called back.

"Then I must have been the one dreaming, for I swore I heard a man's voice asking if you'd seen his pregnant cat . . . er . . . or perhaps it was his pregnant wife? . . ." She emitted a loud, distressed sigh. "Never mind, dear, I think I'm just confused again. Go back to sleep. Sorry if I woke you."

Star glared at him. Daere glared right back.

"Didn't you hear what I said?" he asked, his tone low but threatening. "Or do I have to raise my voice again to convince you?"

"Don't you dare," she hissed.

Sarcasm dripped from his tongue. "Oh, but I dare

just about anything, as you well know. And I'm not leaving this room until you say you'll marry me."

"What makes you think I want to get married? I like my life just the way that it is, thank you."

He rolled his eyes heavenward. "You're going to make me do the whole bit, aren't you? Get down on my knees, beg, plead, promise to love you madly until my dying breath?"

She toyed with the end of the blanket, and she was certain he must hear the sudden wild tattoo of her heart. A thrill of anticipation shot through her.

He only scowled blackly. "Well, you'll not be getting that from me. Maybe from someone like Jake Fontaine, but I'd feel like a damned fool."

To her horror, her eyes suddenly filled with tears. He groaned. "Don't do that, honey. Look. I'm not good with sugarcoated words or even being kind. Sometimes I can be a real coldhearted bastard. We've had our good times together and our share of bad, but I have to admit, you're the only woman who's ever gotten under my skin like you have. You're driving me goddamn insane, lady."

"Should I apologize or clap my hands?" she sniffed. How dare he think that he could just walk in here, more or less tell her that he hoped she wasn't carrying his baby, then in the next breath declare how confused he was about his feelings for her. He sounded as if he were terrified that he might be in love with her. Star *knew* how she felt about him. She loved him! She had since the first moment they'd

427

laid eyes on each other.

"Christ, even the way you hiss at me at times like a she-devil heats my blood," he ground out, his jaw tightening. "Why?" He looked disgusted with himself for revealing so much to her. Yet, once he had begun, he couldn't seem to stop himself. "I even went off by myself just to think and try to figure out what I was going to do about you." He studied her with a mixture of disbelief and puzzlement. "I can't even get you out of my thoughts long enough to find the answer. I envision your beautiful face, your soft body, smell the sweet lilac scent of your hair. You aren't like any other woman I've ever known. I can't second-guess you — hell, I don't really even know who you are!" His eyes narrowed. "Of course, it's the precise reason I find you so damned intriguing. The very same things stir our blood. You live for danger and love bucking the odds, but most of all, you hate like the devil to lose at anything. I'd say we make a helluva team, Star. And any children born of our union would be strong and able to stand on their own in the world."

She studied him covertly. Oh, dear sweet Lord, he must know that she was Raven. What would she tell him if he asked? "What other conclusions did you come to?" she questioned him breathlessly, dreading what he might say next.

"Only that when I walked out of here the other day, I had made up my mind that you'd be better off married to a man like Fontaine. He could settle you down, tame some of your exuberance, maybe even turn you into a lady twenty-four hours of the day, twelve months out of the year."

"What a novel idea," she interjected.

He grinned devilishly. "Yeah, isn't it?" Then he added, "But then I decided there will never be another woman like you to come along in a lifetime, and I'd be a fool to walk out of your life or to change you in any way. We've saved one another's lives. There's a bond between us, it seems." He shifted in the chair and turned his head, throwing his profile in sharp review. The sun peeked over the windowsill. He stared at it, then back at her. Her eyes drank in the sight of him. "We're two of a kind, Star. Nobody else could ever put up with us, let alone *keep* up with us. You'd drive Fontaine right out of his mind." He cleared his throat. "I guess what I'm trying to tell you is that we belong together. Always."

She gazed up at him, wide-eyed, enjoying the moment more than anything she ever had in her life. But suddenly her gaze was diverted by the strangest vision. She could only stare in astonishment as the cactus on the table next to him began to sway and now seemed to be growing, swelling in amazing proportions.

Star tried to convince herself that it was only the effect of the laudanum she had taken earlier, but even when she closed her eyes and quickly opened them again, the cactus was still shaking, as though in the throes of death. This was no trick of her mind. It was really happening. Star tried to open her mouth to warn Daere, who was turned away from the table, but the only sound she could make was a soft gasp.

Daere had become aware of her stillness, and he stared at her in vexation. Slowly, he turned his head and followed the direction of her horror-filled gaze. What he saw prompted him to hurl himself out of the chair. He knew how certain species of spiders liked to nest in cacti, and wasting no time, he scooped up Star in his arms and, turning, hurried toward the door.

Star watched the scene unfold as if in slow motion. The cactus was shuddering as if in the worst agony and, indeed, seemed as though it were laboring to give birth.

"My God, what's happening?" Star cried, clinging to him.

Just as Daere reached the door, the cactus trembled violently and exploded, bits and pieces of spiny flesh splattering the walls and ceiling and pelting them in the back. But something else rained down upon them as well.

Something that lived and breathed and crawled on spindly black legs blurred before her eyes.

Spiders! Tarantula spiders were everywhere! Crawling on the walls, the furniture, the bed where she had just lain, and creeping along her arms, their hairy legs grasping at her night rail. Star stared at the spiders, unable to move or barely breathe. "Alec's pets . . . Alec's pets . . . It's just like that other time," she choked in realization. "Cassondria brought me the cactus earlier this week. She said it was meant as a peace offering, and that she also wished to assure me that Alec had been acting alone when he tried to kill me. He did admit to me in the caverns that he was responsible for Cap's death as well, so I had begun to think that maybe he had been responsible for everything."

With a sweep of his hand, Daere knocked the spiders off them, stomping on as many as he could as he hurtled through the door, cradling Star against him.

Healing sunlight bathed them in a warm golden glow. Star clung to Daere and buried her face against his chest.

"I had always thought he was the one behind Cap's death," Daere said, holding her close. "At least now I know the truth."

"Cassondria almost managed to convince me of her innocence, but now I know she wanted to kill me in the same way they murdered my father. There isn't any doubt in my mind now. She and Alec have been in it together from the very beginning!"

"It's okay, sweetheart. They can never hurt you again," he murmured against her silky head. "Nothing can. I'm here . . . I'll always be here to protect you. I love you, Star. You're the only one who's ever mattered as much to me."

She turned her face up, and as she clung to him, their lips met in a kiss that sealed their hopes and dreams. Suddenly, she knew what path in life she would be taking. Perhaps it wouldn't be straight and maybe not always predictable, but an adventurous journey awaited her nonetheless. It was something that Star, and Raven, had never been able to resist.

But the raven still beguiling all my sad soul
    into smiling,
Straight I wheeled a cushioned seat in front
    of bird, and bust, and door;
Then upon the velvet sinking, I betook my-
    self to linking
Fancy unto fancy, thinking what this omi-
    nous bird of yore—
What this grim, ungainly, ghastly, gaunt,
    and ominous bird of yore
        Meant in croaking "Nevermore."

The Raven, Edgar Allan Poe

Twenty-six

Six weeks later, Daere's and Star's lives had pretty much returned to normal. Well, almost. Life would never become a dull routine for these two people, who looked upon each and every day as a new and exciting adventure.

For Daere, who stood nervously listening to the minister's voice droning on forever, it seemed this was one day he didn't think he would ever forget. It was the biggest adventure of all, one he had been anticipating for weeks.

Star Tremayne was about to become his wife.

Daere had been waiting patiently for the portly clergyman to finally pronounce Star his wife. It seemed like the ceremony had been dragging on forever, and he only wanted it to be done with and to have her all to himself at last.

It had been so long, so damned long since he had held her in his arms and made sweet love to her the entire night through. They had respected Aunt Hilda's wishes and had agreed to a formal wedding and reception, but only if she allowed

434

them to hold the festivities at the Tremayne hacienda.

Since Cassondria had disappeared, along with her bodyguard, it seemed that no immediate threat loomed on Star's horizon. For now, that was enough.

Star had wanted the ceremony to take place in front of her father's fountain of dreams, the very place where she had uncovered the lost will, leaving her the sole heir to the Tremayne fortune. Aunt Hilda had thought it a splendid way to begin a marriage. The will that Cassondria had produced at the time of Benjamin's death had been a forged document, of course, and in light of the original will having been found, the faked one had been declared invalid. Star had finally put to rest her own demons. For now, her life seemed in balance.

After today, Daere intended to do the same with his tortured past. That was, if the clergyman ever finished rambling, so they could get on with the rest of their lives. My God, the planning that had gone into this affair today. Daere really had no idea. It had taken days and weeks to finalize arrangements that would meet with Hilda's approval. During that time, she hadn't allowed him more than a stolen minute alone with Star.

His gaze feasted on Star's beauty. She stood beside him, looking radiant and breathtakingly beautiful in an off-the-shoulder gown of the palest platinum. Tiny seed pearls and crystal bugles adorned the dress and the long sleeves, which were fitted at her wrists. The waistline was narrow, enhancing her slender figure. She wore a lace mantilla covering spiraling curls that had been pinned on top of her head. He thought she had never looked more radiant or desirable.

Star could feel his burning green gaze riveted on her and a tingle of pleasure swept up her spine.

It was a beautiful day for a wedding. The sun streamed down through the spreading branches of the tall, stately trees, splaying across the small group of people who were gathered in the courtyard of the Tremayne estate to celebrate the festive occasion. But neither Star nor Daere were thinking of this, only of later, and what magic the night would yield for them.

The carriages had started arriving shortly after dawn, pulling up in front of the hacienda and turning the reins over to a host of stable boys under the direction of Frank Colby.

Frank was seated in the front row, dressed in a new suit, crisp white shirt, and string tie, but there wasn't any way he'd wear anything other than his trademark red boots. Daere's mother sat beside him, and she looked happier than he had seen her in a long time. Rachel had been reluctant to return to Tequila Bend at first, but Star and Daere had gone to visit her and had finally convinced her that their wedding day wouldn't be complete unless the was able to be there to share in their joy.

It was a select guest list of only twenty-five close friends and relatives, but regardless, no expense had been spared.

The house and courtyard were adorned with baskets of fresh flowers, and their sweet fragrance perfumed the air. Attendants dressed in flowing dresses of lilac taffeta—Juanita's girls—had handed each of the ladies a long stem white rose as she had passed beneath a flower-bedecked arbor to the courtyard.

It was a day of new beginnings, to concentrate on the true meaning of life and the celebration of love they were all witnessing. For Daere and Star, it was a time to look forward to their years ahead as man and wife.

Star was thinking exactly this as she stared up at him, and everything else disappeared from her mind. There was just Daere, and the fierce masculinity of him never failed to take her breath away. And he had never looked more handsome than he did today.

He was dressed in an impeccably tailored suit of dark linen, and the narrow cut of his trousers seemed molded to his long, straight legs. His snow-white shirt was stretched tight across his broad chest, and diamond studs glittered at his wrists. The silky sheen of his thick raven hair caught in the rays of the bright sunshine, gleamed blue-black, and curled over his shirt collar. No doubt, she mused, he had brushed the unruly waves repeatedly in a final effort to tame the wild locks and coax them back into place. To no avail, of course. For which Star was immensely glad. An errant lock had fallen over his slashing brow, lending him a devil-may-care appearance, despite his expensive finery. It was just that "look" that she had fallen in love with. Would forever dream about every night of her life.

She promised herself that later, when they were finally alone, she would be free to run her fingers through his wavy locks as much as she liked, and kiss that well-shaped carnal mouth long and deep and hard. God, she would. All through the night ahead. All through the glorious years that stretched out in front of them.

But today . . . well, she just had to force herself to behave like the proper blushing bride, innocent in the art of passion and nervous about the night yet to unfold.

For Star, just to behave like everyone else had always been difficult in itself, but after having fallen in love with her wild, wicked gunslinger, it had seemed even more of an impossible task. Love welled up within her as she saw him smile slowly, as if he understood just what she had been thinking, feeling. It didn't surprise her to realize it. With joy she accepted this, no longer perceiving it as an intrusion on her private world. This day, and the next after that, would always be theirs alone, for her to share with him.

". . . and so, Daere and Star, by the power vested in me, I now pronounce you man and wife. What God hath joined together, let no man put asunder." The minister grinned broadly at Daere. "You may now kiss your bride."

Daere gathered her close in his arms and bent his head to kiss her gently parted lips. At that moment, he realized just how much she had given to him. Star had taught him to love, to forgive, and that every person on God's earth mattered and had been put here for a reason. He was glad that he had been destined to live out the rest of his days with this woman. She had given him far more than he would ever give her in return.

At that moment, Star was experiencing these very same emotions. She never wanted to be anywhere else but in this man's arms. For her, the dark days were over. She felt reborn.

The strains of the music that Star and Daere had selected drifted on the gentle breeze.

The newlyweds turned to their guests as the minister said, "Ladies and gentlemen, may I present to you Mr. and Mrs. Daere McCalister."

Daere enfolded Star's hand in his and he looked out at the familiar faces of their close friends and family, all smiling, some brushing a tear from their eyes, then he swung his gaze to his wife.

His radiant bride smiled when their eyes met, and a smirk of acknowledgment played around his mouth when he saw her wink saucily at him.

It was so like her to do the unexpected. Without a doubt, life with Star would never be dull.

His heart swelled with his love for her, and he didn't think he'd ever forget this moment. Still, the very best was yet to come. Tonight, after the reception, they would leave on their honeymoon, and he'd have her all to himself.

They would spend a week at the cabin in the mountains, where their love affair had first begun. There would be no one to think about but themselves, and nothing remained that could spoil this very special time in their lives.

Daere and Star McCalister would settle down at long last.

Or would they? Daere was given to wonder later as the wedding guests gathered around to wish the newlyweds farewell as they departed on their honeymoon. Unrealistic and highly improbable, he finally decided. For even as he vowed to himself to protect her always, he strongly suspected that his little hellcat, with her hair like quicksilver and imbued with a temper to match, would remain undaunted by his influence. Star would always blaze her own trail in life. Undoubtedly, one that dazzled like meteor fire and seared anyone who happened to be in her path. She was a woman confident of her abilities — as diverse as they were many — who knew exactly what she wanted from life and how she intended to get there.

How could he ever have thought for a single

moment that his bright, shining Star would ever be content to live out the rest of her life as just an ordinary woman, with only housework and children to fill up the hours of each day? Is that why he had married her? To change the very essence of the woman he had fallen in love with?

Not on your life! Daere was quick to think. A few days of rest and relaxation would be quite sufficient, but then he wanted the rest of their lives to be like the Fourth of July. Just like before.

Riding behind Star on Seguro, Daere smiled faintly as his gaze followed the gently swaying rhythm of her hips. Every minute of every hour was like a new beginning with Star. His smile warmed his eyes. He could hardly wait for sundown.

It was then he intended to reveal his surprise.

For the rest of the journey up the mountainside, Daere McCalister found his eyes drawn to the setting sun.

The cool mountain breeze drifted beneath the partially opened window of the cabin, stirring the filmy white curtains, which fluttered like delicate butterfly wings on the gentle air currents.

On the bed, pale cream sheets remained crisp and unrustled. The bedroom was quiet; the newlyweds had yet to romp there.

For Daere and Star to sanctify their vows, on

this their first night as man and wife, in such a traditional manner was unthinkable, and the prospect had not even been taken into consideration by either of them.

The newlyweds had arrived at the mountain retreat just before dark. It was now nine o'clock. A fire crackled in the hearth, the only light in the main room.

On a rug of thick, lush ermine—a wedding gift from Night Hawk—Daere McCalister lay stretched out, bare-chested, clad in only dark linen trousers, resting his weight on one elbow. An enigmatic smile curved his sensual lips as he waited for his new bride to join him.

Then without a sound, she was there before him, the firelight dancing seductively around her lithe elegance like a siren's song. She had brushed her hair until it fell in silver waves around her slender shoulders, and she was wearing a sheer ivory nightgown through which her bare beauty appeared like smooth alabaster. For a moment, Daere recalled that he had not even seen or heard her cross the room, but there had been many other moments like this in the past and it did not surprise him. She seemed to be able to come and go at will . . . to shift, to change, to be a different woman than the one he'd held only the night before.

These episodes, no matter how bewildering, never failed to heat his blood and leave him feeling exhilarated.

He extended his hand. "Come lay with me," he said. "Be my love, my darling Star."

She seemed to hesitate, watching him assessingly. "First, I have something to say to you. On this of all nights, there should no longer be any secrets between us, Daere."

"Yes, I agree," he replied softly, taking her hand in his.

She drew closer, silent as a jungle cat, and slowly come to her knees before him on the thick, lush rug. "You *are* my life, and the only man I've ever wanted to share every secret desire with."

"It sounds terribly intriguing, darling," he whispered back, drawing her down into the curve of his arm. "But then nothing you do would ever truly surprise me."

"Nothing?" she queried huskily, her teeth nibbling on his earlobe.

"Absolutely nothing," he sighed.

"I must confess, I have been rather nervous about how I was going to tell you this."

He slipped one finger under the strap of her gown and drew it off her shoulder. "Tell me what, pet?" he breathed against her milk-white skin.

Star hid her face in the solidity of his shoulder and drew a calming breath. "I may not exactly be the woman you think I am," she said.

One dark eyebrow rose, and he sighed with mock disappointment. "Had I known before, I may not have married you."

She drew back and looked up at his dark countenance. "You are making a joke of this?"

With sure, deft movements, Daere slipped the gown free of her lovely body and gently laid her back onto the shiny fur. "I am quite serious, my beauty. I didn't ask you to become my wife because you could cook and sew. Quite the contrary." The expression in his eyes was unreadable, but his voice was enchanting. His fingers began a lazy exploration of her slender curves. When she started to protest, he placed a finger against her lips. "Hush now. We are on our honeymoon and should make this night as memorable as possible. Close your eyes . . . Do not open them again, and we will let the magic begin, Star."

Star's eyelids fluttered closed, and she expected to feel the heat of his hands as they caressed her.

Instead, she felt the erotic brush of leather against her bare belly, then heard him say huskily, "Allow me, my darling Raven, to teach you everything you *never* knew about this whip you wield so well."

Her eyes flew open. "Daere, you know," she breathed, overwhelmed with emotion.

"You needn't explain anything to me," he told her gently. "I love you because you're the most exciting woman I've ever met. Don't ever change, for I adore you just the way you are." And bending over her, he kissed her deeply, passionately, and knew that he would love this wild, unpredict-

444

able woman until the end of time.

Throughout the rest of that night he taught her well, indeed, things that Raven had never dreamed could be so pleasurably wonderful.

The leather strands became the sweetness of a lover's whisper as they lay twined about them while they made love in abandoned rapture until the break of dawn.

Taylor—made Romance From Zebra Books

WHISPERED KISSES (3830, $4.99/$5.99)
Beautiful Texas heiress Laura Leigh Webster never imagined that her biggest worry on her African safari would be the handsome Jace Elliot, her tour guide. Laura's guardian, Lord Chadwick Hamilton, warns her of Jace's dangerous past; she simply cannot resist the lure of his strong arms and the passion of his *Whispered Kisses.*

KISS OF THE NIGHT WIND (3831, $4.99/$5.99)
Carrie Sue Strover thought she was leaving trouble behind her when she deserted her brother's outlaw gang to live her life as schoolmarm Carolyn Starns. On her journey, her stagecoach was attacked and she was rescued by handsome T.J. Rogue. T.J. plots to have Carrie lead him to her brother's cohorts who murdered his family. T.J., however, soon succumbs to the beautiful runaway's charms and loving caresses.

FORTUNE'S FLAMES (3825, $4.99/$5.99)
Impatient to begin her journey back home to New Orleans, beautiful Maren James was furious when Captain Hawk delayed the voyage by searching for stowaways. Impatience gave way to uncontrollable desire once the handsome captain searched *her* cabin. He was looking for illegal passengers; what he found was wild passion with a woman he knew was unlike all those he had known before!

PASSIONS WILD AND FREE (3828, $4.99/$5.99)
After seeing her family and home destroyed by the cruel and hateful Epson gang, Randee Hollis swore revenge. She knew she found the perfect man to help her—gunslinger Marsh Logan. Not only strong and brave, Marsh had the ebony hair and light blue eyes to make Randee forget her hate and seek the love and passion that only he could give her.

Available wherever paperbacks are sold, or order direct from the Publisher. Send cover price plus 50¢ per copy for mailing and handling to Zebra Books, Dept. 4187, 475 Park Avenue South, New York, N.Y. 10016. Residents of New York and Tennessee must include sales tax. DO NOT SEND CASH. For a free Zebra/ Pinnacle catalog please write to the above address.

FEEL THE FIRE IN CAROL FINCH'S ROMANCES!

BELOVED BETRAYAL (2346, $3.95)

Sabrina Spencer donned a gray wig and veiled hat before blackmailing rugged Ridge Tanner into guiding her to Fort Canby. But the costume soon became her prison—the beauty had fallen head over heels in love!

LOVE'S HIDDEN TREASURE (2980, $4.50)

Shandra d'Evereux felt her heart throb beneath the stolen map she'd hidden in her bodice when Nolan Elliot swept her out onto the veranda. It was hard to concentrate on her mission with that wily rogue around!

MONTANA MOONFIRE (3263, $4.95)

Just as debutante Victoria Flemming-Cassidy was about to marry an oh-so-suitable mate, the towering preacher, Dru Sullivan flung her over his shoulder and headed West! Suddenly, Tori realized she had been given the best present for a bride: a night of passion with a real man!

THUNDER'S TENDER TOUCH (2809, $4.50)

Refined Piper Malone needed bounty-hunter, Vince Logan to recover her swindled inheritance. She thought she could coolly dismiss him after he did the job, but she never counted on the hot flood of desire she felt whenever he was near!